ROGUE

ALEX SCHULER

WITH KEVIN WEIR

Published by:
Level 4 Press, Inc.
14702 Haven Way
Jamul, CA 91935
www.level4press.com

Library of Congress Control Number: 2019943894
ISBN: 978-1-933769-86-8
Printed in the United States of America

Other books by
ALEX SCHULER

Code Word Access
Faster

DEDICATION

For my family at my side, and the readers at my back.

PROLOGUE

Jonah Wall stood at the precipice of a savage world. The Alaskan wild, the air running cold and unbroken from the Arctic Sea, was a vast white void when the storms picked up, but on a clear day like that one, he could see for miles. An infinite landscape—beautiful and empty, a place that demanded quiet. But in the Natural Petroleum Reserve, it was anything but.

"Sir! It happened again!" a voice shouted. Frankie Moore clomped across the snow toward Jonah, his baby face glowing red beneath a thin layer of grime as he ran, puffing out clouds of vapor.

Another broken bit. Jonah scratched the couple of days of stubble on his cheek and tapped his cigarette out in the ashtray on the picnic table. He stood broad as an oak tree, strong-limbed with pale skin turned to brown bark from working outdoors. Better to cut the smoke break short before his roots sank in and he lost himself in the horizon. He took one last peaceful look at the earth and sky before allowing Frankie to drag his attention back to the rig.

The Nisku 42 was a massive land oil rig, the largest one in North America. A breakthrough for drilling engineering, according to the press releases. Assembled from a couple hundred tractor-trailer loads and built up like a Lego house in the North Slope of Alaska. A mark of power and innovation stuck like a flag into the earth. The newest and fanciest cog in the oil and gas machine.

"Sir? Did you hear me?" One of Frankie's feet hit a patch of ice, sending him forward half a foot before his boots gripped again. He kept his balance, but his hard hat tumbled off his head, coming to rest at Jonah's feet.

"Yes." Jonah scooped up the helmet, shaking the snow clear, and handed it back. "Slow down."

Frankie took the hat and opened his mouth, but Jonah had already brushed past him. Another broken bit meant another headache and another write-up to the company explaining expenses. He put on his own hard hat and adjusted the safety vest he wore over his winter gear.

Frankie hurried behind him. "Are you, uh, excited to see your family?"

"What?" Jonah frowned.

"When we're done, I mean. Five days till the rotation, yeah?" Frankie blanched when he got no response. "I thought you were married."

"I am." Jonah pressed his thumb against his ring finger, feeling the bulge where his band hid beneath his work gloves. "I live local now."

Frankie started to speak, then closed his mouth again. Terrence Walker and Saul Young waited near the door to the drilling floor while Mud Nowak and Aleks Kotov leaned against the railings just above. A six-man drill team looked ridiculous under the scale of the structure.

"Staring at the snow again?" Mud called out from the balcony.

Jonah flipped him the bird. "Where's Darius?"

"Taking another thirty-minute shit. Where else would he be?" Mud was young like Frankie, with a strong jawline, naturally tanned skin, and self-important swagger more suited for a runway than an oil rig. The rest of the team got to calling him "Mud" once he became the pit watcher responsible for the drilling fluid—the mud that brought the cuttings up from the well. Jonah figured it also helped the other guys feel better about working with a pretty boy.

Jonah stopped at the entrance to the drilling floor and looked over at the field office with the snow piled up along the north end. He thought he saw some movement behind the curtains, but it was hard to tell from that distance. Darius Hughes, their resident geologist, swore up and down the drill's path was clear and blamed the first broken bit on the crew's shoddy work. Behind his back, as they often did, the crew called him an asshole. He wasn't an asshole, Jonah figured. He was worse. He was lazy.

"What do ya wanna do?" Mud asked.

Jonah *wanted* to walk into the wilderness. He certainly didn't want to get into another circular argument with Darius pointing at some indecipherable readout. On the other hand, he *needed* to get the job done. "Switch out the bit. Hit it again."

"Man of few words." Mud clapped Aleks on the shoulder. "Love it."

The crew went to work. Frankie rushed by, tightening the strap of his hard hat. When Jonah cast him an eye, he slowed and returned an embarrassed nod as he entered the drilling floor. Jonah chuckled beneath his breath. The kid talked a lot, but he had spirit. Jonah's had broken more years back than he would like to admit, and the slow crawl of time wore on him every day. Thankfully, his team had the energy to pull them through their two-month rotation, and he trusted their skill—even Frankie's. Whatever broke the drill bits, it wasn't their shoddy work.

As the crew returned the drill up the hole, Mud sauntered over to Jonah, hooking one arm over a support strut and leaning in. "What'd Frankie do to piss you off?"

Jonah furrowed his brow. "Nothing. I mean, I'm not pissed off."

"Right." Mud pulled back, taking his arm off the strut. "You might want to tell him that."

Jonah glanced over Mud's shoulder, where Frankie kept his head down and his eyes on the hole. "He's working fine."

"I guess he is." Jonah barely caught a change in Mud's tone but quickly shook it off, and as another roughneck called Mud to come help, he pulled out his phone, uncoiled the earbuds, and popped one in.

While some of his crew listened to music to speed up the clock, Jonah preferred something more calming and loaded up his phone with as many audiobooks as he could fit. He'd gotten through most of them in the month and a half they'd already been out there and was now down to the dry dregs. The narrator, a wizened man with a slight German accent, picked up exactly where Jonah had left off: "When asked about the advancement of the human species, many are tempted to express the wonders of modern medicine, telecommunication, and transportation. Few take the time to consider these same advancements also resulted in the nuclear bomb, chemical weaponry, and environmental destruction."

Frankie detached the massive bit, holding it with two hands and hauling it aside. As he plunked it on the ground, something within the grooves flashed. Jonah frowned and approached. Frankie continued with the switch, unaware of the odd material or Jonah leaning in to investigate.

A silvery substance coated the bit like a thick liquid or gel. Jonah had never seen anything like it come up from the earth. It looked more like mercury than ore. Out of pure curiosity, he gave it a poke before immediately realizing how stupid that was. It could've been acidic or toxic, but as his gloved finger struck the liquid, it hardened, taking on a semi-reflective sheen.

"Stop!" Jonah shouted, holding up his hand. "Get the camera."

All the while, the narrator continued. "Even if one weren't so dramatic, we've seen our rush for advancement result in feelings of isolation and detachment. Our lives are longer, filled to the brim with experience after experience, but what do they mean? Take it all away now, and we would miss it, but a thousand years ago, we could not even have comprehended these technologies. We are living in a completely different world from our ancestors."

Jonah couldn't look away from the substance on the bit as his team sent the down-hole camera into the earth. Every time Jonah touched it, it sealed up like a shell, only to return to its gelatinous form again a minute or so later. When he finally glanced up, he saw his crew crowded around the monitor, jaws agape and eyes wide.

Mud turned from the screen, his face a combination of alarm and confusion. "Jonah, you need to see this."

The tension on the drilling floor could have drowned them. Jonah's heart pounded against his sternum, and the audiobook narrator's voice became distant, as if from underwater: "As you look at the world around you, consider: Is progress the only goal? Is all progress the same? Is there a point where marching forward blindly will send humanity off the cliff?"

In the grainy black-and-white monitor—in the distant depths below the snow and dirt and metal—the camera showed a small cavern with chairs, windows, and a control console that could've fit easily into a science-fiction movie. The walls weren't unworked stone, but smooth, and as the camera swung around, it revealed a closed exit to the tiny room. Jonah's mind stalled at the thought, urging him to stay sane, but there was only one explanation he could conjure.

It looked like a spaceship.

CHAPTER 1

TWO YEARS LATER

Summer had come to Anchorage. Warmth was relative in the northern latitudes, but when Jonah woke to the chirps of song sparrows, it was as clear a sign as packed beaches. And with the added benefit of fewer people.

A beeping sounded through his home, bouncing off bare walls and cold linoleum. Jonah rushed from the bathroom, dressed in only a towel. His new coffeemaker squawked in time with its display; two loud beeps, a pause, and two more in an infinite loop. A gift from Mud, or, rather, a curse. Jonah stomped down the stairs into his kitchen and started hammering buttons on the infernal device.

He scrolled through menus and options before finally finding the button to stop the beeping. He took a breath of relief. Wi-Fi connectivity, phone app, programmable schedule, but no way to make a noise less grating. He grabbed the travel mug from beneath the nozzle and drank down a hit of caffeine. At least the coffee wasn't bad.

He snatched the remote off the couch and turned on the news. The screen instantly lit up with shots of work crews milling around the Nisku 42's former drill site. Jonah paused to take in the images. He hadn't seen the site in person since making his report, as his crew was moved to another site soon after the discovery, but with everything that came in the news after, he was still stricken by what he'd stood over that day. The mere thought of it made his chest tighten.

A spaceship. He'd felt like a fool thinking it at the time, but that's what all the media and experts called it. Its metallic shell flashed in the background, but the station never gave the viewer a clear shot. When the military and men in black suits had arrived, he'd figured the discovery would get covered up. But there it was, a great silver machine dug out from the earth like a piece of ore and shown to God and all the people of the planet. He took a sip of coffee and leaned back on the counter.

The newscaster's smooth voice reported over the scenes. "Efforts continue in Alaska as crews have officially unearthed the final piece of what some officials are calling a spaceship. Reports from the ground are limited, though we are seeing a multinational push from researchers to understand what exactly this structure is."

The shot changed to one of many military vehicles driving atop the Alaskan permafrost. The entire landscape had been torn up and padded down to make room for checkpoints and temporary structures. Soldiers, NASA specialists, and civilian researchers flooded the land like ants over a picnic. And Jonah thought the noise from his coffee machine was bad. The entire point of living in Alaska was the solitude.

"More information is expected to be given at the official unveiling in the next couple of weeks," the newscaster concluded.

Jonah chuckled. That was why they never showed the entire ship, better ratings for the big reveal. He had once lived that life. Why have journalism when they could have spectacle?

He returned upstairs to finish getting dressed, but when he got to his room, the single photo he'd allowed in his spartan home arrested his attention. Him and his boys, Rowan and Ethan. Ethan had his arm out holding the camera, a smile showing a gap where he'd lost a tooth only two days earlier. He'd tripped trying to catch a flyball and tumbled down a small embankment. More subdued, Rowan had his arm around his younger brother. That was a few years back, Ethan a spritely eleven and Rowan a moody fourteen. Now Ethan would be the fourteen-year-old and Rowan a frightening seventeen.

Jonah tugged a shirt over his shoulders and fastened the buttons. Their mother had put them on a late-night flight from Massachusetts, and they were due to arrive that morning. With the rig working him relentlessly, summers were the only time he had to spend with his sons, and he hadn't seen them since the last one. Every year they changed, and he only saw a few frames from the movie of their lives.

A large diesel truck rumbled down the street as Jonah returned to the kitchen. A scrawny man with thin-rimmed glasses and a close-cropped haircut appeared on-screen, talking to a reporter. A chyron scrolled across the screen beneath him.

DARIUS HUGHES: PETROWAVE COMPANY GEOLOGIST

"The readouts showed something down there." The man adjusted his glasses and touched his tie. Sweat glistened against the dark skin above his brow, and Jonah could tell it took everything in him not to constantly wipe it away. "While my crew couldn't hit any oil, I knew there was something important, and we had to keep going at it."

Jonah groaned and shut off the TV, tossing the remote to get lost among the couch cushions. If Darius wanted to stand in the middle of the circus, slowly melting into a puddle, that was his prerogative. Jonah wouldn't be any more comfortable in front of a camera, but he'd also never get himself into that situation. He grabbed his jacket off a hook and his truck keys out of their bowl. The spaceship—whatever it was—was the last thing on his mind.

The Anchorage airport bustled as people dodged around each other and through terminal hallways. In the arrivals area, military personnel escorting scientists with big bags and hard cases cleared paths amid whispers and gawking stares. Within the ocean of travelers, Row and his brother Ethan, each with a hefty backpack in tow, scanned the crowd for a familiar face.

"Oh, cool!" Ethan suddenly took off at a jog, weaving between the bodies, lithe and small enough to sneak through the cracks like a snake. His blond mop of hair bounced as he came to a stop in front of a set of tall glass panels.

There were nine of them of varying height, stretching high over the escalators between them. Each tower contained overlapping images, from blue-green representations of the Alaskan landscape to rectangular fields of copper glass. They'd been there as long as Row could remember, yet Ethan got excited every time they flew in.

Row adjusted the strap of the backpack slung over his shoulder and stepped forward to chase after his brother, only to nearly be knocked down by a family with rolling suitcases. They didn't look back as they cruised by.

He rolled his eyes and flipped up the hood on his sweater, stomping after Ethan. "Don't run off," he said once he caught up. "Mom'll kill me if I lose you before we even get there."

"Oh?" Ethan poked him in the side. "She won't if you lose me later?"

Row grinned and looked at the panels. They were uneven like mountains, and he had to crane his neck to see the tops of them. "That's pretty cool, I guess."

"Imagine if they fell over!" Ethan threw his hands into the air like an explosion. "Smash! Like when Mom dropped that mirror, only bigger."

"Yeah, well, then at least Mom'll kill *you*." He glanced behind him at the rest of the terminal. "Come on. We need to find—"

"Dad!" Ethan took off again, slipping through a gap in the crowd toward a man in a padded jacket who'd appeared from behind a column.

Tall as Row remembered, their father's strength was visible even through the coat's puffy insulation. His sturdiness had comforted Row when he'd been little, but now he thought his dad looked old and worn down. Row watched as Ethan slammed chest-first into his waist and wrapped his arms around him.

"Whoa!" Dad clapped Ethan's shoulders. "You're getting big!"

Ethan laughed and released his grip.

Row took a deep breath, reminding himself it was only for a month, and sauntered over. "Hey, Dad."

"Hey, Rowan." And there it was, Row thought. The familiar wood-enness Dad always adopted when he talked to Row. With his thumbs tucked into his jean pockets, he looked like a cowboy on TV. "You have a good flight?"

"Yeah." Row considered telling him he went by "Row" now, not "Rowan," but there didn't seem to be much of a point. He'd just forget or bug him about it.

Ethan apparently didn't have the same concerns. "He goes by Row now, Dad."

"Oh." Jonah stiffened like he had stepped on a tack. "Did you have a good flight, *Row*? I know those overnights can really suck."

Row rolled his eyes, unwilling to give his dad credit for trying. "It was fine. I slept. I played some Switch."

"Switch." Dad snapped his fingers. "That's Xbox."

"Nintendo."

Dad nodded, but Row knew he had no idea what he was talking about.

"We should get our bags." Ethan smiled, though Row could tell it was forced. Even at fourteen, the kid could feel the tension between Row and their dad.

"Great idea." Dad finally took his thumbs out of his pockets. "I'll pull the truck around and meet you out front."

Row and Ethan wandered to the bag carousel as their dad sped out of the terminal. Row sank even deeper into his hood. Why couldn't Dad just act normal? Talking to him now felt like torture. Everything Dad did came out stilted, like a bad actor on a soap opera. Ethan didn't seem to notice; to him, that was how their dad was. He didn't remember a time before.

"You should be nicer to Dad," Ethan said as they reached the carousel.

"I *am* nice to him." Row looked over at his brother. Ethan stared down at his sneakers, his smile fading. Row squeezed his eyes shut. The last thing he wanted was to ruin Ethan's trip. He clapped his arm around his brother's shoulder and pulled him close. "Hey, aren't you excited about the camping? You know if you keep that face, Mud'll break out his guitar. No one wants that."

Ethan clamped his jaw, but a smile fought its way through. "Do you think Dad'll let us see the spaceship?"

"That's, like, way up north." Row shrugged, even though he had the same hope. Ever since he saw it on the news, it was all he and his friends had talked about. It had taken a full two weeks for Dad to let slip that he was part of the team who found it. Even then, he said it casually, with no real excitement, like describing finding ten dollars in your pocket. But Row would give anything to see the ship up close— finally, something interesting in boring Alaska.

The boys found their luggage and hauled it out to the road, where Jonah waited in his big Ford F-350. Mud was splashed across the side, coating the blue paint all the way up to the windows. Ethan jumped into the passenger seat while Row took the back. They hadn't even left the airport before Row put on his wireless headphones and let the alt-rock fill his ears.

The truck tore down the highway, past thick treelines and families of deer wandering the curb. Nature hugged against the edge of the asphalt, and Row lost track of time watching birds keep pace in the distance before disappearing into the cloud cover.

In the front, Ethan talked excitedly at Dad. Row couldn't hear the words, but Ethan's big gestures and facial expressions spoke volumes. Conversation came easy for his younger brother. Dad nodded along, and while Row still saw that wooden wall, Ethan didn't.

At one point, Dad handed Ethan a pair of boxing gloves. Ethan's face lit up, and he immediately put them on, punching at the dashboard and swaying his head side to side, imitating the fighters he'd seen in movies. Dad caught Row's gaze in the rearview mirror, and Row saw his dad's lips move.

"What?" Row tapped the side of his headphones, shutting the music off, and hung them around his neck.

"I said there's something under my seat." Dad elbowed Ethan gently, giving him an all-too-obvious wink. "Can you dig it out for me? It's really poking me in the ass."

Ethan laughed like it was the funniest joke he'd ever heard. Row ducked down and waited until he was out of sight to roll his eyes. Then he felt underneath the seat until his fingers brushed something, and he pulled an oddly wrapped box onto his lap. The edges were more tape than paper.

"See? I didn't forget you." Dad drummed his fingers along the steering wheel. "First day of summer, gotta celebrate somehow. Right, Row?"

"Right, Dad." He tucked his fingers into the folds and tore the paper away. Inside sat an Nvidia graphics card in its colorful display packaging.

"Frankie, the young guy I work with, said that'll speed your computer up. I don't know how, but Frankie's only a few years older than you. He's got to know what he's talking about."

Row turned the box over in his hands. The card was a few generations old. His system already outclassed anything that GPU could get him, but at least Dad hadn't given him yet another baseball bat. "Thanks. It'll help." He put the box aside. He could strip it for parts.

A green light turned yellow, and they slowed to a stop. A bright red sports car roared up next to them, and Mud smiled from behind mirrored sunglasses.

"Row! That's a Porsche 911!" Ethan excitedly rolled the window down.

"Hey, kids!" Mud shouted. "I heard trouble blew into town."

"Mud!" Ethan leaned out the window and knocked his gloves together. "Check it out!"

Mud lowered his shades. "Pretty cool. Now, make sure you kids give your dad all kinds of hell this summer. He's been working too hard!"

The light turned green, and the Porsche's wheels squealed on the asphalt before Mud tore off, laughing like a madman.

"That's, like, the sickest ride," Ethan enthused. "Do you know how much that costs?" He tapped Dad's shoulder. "Doesn't Mud work for you? Why don't you have a car like that?"

"The truck works fine." Dad revved the engine. "And it doesn't get stuck in the snow."

Ethan looked over his shoulder, tapping his gloves against the side of his head and giving a goofy smile. Row smiled back half-heartedly. If only he could joke and pretend so easily. Maybe then the ocean between him and his father would dry up. Instead, he snapped his headphones over his ears again and zoned out for the rest of the drive.

The truck stopped outside Jonah's wood-paneled split-level, and Ethan jumped out while Row eased himself onto the drive and gazed up at the peaked-roof front, squinting against the sun. The house hadn't changed since last summer, yet Row still expected to find his father living in some log cabin he'd built himself.

"Come on, Row!" Dad called, holding the front door open as Ethan rushed inside. "Don't forget your computer thing."

Row paused mid-step, then spun back to the truck and grabbed the GPU.

Nothing was different on the inside, either. Same bland walls, same single couch with a fifty-five-inch TV—not even a smart one. Row hung his headphones around his neck while Ethan zoomed by, shadowboxing with his new gloves. He'd already tossed his bag haphazardly into the corner.

"You boys remember where the room is?" Dad asked, hanging up his jacket next to the door. "Down that hall right next to the laundry."

"We know, Dad!" Ethan laughed. He slipped his arms through the straps of his bag without removing his boxing gloves. "Same place as last time."

Dad nodded. "Fair enough. But don't get too settled in. We're leaving for the campsite early tomor—"

Sudden beeping cut him off.

"Oh, fu—" His eyes flicked toward Ethan and Row. "Frick." He hurried into the kitchen, dodged around the island, and hammered his fingers on the coffeemaker. "Sorry, this stupid thing won't shut up."

Row spotted a piece of paper stuck to the fridge with the Wi-Fi name and password. He put his bag on the ground, set the GPU on top, then pulled out his phone. Something *had* changed in his dad's house, and, as to be expected, Dad couldn't handle it. Row connected to the internet, opened the camera app, and pushed past his father.

Dad gave him space but peered over Row's shoulder at the screen.

A square QR code sticker sat on the coffeemaker's shell. Row scanned it and quickly downloaded the app. A moment later, the beeping silenced.

"You set the alarm to go off every hour instead of every morning." Row leaned against the counter and hovered his finger over his phone screen without looking at his dad. "When do you want it?"

"I don't want an alarm," Dad said. "I just want the coffee at six-thirty."

"Done." Row stuck this phone in his pocket. "Just because you don't understand something doesn't mean it's stupid."

"I know." Dad leaned against the counter, looking down at the coffeemaker. Quieter, he repeated, "I know, Row."

Row got his bag and GPU and passed Ethan coming out of their room. As with the rest of the house, there wasn't much to it. Two twin beds and a desk with a stool. He immediately unzipped his bag and pulled out his laptop.

"We should call Mom." Ethan poked his head back into the room. "We said we would when we landed."

"Yeah, right." Row placed his laptop on the desk, retrieved his phone from his pocket, and opened the video calling app. It already felt like they'd been in Alaska forever.

The phone only rang once before Mom's face appeared onscreen and her voice came through the speaker. "Hi, Row!"

"I'm here, too!" Ethan called while bouncing cross-legged on his bed. Row turned the camera to him, and he waved with his boxing gloves. "Look what Dad got me."

"Oh . . ." She smiled. "Great. You're already at the house?"

"Yeah." Row turned the camera back on himself and paced. "Dad was waiting at the airport. We didn't have time to call, sorry."

"That's all right." She sat back in a big lounge chair, the one she always read her books in. "Did you have a good flight?"

"Is that your mom?" Dad appeared at the door. Row spun the camera around, and Dad froze at the sight of their mom. It took another second for him to right himself. "Uh, hi, Lorri."

"Hey, Jonah." They had all the rapport of a slug and salt.

"We're having burgers for lunch, so . . ." Dad pointed vaguely in the direction of the grill. "I'm going to get that started. You boys let me know what you want on your buns."

"Thanks," Row and Ethan said in unison.

Row gestured at the gloves still enveloping Ethan's hands. "Take those things off and help Dad. I wanna talk to Mom for a sec."

"Okay." Ethan sounded disappointed, but he tore the Velcro straps open with his teeth and snapped his hands down, sending the gloves bouncing across the room. "Bye, Mom!"

"Call me again before you leave for camping!" she said before Ethan sprinted out of the room.

Row checked to make sure Ethan and Dad were long gone, then eased the door shut. "Mom," he whispered, "how long do I have to be here?"

"Row." Her Mom Voice appeared at lightspeed. "You haven't even been there for a day."

"It's so boring." He flopped onto the stool and booted up his computer.

"You've got that camping trip this week. You love camping."

"Ethan loves camping. I tolerate camping because Ethan loves camping." He launched his internet browser and waited. It lingered on a white screen, trying to load the home page. "Oh, God, and the Wi-Fi's so slow! How am I supposed to hang out with my friends?"

"You can see them when you get back."

His shoulders slumped as he shut the laptop in defeat. "How do you know Dad even wants us here?"

"Of course he does." She sighed, her jaw clenching as it always did when she talked about Dad. "Your father is a . . . complex man. He's got a lot more going on in his big lunkhead than it seems. Just know he loves you."

"Then why is he out here?" Row ran his fingers over the stickers decorating his laptop case. The GPU lay crooked against the side of his bed.

"Maybe you should ask him." Mom leaned in closer to the camera. "On your camping trip."

"Fine." Row laughed and shook his head. Then he glanced out the window above the desk, toward the backyard where his father and brother happily prepared lunch. Maybe he *would* ask Dad why he left. If he could find the words.

CHAPTER 2

Jonah loaded up the boys' camping gear early the next morning. His coffeemaker pressed out hot brew beeplessly after Row's work, and at 6:30 on the dot, he took a full mug out on his porch, looking into the thin treeline separating him from his closest neighbor.

After giving the boys plenty of time to get up on their own, he downed the last of his coffee and headed back inside, checking his watch. 7:12 a.m. He'd told them to set their alarms for seven, though he wouldn't be surprised if they'd slept through them.

He rapped on their bedroom door. "On your feet, boys. I'd like to get to the site before noon."

No answer. He opened the door to find the covers on their twin beds cast aside and the mattresses empty. He scowled. *Odd.*

Ethan's laugh echoed through the open window above the computer desk. Jonah leaned out of the room and spotted the sliding door to the backyard cracked open. The boys must've snuck out while he drank his coffee. Ethan's doing, no doubt. He never liked sleeping.

Jonah followed the cries of joy into the field of wild green he called his backyard. The grass rose to his sons' calves as they squared off, dew soaking their jeans to the knees. They were dressed and ready for the trip and, judging by their wet hair, had even showered. Ethan wore the boxing gloves Jonah had gotten him, taking slow punches at Row while Row danced back and slapped his brother's hands away.

Jonah leaned against the drainpipe coming down from the gutters and watched his sons play-fight. At least they had each other back in Massachusetts. Ethan dropped his hands and lunged at Row's midsection, wrapping his arms around his brother's waist and trying to take him down. Row held his ground against the much smaller boy and let out a whooping laugh.

"I haven't seen *that* move before!" Jonah called out.

"Dad!" Ethan released Row and waved. "I got him out of bed!"

"I can see that."

Row rolled his eyes and playfully shoved Ethan, who spun around on him, one glove over his head and the other one straight out. He swiped his hands up and down, like a flagger directing an aircraft in for a landing, as Row shuffled back.

"You gotta keep your hands up," Jonah said, heading across the backyard. "And plant your feet."

"We're just playing around," Row told him.

"I know, but you can still have a proper stance." Jonah caught Ethan by the shoulder and held him still. "Raise your back heel slightly and put your gloves up, not too close to your face, or else your opponent's gonna knock your own fist into your nose."

Ethan followed his directions. It had been years since Jonah had done any boxing, and then only as a hobby, but it had kept him in shape. There was a time in college when he considered giving it a real go, but he never found much enjoyment in taking punches. Ethan, however, had taken one look at his old gloves on an earlier visit and become obsessed.

Jonah held his hands up as targets. "Give me a swing. Hard as you can."

"Really?" Ethan's eyes lit up.

"Yeah. Just remember, pivot your body. Your power starts from your legs."

Bobbing his head, Ethan focused on Jonah's hands, giving a few test turns with his hips. Steadying himself, he thrust his fist out, striking Jonah's right hand. His entire body followed the punch, with his back leg coming off the ground. He stumbled forward, Jonah catching him before he hit the dirt.

"Pretty good, right?" Ethan grinned up at him.

"Not bad, yeah." Jonah set him on his feet again. "Just keep yourself planted."

Ethan laughed, then stopped with a frown. "Where's Row?"

Jonah scanned the backyard. Row was gone.

"Row!" Ethan walked in a tight circle around Jonah and called to the trees as though he expected his older brother to have suddenly climbed to the top of one of them.

"I'm out front!" Row's yell barely made it to the back.

Ethan skipped across the yard, arms swinging limply at his side. Jonah followed. They circled the house and found Row leaning against the truck's bumper, scrolling through his phone.

"I had to grab my power bank." He indicated the small battery plugged into his phone. "I grabbed my and Ethan's backpacks, too. You wanted to go now, right?"

A dark voice in Jonah's head told him Row hadn't left just to get the power bank and luggage. *How did I mess this up?* He rubbed at the back of his neck. *I was just giving Ethan a few pointers.* He'd have to figure out what he'd done wrong this time, so next time he'd get it right.

"I'll make sure everything's locked up," he said.

After checking the doors and grabbing his own phone, Jonah hopped into the truck where Row and Ethan waited. He watched his eldest through the rearview mirror, sitting in the back seat and focusing out the window.

"Hey, Row. Check it out." He showed him on his phone where he'd downloaded the coffeemaker's app that morning.

"Cool, Dad." Row gave a placating nod.

Well, I'm proud of myself, Jonah thought. He'd only gotten a smartphone because it came with a better phone plan. He'd never scanned a QR code before that morning when he copied what Row had done yesterday.

They drove three hours out of Anchorage to a camping spot near a slow-running river. A couple of men from the drill team and their families were already there, setting up tents or parking trailers, letting their kids have the run of the clearing. They were all Ethan's age or younger, leaving Row the oldest out there.

As Jonah parked his truck in an open spot, Mud exited his travel trailer, hopping down from the raised door. Jonah wasn't surprised to see he'd left his Porsche at home. You needed a truck out here in Alaska, not some impractical toy car.

Mud gestured at Jonah with a beer bottle, shouting, "Look who showed up! You getting old? You're usually the first one here!"

"I'll work on that," Jonah said, dropping the tailgate.

"What kind of comeback . . .? Whatever." Mud chugged the rest of the beer and tossed the bottle into a bag.

The other two roughnecks came over to help Jonah unpack. Terrence was Jonah's age, only leatherier from a long life in the sun. He'd worked rigs in warmer climates and never let the rest of the team forget it. Jonah had no doubt that when a job opened somewhere southward, Terrence would lug his old bones past the forty-ninth parallel. He grabbed some of the lawn chairs from the truck bed.

"Oh, look who's lending a hand!" Saul exclaimed, coming up behind him.

Terrence gave Saul the finger, sauntering off with the lawn chairs.

Saul plucked the cooler of beer from the back like it was filled with foam. He had the big belly of a powerlifter and the grin of a clean-shaven Santa Claus.

Jonah waved him over, indicating his sons as they circled around the front of the truck. "Remember my boys? Ethan and Row."

"What's up, dudes?" Saul's voice hit with the bass of a large drum.

"My own boy, Lon, is over there with Claire." He jerked his head toward a woman with long brown hair tied back in a ponytail and a boy who looked about Ethan's age, both in good shape, like Saul, setting up a tent across the site. "I'm sure he'd be happy to meet ya."

"Why don't you pick out a spot and then meet the other kids?" Jonah handed the boys their sleeping bags.

"You wanna sleep outside?" Ethan asked Row, bouncing on his toes.

"I don't know." Row scanned the clearing.

"It's not supposed to rain tonight," Jonah said. "It's nice to sleep under the stars."

"Speak for yourself." Mud jumped to sit on Jonah's tailgate. "You'll mostly be sleeping under the sun. Night doesn't fall until about eleven."

"Please, Row." Ethan clapped his hands, begging his brother.

Row sighed. "Sure. Let's find a spot."

Ethan took off at a sprint, Row meandering behind. Jonah hoped Row would find some connection with the other kids. Maybe someone who liked computers or video games like him. Though that could be hard to come by. Row had been into the whole tech side of life for years. Even planned on going to MIT for some computer degree. Jonah couldn't remember which one.

"Did you hear back from the others?" he asked Saul.

Saul nodded. "Frankie's gonna stay with his girl in Portland. He hasn't seen her in two months, Don't blame him. And you know Aleks. The day he goes camping is the day Mud here shaves his head."

Mud barked out a loud laugh.

"Bah," Terrence rejoined them. "Let 'em miss out. I've been marinating steaks overnight, and I'm cooking on an open flame once dinner hits."

The men cheered at the thought of the steaks and got to finishing the campsite setup. Jonah kept back, watching his crew and the kids. The yearly camping trip made for high spirits and gave the team something to look forward to. As for Jonah, it forced him to break his isolation for a bit—though he couldn't say he didn't enjoy the time away from his house at least a little.

The day went by with hockey talk and beer. Terrence lit a fire in the evening, hours before the midnight sun would dip along the horizon, and placed a cast-iron pan above the flames. All the time they spent eating steak and corn, there was no mention of the spaceship they'd all found two years earlier. Whether it had been talked out or they preferred to keep conversation manageable, no one brought it up.

Finally, Saul clapped his hands on his knees and pushed himself to his feet, pulling out a Frisbee from beneath his chair and tossing it to his son. "Let's put this energy to use."

The group set their finished plates aside and moved down toward the river, tossing the disc between them. Even Terrence got involved, though it took a bit of prodding from his wife, a tiny woman with hair down to her waist. The kids ran circles around them. Ethan caught a toss from Lon, diving and rolling to his feet, then hurled the disc onward to Terrence's twin daughters. They collided in the air and fell into the grass, laughing.

Jonah stood near the riverside, listening to the water slapping against the stones. A cheer rose behind him, and he turned to see Mud flat on his back, holding the disc proudly in the air. Row sat on a large rock farther downriver, holding his phone sideways and tapping the screen with his thumbs.

For a long while, Jonah looked between Row and the quiet expanse of the Alaskan wilderness stretching before him. He couldn't come up with the words to start a conversation. On the rig, he never felt out of his depth and didn't have to worry about saying something he couldn't take back. Everything could be fixed there, a place where he knew exactly what to do and how to do it. Where he didn't have to worry about taking chances.

Eventually, he cleared his throat and walked over to Row's side. "You should get in the game. Have some fun."

"I am having fun." Row hardly looked up from his phone. "Why don't you get in there?"

"I guess I'm having fun, too."

"Doing what?"

Jonah gestured around them. "Taking in the sights."

Row put his phone down and looked across the river. Wildflowers of purple, pink, and yellow broke up from the dirt and turned to the sun. Clouds billowed through a sapphire sky, their shadows drifting across the mountains like leaves on a lake. The wind blew down the river, creating small ripples with invisible fingers, wrapping around Jonah and Row in the kind of warm embrace the two couldn't share on their own.

"It's beautiful out here," Jonah said. "Even in winter."

"Yeah." Row put his elbows on his knees. "It's nice. Just quiet."

"Do you not like the quiet?"

"Not always."

A Sitka deer meandered out from a pocket of trees a few yards past the far bank. Big, branching antlers rose from its head, and its reddish-brown coat shone in the sunlight. Once it spotted them, it froze, ears out, staring at the troublemakers in its territory.

Row met the deer's gaze, his expression peaceful. Neither of them moved. Even the sound of the others tossing the disc around seemed to fade away. Jonah tried to raise his hand to place it on his son's shoulder, but he couldn't get it beyond his own waist.

Then the buck bolted, and Jonah's hand settled at his side. The moment had passed.

"Dad?" Row frowned.

"What?"

"I . . ." He scratched the back of his neck. "Ethan asked about the spaceship."

"Oh, that." Jonah picked up a rock and tossed it up and down. "I'm not even sure it's a spaceship."

"What else could it be?"

Jonah cast the rock into the river. He didn't have an answer.

"Why aren't you and Mud and the others more excited about it?" Row persisted. "This is a big thing, right?"

"I guess. People have other stuff going on." He leaned back, stretching, and gazed up at the quick-moving clouds. "Whatever comes out of that thing is gonna be beyond us."

"You have no interest in it at all?" Row scooted around to face him.

"Why should I?"

"Because it's . . . it's a . . ." He squeezed his eyes shut, then lay back on the rock. "Never mind."

"Humans will keep being humans, even if we get new toys."

"I thought you'd be more interested in flying off somewhere," Row muttered.

Jonah looked at his son, arms spread wide, supine across the rock with his phone held in one hand. It didn't matter how far Jonah went; the world always lay cold across his shoulders. He didn't need a spaceship to feel distant.

The sun dipped low in the sky, scraping along the far-off mountains in its slow eventide descent. The campers drifted off to their respective sleeping areas. Row followed Ethan to the spot he'd chosen on the edge of the campsite, still in sight of Jonah's tent but where they had privacy and a clear view of the sky.

They lay head-to-head and looked up as the final oranges and yellows faded away. Row wanted nothing more than to sleep, to count down one more day until this terrible trip was over, but he couldn't get his mind to sit still. Usually, he'd be able to put on music, any amount of noise to help him calm down. In the dark stillness, he only had his thoughts.

Fortunately, he also had Ethan.

"Hey," Ethan whispered. "You awake?"

"Yeah." Row turned in his sleeping bag.

Ethan had his arms behind his head, gazing into the burgeoning starfield above. "So, the spaceship. Does that mean aliens exist?"

"I guess so." Row mirrored his brother's position. "But it was buried far underground. Some of the articles I read think it's old. The aliens won't just be walking around Earth."

"Can you imagine flying into space?" Ethan pointed a finger into the sky and moved it from side to side like it was zipping between planets. "You could go anywhere. There's gotta be people somewhere, right?"

"Yeah. Someone built it. They must be super smart."

Ethan reached back and playfully slapped at Row's head. "Not as smart as you."

"Stop." Row smiled and knocked Ethan's hand away. "They built a spaceship—that's super smart."

"Cool!" one of Terrence's twins exclaimed across the campsite.

Neon greens and vibrant purples filled the night sky, the scintillating bands of the Northern Lights framed against the star-filled backdrop. Ethan gasped and even in the dark, Row saw the smile spread across his face.

For a long time, no one said a word. They took in nature's brilliance in rapt silence until Ethan whispered, "I think you'd be happy out there. With people who get you."

Row smiled. "I'm happy right here, Ethan."

Colors danced above them, and Row finally found sleep.

Jonah woke to ringing. At first, he thought it was his demonic coffeemaker until he saw morning light coming through the thin tent fabric. He slapped through his stuff until he found his cell phone. Without glancing at the number, he stabbed the answer button.

"Jon—" He cleared his throat. "Jonah Wall here."

"Hi, Jonah . . . Erin . . . department . . ." The voice cut in and out.

Jonah checked the reception. He had one bar disappearing and reappearing with alarming consistency. "Hold on!"

He unzipped the tent and stumbled into the world.

"Hello . . . Mister . . . Petro . . ." The reception didn't get any better outside.

Mud, brushing his teeth outside his trailer, saw Jonah. He waved and pointed as he spat the toothpaste onto the grass. "There's a spot near the road."

Jonah nodded in thanks and took off at a jog.

"Wait, I need more bars," he said, not knowing if the other end could hear him as he rushed to where the gravel road turned off from the paved highway. Finally, he got a clear sentence.

"Jonah?" the woman said. "Jonah, can you hear me?"

"Yes, I can hear you." The morning chill cut into his T-shirt and boxers. "Sorry."

"That's quite all right." She sounded like someone who remained cheery on company mandate. "This is Erin Meyers from PetroWave's media department. We're looking to have you come up to the dig site for the big reveal next week."

"I didn't think you'd want us there." Jonah rubbed his arms to warm them. *More accurately,* he thought, *I'd hoped you* didn't *want us there.*

"We see nothing better than having the very crew who made the discovery standing on stage."

"On stage . . ." The beginnings of a headache twinged between his eyebrows. "I got my kids; I can't go—"

"Good news." Papers ruffled on her side of the line. "When we couldn't reach your cell yesterday, we called your backup contact. Your wife is thrilled to be involved. We just confirmed her flight out."

Jonah stifled a groan. Great. The first time he'd see Lorri in person in years would be at the site of the ship he'd tried so hard to forget. That was definitely not going to happen if he could help it.

"Look, Erin. I'm not interested in going to any sort of press event. Get someone else."

Erin sighed through the line and took on a firm tone. "I understand, sir. However, I've been told to relay that your continued employment with PetroWave is dependent on your attendance."

Jonah squeezed his eyes shut until he felt the blood pounding behind his eyes. Just like PetroWave, wanting to play hardball. The air rushed from his lungs. "Then I guess I'll be onsite."

"Excellent!" Erin's chipper tone returned. "We're excited to show our wholesome American PetroWave family to the world. See you at the luncheon on Tuesday. I've already emailed you details and will now do the same with your team."

Jonah ended the call and knocked the phone against his head. At least they could finish the camping trip. It was only one day, one trip in front of the cameras then he could vanish once again. He headed back to camp, much slower than his jog to the road. Ethan *had* asked about the spaceship, and even Row had sounded intrigued.

The kids could enjoy it, at least. He snapped a twig off a tree as he passed. *Hell, they'd probably love me for it. That would make the visit worthwhile for them.*

He passed Mud's truck as the rest of the camp awakened, and Mud cast Jonah a side-eye. "What was—"

As if on cue, his phone dinged. Then Saul's. Terrence's sounded as he came out of his RV. The rest of the invitations had arrived.

CHAPTER 3

The earth where the Nisku 42 oil rig once stood was torn apart, excavated to lay bare the enormous egg-like spaceship. As Jonah drove his truck down the switchback road dug into the side of the football field–wide hole, the sounds of celebration filled the air, but he couldn't ignore the military as well as the heavy security present, showing their steel against any threat.

"Whoa!" Ethan pressed his face against the passenger-side window. "Do you think the president is going to be here?"

"Maybe," Jonah grunted. He'd dreaded this moment for the past week. Too many people—politicians, military, reporters, and civilians alike. His palms were already sweating.

"A lot of presidents are gonna be there, Ethan." Row tried to keep his "cool teen" act, but Jonah noticed him craning his neck to see the spaceship's top. "This is a worldwide thing. This is . . . everything."

The truck reached the bottom of the excavation site. Up close, the spaceship seemed ready to swallow them in its silver hull. Some dirt and rock lingered on the shell, but for the most part, it shone unblemished in the high sun, reaching several stories into the sky. Jonah squeezed the steering wheel until his knuckles turned white. He'd known it was big, but there, at its base, it was monstrous—the size of a cruise liner buried beneath the earth.

Official-looking vehicles swarmed the area, ferrying people down from the makeshift helicopter landing pads above before turning around and chugging back up to do it again. Everywhere Jonah looked was movement. He showed his badge to a soldier with a brick-wall demeanor and an automatic rifle and got sent to park next to the news trucks. Already, a crowd swarmed the entrance area, waiting for the banquet to begin.

"Let's find Mom!" Ethan called out as they stopped, throwing his door open.

"Ethan!" Jonah snapped. "This is serious. You can't go running off alone."

Ethan stopped, one foot on the truck's step, then slunk back into his seat. "I'm sorry."

The momentary frustration faded, Jonah still clutching the steering wheel like a life raft. He released his grip and wiggled his tense fingers. He wasn't angry at Ethan and shouldn't take it out on him.

"Stay close." He shut off the engine and stepped out of the safety of his vehicle.

The smells of world cuisine drifted from the mobile kitchens pressed against the spaceship's hull, mixing with gas from the chugging generators to create something less than pleasant. Jonah led his sons away from the parking lot, with a hand guiding each by the shoulder.

Much of the scaffolding used in the excavation had been removed, leaving only a few towers near the front, ensuring most of the ship was photo ready.

"Where's the cockpit?" Row asked, pointing at the smooth silver hull. "How does it fly?"

"Maybe it hovers!" Ethan pulled away before catching himself and settling back down. "Do you know, Dad?"

"No." Jonah hadn't thought to ask. The ship had certainly piqued his curiosity, at least at first, but he didn't want to be involved with it now, nothing that could mess up his solitary, structured life.

They followed the crowd through cement dividers that herded

them toward a massive entrance in the ship's side, big enough to drive a semi-truck through. A thick power cord ran along a ramp from a generator hidden behind the food trucks and appeared to be made of the same silver material as the ship. In fact, the ramp melded so seamlessly with the bottom of the door that there was no visible hinge. Jonah glanced about. *How did they open the ramp? Did they somehow turn the ship on?*

"Jojo!" someone shouted from the crowd.

Jonah only knew one man who called him by that annoying name. He turned toward the sound as Paulie Nichols pushed against the tide, a camera bouncing on its strap against his chest. His buzzcut had turned salt and pepper since Jonah had last seen him, but the crooked smile looked the same as always.

"How long's it been, man?" He punched Jonah's shoulder a little too hard. "Five years?"

"Ten." Jonah guided his boys to the side, catching a confused glance from Row.

"No way. Really? Time's a bitch, damn. I spit out my beer when I saw your name on the guest list." He turned to Row and Ethan and laughed. "These your boys?"

"Yeah." Jonah tapped them on the shoulder in turn. "Row. Ethan. This is Paulie Nichols."

"How do you know our dad?" Ethan asked.

"We used to work together."

"You worked on a rig?"

Paulie snorted like it was the funniest joke he'd ever heard. "No way. Me and him used to dodge bullets in Syria."

"We didn't dodge bullets," Jonah said. "We were reporters. War correspondents."

"I remember some bullets."

"You were a reporter?" Ethan asked Jonah, his eyes wide.

"When you were little." Jonah rubbed the bridge of his nose as his growing headache worsened. When he shut his eyes, the carnage was there to greet him: Dried blood, exposed bone, burning flesh. Atrocities left in the sand, brought back by Paulie's few simple words.

"Your dad was *the* man when it came to war coverage." Paulie squatted closer to Ethan's level. "I've seen him walk casually into zones hotter than the devil's back. Till the paper went digital, of course."

"Well, that was then." Jonah pushed the memories of death into the past, where they belonged.

Paulie rose with a grunt and patted Ethan on the head, prompting a confused look from the boy.

Ethan's eyes darted to his dad, who shook his head in consternation. Paulie had about worn out his welcome, though he didn't seem to realize it.

"I thought I saw Lorri inside." Paulie turned his attention back to Jonah. "Did you not come together?"

Now his welcome was officially worn out. Jonah gave him a flat glare and led his boys toward the ramp. As he glanced back, Paulie shrugged and snapped a few shots of the ship.

"Why haven't you talked more about being a reporter?" Row asked as they stepped onto the incline.

"Not important," Jonah said. "It's the past."

"Right." Row pulled his jacket tighter around him. "It's just the past."

They passed through the entrance into the ship's interior, and all at once, the atmosphere changed. The slight Alaskan chill became a near-perfect warmth, accompanied by soft music from a grand piano on a small stage. The crowd thinned, spreading across the huge open area within. The space had been converted into a banquet hall, with long tables covered in white sheets adorned with elegant delicacies. Ice sculptures were strategically placed on the edges of the hall. Flags of various nations hung on the wall, and in similar places of honor were PetroWave's banners. No mistaking who discovered the ship.

What caught Jonah's eye the most, however, was the strange bend in the floor, a horizontal pathway stretching across and up the room, following the curve of the ship's inner wall. A rope had been set up to prevent anyone from journeying where it became too steep.

A caterer brushed past Jonah, heading back out the entrance. Waitstaff weaved expertly between the guests, offering hors d'oeuvres and champagne to men in elegant suits and women in cocktail dresses.

"I think we're underdressed," Ethan said, pulling at his button-down.

Jonah glanced at his own plaid shirt and khakis. They were the nicest clothes he owned, but among the black ties, he might as well have been a bum. He stuck his hands in his pockets, reminding himself he never wanted to come in the first place, and scanned the crowd for Lorri.

She was already on her way over, a champagne flute in one hand and a fish toast in the other. She had her hair up in a classy bun and wore the thin-rimmed glasses she liked to bring out for parties. Her black dress waved around her knees as she hurried toward them, a smile plastered across her face. Her laminated name tag said "Lorri Wall."

It had been years since he'd seen her dressed like that, one of their last date nights before everything fell apart. Jonah's chest tightened with unignorable regret and guilt.

"Mom!" Ethan rushed forward. "Isn't this awesome?"

"It's pretty cool, boys." She wrapped her arms around both of her sons, squeezing them tight while making sure not to spill her drink or food.

"I'm happy you're here." Row hugged her back.

Jonah shrank away. It had only been a week since they'd seen her, and he'd gotten nowhere near the same reaction at the airport.

Lorri let the boys go and stepped back, frowning as she inspected their clothes, then looked at Jonah.

"Hi, Lorri," was all he could think to say.

"Hi. Uh . . ." She gestured at his khakis and then the boys' outfits. "Didn't read the email, did you?"

"Maybe next time you can discover the spaceship and dress the kids." He clenched his jaw until his teeth hurt.

The boys looked from one parent to the other.

Lorri forced a smile. "Let's just enjoy the party. 'Kay? I got everyone's name tags."

She passed them out, and Jonah saw Row grimace when he read "Rowan Wall." Ethan immediately pinned his to his chest, eyes constantly moving to take in every sight at once.

Jonah spun his name tag between his fingers and scanned the banquet hall, desperate for a beer to calm his nerves. Unfortunately, the bar didn't appear to serve anything but champagne and cocktails. Before he could investigate further, a young woman with an earpiece and a clipboard rushed across the floor, gaze locked with his.

"Mr. Wall." She stopped nearly on his toes. "You're Jonah Wall, yes?"

"Yes?" His instincts told him to run.

"Good, I'm Erin Meyers. We spoke on the phone last week. Come with me." She spun on her heel, expecting him to follow.

"I'm with my family."

"We'll get photos with them after. Right now, we want the drill team who discovered the ship." She clapped her hands. "Come on. The speeches are about to start."

Jonah turned to apologize, but Lorri and the kids were already distracted by an ice carving of a moose. Ethan tried to touch it while Row stared at the catwalks high above them. His family clearly didn't need him, so Jonah clipped his name tag to his shirt and followed the publicist across the room to where the pianist played.

The production crew had set up an eight-foot-tall backdrop for photos, proudly displaying the PetroWave name for all to see. Jonah's rig crew lingered about the display, looking like black flies in cream. Mud resembled James Bond in a tailored black suit, flashing pearly whites at any woman who passed. Saul, Terrence, and Frankie weren't dressed much better than Jonah, but at least they'd put on ties, while Aleks wore an ill-fitting suit, the bagginess turning his gaunt frame into something practically ghost-like. He had a backpack slung over one shoulder.

Frankie tugged at his tie with a sour look, his mouth curled in discomfort.

Mud chuckled. "Better wipe that frown off your face before you give Aleks a run for his money."

"I'm not frowning," Aleks said. "I just think this is a bad idea. This many nations? In one place? You seen how many secret services there are hanging around? This is a spaceship, kids, people don't just get spaceships. I swear you this, someone's getting nuked before this is all over."

Aleks may have been the only one who didn't want to be there as much as Jonah, albeit for different reasons. His nervousness from being around this many people had faded, leaving Jonah empty of energy with only frustration to take its place.

"Any of you seen any beer?" he asked.

The crew shook their heads.

"Lots of bubbly," Mud said. "The bartender's not bad, but, yeah, all liquor here."

"Great."

"You seen Darius?" Terrence asked. "The man's dressed up finer than Mud. You'd think he'd won an award."

"Maybe he thinks he did," Saul said with a wink.

"Gentlemen, over here." Erin shepherded them all into a line, ensuring the company logo stayed clearly visible.

Jonah searched for Lorri, Ethan, or Row somewhere out in the crowd. The mass of press, dignitaries, and security swallowed them up without a trace.

A photographer placed his eye against the viewfinder. "Big smiles, everyone."

"Pretend you're happy," Saul whispered to Jonah. "It'll all be over soon."

Jonah gave a tight smile, the best he could muster, and the camera flashed.

***

After what felt like an hour of having his photo taken, Jonah's eyes started to get sore from all the flashing lights. He posed with his crew, his family, politicians he recognized from TV, and many more he'd never seen before. Every time he thought he might have a minute alone with Lorri or the boys, he was whisked off to another backdrop and another camera person.

He figured he'd finally get to escape once the speeches started, but he was led to sit on the stage in front of an awestruck audience and live news cameras. He and his roughnecks were placed squarely between the president of France and the prime minister of Japan.

With the lights blazing, Jonah could only make out vague shapes in the audience. Not Ethan, not Row, not Lorri. His breath quickened, and he squeezed onto his chair's arm until he thought he might snap it off.

For what felt like hours, he listened to speech after speech. Occasionally someone would gesture at him or call him and his crew up to receive a plaque as if they'd accomplished anything more than tripping over a branch and finding a gold bar. The words blended together until Jonah wasn't sure who was talking anymore.

"A fantastic opportunity to promote change," one said.

"A chance for a new, exciting path," another said.

"Reach beyond what is possible, and strive for new heights."

Nobody said anything beyond useless platitudes and vague aspirations. To Jonah, they sounded like little kids with a new toy, eager to tear it apart and find out how it worked.

Darius was called to the podium and introduced as PetroWave's chief geologist. Terrence was right. He'd dressed like this was the Oscars, with a collar so tight he could barely turn his head. He'd shaved the beard he'd kept while on the rig as well, anything to look less like the roughnecks he worked with. When he finished his own vapid speech about finding the ship, in which he practically claimed to have dug up the ship with his bare hands, he barely acknowledged the crew.

The host's voice boomed over the speakers. "Please welcome our next speaker, CEO of PetroWave, Cora Grey."

"Holy . . ." Mud whispered, bringing Jonah back to attention. "*That's* our CEO?"

A woman with the tall, poised bearing of an empress, her brown hair in a neat bun, took the podium. She pulled at the lapels of her silvery gray suit, smoothing down the edges to razor-sharp points, and smiled comfortably at the cameras like they were old friends passing on the street. Her skirt ended at her knees, long legs tapering to glossy black heels.

"I need to read more newsletters," Mud said.

Jonah nodded.

"Thank you to all the previous speakers," she said, her voice firm and powerful. "As you have heard, it was a PetroWave team who made this wonderful discovery. Which is rather apropos, I think. This ship, this mystery, is far beyond any piece of technology we have ever seen as a species. Centuries more advanced than we are. Though it was discovered in the search for oil, it signifies how PetroWave is always looking to the future and redefining what it means to be leaders in the energy sector."

She paused, leaning forward on the podium.

"You've heard heads of state extoll the opportunity a discovery like this offers, and I'm here to tell you PetroWave will be right alongside them, pushing forward every day to ensure sustainable energy for everyone."

Aleks whispered near Jonah's ear. "That must be why we keep getting work."

Cora's eyes flashed toward them for a moment, and Jonah froze. No way she could have heard Aleks, but he felt a dagger in his chest just the same. Aleks wasn't wrong, of course. For years, PetroWave had talked about promoting renewable energy and mitigating environmental impacts, yet year after year, Jonah saw no policy changes. He couldn't care less if the company wanted to keep pumping dirt, but at least they could be honest about it.

Without missing a beat, Cora Grey continued, but Jonah tuned her out. She came in a prettier package, but she was full of shit, just like the rest.

After Cora left the stage, an old man with white hair buzzed down to quarter-inch points and wrinkles in his dark skin rose from his seat.

"Please welcome our next speaker," the host said. "President Cyril Mbeki of South Africa."

He had to be well into his seventies and, despite the cane tapping with each step, moved easily and with dignity. As he passed Jonah, he glanced at him momentarily. Weariness sat behind his eyes, something Jonah had seen before in the faces of those who lived in war-torn countries.

Mbeki reached the podium and hooked his cane handle on the rim. For a long while, he said nothing, simply staring over the waiting crowd.

"The hope I see in this room makes me proud to stand among you." His accent came with a growl, possibly from a lifetime of smoking—or maybe a life lived hard in other ways. "I fear I may come off as a wet blanket, however. When I was a young man, I witnessed the apartheid government innovate science and technology, only for that same innovation to be used for oppression. The people they governed became cogs in a machine designed to crush them. Though we reach for the stars, now closer than they ever have been, we must not forget how many of our fellow humans still live on the ground."

The audience went quiet, seemingly unsure if this was all President Mbeki intended to say. When he didn't go on, some gave polite applause but no cheers like they had for earlier presenters. A hint of a smile crossed the president's face, the wise old grin of a father to his child. It took courage to speak so directly in a room built of pomp and fiction.

Unfazed by his poor reception, President Mbeki took his cane and

returned to his seat near the edge of the stage. His warning left a mark
on the rest of the proceedings. When the speeches concluded, it felt
like everyone let out a collective breath.

The stage lights dimmed, and Jonah saw the audience for the first
time. He needed to find Lorri and the boys. But as he stood up, a heavy
hand held him to his seat.

"*Un moment*," a Frenchman in a black suit said without looking at him.

The rest of Jonah's crew was similarly held in position, waiting as
the dignitaries moved off the stage first. Saul shrugged and settled back,
shutting his eyes as he waited.

Across the ship, past pried-open doors and carefully placed ladders, Dr.
Dominik Fielding sat with his laptop and gazed up at what he figured
was the engine. As the resident engineer and technology expert, his
job had been chasing the phantom energy surges across the ship for
months, and they all led back to that single point.

The only problem? There was nothing there.

The room was a massive sphere, with a series of three concentric
rings set into the ceiling high above like shrinking halos with a walkway crossing from opposite sides of the outer lip. In the middle, right
above his head, hung a circular portion with a gap in the center, allowing a view of the rings. All in all, the engine room, as he called it, felt
more like the planetarium he used to go to in San Diego.

"Dominik!" his supervisor shouted from the walkway. "I've been
calling you on your radio. You're not supposed to work today. They're
doing that big show."

"I know!" Dominik didn't even look up from his laptop. His radio,
lying beside it, had been muted for the past few hours to avoid distractions. "I'm almost done. I promise."

"I'm not paying you OT. Get out of there!" His supervisor slapped
the wall and headed out himself.

Dominik considered following—he'd looked forward to sneaking free food and drink at the luncheon all week—but he was so close to figuring out the power system. His laptop was plugged into a device designed to measure energy signatures, even types unknown on Earth. Like the one focused in that spherical room, seemingly the source.

Which, for the past three days, he swore was getting stronger.

He adjusted the energy-seeking pads he'd set on the floor, searching for where the signature was strongest. He didn't need overtime. He needed to figure out how the ship worked. He was so close.

CHAPTER 4

Row kept a firm hand on his brother's coat, keeping him from running off the second the speeches were done. They'd been given decent enough spots, just behind the press with the rest of the oil workers' families, but Row found it hard to follow along as each speaker rolled by. For a while, he watched his father sit motionless next to the podium, an unwavering neutral expression stuck across his face as people who'd never met him before heaped praise at his feet.

Everyone spoke in such vague banalities. Row spent most of the time playing Star Builder on his phone; he wanted to see the ship, not listen to boring speeches. By the time the weird guy from South Africa had taken the microphone and shaken things up a bit, he'd added a new power plant to his space station. After that, he only looked up again once the final applause broke.

As he, Ethan, and Mom shuffled through the folding chairs to meet with Dad, Ethan asked, "Do you think this means we'll be going to space soon?"

"I don't know." Mom stretched to see above the crowd. "They sounded pretty excited, though, didn't they?"

"Except for that guy from South Africa." Ethan furrowed his brow. "What was that about?"

"Old people are always scared of technology," Row muttered.

"Row!" Mom said. "Don't be rude."

He rolled his eyes. She didn't say he was wrong.

Up on stage, Cora Grey approached the microphone again. "For anyone interested, we will be running a series of tours of the ship. The first leaves in fifteen minutes, and our expert guide can be found under the PetroWave banner at the entrance of the ship."

A flood of black-suited guards clearing the way for their respective VIPs cut through the crowd, leaving behind an opening for Row to spot his dad lumbering down the stage steps to the ship's floor, his crew chattering behind his back. As Row, Ethan, and Mom approached, one of the crew cracked, "I need a drink before this whole meet 'n' greet." Row didn't recognize him, which meant he must've been Aleks, the only one who never went on their regular camping trips.

"I'm with you there," Mud said. He touched Dad on the shoulder and nodded toward Mom. "You married folks have fun."

Ethan rushed into Dad's arms. "That was so cool, Dad! Everyone was talking about you."

"I'm glad you enjoyed it." He spoke slowly, sounding almost bored.

Mud and Aleks slid off with the crowd while Saul and Terrence greeted their own families. Frankie, the only crew member wearing overalls, wrapped an arm around a woman who must've been his girlfriend.

Dad put Ethan back on his feet, and Saul's son, Lon, clapped him on the shoulder. "Hey, Ethan." He gestured at Terrence's twins. "We were gonna go check out where the floor starts to curve. Wanna come?"

"Hundred percent!" And like that, his boundless energy found a new target. Ethan turned to Dad. "Is that cool?"

"I . . . don't know." Dad scratched the back of his neck. "I have this meeting with some people from the company, but I thought we'd go back to the hotel soon."

"We're in a spaceship, Jonah," Mom chided. "I know you don't want to be here, but let the kids enjoy it a little."

Dad settled back on his heels, and Row's stomach churned. He hated seeing his parents fight, and even this simmering tension got his guts in a knot. A little part of him still dreamed his parents could work out their problems and their family could come back together, but in only a few minutes, they always ended up bickering.

"Let's go check out the room." Mom smiled at Ethan, then glanced over her shoulder. "Row, you wanna come with us?"

"I'm good." Row still wanted to see the ship, but now that he had the freedom to, it all seemed a bit overwhelming. During the speeches, the world leaders and company heads and whoever had barely mentioned it; did anyone even know anything about this thing? Or did they just not care?

Lorri set her jaw, looking like for a moment she would say something until Ethan sprinted off.

"Come on!" he shouted, leading the kids in a mighty rush. "Hot drop!"

"Wait! Don't run!" Mom chased after them, her heels clicking on the smooth floor.

Row felt a soft smack on his head and looked up into Dad's disappointed face.

"Come on, Row," he said. "We're in a spaceship. I thought you'd get a kick out of all this. Wasn't everyone just talking about all this stuff?"

"No one's talking about the ship. They're talking about themselves."

"I know. But your mom's right. Have some fun."

"What about you?" A sudden surge of courage took him. "I saw you on that stage. You were miserable."

"I'm not miserable. I'm . . ." Dad ran his hand along his chin stubble. "I have to be here. It's not my choice."

Row shrugged. "Guess we finally have something in common."

Dad's face fell, and he looked away. Not angry, not sad, at least not in a way Row could tell. Just distant.

"We're starting the tour in two minutes!" a young man with an American flag pin shouted from nearby. "This could be your only chance to see the back passageways of a real spaceship."

"I guess there's always the tour." Row tucked his phone away and spun on his heel. He took the name tag off—it wasn't even the right name anyway—and shoved it into his pocket.

"All right, everyone, stay close," the tour guide said with chirpy cheeriness. "The halls of the spaceship can get confusing, so make sure you keep me in your sight—and stay on this side of any yellow tape—and we're sure to have a fun time."

Row cocked an eyebrow. Someone had forgotten to tell the guide he wasn't leading a pack of camera-snapping tourists. Still, one of the dozen or so people gave a cheer in a language Row didn't recognize. The tour guide smiled and, with a wave, marched the group toward an open bulkhead door behind the stage.

The temperature dropped once they left the main luncheon. Regularly spaced construction lamps lit the halls beyond, which smelled dank and earthy like an old cave. From reading the news reports, Row knew the ship had been airtight before the drill pierced its bridge, so it had to be a recent phenomenon, or else he was smelling the musty odor of something ancient.

Something thumped behind him, and he turned to see a Black girl about his age in an electric wheelchair coming through the bulkhead. The rear wheels made the same thump as they crossed over the narrow door seam from the banquet room into the halls.

"What's up?" she said, steering the chair next to him with a small stick on the armrest. "Your dad's Jonah Wall, yeah?"

"Yeah?" Row tried to keep his eyes forward as they walked, but he couldn't help glancing over at her.

Her braided hair was cinched high up the back of her head before falling over her shoulders like a dark waterfall. Even when talking, she never stopped smiling. Row couldn't ignore how thin she looked. Her shirt and jacket hung off her like melting wax.

"That's so cool!" She flipped her braids back over her shoulder. "So, he, like, really discovered the spaceship? He was the first one to see it? What was that like? What did he say?"

"He didn't really say much."

"Really? Oh, my God! I would've told everyone. I wouldn't stop telling people. But I guess that's what you get from oil drillers. They're real manly-men types, yeah? Strong and silent, yeah? Old school, yeah? Suppose they would be, in a dying industry. But finding a spaceship? Underground? Wow."

Row could barely get a word in edgewise—if he even knew what to say or what question to answer.

The tour guide went on, pointing at doors and walkways as they passed. "When the first teams entered the ship, they found most doors were already opened. Experts surmise it was a security system, ensuring that no one would get trapped in case of power failure. The closed doors, however, have proven to be a tough nut to crack, as we don't want to damage any of the potentially delicate systems."

"How did they open the exterior door?" a tall man with a German accent asked.

"Mysteriously enough, it opened when the first team approached the ship." He wiggled his fingers and emitted a ghostly "oooooo."

"So, are you Rowan or Ethan?" the girl in the wheelchair asked.

"Rowan. I mean, Row." He took a moment before doing a double take. "How did you know that?"

"My dad had files on everyone who came to this event." She slapped her forehead. "Oh, duh! I forgot to introduce myself. Our dads are both famous, though your dad is more famous right now. My dad is famous more of the time. Ugh, sorry. Starting over." She extended a hand. "I'm Keneilwe Mbeki. But call me Kiki. I like Kiki. And I'll call you Row."

"Right. Yeah." He gently shook her hand. "Your dad's the president of South Africa."

"Yep, yep, yep. He gave that truly rousing speech."

"I thought it was . . . nice."

She huffed. "Dad's never been good with technology. He talks a lot about the 'simplicity of times long ago.' I don't think he considers that in the times he talks about I would be long dead. No medicine or anything like that." She laughed nervously and, for the first time, seemed at a loss for words.

The two of them continued in silence for a time, the tour guide giving a wholehearted attempt at making the metal halls feel interesting, though they were just smooth, interrupted by the occasional locked panel door. Eventually, Kiki perked up and smiled again.

"He just doesn't think about it is all," she said. "He's very busy. He's like your dad. Very strong, very silent, very busy. But we love each other."

"My dad . . ." Row scrunched his face. "It never feels like we're on the same page. I think he hates me."

"Oh, no. I'm sure he doesn't hate you. I bet he just, like, doesn't get you. Maybe he's just disappointed!" Her eyes went wide. "I mean, he's worried about you. My dad worries about me all the time. I don't know if you noticed, but . . ." She looked around conspiratorially and leaned toward him. "I'm in a wheelchair."

Row blinked. "Yeah."

"I know. I hide it so well." She grinned and settled back. "I have muscular dystrophy. It's a degenerative disease. But it's cool. I got this sweet chair. If I didn't have this thing, I'd be, what? Getting pushed around? Crawling on the ground? Yeah, that would suck."

She laughed again, harder this time. Row bobbed his head. *I'm not sure if I'm catching the dark humor,* he thought.

"Is that a question at the back?" the tour guide asked.

"Nope, sorry. Just showing my new friend something," Kiki called to the front of the group. Then she turned back to Row and said in a slightly quieter voice, "Anyway, do you know what kind of drill your dad used to get through the ship? Because I thought a spaceship that flies through space needs to be tough. Are oil drills really that strong?"

Row had no idea, and he didn't care. But the tour group was too tightly packed for him to escape by moving forward, and Kiki could easily keep pace with him in that high-tech wheelchair if he turned back. All he could do was nod politely at her questions and hope the tour didn't last much longer.

***

Jonah leaned on the bar, a second rum and Coke nestled in his hand as he listened to the pianist plunk away on the third or fourth song that sounded exactly the same. The event had gone worse than he ever could've imagined. It would've been better for him to never speak at all; every time he opened his mouth, he only made Lorri or Row madder at him. At least on the camping trips, the other guys could distract the kids.

He touched the cold glass to his forehead. What kind of father dreaded time with his sons? The one who kept failing, he told himself. He finished the last drop of his drink and bowed his head only to see an elegant black high heel land next to his work boots. He traced the curve of the legs up to the skirt and the hips, to the jacket, and to Cora Grey regarding him with a tight smile.

"You must be Jonah Wall," she said.

"Yup." He fingered the lip of the empty glass.

"When we planned this whole soiree, I wanted you to give a speech, but my media team told me you're not the talkative type." She took in a deep breath. "Guess they're right."

"Yup."

"All the same. We're happy you can be here. It's a big day."

He scoffed, his head starting to buzz. It was good rum. "For the company?"

"For the world, Mr. Wall."

"I'm sure PetroWave really cares about the world."

Cora cocked her head. "I'm afraid I don't know what you mean."

"Greenwashing." He tapped the glass on the counter.

"Excuse me?"

"That speech you gave up there. Renewable energy. Carbon footprint."

"I'm aware of what greenwashing is." She straightened her spine.

Jonah couldn't imagine she held herself much differently talking to shareholders. "PetroWave has been dedicated to—"

"Save me the corporate bullshit. I've worked here for almost ten years; I've heard it all."

She narrowed her eyes and snapped her jacket tighter over her shoulders. "Are you saying you want us to roll back on drilling? That's your livelihood, you know."

"What I'm saying is, don't put a dog in a crown and call it a king." Jonah locked eyes with her for the first time. "Either own up to your ideals or stop lying about them."

Cora set her jaw. Something flickered behind her blue eyes, a moment of softness, before it disappeared. She nodded curtly and brushed past him, leaving the floral scent of her perfume behind long after she'd vanished.

Jonah realized that come tomorrow, he'd probably regret finally speaking his mind.

The tour entered a thin room lined with slats sticking out from the walls. The guide gave one a firm pat. "Our best guess is this is a sort of bunk room," he said. "We've found at least fifty just like it all along this floor. It gives a fair guess at how many aliens lived on this ship and even their approximate size. That being just shorter than us."

"Assuming they look anything like us," Kiki whispered to Row.

Row grunted like he heard her, but his mind had drifted elsewhere. He gazed down the dim hall that passed the bunk room, where a piece of yellow warning tape told visitors to stay away. There had to be something interesting down there. He stood on a spaceship, after all, it couldn't all be boring bunk rooms. He'd just have to sneak off. But what if someone caught him?

His stomach turned, fighting his impatient feet. *I should stay.* He pulled at his jacket's hem. *I don't want to get in trouble.*

"Come on," Kiki said as though she'd read his mind. "This is boring. Let's see what's down there."

"I don't think so." Even if he did end up sneaking off, he didn't want to do it with the non-stop talker. He wanted to be alone. "That's not a good idea."

"You'd rather listen to the living embodiment of beige talk about beds?" She drifted backward silently into the hall. "Come on. This ship must be more interesting than they're making it seem."

Row looked at the guide, then at Kiki heading down the corridor. He held firm. The tour may have been boring, but his mom would lose her mind if he got lost.

Then again, Kiki was the daughter of the president of South Africa. If she got lost, and they learned Row had abandoned her, he could be in even bigger trouble. And how could she get in trouble? She was a dignitary. *It would be irresponsible to let her go on her own.*

With enough excuses to settle his mind, he took a few casual steps back out of the room, then spun and raced after her.

She waited at the yellow construction tape. "I knew you were more fun than you looked."

"I promise, I'm not." He lifted the tape and let her under before following.

Off the beaten path, the construction lamps became rarer, leaving large stretches of the hall in near pitch black with only the next light as a beacon. Kiki's wheelchair glided silently, but each of Row's footsteps pounded like a sledgehammer. He didn't belong there. He should turn back.

He didn't. Kiki kept at his side, a ray of sunshine in the dark, basking in amazement at the cool gray halls. Somehow, her presence calmed him and urged him to keep walking. He didn't want her thinking he was a coward, after all. She looked to be about his age, but he'd never met anyone with so much energy.

Voices echoed from ahead, and they slowed.

". . . a non-Newtonian fluid can change its viscosity when under force," a woman's voice said.

"I know what a non-Newtonian fluid can do," a deeper voice replied. "That's YouTube-level stuff."

The conversation came from an open door, where harsh yellow light flooded into the hall. Row slowed his steps, easing his left foot silently to the ground.

"We should go back," he whispered to Kiki.

She shook her head. "We're too far. Just go quick and quiet."

Row hesitated, looking up and down the hall. Kiki shot forward without him.

"You just looked confused when I said it," the woman said with no noticeable accent, so Row figured she must be American or Canadian.

"I wasn't confused; I was trying to stifle a yawn." The man was clearly British. "And more to the point, are you implying the hull is made of a fluid?"

Kiki wheeled up to the edge of the light and turned her chair, peering into the room. Row, despite all his misgivings, crept forward and joined her. The space had been filled with all sorts of expensive equipment exhibiting screens and lights and readouts. Mom liked to watch TV procedurals, and Row recognized some pieces from the background of their lab scenes, but other, larger devices looked like they'd have been more at home on a spaceship of their own.

The scientists, or whoever they were, hovered over something that looked like a tall microwave, peering through a transparent panel at what was inside.

The woman was short, with a round face and nearly platinum blond hair wrapped up in a bun. "It's clearly not made of fluid," she said, pushing thick-rimmed glasses up her nose. "But of something that gets stronger the harder it's hit."

"Possibly." The male scientist stroked his neatly trimmed beard. He was tall and built like a garden rake. "If it's some sort of reactive material, that would explain how it could survive in space, but the drill was able to pierce through it."

"And possibly how it repaired itself afterward!" She clapped her hands in excitement. "We should tell Dr. Cummings first thing tomorrow."

"Indeed."

Part of Row wanted to creep in and see what they were looking at, but Kiki pushed her stick and glided past the door, so he chased after, making sure to step lightly.

"Maybe don't start with the non-Newtonian fluid thing, though," he heard the male scientist say.

"I was trying to speak to your level." A snort echoed into the hallway.

"I told you it's a lot more interesting back here," Kiki said.

"Yeah." Row glanced back at the lab. He'd already learned much more in a minute than the tour had given him in half an hour.

"Did they say the ship repaired the hole your dad put in it? Does that mean it's alive?"

"I've heard of self-healing materials, but to create an entire ship out of something like that is amazing." Row's mind ran wild with what other strange and wonderful technologies the ship might hold. PetroWave should've had those two scientists give the presentation if they wanted people to care. "That must be why the ship held up so well after being underground. It wouldn't be affected by erosion or metal fatigue."

"You sound smart. How do you know all that?"

"I, uh . . ." He hoped the shadows hid the redness in his cheeks. "I just read it online. I get bored easily. It's lame, I know."

"No, it's cool!"

"My dad would tell me to get outside more."

"Ugh." She threw her head back in playful disgust. "I've been outside. I don't know what all the hype is about."

Row burst out laughing, and Kiki joined. He was surprised at how much fun he was having, given how boring the afternoon had started.

They came upon another door and shared a look before cautiously

entering. The room, if it could be called that, seemed to have no bound-
aries. An expansive catwalk stretched before them, its crossing metal
walkways extending beyond the reach of the entryway lamps and into
the darkness. Row peered over the railing, and his head spun as he
looked down multiple stories.

"Do you think the aliens can walk on walls?" Kiki asked.

"I dunno." He wet his dry lips with his tongue. "Why?"

"How else would they walk on that?" She pointed to the right,
where the catwalk split in two, curving up and out of view toward
another walkway above them. It reminded Row of the sloping floor
where the banquet had been held.

"I don't know. We don't know anything about the people who made
this. Maybe they could fly."

"Oh, like Superman." Kiki lifted a fist like she was about to take off.

Row looked over the edge again, white-knuckling the railing.
Several stories down, barely reached by the lights, were four metallic
doughnuts set in a row. From this height, they looked no bigger than
a foot in diameter, which meant they had to be huge up close, and
each one had a thin tube coming out of one side, pointing at round
impressions—holes?—in the opposite wall below.

"They're snails," Kiki said, looking through the lower gap in
the railing.

"What?" Row glanced around, wondering where she saw snails.

She pointed at the doughnuts. "See? They've got the circle and the
skinny tube. Like a snail."

"I guess." If Row turned his head, he could almost see what she was
talking about. "That snail would have a tiny head."

"Fine." She turned her wheelchair and wheeled across the precari-
ous catwalk without blinking. "You tell me what you think it is."

Row squinted his eyes, trying to make out anything in the shadows.
On the back of one of the snails was a series of concentric circles, like
a bullseye. The next had what looked like a Y with a diamond around
it, while the third had some crooked crescent moon. The last one, the

farthest away and the hardest to see, only had a thick-lined X. The symbols didn't do much to help Row understand the donuts' purpose; they might as well have been snails.

Kiki had almost left the nearest lamp's glow by the time Row looked up. He hurried after her, keeping one hand on the railing as he went. His eyes were locked on the back of Kiki's head, where her braids wrapped around the nape of her neck and took on a brownish color. If he looked down, he'd never start moving again.

Just keep following Kiki, he told himself. She hadn't steered him wrong yet.

Dominik couldn't believe what he was seeing. Everywhere he moved the pads, he found an energy signal in the form of a series of beeps and a recorded wave on his computer screen. A few weeks earlier, he'd been crawling around the engine room's sphere, sliding the pads across the floor like a dowsing rod seeking water. The energy was everywhere, flowing like raging rapids through the wires beneath the floor. What could be causing it? What did it mean?

"Wow!" A man with a buzzcut and a camera appeared on the upper lip of one of the entrances to the spherical room, below the catwalk, snapping pictures of the rings above Dominik's head.

"Hey!" Dominik flew to his feet, nearly knocking his laptop over. "This area's off-limits."

"Naw, it's cool." The man tapped a laminated pass on his vest, too far away and too small for Dominik to read. "Paul Nichols. I'm press."

"Okay. Yeah, but . . ." Dominik rubbed his eyes. "It's also off-limits to press. The party's back the way you came."

"It's fine! We got a senator here, and we're just gonna use it as a backdrop. In and out. Real quick." He waved to someone outside who Dominik couldn't see and gestured at the catwalk and platform in the upper center of the room. "Come on! I found a good place. Could even get up to that walkway up there, I bet."

"No!" Dominik shouted. "No more people here!" But it was like talking to a brick wall.

A white-haired man with deep wrinkles walked into view, a cigar clutched between his teeth. He nodded at the rings hanging above him and pulled a metal lighter out of his pocket.

"Hey!" Dominik ran to the bottom of the ladder that climbed the side of the bowl up to the lip. "You are *not* smoking in here, no matter *who* you are!"

The senator either didn't hear him or didn't care. He flicked the lighter and brought it to his cigar. Dominik's equipment shrieked. He hurried back in time to see his readings register a sudden energy spike on the screen.

Narrow slits appeared in the walls behind the senator and let out a deep bass rumble. The guy with the press pass covered his ears as sound waves doused the senator's lighter and cigar.

"What the hell was that?" the reporter asked, looking back as the wall closed again behind him. He put his hand on the newly smooth surface.

"Get out!" Dominik's face burned red. He stomped toward the lip and gestured angrily at the unauthorized visitors, aggressively waving his hand. "Get out now!"

"Fine! Jeez." The reporter snapped another picture of the rings and left, taking the bewildered senator with him.

Dominik huffed. His heart beat like horse hooves, and his face felt like a campfire. Even with two dozen nations' security on-site, nothing could stop the arrogance of some people. He didn't even have time to marvel at the sonic fire suppression, not while his equipment screamed at him.

The readings had skyrocketed off the charts. He had assumed the recent energy signatures were already displaying the ship's full power, given how high they were. But when he tried decreasing the sensor's sensitivity, it became clear that what he'd seen before was just a trickle. Judging by how loudly the sensor was still beeping, the signatures were getting stronger.

He snatched his radio from next to his laptop. "This is Dominik in the engine room. Something's happening; the power to the ship is increasing, and I think it's turning on. We should evacuate everyone until we know it's safe."

He waited. No one replied.

"Hello? I'm an engineer in the rear of the ship. It's turning on. Does anyone hear me?"

Nothing but dead air. He wondered if the surging energy had disrupted the radio signals. The floor rumbled, and strange, guttural whines filled the room. The walkway above him retracted into the walls, leaving the center platform somehow floating in space. His legs shook, and not just from the vibrations now rattling the engine room. He collected his jacket and laptop and headed for the ladder out of the bowl, still clutching the radio.

"This is Dominik. Please respond." His head swooned like air was being pumped in through his ear, and he couldn't control his breathing. "Listen to me. The ship is active!"

Finger on the call button, eyes on the ladder, Dominik never saw the rings descend from the ceiling and begin to spin. The outermost swept down, barely skirting the pristine metal bowl. All Dominik heard was the rushing of air, and he was gone.

CHAPTER 5

A
t first, Jonah thought someone had started one of the big excavators outside and accidentally left it running. A dull hum filled the banquet room, so slight and small he wasn't sure when it started. The pianist played through, but even she looked around as though searching for the source of the sound. Jonah wandered through the hall, heading for the appetizers; the actual luncheon wasn't set to start for another twenty minutes, and he was starving.

When he got to the hors d'oeuvres, he skewered some smoked shrimp with a toothpick from a small container on the table. He'd given up on the day; at the very least, he could fill up on meat and cheese until he got sick. As he put away his third bruschetta, he saw the table's ice sculpture, one of a bear rearing up on its back legs, begin to move. He stopped, crumbs lingering on his lips, and watched as the sculpture vibrated across its drip tray.

Jonah touched the bear's leg. It trembled beneath his fingers. He opened his mouth to tell someone, but before he got a word out, it reached the edge of the table and toppled over, exploding across the floor like a frozen splash. A woman yelped in surprise, and all eyes turned to Jonah.

"Sorry," he said with a grimace, as if he were guilty of knocking it over.

A moment later, a champagne glass on a nearby table smashed, then three more. The hum turned to a roar, and no one could ignore the steady vibrations shaking the room.

A man in military gear snatched the microphone off its stand and stood at the edge of the stage. "Attention! All attendees must calmly but quickly make their way to the exit. Please follow the directions of our personnel, and they'll lead you to the safety point."

He'd barely finished the words when the room burst into motion. People rushed for the one large exit, taking the suggestion of quickly over calmly. Guards with their charges, dignitaries and the like, pushed through the crowd, ensuring their own people were safe first and coming into verbal conflict with the others trying for the same.

Jonah jumped on a table and searched for familiar faces. A series of lights built into the walls came on, outshining the generator-powered lamps and making the banquet hall far brighter than before. Military flanked both sides of the door, urging everyone onward. Cora stood near the stage, shouting into her cell and gesticulating wildly. Jonah didn't have a moment to wonder what she was so angry about. Instead, he spotted Lorri and Ethan rushing in from the back with Lon and Terrence's twins. His heart thumped against his sternum. He leaped off the table and rushed to meet them.

"Jonah," Lorri said, her face pale. "What's going on?"

"I don't know." He turned back to the exit. The military had already herded most people out, but a few stragglers, like them, remained in the hall.

"Where's Row?" Lorri asked, her brow creased with worry.

"He went with a tour. Go outside with the kids. I'll find him and meet you there."

"But Dad!" Ethan pulled at Jonah's coat. "I don't wanna go without Row. What if the aliens get him?"

Jonah knelt and put his hand on Ethan's shoulder. "I'll find him, I promise. But you have to protect your mom and the other kids, okay? I'm trusting you with this."

Ethan sniffed and nodded, holding onto his mom's hand with all

his might, as he had when he was much younger. Lorri gave Jonah a
look of trust, a small smile he hadn't seen in years, and headed for the
entrance. He watched her go, joined by Saul's and Terrence's wives, as
well as Frankie's girlfriend, until he noticed the American flag–wearing
tour guide hurrying in the same direction with a crowd of people.

"Hey! Wait!" Jonah chased after him.

The tour guide stopped and spun around, bewildered. The group
he led carried on without him. Row wasn't among them.

"My son went with you on the tour." Jonah ran his fingers through
his hair, panic rising in his chest. "He's about seventeen. Dirty blond
hair. He's wearing a windbreaker."

"Yeah, he was with the girl in the wheelchair." The guide kept glancing at the exit. "They left partway through. I thought they came back.
Sorry, but I . . ." He didn't finish the sentence, just ran off.

Jonah spun around the room, looking for any sign of Row hiding
among the luncheon tables and decorations. If Row had left the tour
early, he might not have come looking for Jonah, but he wouldn't have
hidden from his mom. Where was he? Could he be outside already?

"Jonah!"

He turned to find Saul and the crew filing into the banquet room
from another door at the back. A couple of cameramen, their rigs
slung over their shoulders, hurried past, barely glancing at Jonah as
they made their escape.

"What the hell's going on?" Saul's eyes landed on the smashed ice
sculpture on the floor.

Darius shoved his way through the group, nearly stumbling into
Jonah's chest. "I was having a very interesting talk with Anderson
Cooper when everything started shaking!" Even in an emergency, he
couldn't help name-dropping.

"Your families are outside with Lorri." Jonah stepped around them,
homing in on the door he saw the tour come through moments ago.
"But I can't find Row. I can't leave without him."

"The military is evacuating people." Darius pulled at his tight collar. "We need to go!"

The floor shifted beneath their feet. Another ice sculpture toppled over, scattering shards across the floor.

"Oh, shit!" Frankie yelled, pointing at the entrance.

The drawbridge-like ramp they'd ascended to enter the ship had begun to rise. The military personnel started pushing the last people through. A few leaped out with them as self-preservation took control.

Adrenaline and fear shot through Jonah's body.

They were about to be sealed in.

The rumbling was Row's first sign that something was wrong, but he knew they were in trouble once they took the next turn, sure it would take them back to the large room with the snails, and found only a dead end.

"Was it supposed to be a left or a right?" Kiki asked, reversing into the hall they came from. "I can't tell what anything looks like in the dark!" The generator-powered lamps were few and far between in this deeper part of the ship, making it difficult for Row and Kiki to keep their bearings.

As if in reply, the built-in panel lights above them flashed on, glowing a cool white.

"Did you just . . ." Row touched the cold metal of the wall, which he could now see clearly for the first time.

"Turn the lights on? I don't know how I could have." Kiki's laugh echoed down the empty passageway.

What Row had previously thought was a dead end opened in the newly lit corridor, revealing a large, dark room filled with consoles and chairs. As he and Kiki went inside, the lights turned on in reply. Panels glowed blue, green, and red, making the room a vibrant display of colors. Holograms with strange markings appeared in the air as they

passed by. The room itself was made up of multiple low levels, connected by single stairsteps and a subtle ramp curving around the wall.

"It's the bridge," Row said, barely able to keep his jaw off the floor.
"It has to be." He'd played so many science-fiction video games, flying polygons through digital stars, but nothing prepared him for the
awe-inspiring feeling of standing in a real spaceship's bridge.

Kiki approached one of the consoles on the back wall. She reached
for an icon on the screen, only to stop herself and pull her hand back.
"That's probably not a good idea."

Row laughed. He stepped down onto the lowest level, closest to the
far wall across from the entrance. In a flash, the wall went transparent,
becoming a floor-to-ceiling window that spread from one edge of the
room to the other. They could see the remains of the scaffolding still
propped along the ship's exterior. Below that, people crowded, some
huddled together, others rushing around doing who-knows-what.

"What do you think is happening out there?" Kiki asked, joining
him at the window.

Row frowned. A tickling dread crept up his spine. He'd been so lost
in the immediate splendor of the functioning bridge that he'd forgotten all about the strange rumbling that had led them there.

Ethan let his mom lead him toward the parking lot while the military
men pushed the crowd back, but his head kept swiveling back to the
entrance ramp, which had begun to lift like a drawbridge. As the metal
slab tore itself from the earth, raining dirt on the soldiers who stood
nearby, a short train of harried-looking guests jumped to the earth
below, followed by a few last soldiers. But not his dad or Row. Where
were they?

"Kiki!" a voice cried out, and Ethan saw the African president who
gave the weird speech earlier hobble past a group of guards and soldiers,
his cane clutched in the air by its middle instead of supporting his steps

as it had been earlier. He moved surprisingly well for an old guy, and Ethan was astonished to see him dive chest first onto the ramp when it was already four feet off the ground and vanish inside the ship.

The ramp continued its course, cutting the thick power cords that had serviced the event and finally sealing seamlessly into the ship's side. In the blink of an eye, Ethan could no longer make out where the door had just been.

"Get a saw!" a soldier yelled, but Ethan couldn't see what good that would do.

He was searching the crowd for his dad and brother when suddenly, the front of the ship, whose egg-like exterior tapered to a point, turned from metal to glass, and there was Row. Inside the ship, looking down like an alien ruler.

"Whoa," he whispered, then said more loudly, "Mom!" But when he turned, she was nowhere to be seen.

A man in a suit shoved past, nearly sending Ethan onto the dirt. He frowned and looked up again for his brother. Row was still in the window, only now, a girl was with him. Ethan didn't recognize her, but it wasn't fair. If Row got to stay on the ship, why didn't he?

The soldiers were so focused on the door that Ethan slipped over to the scaffolding unnoticed. He circled the structure, then grabbed the lowest rung of the supports. The metal bit coldly into his skin. He pulled his coat sleeves over his hands and started climbing.

"What's he doing?" Row had been relieved to spot his mom and brother outside the ship, but that was wiped away as Ethan started to climb the scaffolding. Row cupped his hands against the window and shouted, "Go back! Get away from the ship!" but Ethan's focus didn't waver.

"I don't think he can hear you," Kiki said.

"I know!" Row punched the translucent material, immediately regretting it as his knuckles flared with pain. "But it's dangerous!"

Ethan traversed each level with an apparent disregard for his safety. The wind pulled hard against his coat, threatening to tear it right off his body, but still he looked up at his brother with determination.

The rumbling had morphed into a roar within the ship, and Row tugged at his hair in panic. He nearly pulled a fistful out when his hand shot forward suddenly. "Go back!" He pointed at Ethan, then at the ground, hoping to convey the message wordlessly.

"Yeah!" Kiki pounded on the window. "Go away!"

Row's throat cracked, but he kept shouting. It made no difference. Ethan reached the scaffolding level with the window and knocked excitedly. They saw his knuckles hit the transparent material but couldn't hear a sound. Ethan's mouth opened in what had to be a shout, but again they heard nothing. The window was soundproof.

Row put on his most serious expression and mouthed as clearly as he could, "Leave. Now."

Ethan must have understood this time, but he shook his head. Row glared at his brother, then turned on his heel and ran for the door. Maybe if he left the bridge, Ethan would climb back down the scaffolding. Maybe they could find each other outside, and their parents. Maybe this rumbling would stop, and everything would be okay.

When Lorri finally located Ethan again, she unleashed a terrified scream. How had he managed to get to the top of that scaffolding and—wait. Was that Row in the window? *He's still on the ship?* Both her boys were in danger, and her focus narrowed to them alone.

She raced toward the ship's nose, but an arm snaked around her waist, and she collapsed forward with an *ooph*.

"Stop!" she cried when she'd recovered her breath, clawing at the soldier's grip with her manicured nails. "My sons are up there! Ethan! Row!"

"You have to stay back, ma'am." The soldier shoved her back into the crowd and held the line.

"Ethan!" Lorri's yell was barely audible over the roar from the ship, and the excavation site was a furious cacophony. A terrible whine and a shower of sparks rained down near the former entrance where a soldier with a cement saw tried to hack through the shell, and Lorri continued to call out to her sons.

Her cries were swallowed up as the ship began to shake. Small rocks in the area lifted into the air, drifting toward the silver hull.

"Ethan! Row!" Lorri's voice suddenly sliced through the unexpected silence.

Then an explosion of sound that would put a thunderclap to shame ripped over the crowd. A pulse of force hit Lorri square in the chest, rattling her bones. She instinctively braced her lower body and squeezed her eyes shut, engulfed in silence. When she opened her eyes again, the world fell out beneath her. Somebody screamed. It could've been her.

Blood coated the dirt. Soldiers close to the ship were sheared cleanly in half. The scaffolding creaked against its own weight, suddenly missing many of its supporting struts. One of the catering trucks looked like an invisible giant had taken a bite out of it. And the ship . . .

The ship was gone.

CHAPTER 6

Jonah rubbed the soreness from his ears. A minute earlier, they'd suddenly popped, and he felt a weird shift in his stomach. It didn't help that Darius was hammering his fists against the metal of what just moments ago had been the entrance ramp. "Open up!" he shouted. "Come on and open up!"

"Maybe it'll open if you tell it who you are," Mud said, leaning next to him. "Come on, Darius the Spaceship Hunter. Let it know who's boss."

"Can you shut up for one second? Seriously?"

"I don't have reception." Cora Grey stomped over from the stage, holding up her phone. "Anyone else?"

Terrence and Saul pulled out their phones and frowned. Darius quickly stopped pounding and slipped his phone from his jacket pocket, consternation replacing annoyance as he poked at the screen futilely. Jonah didn't bother checking his own phone; he could tell by his crew's expressions what he'd find.

He glanced around the room to take stock. About twenty people remained in the hall, most of them military—Air Force by their uniforms. They hadn't dressed for the party; instead, they wore their fatigues and had rifles at their sides. His drill crew were all still on board, plus Cora. They'd been joined at the last minute by Cyril Mbeki, the elderly president of South Africa, who'd taken a heroic dive into the ship moments before it sealed tight. He continued to surprise.

"Are you all right, sir?" one of the Air Force officers asked President Mbeki, helping him to his feet. The soldier was strong-jawed, with light-brown skin and an unwavering gaze. He brushed some of the dust from Mbeki's shoulders and held him firm. He appeared to be a lieutenant colonel, judging by the silver leaf insignia on his jacket.

"I'm fine." Mbeki clutched onto his cane tightly, and Jonah wondered if he'd hurt himself on his unexpected entrance. "I'm looking for my daughter. She's sixteen and in a wheelchair."

Jonah perked up at the mention of the wheelchair. "I think she may be with my son. They got separated from the tour."

"Then we'll have to find them together." Mbeki hobbled forward on his cane.

"No one's going anywhere," the officer said. "I'm Lieutenant Colonel Christopher Rivera. That means I'm the highest-ranking officer on this side of the door, and we aren't going anywhere until I can contact the command structure outside."

"And can you?" Jonah asked.

Rivera bit his tongue. "The radios are down."

"Then I'm going to find my son." Jonah offered the South African president a hand, but he waved it off.

"I said, we stay put." Rivera stepped in their way. The rest of the Air Force personnel approached, rifles held at their sides. They had the same jitter in their step and darting gaze as the rest, but they were armed, and that gave them enough semblance of power.

Mbeki met Rivera face-to-face, a calm but stern expression on his face, one of a man who was used to leading. "I will not stand by while my daughter is lost out there. If you're going to shoot me for that, I suggest you do it quickly."

"Gentlemen." Cora inserted herself between the pair. "Compose yourselves."

"We're not going to shoot anyone, sir," Rivera said. The *sir* had more venom than the first time. "We just need to keep people safe and together. The best minds in the world are out there working their way in. There's nothing to worry about."

"Dad!" Row sprinted into the hall at high speed, knocking over one of the tables he couldn't dodge around. At his back, Kiki pushed her wheelchair to top speed, beating Row to the group congregated at the door.

"Kiki!" Mbeki threw his arms around her.

"Are you all right?" Jonah asked.

"You have to come with us!" Row's face was flushed with exertion, and he barely looked at his father before turning on his heel and heading back the way he came. "Now!"

Kiki pulled herself out of her father's arms. Her eyes were wide. "Come on, Daddy. We're not where we are."

"What do you mean?" He reached for her again, but she'd already thrown the chair in full reverse.

The kids had come in with such fire and intensity that not even Rivera had time to stop them. Jonah took chase after Row and Kiki, and everyone else followed suit.

"What do you mean we're not where we are?" Jonah asked Kiki, racing to keep up with her motorized chair.

"Well . . . we're in a spaceship." She swallowed hard. "Right?"

Jonah's skin went cold. She couldn't be talking about what he thought she was talking about. His mind practically overflowed with questions, but he didn't know how to ask them—or if Kiki would even know the answers—until they arrived in a large room near the front of the ship. Jonah recognized it as the first piece he saw through the drill cam two years earlier, only now fully lit and covered in blinking consoles. If only that were the last surprise. Row and Kiki stopped at the window. They didn't have to say a word.

It wasn't Earth outside—at least, not somewhere on Earth Jonah recognized. Stretching around and away from the ship was a dark and blasted landscape of orange-red rust and gray industrial ruins. Short skeletons of collapsing structures leaned against each other, spilling their walls out and displaying their interiors, others resting at an angle. They had recognizable floors, and though they were too decayed to make out their original structure, they seemed more rounded in design than the buildings back home. Something shimmered above them. The sky was a hazy yellow hue, stretching far off into the horizon.

They were inside a dome, Jonah suddenly realized. A dome on a world unlike any they could imagine. Beyond the ruins, beyond the hexagonal pattern of the barely visible shield, was a barren landscape of orange dirt and jagged stone.

Jonah's eyes glazed over, unable to take it all in, until he noticed a thick pad of red smeared across the right side of the window. In the center, stuck in place by the sticky mass, was a name tag, just like his own. This one said "Ethan Wall."

Row caught his father's gaze and followed it.

Row saw the blood.

He saw the name tag.

He screamed.

"Ethan was . . . he was climbing outside the ship to get to me . . ." Row's voice cracked.

Jonah's mind shut down. He suddenly stood three feet behind himself, watching the back of his head as he stared at the crimson horror, the pieces finally falling into place. Row choked and sprinted out of the room, and Jonah barely heard him leave. Kiki started after Row, but Mbeki held her chair back. She couldn't help him. Only Jonah could, and he couldn't yet bring himself all the way back to reality.

Aleks' voice filtered in, strained and angry. ". . . shouldn't have come! This is exactly what I thought would happen!"

"You thought we would get shot to space?" Saul asked.

"Because this is the plan. They want to test the ship, right? So first they send us up into space, then they grab us, put us in a hole, and stick needles in our brains to figure out what crazy cosmic radiation hit us."

Saul shoved him against a console. "I've had enough of your

paranoid shit, Aleks!" Aleks froze, eyes like headlights. A couple of
airmen held him by the arms and pulled him away, almost losing him
a couple of times as he struggled.

"How do we get home?" Frankie asked, barely more than a
mouse's squeak.

"This isn't happening," Terrence said. He kept touching his face
and arms, pacing back and forth in front of the window. "This is . . . a
screen. It's just showing us a . . . a movie."

Darius stumbled forward, tapping the red smear. "Yeah, a fun movie with blood on the lens. Oh, God, we're all dead! I'm going to die
in space."

"Everyone, shut up!" Rivera stepped in front of the group. He
grabbed Terrence by his shirt and tossed him at one of his airmen.
"Take your asses back to the banquet hall. Civilians stay seated while my
team locks down the area, and *nobody* is walking off anymore. Got it?"

Saul struggled against the airmen, who kept their grips firm on his
upper arms. "Who put you in charge?"

"This isn't a conversation." Even though Saul had ten pounds of
muscle on him, Rivera approached and met his furious gaze without
blinking. "Back to the hall."

Saul snorted through his nose like a bull but relaxed. The airmen
released him and escorted him out of the bridge, taking the rest of the
drill crew with him. Mbeki urged Kiki out, leaving only Cora and
Jonah, who stood still as a statue. His body had gone cold. No more
thoughts were polluting his mind, only the crystal-clear horror of his
youngest son's bloody name tag.

Rivera curled his lip, and with heavy, plodding footsteps, he circled
Jonah. His gaze flicked down to the name tag. "Jonah Wall. I saw you
on stage. I know you wanna play the big man for your team, but I'm
in charge here. Back to the hall. For your own safety."

Jonah didn't move. He wasn't afraid of the soldier, and he wasn't in
the mood for orders.

"Listen." Rivera leaned in until Jonah felt his breath on his face.

"Either you walk the line, or I'm dragging your unconscious body over it. I'm not playing around."

Jonah clenched his fist. "No."

"Okay!" Cora busted in, crossing her arms, and faced Rivera. "Colonel, if you want to order your soldiers around, perhaps you should follow them."

"I am the highest-ranking officer—"

"We are not in the military, and this is not a military operation." She kept a placating smile across her face, but her words struck like sledgehammers. "I have four brothers in the military, so your deep-voice bravado doesn't work on me. All the same, Mr. Wall's not a threat to anyone. Agreed?"

Rivera looked Jonah over. Then scoffed. "Agreed. But no wandering the ship. Everyone's either here or the hall." He glared at Jonah and marched out of the bridge, kicking one of the consoles as he passed.

Cora let out a breath. She turned to Jonah, but he didn't look back at her. Whether he'd been left alone or Christopher had laid him flat, it didn't matter. Maybe if he'd taken the punch, he could've woken up from the nightmare. Instead, his mind reeled in an endless loop of horror.

The ship creaked, and Cora jumped. She took a breath like she was about to say something, but instead, her eyes darted to the smear of blood, then back to Jonah, then she left without a word. Her heels clicked down the metal hallways and vanished into the ship, leaving Jonah alone, gaping at an alien landscape and trapped in the cage of his mind.

Row hadn't stopped running since he left the bridge. Ethan couldn't be dead. Row had turned just as the ship apparently moved, glancing back to make sure Ethan had climbed down, and seen him vanish before the scenery changed, so fast it was like he was flying. He hadn't noticed the blood where his brother had once stood. Or his name tag. He should've. He was supposed to take care of him.

Ethan couldn't be dead.

He turned a corner so fast his feet nearly left the ground. Once the ship had powered up, doors opened across it, letting him pass through areas he and Kiki hadn't seen on their first trek to the bridge. He cut through a bunk room, down a ramp, and into the former banquet hall. He didn't know where he was going or what he would do when he got there. He just needed to be there fast.

The main door loomed before him, meshed seamlessly into the dark-gray walls. Row slammed his shoulder against it, kicked it, anything to get it open. A fly against a castle wall, but he kept battering until his arms and legs got sore.

"Hey, kid!" Mud shouted, coming in with the rest of the drill crew, followed by President Mbeki, Kiki, and Colonel Rivera's airmen. He pulled his tie loose and tossed his jacket aside. "You're gonna hurt yourself. Settle down."

"I need to find Ethan!" Row shouted, bashing himself against the unkind metal again. "He's hurt!"

The crew slowed as they approached. "Row, he's . . ." Mud started but couldn't finish. He shared a look with the roughnecks and airmen. They'd all seen the blood, the amount of it, but none of them could say the obvious. Mbeki held Kiki's hand.

Row threw himself at the door again and again. His eyes burned, but he fought back the tears. There was no need to cry, not when Ethan was still alive. The repeated thump of his sore body against the metal was the only sound when Rivera arrived.

"What's going on here?" he demanded. He spotted Row and frowned, then pointed at his airmen. "Get these people into seats."

Row struck the door again, and this time it shifted. It opened about a foot, letting in a rim of light on three sides. The metal groaned, the ramp began descending, and yellow light spilled into the room. The airmen drew their rifles. Row stumbled back, his jaw hanging open as they took in their surroundings.

"Oh, God," Terrence said, clutching his head. "It's real."

The landscape looked as it had from the bridge, only now as a sharp reality. What was new from this angle was the massive pit. Strange, ruined buildings like those they'd seen earlier rimmed the exterior of an infinite black hole a half-mile wide. Some structures crumbled over the edge, while others held on by their foundations at treacherous angles. The ship itself sat on a large circular platform situated at the edge of the pit. There were others like it ringing the sides, though they were empty, and most had cracked in half or were barely recognizable as platforms. Those still intact seemed to be similar in size to the one the ship rested on, like they were made to function as landing pads.

The ramp's tip finally touched down, and a chunk of the landing pad cracked off, tumbling into the darkness. They never heard it land.

"Holy cow." Kiki rolled forward with her mouth open, her eyes raised to the shimmering in the sky. "I think this whole place is in some kind of force field!"

"Kiki!" Mbeki tapped his cane. "Get back here. It's dangerous."

Kiki reversed her wheelchair, but she couldn't stop peering outside. "But look at where we are. Maybe we should check things out?"

"Absolutely not!" He broke into a coughing fit. Kiki rushed to his side, and he held on to her chair for support. "We don't know what could be out there," he eked once he had control again.

Row crept to the edge of the ramp, away from the bickering. A crack in the landing pad ran perpendicular to the ship's hull, just underneath the end of the ramp, leaving a six- or seven-foot gap to the far side, where another piece of the landing pad met the edge of the pit. Even if they wanted to leave, they'd have to find a way across that first.

"Your father's right." Rivera spoke to Kiki and handed his rifle to one of his airmen. "No one's leaving this ship."

"I think we should." Saul pushed off the table he'd been leaning against.

"Are you out of your mind?" Darius challenged.

"I can't just sit here!" He rubbed his eyes. "I can't keep thinking about Lon and Claire. I need to do something."

"I agree." Mud bounced on his toes. He'd gone pale and kept rubbing his wrists. "Maybe something could help us out there. It's better than being in this damn ship." He punched Frankie in the shoulder a little too hard. "How about you, Frank? Could be a fun story for your girl back home."

Frankie mumbled something. Mud's forced grin faded for a moment. He looked to Terrence, who was pacing, stopping to look out the door, then pacing again. No help there. He turned to Aleks, squatting against the edge of the room.

"Come on." Mud walked over, his arms open and inviting. "You never wanted to be on this ship in the first place."

"I'm trying to figure out what they want us to do," Aleks said into his hands. "Are we supposed to leave or stay? Or does it not matter?"

Mud threw his hands in the air. Row ignored their debate; he had different considerations standing out on the ramp. Large clumps of dirt sat across the chasm, along with bits of twisted metal and chunks of wood. A long rod lying halfway across the gap had twisted itself nearly into a knot, but there were still recognizable rung-like loops dotting its side. It was the scaffolding.

The ship couldn't have flown anywhere in such a short time and with barely a bump to those inside. It had to have teleported, bringing the surroundings with it. That included some pink pieces of mush that made Row's stomach turn.

He spotted a narrow path off to the side of the end of the ramp, ringing the ship and disappearing somewhere around the nose. There could be a way forward in that direction. He stood with the toes of his shoes hanging over the lip, focusing down on the cracking landing pad a few feet down.

Ethan could've gone in that direction. He had to be hurt. Row clenched his jaw until his teeth ached. There was so much blood. He had to find him quickly.

He stepped forward, only to get tugged by his collar as Rivera dragged him back up the ramp.

"We are not exploring the surface." He handed Row off to Mud, then snapped his jacket's lapels and looked to Cora, who'd followed the rest of the group from the bridge. "Control your employees."

Cora sighed and pushed a strand of hair out of her eyes. "Gentlemen, our esteemed officer of the Air Force is correct. There's no sense wandering out there when we don't know what to expect."

Mud scoffed. "We get sent across space, and the CEO is as cold as ever. Do you ever feel any emotions?"

"I'm starting to feel one now." She smiled like Mud was a child needing to be scolded. "Mr. Nowak, if you want to do something, I suggest you figure out how much food is left from the luncheon."

"My friends call me Mud."

"That's very interesting, Mr. Nowak."

Mud marched off, grumbling under his breath. Terrence and Frankie followed. Saul shifted in his spot. Row had always thought he was the one roughneck stronger than his dad, but now he looked more like a large child, barely holding on as emotions swelled inside him. Dad, on the other hand, had stood there like a stone, a blank expression carved into his face. How could he not feel anything? How could he not care if Ethan was hurt? Ethan was the one Dad connected with; how would he have felt if it were Row?

Kiki helped Mbeki, who struggled more with his cane than before, to a chair and glanced back, meeting Row with sad eyes. He turned away. He didn't want pity. He didn't need it.

Because Ethan couldn't be dead.

CHAPTER 7

Time had no more meaning, not with a sky that hid all hints of a sun. Jonah wasn't even sure what sun it would be. He sat on one of the chairs in the bridge, staring at Ethan's name tag like he could reverse time and go back to when it rested crookedly on his son's deep-blue jacket. The longer he looked at it, the more it became a false memory he lived in.

He'd seen dead children before. He'd seen tiny body parts blown across streets or burned to fetid crisps with their parents' arms wrapped around them in a final embrace, but he had always been able to . . . distance himself, somehow, by telling himself it was just part of the job. But he wasn't a journalist anymore, and he'd lost his youngest son. Jonah never got a chance to hold Ethan at the end.

At some point, Mud and Saul returned to the bridge. They came in hot, but seeing Jonah sitting in a chair, hands clasped on his lap, they cooled off fast. For a few minutes, no one said anything until finally, Saul cleared his throat.

"We need you out there, Jonah," he said.

Jonah barely glanced at him.

"No one knows what they're doing. No one knows what we *should* be doing." He leaned on the console. Jonah ventured another glance and saw his eyes were puffy and rimmed with red from crying. "Even that Air Force guy is barking orders just to bark orders. People are getting restless."

"And what can I do?" Even muttering those words left Jonah exhausted.

"Anything, dude," Mud said. "You always have an idea."

"Does this look like a rig? Does this look like Earth?"

"Then what do we do?"

Jonah shut his eyes. "I guess we die."

Saul recoiled. Mud turned his back, pacing back and forth across the bridge. "Goddamn it. Is this what you spend all that time in the snow fields thinking about? Giving up?"

"I didn't realize keeping your spirits up powers spaceships." He should've shut the door or gone someplace where no one could've found him.

"You got a kid back there." Saul turned Jonah's chair to face him. "Row needs to see his father standing on his two feet."

"He doesn't need anything from me. He never did. Every time I'm in his life, it gets worse. You talk to him. You know how to."

"No one knows how to talk about this." Saul glanced at the blood on the window. "It's a tragedy, Jonah. You and Row need each other."

"It's not a tragedy. It's life." He winced at his own words. "That's why I can't talk to him." Try as he might, Jonah could never fully escape other people. Even on another planet.

Saul shrugged at Mud. They seemed to have no more words for him, not that he would listen. Mud sniffed, looking out the window with shaking hands once again.

A head peeked through the door. Not a roughneck or a soldier, but a thin-faced man with a neat black beard. Seeing the trio inside, he stepped into full view and adjusted his button-up shirt's collar. A shorter woman with a platinum-blond bun appeared beside him. They both gawked past Saul and Mud at the non-Earth landscape beyond.

"Hi," the man said, tapping his fingertips together. "Question, it may seem silly, but are we in space?"

"Who are you?" Saul asked.

"I'm Dr. Emily Cooper." The woman stepped forward. "My associate's Dr. Samuel Young. We were working onboard and, um . . ." She pointed out the window. "That looks . . . not like Earth."

"The ship moved. We think. Didn't you feel all that shaking beforehand?"

"We were working." She glanced at Dr. Young before they both turned away. "The ship's very complex."

"Do you know how to work it?" Mud asked.

"Work it? Work it how?" Dr. Cooper queried.

"Make it fly or something!"

"That's not the kind of work we were doing."

"I'm sorry," Dr. Young said. "Is it just us?"

"No." Saul clapped Mud on the shoulder. "We'll bring you to the rest."

Dr. Cooper leaned around Saul's wide frame, seeing Jonah slumped in his chair. "What about him?"

"Best to leave him be," Saul said without looking back. He left with Mud and the scientists.

Jonah was grateful to be alone again.

The tension in the banquet hall had not diminished. Cora found it silly to continue calling the area that, the banquet a long-over failure, but part of her was afraid calling it the loading dock, or whatever it was, would be admitting they had really traveled through space. Then again, it might be time to do just that.

The airmen held position near the door, but even their discipline faltered as they gazed at the yellow world outside the ship. The roughnecks, meanwhile, had taken to bickering back and forth like birds. Some wanted to go out; some wanted to stay in. Mud and Saul had wandered off in a huff half an hour earlier. Colonel Rivera, for all his bluster, had given up on trying to control them. He paced through his airmen, checking uniforms and guns, but Cora saw the shake in his hands and fear in his eyes. She was always good at reading people.

As for herself, her heart sank every time she looked down the ramp. Everyone knew the situation they were in, but no one dared to say it. They were lost souls shipwrecked on an island a million miles from anywhere on a map, past a threshold of technology no human could fathom reaching in a century. No one was coming to get them.

Cora kept herself busy, haunting the edges of the room and keeping an eye on the mood. The poor boy, Row, sat at the ramp, his head in his hands. She couldn't imagine what stormed inside his head. President Mbeki and his daughter had landed at one of the tables, the vibrant white tablecloth Cora had picked out cast aside. She'd selected the coverings specifically to evoke the way the spaceship looked under direct sunlight. Earth sunlight, she reminded herself. Like they were supposed to be still experiencing now.

She approached them and crouched at Mbeki's side. "How are you feeling, President Mbeki?"

"Cyril. And I am fine. Thank you." He patted his chest. "This body isn't what it used to be, though."

"You made quite a dive into the ship. That was a brave choice. I hope you're not regretting it."

"I would not leave my daughter to face a danger like this alone." He took Kiki's hand and squeezed gently. "We're always stronger together."

Kiki smiled at him, then turned to Cora. "Excuse me, Ms. Grey?"

"Cora." She smiled back. "Please."

"Right." She stared at the floor and stuck the tip of her tongue out, working her thoughts into words. "What do we do now?"

Cora blinked. Kiki truly had a way of speaking directly. "We keep each other's spirits up."

"If you don't know, say you don't know." Kiki sounded exasperated. She turned her chair to face the table.

Mbeki cast Cora an apologetic look, but Kiki had a point. She left them to rest and wandered to the back of the room, where the floor began to curve into the far corridor. The organizers had blocked it off with rope to keep the dignitaries and their guests from getting hurt. She had always thought it was strange that the ship was built in such an inaccessible way, with flooring that angled in a way no regular person could reach unless they had the ability to walk on walls.

As she approached the curve, her stomach churned, not painfully, but as it would when an airplane banked. She kept walking, expecting the curve to become too steep for her to continue, yet each step came as easily as the one before. She ducked under the rope and walked until she could look back and see the tables and chairs spreading vertically up a wall that had moments ago been the floor. The view twisted her mind in knots, and try as she might, she couldn't think of a single logical explanation for the phenomenon. The ship only got stranger with time.

Saul and Mud came in from the path to the bridge, appearing to Cora to defy gravity. They brought with them two new faces. Cora didn't recognize them from the guest list, so they must've been part of the team investigating the ship. She hurried back to join them, wavering slightly as she reoriented to the new gravity.

"This is Dr. Cooper and Dr. Young." Saul indicated the scientists in turn. "Doctors, this is, well, everyone, I guess."

"Damn." Dr. Young ignored the group and approached the ramp instead. "That is not Earth. That is certainly not Earth. How is that not Earth?"

"Isn't that for you to find out?" Rivera—he didn't look much like a Christopher, Cora thought—asked, striding over. "You're the eggheads working on the ship."

"As we told your friend," Dr. Cooper said calmly, "that's not our job. There was a team of engineers working on that. I'm an astrophysicist; Samuel's a biologist, for God's sake."

"Then make it your job." Christopher loomed over her with clenched teeth, his fear showing.

Cora had half a mind to step in, but the other half of the group clearly agreed with Christopher. No one else had any idea how the ship worked; at least the scientists got their hands in its guts.

"I think I hear something out there!" They all turned to an airman who had stationed himself by the exit. They froze, listening intently.

Metal creaked outside. Then, through that, came a distant voice.

"Help!" The voice barely made it to the ramp. "Somebody please help!"

"Row's gone!" Kiki wheeled up to the ramp, where Row had minutes earlier been sitting motionless.

"Help!" he shouted again, his voice bouncing through the tangled weave of stone and metal.

The roughnecks ran forward until Christopher stepped in their way. "We're not leaving the ship!"

"There's a kid out there!" Mud took a step only to have Christopher shove him roughly to the ground.

"And there are people in here!" Christopher brought his rifle to his shoulder, and though he kept the barrel pointed at the ground, the threat was clear.

"We have to help him!" Kiki said. Cyril stepped in front of her chair to shield her from the confrontation.

"Can anyone hear me?" Something crashed, and Row screamed. He made no further sound.

Cora noticed Jonah hadn't come back with Saul and Mud. While the roughnecks stood toe-to-toe with Christopher and his airmen, she set her jaw. Row had probably gone to find out what had happened to his brother. Someone had to go after him, but if she pushed, she'd make an enemy of Christopher. Too soon for that. She sprinted toward the bridge. Jonah needed to be there. He needed to know what was going on.

The passageways blew by in a blur until she skidded into the bridge. Jonah was slumped in one of the chairs, his eyes closed while he took slow breaths.

Cora called his name. Then, when he didn't respond, she rushed to his side. "There's fighting in the banquet—the loading dock, Row's in trouble. He went outside the ship!"

Jonah's eyes popped open. He jumped up and took off at a dead run. Cora chased after him but found herself wobbling on her heels.

"Shit." She kicked them off and grabbed them in one hand, racing after Jonah's fleeting form in her bare feet.

Jonah burst into the loading dock like a cannonball. His crew was squaring off with Rivera, backed up by a couple of his airmen, keeping them from approaching the ramp. As he moved forward, he heard a shout echoing from outside.

"Help! Someone!"

Jonah's chest seized. Row's voice—distant and muddled but without a doubt his. His vision narrowed until all he could see was the ramp and the twisted structures past it. Every dark thought that had crossed his mind for the past few hours since the ship had moved vanished until the only thing in his head was finding Row. He couldn't lose him, too.

He brushed past his crew and found his path stopped by Rivera, who gripped his rifle and commanded him, "Go back."

Jonah stepped around him without a word.

Rivera put an arm around Jonah's chest, physically holding him back. "I'm not risking my men for some kid! I gave my order, so no one leaves the ship!"

"I'm not asking you to risk your men." Jonah shoved his arm away. "I'm going out there to get my son. Alone, if I have to."

"Not alone." Saul appeared at his side. Mud, Terrence, Frankie, and Aleks joined him, and even Darius sidled up, muttering, "This is a bad idea," quietly enough he may have thought no one heard.

Jonah cast Rivera a long glare, urging him to try something. The soldier's gaze flicked between Jonah and his crew. Then he looked back at his own men, but they'd given space. Rivera paled, seeing his side falter in his orders.

As Row kept shouting, Jonah bumped Rivera's shoulder and exited onto the ramp. The destruction of the strange outpost became more real without the window in his way. The air smelled acidic and stale, nothing like anywhere he had ever been on Earth, and he winced as it filled his nostrils. He would have to get used to it.

"Row!" he shouted, standing at the ramp's lip, where the edge of the landing pad crumbled into a dark pit below.

"Dad!" Row shouted back. The ruins swallowed his words, making it hard to pinpoint his location.

"I'm coming!" Jonah paced the edge. It was at least an eight-foot jump over the chasm. A workable path on the pad below the ramp led along the side of the ship and disappeared at the bow. Somehow Row had to have gotten out, but with how fragile the landing pad and surrounding structures seemed, there was no assurance the same path would exist for Jonah.

"Out of the way," Rivera said. Four airmen brought one of the longer banquet tables and laid it across the gap. He leaned toward Jonah, thrusting a finger toward his chest. "You're not in charge of this operation, hero."

Jonah didn't care who was in charge. He just wanted his son. The airmen who'd placed the banquet table crossed first. The first, a tall, skinny man, took a step, and the table bowed under his weight, threatening to drop him into the darkness below. For a moment, everyone froze, but then he was across, and the other soldiers followed.

Jonah went next. He kept his eyes forward and slid his feet carefully across the plastic. They had held the ice sculptures, he reminded himself, but that thought vanished as the metal supports creaked. A soldier put out her hand. He took it and pulled himself onto firm land, patting his chest until his heart slowed.

One by one, they crossed. Even big Saul made the trek without cracking the table. Rivera left the other half of his airmen behind to watch over Kiki and Mbeki, joining the seven across the chasm. The scientists, too, waited on the ship.

To Jonah's surprise, however, Cora hurried down the ramp and across the table. She moved quicker than before, and when he looked down, he saw why. She'd traded out her heels for slip-on flats. Lorri always did expound on the benefit of spare shoes for formal events.

"Come on, Mr. Wall," she said, wrinkling her nose at the smell.

Turned out even the CEO could surprise him.

Jonah jumped onto a pile of rubble fallen off a nearby structure and scanned the area. Hundreds of dull-gray structures, each about the size of an office building, barely held onto themselves around the massive central pit. Fallen debris from those decaying edifices littered their path. All sorts of things could've happened to Row. He could've been pinned by falling rubble; he could've tripped into a hole; every hypothetical struck Jonah in the heart like a knife.

"Row!" he shouted. "Where are you? Make some noise!"

"I'm here!" Row shouted back, his voice sounding weaker than before.

Jonah slid down the rubble and descended the stairs that led away from the pit's edge, avoiding the sections where pieces had crumbled, sometimes skipping a stair entirely and hoping he didn't trip. His companions stayed close, watching their steps as each foot creaked on the unsound stairs until they reached the outpost streets, and the pit was out of sight, for the moment.

As they entered onto a crumbling road, a light began to glow on the outside of one of the buildings, then another as they walked farther, only to burst and burn out.

"It's waking up," Aleks said.

"Don't be so creepy." Mud slapped the back of his head.

"It is, though."

Jonah shouted for Row, and a few tense seconds passed before he shouted back, his voice still faint. The utter silence outside of that momentary call and response made his skin crawl.

How could he get so far? He thought. *Did he fall?* The buildings to his right dropped away, revealing the pit once again, closer this time. The outpost had been built in layers, those once underground now exposed to the sky. Some parts of the upper levels stuck farther into the central pit than the lower ones. If Row had journeyed out there and something broke beneath his feet, who knew how far he could have tumbled?

The airmen kept their rifles raised, scanning every window and doorway they passed, lingering on the shadows cast inside, daring something to move within while hoping nothing did. Whatever the place was, it wasn't a city or an outpost. It was a cemetery. And they walked on the graves.

"This looks familiar," one of the airmen said. The same one who'd helped Jonah across the table, a young Black soldier with a badge on her chest naming her Booker.

"You been on a lot of alien planets?" Mud chirped.

"No, but . . ." She wetted her dry lips. "Everything looks human."

Jonah understood what she meant. He could almost pick out what the buildings were. He saw tables inside, or machinery, set up in what had to be workshops. The streets they walked down had a familiar width and comfort to them, though abandoned. It all felt like Earth, save for the hazy yellow sky beyond the dome. Not to mention the dome.

"Row!" Jonah shouted again.

"Dad!" He sounded closer.

Jonah took a hard right through a collapsed wall and onto an outcropping over the pit. His pulse beat in time with his footsteps. He reached the edge of the cliff and looked down off the crumbling side, his breath catching in his throat at the sheer drop. He couldn't see the bottom.

Row hung from a stone slab, desperately clinging to a hold in the rock with both hands, his feet dangling into space, and the yawning dark chasm awaited below.

CHAPTER 8

The slab looked to have once been a floor, now a deadly slide ready to send unlucky passersby into the pit. Row had wrapped himself around a piece of rebar sticking out from the stone. Blood oozed out of a cut on his cheek, and his tumble had torn off pieces of his jacket.

"Dad!" he shouted, seeing Jonah appear above him.

"Hold on!" Jonah glanced about, searching desperately for another path or even a few handholds. "I'll find a way down."

A wrenching sound filled the air. Jonah turned back to see a chunk of the outcropping break away, creating a chasm between two halves of the group that had followed him. Everyone ducked out of the way, showered with dust and shattered rocks. Jonah, Cora, and his drill crew were on one side, along with Booker. Rivera and the rest of his airmen were on the other.

The rubble from the collapse thumped down toward Row, who screamed and ducked as stone chunks bigger than him thundered over his head. The rebar creaked and bent, and he slid a few inches, nearly losing his grip.

"Stop!" Jonah shouted at the group behind him. He pointed at Rivera. "Keep your people there!"

Then he crept closer to the edge and sat on the lip, dangling his feet carefully to find purchase. He eased down, planting his foot on a piece of rebar and twisting around until he could descend it like a ladder.

He tested a foot on the broken floor jutting into the dark. It was steep, but it had grip. Row hung about a dozen feet out. If Jonah could get there without slipping, he could pull him into a safer position.

Jonah's hands felt dangerously sweaty; one wrong move would mean certain death. For him and probably Row, too. And he couldn't lose another son.

He readied himself to step onto the floor.

"Wait." Booker caught his arm. She took the strap off her rifle and wrapped one half around his right wrist and the other around hers, pulling it tight. "Just move slow."

Jonah nodded. His stomach might have been full of rocks, but he clambered onto the slab all the same. He sat and pressed his heels into the stone. When he pulled on the strap, Booker pulled back, bracing him as he slid forward.

Row released one hand from the rebar and reached out, only to quickly pull it back.

"Just wait there," Jonah said, keeping his voice as level as he could. The infinite pit taunted him in its stillness, waiting patiently to consume them both.

Eventually, Booker had to climb onto the slab as well. Frankie grasped her belt while Mud clutched his overalls, Terrence linked arms with Mud, and Saul took firm hold of Terrence's belt while anchoring himself on the rebar ladder. Cora and Aleks supported Saul to make sure he didn't slip off the ladder. The human chain held steady as Jonah crept closer.

"Come on, Row!" Jonah stretched his free hand out until he could almost touch his son.

Row took some deep breaths, then threw himself forward, grabbing a fistful of Jonah's sleeve. Fire filled Jonah's stomach, and he closed a hand around Row's wrist and pulled, bringing Row to his side.

"Go," he said, bracing a foot in a crack.

Row climbed up the team's bodies, using them as a guide rope until back on safe ground. In turn, everyone pulled on the one they supported, half-dragging Jonah, Booker, and Frankie off the slab. Jonah collapsed to his knees, catching his breath while his pulse raced out of control. Row clutched his hands to his chest, leaning against Saul for support.

"What the hell were you thinking?" Jonah gasped, still out of breath. "Why would you leave the ship? Something could have happened to you!"

"I was trying to find Ethan . . ." He turned away.

"Ethan's dead!" Jonah already hated himself for admitting it, but he was trying to make sense of what Row had done.

"I know!" Tears filled Row's eyes. He opened his hands, revealing a scrap of fabric, dark blue with the hint of a white pattern. Blood coated half. "It's his. I found it outside the ship, and I thought he might be out here, but . . ." He squeezed his eyes until the tears flowed freely down his cheeks. "Why don't you care!?"

Jonah's skin went cold. Half a dozen pairs of eyes turned to him. "I—"

"He loved you!" Row pushed away from Saul and threw the fabric into Jonah's chest. "How could you accept it so easily? Why wouldn't you want to find him? You're a monster!"

A voice in the back of Jonah's mind screamed at him to say something. To tell Row how he felt seeing Ethan's blood plastered across the window of the ship. How his heart had shattered.

I'm sorry, he thought. *I'm sorry. Don't tell me I'm a monster when I'm sorry.*

But he never said it. He just sat there, a vacuous shell, and Row turned from him again. Jonah picked up the fabric and squeezed it in his hands.

"Hey!" Rivera shouted from above. "Are we done?"

"Yes, sir." Booker stepped carefully around Row to peer up the makeshift rebar ladder. The rest of the airmen looked down. "Everyone's fine; we'll be up—"

She vanished. The ground crumbled like a cookie beneath her.

"Booker!" Rivera shouted.

Jonah and his team scrambled back from the edge before it cracked any more. Jonah chanced a glance into the newly created hole where Booker had fallen. They were standing on the upper levels of a massive, mechanical operation. Great machines with conveyor belts and arms roared to life, shaking off the dust of ages past. Booker lay atop a metal structure being fed by four belts, clutching her leg and screaming. Even from fifty feet away, Jonah could see the terrible bend in her bone.

"Stay there, Sergeant," Rivera said. "We'll find a way down!" He ran out of view.

An articulated lifting arm unfurled above Booker, only to struggle against its joints until part of it broke off, slamming into the machine only a few feet from her head. It wouldn't be long before the entire operation tore itself apart. They didn't have time to find a way down.

"We need to help her!" Row cried, anguished.

Jonah spotted a platform moving below them. It hovered mid-air, slowly drifting from one side of the work floor to the other, passing only ten feet below their position. Close enough to drop to.

"There." He pointed it out to the team. "That'll take us down faster."

"Absolutely not!" Cora snapped. "This place is a deathtrap. You don't even know if that thing will hold us. It's floating, for God's sake."

"Then I'll jump first."

"Mr. Wall. You still work for me."

"Call HR."

Booker had gone quiet. The rocks returned to Jonah's stomach, telling him to keep his feet on solid ground. Instead, he took three deep breaths, counting out the seconds until the platform passed under him again. It was at least a fifteen-foot square, with a sturdy-looking railing around the perimeter. It had to be designed to hold large weights.

For a second, his heavy stomach lurched into his throat, but it slammed back into place as his feet struck metal. He crumpled to his side, sending up a puff of dirt. His knees screamed, a reminder that he wasn't as young as he used to be, but at least he hadn't missed. He hauled himself back to his feet using the railing as support; his hand came away covered in caked grime.

A series of shocks shook the platform as the others joined him. Row was first, making a lighter and smoother landing than his dad had, then Mud, Frankie, Terrence, Saul, and Aleks followed in a mass of flailing limbs. Even Cora took the plunge, brushing the dust off her skirt as she got to her feet.

"You didn't *all* have to come," Jonah said, wishing they hadn't, especially Row.

"You didn't listen to me." Cora scowled as she found a tear on the side of her skirt.

"This isn't a boardroom." Jonah massaged his shoulder, the one that had struck the platform. "You're not in charge here."

"I'm not . . ." She clasped her hands in front of her face and took a deep breath. "I'm not getting in a pissing contest with you. I just need you and your crew to think. How are we getting out of here?"

Jonah looked around. The expansive pit stretched to their right, and the layers of the outpost hung above. "We'll . . . figure something out. You jumped down, too."

"Yes." She clenched her jaw and turned up her nose like she'd caught a bad smell. "I certainly did. Now I'm stuck down here with all of you."

"Technically, not all of us." Mud thumbed back at the upper level.

Darius waved his arms like one would at a passing cruise liner. "You look more than capable!" he called. "I'll see you back at the ship!"

Jonah wasn't surprised the flaky geologist had bailed, only that he'd gone as far as he had.

The platform drifted above the operation, giving them a bird's-eye view. He could vaguely guess at the purpose of a couple of pieces of machinery, such as the belt that ended at a gigantic bucket lifting in the same floating motion as their platform.

"It's a mine," Cora said, leaning on the railing. "Whatever these things were, they were mining the planet."

Their platform dipped as the bucket, long empty after however long the mine had been abandoned, drifted over their heads, showing nothing beneath but some vented pads attached to the bottom that ruffled their hair as it moved on.

"*Star Wars*," Cora whispered, barely audible.

"What was that?" Jonah asked.

"Nothing." She cleared her throat and looked off the platform.

Jonah followed her gaze. Out of the side of the building and down, where the walls had long since fallen away, he could see the underside of the pit for the first time, a cave-like area that didn't look like it boded well for the structural integrity of the buildings still standing on the ground above it. The area beneath the outpost had been hollowed out. Whatever they were mining, they had mined too much, leaving the ground a shell. Hundreds of hovering platforms like the one they stood on buzzed near them just beneath the surface within the hollow, leaving behind clouds of ancient filth. Most were empty, but some held large metal boxes and transported them across the pit.

"Hell." Terrence stroked his chin. "Aleks was right. This place turned on when we got here."

"I hate when I'm right." Aleks shut his eyes.

More of the vented pads, some more than twenty feet in diameter, were stuck to the underside of the cave's ceiling. A section of buildings broke away from the rest, the ground on which they stood supported by the pads and floating free in the darkness. Whatever those pads were, they were the only things keeping parts of the mine from collapsing.

The platform drifted down the other side of the building, slotting into an empty section next to a conveyer at the bottom of the pit. The air pulsed, then an invisible force shoved them off the platform, landing them in a heap on the belt.

"That was fun," Mud growled, extricating himself from Frankie.

Jonah eased himself off the belt and onto the ground. He turned back to help Row down, only for him to ignore his dad's hand and jump down himself. Jonah sighed. Row hadn't said a word to him since he'd pulled him off the slab. But he didn't need to hear his words. He just needed him to be alive, even if his silence hurt. He watched Row swing himself under a railing and hurry across the dusty ground. Even after everything that had happened, Row kept moving, no matter the danger.

They snaked through the winding rubble, dodging quickly collapsing machinery. Jonah started to push himself to the front of the group, past Saul, but Saul suddenly clutched his collar and pulled him back.

"Wait!" he shouted.

A metallic arm dropped from the sky like a guillotine, smashing through the conveyor belts and bending them into sharp Vs before slamming against the ground. Jonah blinked, dizzy as he gaped at the spot where he'd nearly died.

"We better get out of here fast." He patted Saul's hand, then pulled himself away, gently stepping out of his grasp. Row looked at him with concern, but once he saw Jonah look back, he turned away. Jonah wanted to say something, anything, but the words stuck in his throat.

They reached the central machine, and Jonah, Mud, and Saul climbed the stairs to the raised piece of machinery Booker had fallen onto. It looked like a control panel: no levers or buttons, only a flat piece of transparent material with various shapes and lights across it.

"Stay down there," he told the others. "Frankie, see if you can find us a way out."

"I'll do it." Row headed off before anyone could protest.

Jonah figured he wanted some space, but considering the trouble he'd gotten into the last time he'd wandered off alone . . . "Frankie." He pointed at Row as his son hopped over a conveyor belt. "Keep an eye on him."

Frankie nodded and rushed off. Meanwhile, Saul and Mud boosted Jonah onto the top of the machine, where Booker lay motionless within a dent she had made on impact, her leg bent oddly within her uniform pants. Blood pooled beneath her. She didn't react as Jonah crept closer. Mud clambered up behind him.

"Oh, shit," he said. "She doesn't look good."

An understatement. Jonah leaned in, praying they weren't too late. Booker's chest hardly rose and fell. But she was breathing, shallow as it was.

"Hey." Jonah gently tapped her face. "You still with us?"

Her eyes fluttered open. "Sir."

"No. Jonah. We're going to get you out of here, but you need to stay awake."

"What happened to my leg?"

"Don't worry about it." He motioned for Mud to circle to the other side. "What's your name? I don't think I ever caught it."

"Staff Sergeant . . . Monica Booker."

"Monica. We're going to move you. It's going to hurt."

She squeezed her eyes shut, then nodded. Jonah and Mud each took an arm with one hand, their other hands supporting her shoulders, and pulled. She screamed in pain. Mud's eyes widened, but they didn't have time to be gentle. They dragged her out of her impact crater and took her to the edge overlooking the control panel.

"Terrence, get up here," Saul commanded.

Then, careful as they could, Jonah and Mud transferred Staff Sergeant Monica Booker down to Saul and Terrence, who then carried her down the steps with Aleks and Cora. All the way, Booker wailed, the noise bouncing off the walls and up to the top of the dome. At least screaming meant she was still alive, Jonah figured, climbing down from the machine.

They were just laying her at the foot of the stairs when another chunk of the pit's wall broke off, smashing into a device and sending it spiraling into nothingness. They were running out of safe ground. Jonah scooped Booker into his arms. "I can carry her."

Saul put a hand on his shoulder.

"I have her." Jonah shrugged him away.

"Jonah."

"I have her."

Saul was stronger, no doubt, but Booker had come out there to save Jonah's son. She'd wrapped her strap around his wrist and held him as he climbed down, and she got hurt for all her trouble. Whether for penance or to pay a debt, Jonah had to be the one to carry her.

"Over here!" Row waved at the group through a gap between two large, rusted cylinders, Frankie poking his head out right behind him. "I found a way up."

They led the group to a collapsed crane that had punched a hole through the wall of the operation building. Outside was an ascending street, not unlike the one they'd walked aboveground. They had no way of knowing if it would lead them back to the ship, but it was better than staying in the crumbling mining operation. Saul took the lead as they began their journey up.

"This place is ancient." Aleks gazed at the platforms moving across the pit. "How's it still working?"

"If these are the same people who made the ship, they're highly advanced," Cora said. "It all must be completely automated. I can't imagine they'd want to dig under their own city."

"But then where did they go?"

The questions hung over their heads, no one brave enough to hazard a guess. Jonah watched the ruins pass by out of the corner of his eye as he cradled Booker, careful not to accidentally knock her against any of the crumbled walls. A couple of lights still flickered on as they walked past, but most stayed dead.

Something about the destruction put knots in his gut—more than decay, more than abandonment. There were holes punched through concrete-like stonework and large craters in the middle of the street. He'd seen scars like that before, in war-torn villages in far-off deserts in the Middle East.

They eventually came to a platform like the one they'd ridden in the mining operation; only, it was smaller with a simple square box on one of the railings. Row stepped onto the narrow catwalk around it to inspect the box. It lit up as he approached.

"I think this is an elevator." He pointed at the overhang above them. "See?"

"I'm good with not walking," Terrence said, joining Row with a grunt. His bones were weary.

Jonah looked ahead, where the street continued. Many more platforms lay strewn between the buildings. Unlike the others, those hadn't turned on for some reason. They circled a mound of something sharp and irregular, too difficult to make out in the shadows cast by the surrounding structure.

"Take her." Jonah gently passed Booker to Saul. "Give me a second. Stay here."

He approached the strange shapes, his skin feeling electric, his arm hairs standing on end. Once he'd stepped into the shadows, his eyes adjusted. Thick, brown sticks and lumps filled a pit dug into the street. They never looked like they did in movies, but Jonah had seen a pit like that before. A dense poison crawled into his stomach until the feeling deadened, as it always did when looking upon the horrors of existence.

"My God." Cora had followed him. She held her hand to her mouth, fingers trembling. "Are those bones?"

Hundreds, if not thousands, filled the pit. A mass grave left open to the world. Jonah crouched and picked up a small joint from the edge.

"Are these . . . human?" Cora backed away. "They look human. But they can't be."

"Maybe." Jonah pocketed it and turned away. "We need to keep moving. There's nothing else here."

"Doesn't this freak you out?"

Jonah didn't break his gait. ". . .Not anymore."

Cora's face had gone pale as a snowstorm, but she returned to the lift all the same.

"What was it?" Aleks asked.

Neither of them said anything.

Row squinted at the box attached to the railing. Seven symbols

glowed on it. He tapped the top one. It flashed, and the platform began to rise. Jonah glanced over at the mass grave, once again hidden
in shadows.

For something like that to be left undisturbed for so long meant
that whatever had happened to those people was the last thing to happen on the planet. No one came back. Was this where the ship came
from? Was that why it had returned?

Cold fingers crawled up Jonah's spine. He'd been right, the outpost
was a grave. One ready to bury them next.

CHAPTER 9

The lift hummed as it ascended, infuriatingly slowly. The edge of the chasm was visible, but only barely, multiple stories up. Occasionally a clatter rose as more of the outpost fell apart. For a long time, those were the only sounds.

A weight fell upon Jonah's shoulders and spread throughout his body as he rested against the railing. He'd been wound so tightly for so long that something had to break eventually. He looked to Row, trying to get a sense of how his son was feeling, but Row never even glanced back.

Something snapped like a lightning strike, and every head turned. The mining operation they were in a few minutes earlier tilted, then shattered, pulling down the buildings atop it like a sweater unraveling into its threads. Everything they had once stood on, where they had saved Row above and Booker below, vanished into the abyss. Fortunately, the elevator they were in ran along the edge of the pit, or the debris would crush them as well.

Mud grabbed the railing and gawked at the instant destruction. "Dude, what do we do if that happens to the ship?"

"It's not going to happen to the ship," Cora said confidently.

"How do you know that? It's hanging right over a pit, and the only bridge is a table."

"Fine. I don't know." She sent him a flat look, her mouth a thin line. "Does that make you feel better?"

Mud swallowed hard. "I liked you better when you were emotionless."

The lift reached the top, and everyone, save Saul, rushed off, new energy in their steps since any one of them could be their last. Saul delicately stepped onto the street, keeping Booker cradled carefully in his arms. Even aboveground again, it didn't seem safe, so they moved heedlessly between crumbling structures to get away from the imploding mine.

When they came to a split in the road, Jonah directed them left without hesitation. Despite the twisting labyrinth, he never lost his sense of direction.

Though it didn't help when they came upon a two-story pile of rubble. One structure had fallen against the other across the street, dumping its walls and contents into their path. Jonah prodded an outside wall until he found a sizeable gap, about two shoulder widths wide. He stuck his head in. While most of the interior was a patchwork of light beams, the other side glowed steadily, suggesting a way out.

"We'll have to go through here," he said, stepping inside. "Watch your heads."

"Great, I guess now we can get crushed to death instead of falling," Terrence muttered.

Metal whined, and everyone froze. Silence followed. Jonah let out an unsteady breath and wiped a sweaty hand on his pants. The path curved through what was once a window. Jonah braced himself on the sill and hiked a leg over. His foot caught for a second, and he stumbled forward, catching himself against something cold and silver.

It looked like the ship, and for a second, panic gripped him as he worried their vessel had been buried, but then he realized this hull was smaller. Much smaller, in fact, as if it were the personal size to their ship's large. The building had pinned it halfway into the street, but it showed barely a blemish.

"What're those?" Saul asked, his gaze fixed on something on the ground.

Jonah stepped back. Tiny boxes, no bigger than Rubik's Cubes, littered the area around the small ship.

"I don't know." Jonah knelt to take a closer look.

The cubes appeared to be rocks but with edges too clean to be unworked. They also had a strange texture; the best Jonah could compare it to was when he worked a rig down in Alberta some years back, and one of his crew found a fossilized trilobite.

"Hey!" Aleks shouted from the back. "Someone wanna keep moving before we get a half-ton of rocks brought down on our heads?"

Jonah left the ship and the strange boxes behind; not every mystery on this planet could be solved. They finally exited the collapsed structure near the edge of the dome, which shimmered strangely, almost like a hologram. Standing that close, it didn't look like glass or plastic; it was more akin to faint lightning in hexagonal patterns. Beyond, a dull-orange landscape of rock and dust disappeared into the haze.

Off in the distance, near where a mountain ridge shot up from the flat plains, Jonah saw another dome like the one they stood in, with buildings silhouetted within. He couldn't imagine it had fared any better than their own.

One of the lights, a large bulb on a metal pole, broke from the building next to him and shattered across the street. It was only then he noticed the tremor in the ground.

"It's going to cave in!" Mud shouted.

Much worse than that, a familiar hum soon came clear. Jonah snapped to attention. "The ship!"

A wave of realization washed over the group. Frankie, the quickest, took off, with everyone else not far behind. Jonah held back. Row was his priority, with Saul lumbering on with Booker a close second. The ship came into view—but they were on the wrong side from the entrance. The twisting walk from the mining operation below had deposited them at the far end of the landing pad. The ship's rumbling carried into the ground. Frankie, head down at full speed, jumped aside as a piece of the pad broke away.

"Go around the front!" Jonah shouted. "There's a path."

Frankie let out a raspy—but affirmative—huff and aimed left. The roughnecks darted through the ship's shadow beneath the nose. The ship barely touched the pad, almost seeming to hover just above it. It balanced impossibly considering its size, so when Jonah had to cut close to its silver shell to avoid tumbling into the chasm, he feared he might touch it and send it toppling over.

As they came around the front, they spotted Darius standing on the ramp in the distance, whipping his head from side to side. Once he caught sight of them, he cupped his hands to either side of his mouth. "The ship's starting up! You have to get inside!"

Jonah's instincts told him to run as fast as he could, but he held back and waited for Row and Saul until they passed him. The crack in the landing pad next to the ship kept him at a reasonable pace to avoid slipping into it. With the operation fully awake, he could see lights far below, many from the floating platforms, now visible from his vantage point, beginning their ancient processes. Still, it was a long way down with no bottom in sight.

He and his crew kept single file, creeping along until their path widened and Frankie could sprint off again, the others matching him. Coming in from the side, they would have to jump or climb onto the top of the ramp four feet off the ground. Frankie, full of adrenaline, leapt from the landing pad clean onto the ramp.

"Where're the soldiers?" Darius asked, catching Frankie by the shoulder to steady him. "They're not back."

"You got here first?" Jonah made his way to the front of the group and took Frankie's hand and climbed onto the slope. He looked across the table-bridge but saw no sign of Rivera or his airmen. Surely, they weren't still looking for Monica Booker. Jonah had hoped to meet them on the way up, but the mess of it all distracted him. Row pulled himself onto the ramp and followed Jonah's gaze into the outpost.

"Get inside," Jonah ordered, striding across the table-bridge.

Row nodded, wide-eyed with fear, and backed into the ship with the rest of the roughnecks clambering up the side of the ramp. Jonah scaled the rubble he had used to scout the outpost before they left the landing pad the first time, now searching for any sign of human movement. Rivera had been a bit of an ass, but Jonah didn't want to leave the airmen behind if the ship was about to jump again.

A minute later, Rivera appeared on the path below the landing pad, arms pumping and rifle bouncing against his back as he ran. His six airmen weren't far behind.

"Jonah!" Mud shouted as the ramp began to lift.

"The table!" Jonah pointed at the makeshift bridge, now tilting as the ramp closed.

Mud grimaced but sprinted up the quickly steepening floor. He put his foot against the table and kicked it across the gap toward Jonah, where it skidded across the dirt. It was too short to span the chasm without the ramp making up the distance, but the gap narrowed where Jonah and his team had come in. He grabbed the table and dragged it down to where it could make the gap. It was heavier than it looked, and when he reached the best spot, he had to brace the table against his waist and tip it back. His arm muscles strained as he tilted the table up, then slammed it down across the crack, giving them a way back.

"Get inside now!" Mud slapped the ship's hull.

Jonah looked back to see Rivera bounding up the landing pad stairs. His face glowed bright red, but his feet didn't falter. Jonah hurried across the new bridge and sprinted down the ship's length. He jumped through the quickly closing gap, Mud grabbing one arm and pulling him in, while his other elbow bumped against the side of the ramp. He winced as it flared in pain.

The table jumped as Rivera thundered across. He bounced into the outside of the ship, pushing off it and digging his boots into the ground again as he completed the right angle and raced for the opening. His form had gone sloppy, and his breath came out ragged and strained.

He leaped toward the ramp but only got one foot up as he attempted to twist through the quickly narrowing gap. Jonah grasped him by the back of his jacket and pulled him inside.

The next airman didn't bother trying to jump, instead reaching up like a toddler toward his mother. Jonah extended a hand and hoisted him up into the ship. Plastic snapped, and Jonah looked up to see the table break in half. A pair of soldiers—the last two to cross—dropped forward, the one in back, a short, stocky man with a shock of red hair, vanishing into the pit while the first, brunette and tall, cracked his head on the chasm's edge with a wet sound and lost his balance, disappearing into the darkness as well. The three who'd just crossed looked back in horror but didn't stop moving toward the ship and the door that was continuing to close.

"Don't slow down!" Jonah shouted even though the ramp was nearly vertical.

The closest soldier leapt up, landing halfway on the lip. Jonah clutched him by the shoulders and pulled, but something on the guy's uniform must have gotten stuck because he couldn't get him inside any farther. He braced both feet and leaned back.

"You have to get out of there!" Saul screamed from inside the ship. "You don't have time!"

"One more second!" Jonah reached forward with one hand and seized the soldier by the back of his belt. The men still outside pushed up against his boots.

"Jonah! Now!" Jonah felt Saul's arms wrap around his waist, and he was yanked back, losing his grip on the belt just as the door slammed shut.

Blood spurted across the floor and wall. Jonah recoiled, scooting backward, his feet sliding on the floor. Where the soldier had been were two arms, unmoving fingers tensed for something to grab onto.

"Oh, shit, oh, shit." Row repeated over and over.

Kiki and her father drew near. Cora spun on her heel. "President Mbeki! Get her out of here!"

He caught Kiki with one arm. Frantic fists pounded against the outside of the door, but there was nothing any of them could do.

"Damn it!" Rivera punched the floor. He glared at Row. "I *told* you to stay on the ship! I *told* you it was for everyone's safety!" He rose to his feet, teeth bared like a wild animal. "Those deaths are on your head."

Row's jaw waved.

"From now on, we are doing what I say when I say it." Rivera released his rifle from his back and held it at his side. "This ship's now under martial law."

"No." Jonah stepped between him and Row.

One of Rivera's eyes twitched. "Excuse me?"

"We're not soldiers; you don't get to order us around. I'm sorry about your people. I truly am. This ship has already taken my youngest son, and I won't let you turn it into a gulag because of your own grief."

"Is that so? Fine." He raised his weapon to Jonah's chest, his eyes narrowed and jaw set. He looked unnervingly calm. "Jonah Wall, you are under arrest. Your and your son's actions have led to the deaths of five good Air Force servicemen and women. You will be held here and tried formally when we return—" Rivera balked at his own words, clearly unsure how to finish.

"To Earth?" Jonah grunted. "You might be surprised to know you're not the first person to point a gun at me."

"Sir." Booker pushed herself up on the table where Saul had placed her. Her words could barely make it out of her throat, and her eyes stayed mostly closed. "It's my fault. We rescued the kid just fine, but I wasn't looking where I stepped. I fell through because of my own damn bad luck."

"No." Rivera pushed out his jaw. "This ship needs control. It needs—"

Jonah pushed the rifle's barrel away and socked Rivera across the face. He dropped, leaving the gun in Jonah's grasp. The rest of the soldiers raised their weapons, aiming them between Jonah and the rest of the roughnecks. Rivera had lost almost half his crew. Only eight remained—including the injured Booker—leaving the sides much more evenly matched than before. Tense glances were exchanged. Fingers tapped against trigger guards. The humming of the ship grew louder.

"Enough!" President Mbeki slammed his cane into the floor, breaking the tension. "We are not wild animals! We are human beings, and we are in this together." He started to cough, but when Cora moved to support him, he waved her off. "This trial can only be overcome by working together. If we keep at each other's throats, we will all crumble."

Saul released his headlock on a soldier. Another airman lowered his rifle; no one dared to fight after Mbeki's strong words. Jonah's fire had been quelled. He offered his hand to Rivera.

"I am sorry about your people," he said. "They deserve better. We all do."

Rivera ignored Jonah's help, rolling onto his feet and cracking his jaw instead. "Give me my service weapon."

Jonah tilted his head back. Surely even Rivera wasn't insane enough to shoot him in front of everyone. He squared up and offered the rifle.

Rivera snatched it and swung it over his shoulder. "Someone patch up Sergeant Booker's leg." He took a step, then stopped and leaned into Jonah's ear. "Take care of your people. I'll take care of mine." He thrust his shoulder against Jonah's and moved on.

The airmen carried Booker out of the room while the rest of the group slowly dispersed. Saul took a cloth off one of the tables and laid it over the grisly sight at the door. It covered the arms, but the blood had shot a good six feet up the wall. Nothing to do there.

Occasionally something thumped against the ship's hull. The two airmen were still outside, but there wasn't a visible panel or button anywhere that might open the door. Judging from the previous event, they'd jump soon, leaving those two poor souls behind. Stranded on a crumbling planet with not even a ship to give them shelter. Jonah couldn't remember the last time he'd felt so hopeless.

Row stepped beside him, his eyes focused on the blood coating the door. "Dad, I—"

"What were you thinking?"

"I wanted to find Ethan."

"You knew it was dangerous. Your actions don't just affect you. We're all stuck here together."

Row narrowed his eyes, fighting back the tears already welling. "You didn't have to come to get me."

"Yes, I did." *Because you're my son.*

Row huffed and stomped off, hiding his face in his hands. Kiki, after checking to make sure her father had recovered from his coughing fit, wheeled after him. Jonah was glad Row had someone to talk to. Something heavy settled in his gut. *Why can't I be the one he talks to? Why is this so hard?*

He pulled out the piece of Ethan's shirt and held it between his fingers. Such a small thing sent Row running, not a thought or a care, just a driving force to find his brother. How could he scold him for that? Jonah once dove headlong into every firefight and bombed-out building, ensuring the world never forgot the cost of war. For a long time, Jonah and Row had floated past each other with nothing to say. Now, as Row dove into danger as Jonah once had and faced the same tragic outcomes, Jonah could only watch and wonder if he was feeling pride or worry that his son could be just like him.

CHAPTER 10

Row stomped through the ship's back halls, Kiki wheeling at his heels. He had no destination in mind. He just couldn't be near his father or the blood coating the door. Colonel Rivera was right; it was his fault those people died. His legs wobbled like they might give out, but he kept going, trying to ignore the tears still pricking at his eyes.

"What was it like out there?" Kiki asked. "I saw these flying things zooming around after you all left. They looked like drones but bigger. They probably had repulsors or something on them, right? I've seen those on TV shows. Did they have repulsors?"

"Maybe?" Row glanced at her, her excited expression telling him she was waiting for more. "We rode on one."

"Whoa! That's awesome!"

"It was pretty cool." And it had been, after the adrenaline from nearly falling into the mine had faded. Row wished it was the right time to get excited by the fascinating technology he'd seen.

Kiki's face told him to keep going, but Row didn't have the energy. He'd left the ship to find Ethan, but he'd found nothing but death. With only the spaceship humming, his mind wrapped itself into knots following macabre lines of thought. He needed sound.

"One of them flew over our heads, and I could feel the gravity pushing down on me," he said, keeping his eyes on his feet. "And when it lowered, it had this weird invisible force that pushed us. I think they were cargo lifts. Cora said it looked like a mining operation, so I bet those lifts moved ore to be processed in that factory." He couldn't stop a smile. "The entire thing was still working! It's almost hollowed out the ground beneath us. It's terrifying but . . . so cool."

"Maybe this was a mining ship." She eased off her stick. "It's mostly space for cargo. That tour guide didn't show us anywhere near the coolest stuff."

"Have you been looking around?"

"I wasn't going to take a nap or anything while you had all the fun." A sly grin spread across her face. "Come with me."

She spun her chair and zoomed off down an adjoining corridor. Row watched her braids bounce off her backrest. No matter what happened, that smile never left her face, and Row had to admit he was a little envious of her seemingly unshakeable optimism. Her energy broke through any wall in its way, and Row walked lighter when she was around.

"Come on!" she shouted.

Row chased after. She didn't slow, and he had to jog to keep from losing her. She stopped at an innocuous door with a series of the now familiar symbols across the surface. It had to be the language of whoever flew the ship.

Kiki reached forward, then paused. "Touch the edge."

"What?" A rim went around the outside of the door. It looked harmless enough, but after falling through a couple of levels of infrastructure, Row had learned better than to touch things he didn't know.

"Trust me. Run your finger along the edge."

Row narrowed his eyes, then eased his hand forward and swiped his fingers down the door's frame, then jumped back. A light flashed where his skin had touched the rim, and a whirring came from behind the wall.

"Uh . . ." Row braced himself nervously.

"Just wait."

The whirring stopped, and the door slid open, revealing a small, brightly lit room. An elevator.

Kiki burst out laughing. "You should've seen your face!" She nearly fell out of her chair.

"Okay, fine." Row tensed his jaw to keep a smile from breaking through. "It's an elevator. Cool."

"It *is* cool." She wheeled inside. "I found at least twelve of these doors. There're probably more elsewhere because this one only has four symbols."

Row joined her. Just like the rest of the ship, the elevator was seamless metal. She waved her hand over a four-part grid. Within each was a different symbol: one that looked like a jar, one a jagged line, one a squished O, and the last a cross with an additional tail on the left arm.

"I rode it around for a while," she said. "They go to the bridge"— she pointed at each symbol in turn—"that big room we had lunch in, I think the engine room, and that large dark room with the catwalks. So, you can enter it from all kinds of places, but only get to those four rooms, I guess. I don't know why."

"It's a spaceship. Haven't you ever watched *Star Trek*? It's probably voice-activated." He couldn't help but feel some excitement at the prospect. "Too bad we don't know the language. The panel's just shortcuts."

"But you're guessing."

"We're all guessing."

She shrugged, then tapped the jar icon. "Next stop on the tour." The door shut, and the elevator whirred.

"How long does it—" The doors opened before he finished. He hadn't even felt the elevator move.

"Not long." She wheeled out.

Row peeked into the hall the elevator had revealed. He was pretty sure they were around the corner from the bridge. He recognized the construction lamps that were the sole light source before the ship took over and cut them off from the generator.

In the bridge, Kiki circled around to one of the left consoles. She waited until Row stepped into the middle of the room and gave her a confused look before grinning and tapping an icon. The lights dimmed and a translucent cloud formed around Row. He jumped back.

"It's just a hologram," Kiki said. "But isn't it beautiful?"

Thousands of pinpoint lights glowed within the cloud. Like someone had taken a piece of the night sky and immersed him in it. "What is it?"

"I have no idea." She reached out for the halo, and her hand passed right through. "I've been on a ship before, and I figured if those consoles at the front were for the helmsmen, I could fool around with some of these back ones. There are more symbols on them, but I avoided anything with too long of a name. Most didn't work but this . . . I had to show you this."

A smile blossomed across Row's face. He couldn't believe Kiki figured all that out in such a brief time. The elevators, the hologram . . . there had to be more to find.

"Have you checked out any of the other panels?" He spun around and saw the blood still smeared across the window, Ethan's name tag in the center. A cold knife cut into his stomach.

"Uh, hey, check this out, Row!" In his periphery, he saw the entire hologram display spin; Kiki must have manipulated it somehow. But Row couldn't break his gaze from the window.

He drifted forward, his feet moving on their own. The first time he'd seen the blood, his mind had become a blur, winding around itself until his thoughts stuck to each other like old pieces of candy. The smear had been huge, coating the window from top to bottom. Now it wasn't much bigger than Ethan himself.

"I'm sorry about your brother." Kiki's words floated to him from across the room.

The knife in his gut twisted. He clutched at where he swore there should be a wound but found no hilt, no gash, nothing. He finally turned away from the blood and back to Kiki. "It hurts so much."

"My mom died a few years back. Cancer." Kiki played with the braids hanging over her shoulder. "I'm used to pain, but it was something else. Felt like someone ripped something out of me. Eventually, I got used to it, too, though."

"I don't want to get used to this. I want it to hurt. If I let it fade away, then I'll be just like my dad, moving on like he never cared at all." He turned away so she wouldn't see him cry. Men weren't supposed to cry.

Kiki wheeled down the little ramp to the front of the bridge. "My dad never talked about it after my mom died," she said. "He marched on, a leader for South Africa, but I still wished he could be my dad for just a little bit and grieve with me. From time to time, when he thought I was asleep, I found him standing on the veranda where they used to talk for hours. When she was at her weakest, he would take her out there and watch the clouds roll by." An almost wistful expression crossed her face. "People grieve in their own way. Maybe your dad is grieving in his."

The pain in Row's stomach subsided but didn't leave, ebbing until it was like a distant pulse. All he knew of his father was the man who ran away. A man Row couldn't even talk to. A man who preferred the company of empty walls. On that last point, he couldn't blame him; sometimes Row preferred empty walls, too.

"Row." Kiki rested her hands in her lap. "Wanna figure out how the ship works with me?"

"No, I . . ." He twirled a loose thread from his torn jacket around his finger. "I don't think . . ."

Then he looked up at the blood. Ethan always believed Row was smart, that he could do anything he put his mind to. Ethan always looked forward. Standing around crying would not honor his memory.

"Okay." He wiped the tears from his eyes and faced the bridge. "Those adults out there are useless. Let's figure this out."

***

The atmosphere in the loading dock shifted from fear to despair. The ship's hum had become a dull background noise to the group's existence. The roughnecks found a deck of cards in one of the bags left behind in the evacuation and started a friendly game of Hearts. Or tried to, at least. Saul and Mud were the only two with any focus. The rest either needed constant prodding or were distracted by Terrence, who lay flat on his back, staring at the ceiling.

No one had seen the airmen since the confrontation at the door. Cora worried about what that would mean for the rest of them. She had a talent for reading people—which came in handy in business meetings—and Christopher was bad news all the way down. And he had the loyalty of his team, a dangerous concoction when combined with the fear she saw after Jonah knocked him down.

Jonah had barely moved in the hours since returning from their little adventure. He had transferred the dismembered arms into a corner they could ignore and covered them with half a dozen sheets before plunking himself down against the entrance. It was like he didn't even realize the powder keg he'd set off with Rivera. Someone had to tell him.

Cora rose to her feet and headed over. "You know," she said, leaning against the smooth metal wall, "the door closing was the last thing to happen before we jumped last time. Maybe we already did again."

"We haven't." Jonah kept his eyes on the space between his knees.

"How do you know?"

As if to answer, a thump came from outside the door—one of the airmen trapped on the surface.

"Ah," Cora said. "They're still a bit hopeful, I guess."

"Maybe it makes them feel better."

Cora chewed on the inside of her cheek. "You need to stand up."

He gazed straight forward.

"Listen." She leaned over him. "For some reason, God knows why, these people listen to you. They look to you for motivation. You moping around like a depressed donkey is helping no one."

"I don't want to be their leader."

"I give less than a shit what you want. Your problems are not mine, but those men followed you into hell without question. You jump down to rescue someone; they do, too. You start throwing fists at armed soldiers, and they are following your lead no matter what. Take some responsibility for that."

"God, you're annoying."

A sensation like a lightning bolt struck Cora's chest. She smiled, but it never quite reached her eyes. "I'm annoying? I would love for those men to listen to a fraction of what I say. You're aloof, and they call you stoic and cool. But me? I'm emotionless. Cold. Now here's the part you need to get. I don't care about that. I care that we are trapped on a spaceship, and the least we can do is not tear each other apart."

Jonah lowered his head, but Cora didn't stop.

"And what's all this?" She waved her hand over his slouching figure at the door. "Is this punishment? Are you flogging yourself for your own misery?" She scoffed. "I'm annoying? You're infuriating."

"Excuse me?" a meek voice said behind her.

"What?" She spun around to find Dr. Cooper.

"Oh, well . . ." The scientist pushed a stray lock of hair behind her ear. "Dr. Emily Cooper, from the lab. Remember?"

"Yes, I remember." Cora massaged the tension headache growing in her brow. "What is it?"

"Samuel—Dr. Young, I mean—found something we need you to see." Dr. Cooper's gaze shifted between Cora and Jonah. "You seem to be the ones calling the shots."

"Look at that, Mr. Wall." Cora clutched her hands to her chest. "Everyone likes you."

Jonah grunted and pushed himself to his feet. "What is it?"

"Dr. Young will explain."

Cora and Jonah followed her into the back of the ship, where a lab had been set up in one of the side rooms. At least, Cora thought it might be a lab, judging by the very human-looking computers and other equipment littering the area. As they approached, a small, white dome whirred along the floor. Cora danced aside, but it corrected to her movements and shifted away on its own.

"What is that?" Jonah asked.

"We think it's a cleaning robot," Dr. Cooper said as the little dome took a hard right into the wall, moving up to the ceiling like gravity didn't exist. "This place has been changing since it turned on. I'm worried about what other systems will start appearing as it shakes the cobwebs off. One bright side is I believe I found a room for waste."

"You mean a garbage disposal?"

"Human waste."

"So, you found a bathroom."

"Yes. Bathrooms are very important. People need bathrooms."

Dr. Young looked up from his microscope as they entered the lab. "Ah, you told them about the bathroom. Good, we need to spread that around."

The scientists' gear packed the space, but Cora noticed a second room to their left, mostly untouched by the multitudes of equipment, save for a large battery generator. It looked sizeable and could probably run for many hours. She hoped the scientists were using that time well.

Just behind the generator was what Cora could only imagine was a bed. A flat rectangle with plush material in the middle. It didn't look exactly like a mattress she was used to seeing, but she couldn't imagine what else it could be.

"Was this a bedroom?" she asked.

"Living quarters." Rivera's voice pierced the room, and Cora swiveled to find him leaning against a decorative partition on the far side. "There's a sink over here."

Cora stiffened in surprise. She hadn't seen him. But now, she also spotted his rifle leaning against the wall, inches from his grasp.

"How's Sergeant Booker?" Jonah asked. His expression was neutral, but Cora noticed he never took his eyes off Christopher.

"She's fine." He sniffed and motioned at Dr. Young. "We're all here. What's this about?"

"I don't know if you noticed, but the ship has been waking up." Dr. Young plucked a pen from a cup and held it between his fingers. "Lucky for us because it has opened new rooms for us to search. Dr. Cooper already told you about the bathroom, which, as it is pertinent to our conversation, is rife with DNA. Ancient DNA."

Cora frowned. "You found alien waste?"

"That's where things get interesting! Firstly, I dated it at about fifty thousand years old, judging by the general wear and tear and the density of the bone."

"Jesus," Jonah said under his breath.

That was an understatement. Cora knew the ship had to be old just by where it was uncovered in the Earth's crust, but its pristine state threw off any predictions.

"That's one hell of an engineering feat to still work after fifty millennia," Christopher said, picking his teeth.

Cora could say the same about the mining operation. That it functioned at all after that much time, even if it was destroying itself, boggled her mind. Whoever these aliens were, they eclipsed humanity completely.

"And secondly," Dr. Young continued, his face lighting up, "and this is the cool part: this DNA is human. The genetic sequencing lines up."

It felt like the air had been sucked out of the room. Christopher froze with his pinky nail in his teeth. Cora blinked rapidly, her mind going blank. A single bark of laughter left her throat.

Jonah stepped closer. "Are you saying humans were on this ship fifty thousand years ago?"

"Humans-ish." Dr. Young scratched his head and squinted. "Homo sapiens-ish. Fifty thousand years is a long time, but I'm confident enough to call it human . . . ish."

Cora rolled from her toes to her heels. The information came like a punch to her sternum. It was a concept she would have never considered, but what could she do with it?

"So . . ." She took a deep breath. "One of our ancestors entered the ship and used the facilities."

"The room was sealed." Dr. Young snatched the pen off the counter and tossed it back into the cup. "But yes, that is a possibility."

"How does this help us get home?" Christopher pushed himself off the partition.

"It doesn't?" Dr. Young glanced at Dr. Cooper for support. "But it's an important part of uncovering the truth behind this ship."

Christopher growled, swinging his rifle over his shoulder and sending Jonah the evil eye as he stomped out.

"I hate to agree with him," Jonah said. "But all this means nothing if we can't get back to Earth."

"We've told you," Dr. Cooper said, "that's not what we do. We theorize and experiment; we don't fly spaceships. I'm trying to figure out how the engine works, but if I explain the chemical makeup of gasoline, that doesn't tell you how to drive a car. Ask the people poking around the bridge. They seem to be getting a grasp on things."

Cora perked up. "Who's on the bridge?"

"The girl in the wheelchair and the kid who ran off." Dr. Cooper picked up a clipboard. "They came by asking about power systems. I loaned them one of our energy detectors."

"What is he doing now?" Jonah mumbled. He dug in his pockets and tossed the bone joint he took from the planet's surface at Dr. Young. "I found this bone back there, outside the ship. I hope it can help you uncover the truth, or whatever." He took off out of the lab.

Cora began to follow but paused. "Human. You're confident about that?"

"I don't know how to fly a spaceship," Dr. Young said. "But this is what I do, study the biology of things. If they were human, that could be why the ship is responding to us."

Cora nodded. The facts did little to calm her nerves. It was one thing to believe aliens visited Earth in the distant past, it was entirely another to say humans, or at least ancestors of humans, did and were advanced enough to build a spaceship. If that was the case, Cora wondered, where did they all go?

CHAPTER II

Jonah stepped into the bridge to find it alight with holograms. Some were cloudy with lights drifting through, like a 3D galaxy aglow with stars, while others had sharp edges with spinning displays and strange symbols, some in sequences long enough to be words. They overlapped in strange ways, becoming unreadable even if Jonah knew the language. Row and Kiki jumped between consoles, tapping against the panels while shouting at each other.

"Try that red one again," Row said.

"It just makes the squiggly thing move." Kiki rushed around to a panel on the back wall. "I'm gonna do the blue triangle."

"What is going on here?" Jonah asked, swiping at a blue-white bar hovering near his head. The front window turned black.

"That's the opacity control." Kiki wheeled past him, dragging her finger along the hologram and turning the window transparent again before carrying on without slowing.

"We're figuring out how this works." Row tapped a few of the consoles, and the projections vanished. "Don't worry. We're avoiding the ones that look like actual ship controls."

"You don't know what any of this is," Jonah said. "You shouldn't fool around with it."

"No one knows what it is. But it's better than sitting around waiting to die." He grabbed his jacket off the back of a chair and pulled out his phone, holding it up for Jonah. "What do you see?"

Jonah squinted at the screen. Row's background was the album art of some indie rock band he'd never heard of. The time was just after eleven at night, or at least that was what it was in Alaska. "I don't know. You don't have reception."

"But I do have power." He tapped the case next to the battery symbol where a lightning bolt flashed. "And it's charging."

"How?"

"My phone has wireless charging. Usually, I put it on a pad, but whatever's powering this ship is everywhere." He shook the phone in the air. "And it's compatible. Don't you see how incredible that is?"

"My wheelchair, too," Kiki said. "I have a dock it charges in at home, but here I haven't lost a single percent."

"There aren't any wires either." Row tossed his phone back on the chair before running his fingers along the wall. "Whatever this ship is made of also carries the current. It's one big seamless machine."

Jonah hadn't seen Row smile like that since they'd lived in Massachusetts before the paper laid him off, and he hadn't seen him move with that much energy since he was a toddler, at least before the group's earlier adventure in the collapsing mine. It may have been dangerous to poke around the ship's bridge, but at least Row was no longer focused on Ethan's death.

"Now watch this." Row slid past a chair and hurried for a glowing panel in the back wall. "Kiki, turn off the holograms."

The girl zoomed by, tapping buttons on consoles as she passed until the mess of semi-translucent data disappeared. Row danced his fingers across the panel in the back corner. Jonah couldn't have been out of sorts for that long, but already the pair moved around the bridge like it was their home.

"Anything we pull up on these screens can be shown in the holograms." Row pressed a finger on the panel and flicked up. A square with symbols down the edges appeared in front of Jonah. "I think this one's useful."

"What is it?" Jonah asked. A line moved slowly across the bottom of the square. Occasionally it became valleys and hills, lingering as they traveled from right to left before drifting off the hologram.

"We're pretty sure it's power consumption. Kiki."

Kiki nodded and rolled around the room again, turning the holograms back on. With each one she hit, the line on the graph moved higher. Jonah was impressed. Without reading the language, the kids had used reasoning to work out what the alien tech meant. He'd spent hours in that room and barely got off the chair.

"We're pretty zoomed in, timewise." Row dragged his finger across the console. The graph shrank, showing a steep and steady increase in power over time. "It's been going up like this for . . . well, I don't understand the time scale, but I assume since the ship started shaking. Now let's go back a little bit earlier."

The spike zipped away, leaving the graph at a steady low level for a long time until it suddenly shot right to the top. Even Jonah, with his complete lack of computer skills, could guess what that was.

"That's the ship leaving Earth," Row confirmed. He played with the settings until both spikes showed on the graph. "Using that as a reference, we can expect . . . well . . ." He held up one finger, waited, then dropped it. "This."

Jonah's ears popped like they had the first time the ship jumped, and the rocky landscape outside transformed into an open ocean. Foamy water splashed against the window as the waves raged under a dark blue sky. As opposed to the yellow planet they came from, this one could easily have been Earth.

But as Jonah approached the window, the waves consuming the ship died down, revealing thousands of identical flat structures across the water's surface as far as the eye could see. Landing pads, same as the ones they'd just left behind. Jonah's moment of hope that they'd somehow returned home washed away with the waves. In the distance, a storm brewed, the dark clouds and flashing lightning strikingly similar to those on Earth.

"Uh-oh." Kiki peered at a readout near the window. "Uh, Row, that thing you said might happen, well, happened."

Row dashed across the bridge, grabbing his jacket as he passed, and looked over Kiki's shoulder. Jonah joined them in looking at a horizontal bar projected across the console's smooth metal. A sliver on the left-hand side was filled in darker, not much more than a knuckle wide. Above it was a symbol Jonah could only describe as an angry bee. Row winced when he saw it.

"Row?" Jonah couldn't see what was so upsetting.

"When we were on Earth, the display had turned on, and I noticed this bar was here." Row pointed to a spot just left of center. "I only noticed because . . ." He swallowed hard.

Jonah glanced up. They stood beneath the blood smear. The water had already begun to wash it away, but Ethan's name tag was still stuck in the middle.

"Anyway." Row cleared his throat. "After that first jump, it went here." He slid his finger to the left. "Now it's there." His finger indicated the current sliver. "It's fuel. It has to be. And we're almost out."

A chill ran down Jonah's spine as another big wave slammed against the window. The ship shook in reply.

Row and Kiki had made bigger strides in getting them home than anyone else, even those stupid scientists. If they wanted to keep the dream alive, they needed to keep the ship running.

"We need to figure out how to refuel," Jonah said. "Maybe there's something here."

"You want to leave the ship again?" Row laughed, shaking his head. "No one's controlling this thing. It's going to jump whether we're on it or not." He pointed at the graph. "Look, it's already powering back up."

"Judging from last time, that's still at least a few hours, right?"

"Maybe!" Row threw his hands in the air. "It's changing all the time! I can't predict it."

Jonah leaned on a console. "Do we have enough fuel for the next jump?"

"I don't know."

"We can't let this ship die, not when we're so close to figuring it out." He rubbed his eyes. "I mean, not when *you're* so close to figuring it out."

Row shuffled his feet. "Thanks, Dad."

Jonah pursed his lips, uncomfortable. All he had to say was that he was proud of him. He was, wasn't he? Row had achieved so much in such a short amount of time, but every time the words approached Jonah's lips, they felt hollow. Foolish. Plastic. "This is really cool."

"Yeah." Row shoved his hands into his pockets. "It is. We should, uh, tell the others we moved." He headed toward the exit.

Jonah slapped himself mentally. What was wrong with him?

Kiki showed him an elevator outside the bridge that took all three of them to the loading dock. Once he stepped out, his head spun. The loading dock he'd spent most of his time in sat far to his right—and up a curve that made him feel like he was standing on the ceiling.

"I wouldn't worry too much about gravity here," Kiki said, wheeling herself along the curve.

Jonah took careful steps, but he was able to walk along the curved floor without trouble. He closed his eyes to keep the dizziness away; he didn't like his mind tangling itself up trying to figure this out. Row seemed similarly hesitant, keeping his eyes focused on the ceiling.

The drill crew was crowded around the loading dock door with Cora while the airmen kept a decent distance away. They'd removed their uniform jackets, leaving them in sand-colored T-shirts.

Mbeki, who'd been sitting at one of the banquet tables, pushed his cane onto the floor and forced himself to his feet. He staggered slightly at first, then held himself firm. "Kiki, where have you been?"

"Daddy, this ship is amazing!" Kiki wheeled up right in front of him, practically vibrating with excitement. "Row and I figured out how to work a bunch of the bridge. You need to let me show you."

"Maybe." He rubbed his wrist and let out a long exhalation. Jonah couldn't help but notice he was a far cry from the steadfast man who'd stood at the podium and urged caution only earlier that day.

"Hey." Saul waved Jonah over to the once-again-open entrance. "Looks like we moved again."

"I know. Row found out we're running low on fuel. We need to find some, whatever it may be."

"That might be harder than you think." Saul stepped aside, letting Jonah see the exit.

The ramp had lowered—directly into the water. The ship was submerged halfway up the hull, and waves slapped against the dock's threshold, covering Jonah's boots in a white spray. The breeze snaked through his coat, cold and salty. There was no sign of anything out there but the circle of landing pads and open ocean.

"No way!" Row rushed forward, stopping as a wave splashed over his shoes. "The ship is automated. Why would it bring us here if it's so low on fuel?"

"Who knows?" Mud crouched and cleaned some of the dirt from the mining planet off his hands in the water. "The last planet fell apart. Maybe this one flooded."

Jonah ran his fingers through his hair. If the ship couldn't make the next jump, they were literally dead in the water.

"I see something." Row pointed about a yard out from the ramp. "There, under the water!"

The drill crew piled forward. As the next wave crested, Jonah spotted an amber glow below the surface. Distant, but undeniable.

"There's another!" Frankie shouted.

"I see three!" Terrence added.

"It's a path." Row stumbled back. "I knew there couldn't be nothing here! If we're going to find fuel, that's where it will be."

"God," Rivera moaned. "Does that kid ever shut up?"

"Hey." Jonah pulled Row aside, shifting so he stood protectively in front of his son. Glaring at Rivera, he spat, "You wanna get knocked out again?"

"I would love to see you try." Rivera loosely cradled his rifle. The rest of his team laughed. Booker wasn't among them. Jonah hoped she hadn't been left alone after seeing how severe her injuries seemed on the mining planet.

Jonah had more important things to deal with. He faced his crew, who were waiting expectantly for his next words. The waves, too, slowed as if the planet sat in attendance.

"None of us want to be here." He winced. Not a good start. "Dr. Young says whoever used this ship before was . . . was human."

A hushed murmur ran through the group. Some of Rivera's team whispered to each other, and he snapped his fingers to shut them up.

"That means this ship belongs to us. This is not a monster; it's a machine. We can figure it out, we can take control, and we can get home. We're learning more about it all the time, but it's running out of power." He let out a breath. "So am I. It's been a long day, and I don't know about you, but I'm not ready to sleep yet. Row says the ship knows what it's doing, so there must be a way to get down to whatever is under the water. We spread out, find what that is, and get ourselves some fuel. We're roughnecks, after all!"

Saul pounded his chest, and the group cheered. Jonah's insides vibrated, but he held himself steady and stalwart like a rock. The ocean, vast and deep as it was, contained nothing he couldn't handle with his team. Cora crossed her arms and gave him a smug smile.

"Don't start," Jonah said, shooing her away.

Lightning struck in the distance, the rising waves telling of the oncoming storm.

Christopher led his unit away from the loading dock. The entire meeting had been nothing but a waste of time, spinning yarns about naïve dreams—children holding to optimism against the raw and bloody truth of reality. There was no time for that in war.

"Do you think they can really figure the ship out?" Airman Nathan Klondike peered at his commander earnestly. Christopher remembered him getting transferred in a couple of weeks earlier. A fresh-faced kid with the barest beginnings of a beard on his chin.

"There's no figuring this ship out." He spat onto the floor as they took a corner. A little white dome glided by, cleaning the spot before carrying on. "He's telling them what they want to hear so they'll do what he says."

"But . . . what if we can get back to Earth?"

Christopher turned on a dime and slammed his forearm into the airman's chest, pinning him to the wall. "We're not going back to Earth! This is our world now! He's not sending them down there for fuel; he's sending them down for supplies. And the one with supplies is the one who rules. Understand?"

Klondike coughed. "Yes, sir."

"Good." He stepped back, letting the airman collapse to the floor, then eyed the rest. No one made a move. They wouldn't dare. "Jonah Wall will get everyone killed if he's allowed to keep leading. Him and that damn kid of his. He's not strong enough. Only I can ensure we get through this."

The unit bobbed their heads. Christopher smirked. All he needed was a devoted few. They could make a new life on the ship, carving out their spot among the stars. Trying to control the ship was futile, and people always crumbled under enough pressure. Soon enough, Jonah would feel it, too. Christopher helped Klondike to his feet, and he and his men returned to the bunk room they'd made their home in.

He passed his rifle off to one of his subordinates as he approached the wall of bunks. "How're you feeling, Sergeant Booker?"

Booker looked up from the slat she'd been handcuffed to. Her leg had been bound in an emergency splint, but she still dripped the occasional bead of blood to the floor. Between the cuffs and the position of her leg, it was impossible to lie down, forcing her to sit straight up on the hard metal.

"Better, sir," she said, her voice hoarse and strained.

"Good." He grabbed a plastic water bottle he'd taken from the luncheon and tossed it at her. "Well enough to remember what team you're on, I hope?"

Booker tore off the lid and greedily gulped down the contents. Only once it was entirely drained did she take a breath. "Yes, sir."

He smiled and passed the cuff keys to one of his subordinates.

Pressure, that's all it took.

CHAPTER 12

I took just over an hour before Row stood assessing their only chance at fuel. Or at least that's what he believed. The whole group, minus Rivera and his people, had discovered a wide room across most of the ship's lower aft, filled with a dozen egg-shaped pods about the size of hatchbacks set into indents in the floor. Everyone congregated within, except for Rivera and his men. They all had yet to leave the bunk room. Even President Mbeki had lugged himself down the halls using his daughter's wheelchair as support. Every time Row saw him, he seemed a little more withered, stretching into a thin sheet of who he was.

Now they investigated the spaces below the pods, which had opened shortly after they entered the room a few moments earlier to reveal the ocean below.

"It's a moon pool," Cora said, peering into the dark water under one of the pods. "Off-shore rigs used them to move equipment into the water."

"This area only got power when we jumped here." Row slipped past Jonah and approached the first pod. "The ship's prioritizing, so this area must have something to do with the planet."

As he came around the left side, a piece of the pod's shell hinged open and unfurled at his feet, creating a ramp just like on the larger ship. The front quarter of the pod's top turned transparent. The inside had four seats and some space to move around. Most of the back end wasn't accessible.

"Could be an engine," Aleks said.

"Or a trunk." Saul patted the back of another pod. "When's the last time you saw an engine in this whole mess?"

Row peered around the back of the pod he'd been inspecting. If it was a trunk, it was for carrying something big. Dad stepped onto the ramp and peered inside. The lights glowed, and the console in front of the driver's seat flashed blue.

"Looks good." Even Dad didn't sound like he believed that. Still, he slapped the top like it was an old Camaro. "Hop in, guys. Let's get ourselves some fuel."

Row stepped forward, but Dad caught him before he touched the ramp.

"It's best if you stay here."

"I'm not staying on this ship if Rivera's still here." Row's skin went cold as he remembered the glare he got after the debacle on the mining planet. "I can figure this pod out."

"I'm coming, too." Kiki wheeled up next to Row.

Jonah groaned. "This isn't a field trip."

"I helped Row with the bridge." She bounced in her chair. "Let me go."

Jonah looked to Mbeki for help.

"Let her go." He rested both hands on his cane. "I sometimes forget how old she's become."

Kiki lit up. She touched Row's arm, and he was pleasantly surprised that he didn't mind. He was glad to spend more time with her after the discoveries they'd made on the bridge and in the rest of the ship. Jonah stepped aside, only for Cora to be the first one in. Row saw him hesitate, but he barely got his mouth open before she spun on him.

"Don't try with me," she said. "I may not be a roughneck, but I know how to find fuel." Then her tone softened. "You made a very inspiring speech. Come on, kids."

Kiki followed her inside. There was just enough room between the seat rows for her wheelchair to fit. Row took a moment with his dad.

"Saul," Jonah said. "Take the guys in another pod."

Mud clapped his hands and stepped back. "You guys have fun." I'm keeping out of this one. That pod looks tight, and, honestly, I smelled you all enough on the rig."

"Me, too." Darius looked like he'd eaten a rotten lemon. "This is not my jam."

"Suit yourself. Not enough room for you duds, anyway." Saul tipped his head, and Frankie, Terrence, and Aleks followed him to the second pod. As Saul approached, its ramp came down, and the lights lit up the same as the first.

"Watch yourselves." Jonah rested a hand on the pod's shell and glanced at the people staying behind. "This ship can still be dangerous."

"We can manage," Mbeki said, leaning on his cane. "You watch out for my daughter."

Jonah nodded and stepped into the pod. Behind him, Row lingered for a moment, the realization of what he was about to do gripping his chest. He'd run out of the ship before without a thought. Now, all he could do was sink into the mire of his mind. What if the pods broke? What if they didn't start up in the first place? What if something more dangerous was down there? What if the ship jumped while they were gone?

"Hey." Kiki appeared at the door. "Come on!"

The fearful thoughts melted away, replaced by a warm glow. Row headed up the ramp.

"What were you doing out there?" Kiki asked.

"Just, uh, thinking." He took the seat nearest her wheelchair.

"What were you thinking about?" She cocked her head, her braids falling across her neck and chest like an embracing arm.

Row turned red. "Nothing."

"What do we do now?" Jonah sat at the front of the pod, in front of the console, but there was no yoke or control stick. He hovered his hands over the various symbols and icons on the console, fingers twitching.

"I don't know." Row looked over his shoulder. He'd been studying the alien language for hours, and while some symbols looked like the ones in the bridge, he and Kiki hadn't yet figured out what "go" was.

A faint image glowed on the window above Row's chair. It was a simply drawn egg with a wavy line above. Row pressed his hand against it, and it lit up.

"Did that do anything?" he asked.

The team in the other pod suddenly perked up and looked around.

Row stood so he could see the other pod better, keeping his hand on the glass, and tested his theory. "Can you hear me, Saul?"

A lightbulb seemed to go off in Saul's head, and he looked at their pod. He let out a laugh audible through the open ramp door and pressed his hand against his own window.

"We can hear you." His voice came from the walls. "Any idea how to make this thing move?"

Kiki indicated something to Jonah. "How about the big middle button?"

Right in front of him sat a pulsing blue circle with an upward-facing arrow inside.

Row's hand was still pressed to the window, and he described the button to Saul.

"Sounds good to me," Saul said.

"What's the harm?" Jonah muttered. He tapped the icon, and it faded away.

A second later, the door shut. A second after that, the pod dropped into the water, smoothly gliding below the surface. Saul's followed. Darkness surrounded them. There was only the faintest glow distorted against the waves above and the interior lights from the second pod. Their tiny ship hummed, and a headlight burst out from somewhere on its front, showing where the landing pad had dipped into the water. The headlight turned to face the beacons Row had spotted and moved forward, the only sound being the water rushing past the metal shell.

There was no telling how fast they went. Beacon lights blurred past, the only break from the ever-present darkness. Something large shot past on their left, and Row's heart leaped into his throat. Then something massive appeared on their right, only for a moment before it was gone. He wanted to think they were just large fish, but his mind kept wandering to those documentaries he occasionally watched about what lurked in the depths of Earth's oceans. Who knew what monsters an alien ocean could be hiding?

Finally, the pods stopped. A light flickered on outside. Row peered out the window, wondering what kind of beast he'd see.

It was a pipe. A simple tube with a light hanging above it, similar in size to the industrial pipes in sewer systems. Another light came on, showing more pipes. One by one, the exterior world lit up, until it shone as bright as daylight. They were surrounded by large metal structures with piping running through their walls.

One building was a large cylinder, slowly rising from the darkness. An orange glow rimmed the bottom of the cylinder for a second at its apex before it dropped and let out a dull boom on impact.

"This may sound crazy . . ." Cora started.

"It looks like a refinery," Jonah finished.

Row nodded in silent agreement. A highly advanced refinery—underwater—but a refinery all the same. Once the lights outside finished turning on, the pods shut off their own headlights and resumed moving.

"How're we supposed to find fuel down here?" Aleks asked through the comms. "We can't even drive these things."

Row opened the line. "Maybe I can find a way to get control. Hold on." He squeezed himself in next to Jonah's seat and inspected the console.

The pods reached the end of the lengthy stretch of buildings and dipped lower, following the pipes. Just like the mining operation before, their presence woke up the water planet. They passed under an enclosed walkway between two buildings, its glass-like walls holding against the crushing depths. Through the windows, they saw benches and hanging lights, architecture that spoke of peaceful residences even that far beneath the surface. A place where people could rest and gaze at the sea.

People lived here, Row thought. *They must have. A city underwater.*

They turned a corner and saw a spaceship, like the one that had jumped them there, suspended between two buildings. It had crushed their tops on its descent, nearly splitting the taller and wider structure in two.

"That's not reassuring." Cora gripped her armrests with both hands.

Row, thinking logically, found an icon on the console. It was like the upward arrow that had started them moving but had a bracket on either side. He'd noticed it earlier; it hadn't stopped flashing since they entered the water. He tapped it, and the pod slowed. A control stick unfolded from beneath the console, and the panel's layout changed.

"What now?" Jonah grasped the stick awkwardly with one hand. A panel flipped out on his armrest, showing the same upward arrow at the top.

"Think that's your speed control," Row said.

Jonah pressed a finger on the panel, but nothing happened. He frowned and flicked his finger up. A bar filled the panel, and the pod launched forward, straight at a wall. Jonah took the stick in both hands and jerked the ship in a hard right, bouncing them off the building. Row dove over his dad's lap and swiped the thrust off.

"What the hell was that?" Aleks shouted through the comm.

Row stumbled over to the window. "We figured out how to take control. There's an icon on the—"

"Let's just follow what the pod wants. Try not to crash before we get the fuel," Saul said.

Dad pressed his finger against the panel again and, slowly this time, moved it up. Saul's pod took the lead, and the other followed it downward.

They reached a ridge, and Saul's pod continued down, but Dad drove theirs forward, taking them high above the sights. Row pressed himself against the window, and his jaw dropped.

An underwater civilization spread out to where the lights faded. Tall rectangular structures poked up from the seafloor, small fish-like creatures flitting past their glowing windows. Drain the water, and it could have easily been confused with a city on Earth—except for the holographic signs printed in the alien language that glowed against the interconnected buildings' exteriors.

Dad pushed forward on the stick, dropping them between two spires that twisted around each other in a double helix. Row rushed to the other side of the pod, where he saw a dome with hexagonal imprints, much like the dome on the mining outpost, covering a couple of acres of what had to have once been farmland, going by the orderly lines into which the land had been divided and the remnants of what Row thought could have been tractors with a few too many wheels. The dome had cracked long ago, however, allowing seaweed to spread within and otherworldly crustaceans to skitter through its remains, the ruined vehicles covered in plant life. The cities had been striking from a distance, but the closer they got, the clearer Row spotted the decay: the homes were filled with water that had seeped through cracks and holes in the walls, and barnacles had overtaken the surfaces.

Once Saul's pod came back into view, Dad followed it into a stone tunnel choked with seaweed. It reached out like green arms, brushing its fingers against their metal hull. They took a right at an intersection and re-emerged a few moments later out the end of the tunnel. The buildings barely stood two stories high there; the tops were jagged, some with remnants of walls still holding to them, suggesting anything higher had crumbled to dust, with one exception. A tall tower, sticking up like a black obelisk, had a hole punched clean through the middle, leaving its lower edges on spindly legs.

Row felt a profound sense of loss. The civilization that had come before was advanced beyond his wildest dreams, and there it lay in the muck in a dark ocean.

They had so much amazing technology. He slunk back to his chair. *How could they abandon it?*

Row had always believed life on Earth, for everyone, not just him, could only be made better by faster advancement of technologies. Space flight, quantum computing, and super-crops, they were all supposed to save humanity. On this planet, he'd found the most advanced civilization he could imagine, but even all their technology couldn't save them from the abyss. Was Earth doomed to the same fate?

Kiki, seeing the dour look on his face, reached over and squeezed his hand. Despite his sadness, he couldn't help but smile at her, and he couldn't stop the blush he felt climbing his face.

Saul's pod eventually led them to a large domed building, a perfect circle in the center of the ruins. A cylindrical silo, much like the ones they saw in the first refinery they passed through, was attached to it through an enclosed walkway and a series of piping. Saul's pod dipped into a short tunnel underneath, while Dad took theirs through a hole in the dome.

Hundreds of metal enclosures ran along the inside wall in three layers. Row briefly wondered if it was some sort of prison until Saul's pod turned around and backed into a spot below one. Water pulsed outside the vehicle, holding it in position as the back popped open.

Dad maneuvered them below for a better angle. They watched as water rushed into the pod's open back and a tube opened under the enclosure. Nothing came out. A couple of seconds passed before the trunk shut, the tube retreated into the enclosure, and the pod moved back toward the walkway.

"Was that good?" Saul's voice came over the comm. "Was that supposed to happen?"

Dad motioned for Row to open the line. "Your guess is as good as mine. Keep your pod moving. We'll check it out." He tapped the autopilot, and the stick and panel retreated to where they had come from. The pod turned and backed into the space next to the one the other had just left. Just like they'd seen happen with the other pod, the back opened, water rushed in, and a tube lowered from the bottom of the enclosure.

A flashing light appeared on the back wall. Row pressed his hand against it, and the metal turned transparent, allowing him to see into the trunk.

"It's just water," he said. "Nothing's coming out of the tube."

The process completed, the pod pulled out and began following Saul's pod toward what appeared to be the exit tunnel. Dad took back control and brought the pod above the dome. The second pod was nowhere in sight, presumably on its way home, job done.

Dad let go of the stick and turned his chair to look at Row. Kiki and Cora did the same. All eyes were on him, and he had no idea what to say. It didn't make any sense. Why would the pods be automated to do something so pointless? What was the purpose of filling the trunk with seawater?

He looked out the window. Like everything else, the building below them was in a state of decay. The hole Dad had entered the dome through was clearly not there by design. Now that he thought about it, if it wasn't there, the structure probably would've functioned like the pod dock on the ship. A moon pool.

"It's not supposed to be flooded." An idea was taking shape, and Row knew he was right. "It's broken. I think—"

Row was thrown off his feet as something struck the pod from below. The water outside frothed and roiled, and Kiki tumbled out of her wheelchair, which smashed into the wall and ceiling as the pod tumbled over and over until coming to a hard stop, embedded in the rubble on the ocean floor.

"Everyone okay?" Jonah asked, pushing himself off the console he'd slammed into chest-first.

"Enough." Cora stood and braced a hand on the wall. She clutched her ribs and looked out the window. Then her face went pale. "Oh, God."

Out from the gloomy depths loomed a great, white serpent.

CHAPTER 13

The beast swayed its extensive body through the water, circling the pod. Its snout came to a sharp point, with tusks creating a jagged cage along the sides. Pale gray flesh with green kelp-like highlights stretched thin across its bones and, in a certain light, became almost translucent as though a reanimated skeleton hunted them. Tendrils floated in the ocean currents along its body, and a fin ran the length of its spine, disappearing down its long tail into the darkness beyond.

Adrenaline spiked in Jonah's chest. He jumped for the stick and dragged his finger up the thrust panel. The pod shot forward. The serpent opened its mouth, revealing messy rows of needle-like teeth. Jonah pushed the stick, driving them beneath its maw and skirting its shimmering body.

The serpent whipped around. Jonah dodged through its winding form, brushing one of the tendrils before bursting free. He aimed for the rubble beneath the taller tower and dipped low. Behind the pod, the sea monster tore up the seafloor, creating clouds of obscuring dust.

"What about the fuel?" Row asked, helping Kiki back into her chair.

"Forget the fuel!" Jonah shouted, scraping the side of the pod against a piece of wall, sending barnacles in all directions. "This thing's going to crack us like an egg!"

The ground below them lifted, then exploded into a toothy mouth. Jonah pulled hard left, bouncing off the back of a second creature that appeared out of nowhere, serpentine like the first but with a snub nose and interlocking plates down its back. Crustaceans with long, lanky legs leaped from its carapace or were thrown aside in its thrashing.

Jonah blasted off toward the seaweed tunnel, his finger in the middle of the thrust panel, sweat collecting at the point of contact. He wanted to go faster, but his instincts refused to let him move that finger. He wasn't a pilot; too fast, and he'd surely smash them into pieces.

"Dad!" Row shouted.

The plated serpent caught up to them, clamping its teeth around the pod. They were too close to the tunnel, however, and it only struck the edges, spitting the ship out on impact. Jonah took a breath and tried to ignore his racing heart.

The reptile thrashed against the tunnel's entrance. Its plates vibrated, and the water around it bubbled. Then it burst forth, tearing through the stone. Seaweed stuck to the sides of its mouth as it opened wide, ready to snap them up again.

"Move!" Cora demanded.

"You think you can do better?" Jonah shouted back.

"Yes!"

He let her take the stick, and she had barely touched it before slamming the thrust to full. Jonah stumbled back, catching himself on his seat. The pod left the plated serpent in its wake. They took a left at the intersection and exploded out of the tunnel, the pressure rattling the debris on either side. They shot high into the city—and directly toward the bone serpent.

Cora shut off the thrust, banked hard to the right, and slammed the thrust back to full. The pod shot clear, and the serpent snapped its teeth where they had just been. Below them, the plated serpent tore itself free from the tunnel and homed in on them.

"You better sit down," she said to Jonah. "This is going to get tricky." She dove into the most crowded parts of the city below.

Jonah followed her advice and retreated to an empty seat. Row sat next to Kiki, holding hands as they pressed themselves under the side console.

"It's going to be okay." Jonah grasped Kiki's chair so it didn't tumble about. He hoped he wasn't lying to everyone else or himself.

Cora flew at a speed Jonah couldn't imagine. She slipped through a crack in a building's foundation and came out into a massive atrium surrounded by mostly broken windows. A monorail circled between the floors, pushing through despite the water.

The bone serpent smashed through the glass, taking hold of the train and tearing it out the other side of the atrium. Large pieces of metal and glass rained down, and Cora danced the pod among the wreckage, her tongue stuck between her teeth.

"Stop!" Row stumbled out from under the console and steadied himself on Cora's chair. "We need to stop."

"What?" Cora looked away for a moment, and when she looked back, a piece of the monorail track was coming right for them. She put the pod into a spin, taking a scrape along the vessel's bottom but avoiding the worst of it. "What do you mean, stop?"

"These things must be blind." He pointed at the bone serpent thrashing with the train. "They're reacting to movement."

"Sounds good. Just not right now!" She turned through the hole the bone serpent had made just as the plated one came smashing through the other side.

She cut low along a street, the plated serpent right on their tail. Cora gave the pod all she had, pushing it into the center of the buildings and then pulling back.

The plated serpent slammed into the base of the building and got swallowed up for a moment, then burst through a window ten stories up. It weaved in and out of the walls, rubble raining down in its wake. Every piece that hit the seafloor sent another cloud of dust into the water until murkiness practically engulfed the city. A good place to hide if there wasn't a danger of getting hit by debris.

They could hear the serpents swimming near them, slamming into the buildings, until one half of a building floated down right in front of the pod. A moment later came a watery shriek, like the rubble had clipped a serpent, stunning it for a moment.

A moment was all they needed. Cora wrenched the stick to the side and settled the pod snuggly against a building. Row jumped forward and slapped the activation icon. The pod went dark, and the humming disappeared. The only light that remained came from the city; the only sound from the serpents tearing it apart on their hunt.

"How can you drive like that?" Row whispered.

Cora sighed and leaned back in her chair. "I spent a lot of time at the arcade near my house growing up."

Row started to laugh but stopped short when the bone serpent lashed its tail at the wall above them, slicing a deep gash in the structure. They all froze, but it carried on, snapping at the plated serpent if it got too close.

Jonah rested his elbows on his knees, forcing his stomach not to relieve its contents onto his shoes.

They were safe, but they were trapped.

The storm had come on slow, but before long, it soaked everything too close to the ship's open loading dock door. The only bright side, Mud figured, was he could use it to sweep away those gruesome, dismembered arms.

"How long do you think they'll be gone for?" Darius asked from his position near the stage. He'd refused to get any closer, claiming he'd get pulled out to sea.

"Who knows?" Mud kicked at the water, watching the blood-soaked cloth sink below the waves, taking its disgusting contents with it. "I've got a bit of a different concern. Them soldiers are starting to act odd, right, Rock Doc?"

"You know that's not my name." Darius picked at a loose thread on his pants. "Yeah, but what're we gonna do? They've got guns."

"Exactamundo. That's what worries me the most." Lightning forked across the sky. Mud shivered as a cold breeze cut through his shirt, then spun about. "I may have a solution for that. Wanna see?"

"Not really, honestly." Darius pulled his knees up to his chest. "You do whatever you want, man. Leave me out of it."

"Come on." Mud stomped over and slapped the stage next to Darius. "You heard Jonah, this ship belongs to us, and that Rivera guy is one bad mood away from putting us all in cages."

Darius raised his head. "Fine. What's the plan?"

Mud led him to a room directly off the side of the loading dock, slightly up the disorientating curved floor. The space was thin but long, with identical metal staffs hanging off hooks down one wall while the other had sleeves of hockey-puck-sized black disks.

Darius tapped an alien word printed onto the sleeves. "What's this?"

"I have no idea." Mud took one of the staffs down. "But *this* is cool."

A D-shaped handle hovered near his waist, about halfway up the length. He touched the left side of it, and out flipped four parallel rods from the central axis, two at the top and two at the bottom, creating the edges of an invisible box. Rather than sitting on the ground, it floated a couple of inches just above it.

"Is it a forklift?" Darius asked.

Mud shook his head, but he could see where Darius got that impression. It was what he'd thought when he first found them. He tapped his thumb on the top of the handle, and lights turned on down the length of the rods, joined by a slight hum that faded in seconds.

"Watch this," Mud said, digging in his pockets. He found a quarter and flicked it at the device.

As soon as the coin crossed the edge of the rods, it stopped, hanging perfectly mid-rotation. Darius did a double take, and Mud smirked.

Exactly, Mr. Rock Doc. He reached forward and pushed the coin. It moved with his finger, but once he pulled away, it stopped, suspended in space.

"That is cool, I admit." Darius frowned. "But what do we do with it?"

Mud shook off the tingling sensation left behind by the device's field. "I thought that was obvious. They have a bunch of guns; we have a way to carry stuff without being heard. We steal their guns."

"I suppose you can call that a plan," Mud turned around and saw President Mbeki—Cyril, if Mud remembered correctly, though he didn't think he could call him by his first name to his face—leaning against the door.

Darius stood straight like a pencil. Mud stuttered over his words, unable to pick which lie to tell.

"If you force a confrontation, wild animals can react badly." Cyril coughed into his handkerchief. "Have you considered that?"

"I have," Mud said. "But they're already reacting badly. It's only been ten hours. What about when the food from the luncheon runs out? What happens when things get really dire, and they have all the power?"

"Then you strike first?"

"I don't wanna strike at all. I just don't want those jackboots going Donner Party on us without having a chance to defend myself."

"I can't support your dramatics. Though it may be time for me to have a talk with Colonel Rivera and his people, and that will take a few minutes of their time." Cyril pressed his hands onto his cane and hobbled off.

Mud dropped his gaze. Cyril was right. The airmen were intimidating, but they hadn't done anything outright aggressive. Taking their guns could cause more problems than it potentially solved. He eyed the staff in disappointment, but a thought niggled at the back of his mind. Why had Mbeki told them he was going to talk to Rivera? *That will take a few minutes of their time.*

A shot fired in his brain. Mud collapsed the outer rods on the staff. "We gotta go!"

"What?" Darius looked around in confusion.

"He's going to distract them, pull them away from their guns."

"Oh." Darius's round face lit up. "Oh!"

They sprinted across the loading dock; the staff tucked under Mud's arm. They would have to circle through the back halls to approach the bunk room the airmen occupied from the other side. Mud wasn't going to lose his one chance. He wasn't tough, violent, or even all that smart, but Rivera had threatened Row. A child. That made Rivera a wild card.

Mud didn't have kids of his own, figured he never would. But he'd seen Jonah's, Saul's, and Terrence's grow up. If he couldn't stand up for them, what good was he? A pretty face who liked to crack jokes? Nuh-uh.

They came upon the corner leading to the soldiers' room, and Mud slowed, holding out an arm to stop Darius. Then, he put a finger to his lips and crept forward.

"There has been tension on the ship," Cyril said from down the hall. "I'd appreciate it if you'd lend me your ear to discuss it."

Mud peeked around the corner. Cyril stood at the door to the bunk room, one hand on his cane and the other holding his handkerchief to his chest.

"President Mbeki." Rivera's voice floated through the doorway. Mud thought he sounded tired. "I'm not the one who needs to understand his position. Jonah Wall is—"

"I have counseled generals and been counseled by them. Let your people and us talk openly, and perhaps we can discover a way forward for peace."

"I don't think I can do this," Darius whispered at Mud's back.

"Are you kidding me?" Mud turned in disbelief. "We're already here."

"Exactly. You have the staff, the lifter, whatever you want to call it. You barely need me at all." He backed up, and Mud grabbed him by the shirt.

"I knew you were obnoxious, but I didn't realize you were a coward, too. You gonna tell everyone you singlehandedly took Rivera down and stole all his guns, just like you singlehandedly dug up this spaceship?"

"Oh, my God. Are you actually angry about that?"

"Yes!" It took every ounce of self-control Mud had—and there wasn't much—not to start yelling. "I know Jonah and the others don't care, but I *did* want to be known as the guy who found a spaceship. I don't have a whole lot going in my life. I would've liked to do the interviews."

"Yeah, well, I wanted it, too." Darius tore his shirt out of Mud's grasp, popping two of the buttons. "All I get is shit. PetroWave is constantly on my ass. If I don't find oil, it's all I hear about, but get us a good dig, and it's silence. And you guys, don't even get me started on you guys. Whether I tell you to dig or tell you to move, you hate me. You don't even invite me on those camping trips I know you take." He plucked at the fraying hem of his finely tailored shirt. "I just wanted a win, okay? I'm sorry I shut you out."

Mud pursed his lips. Darius had always been the man in the deluxe trailer, the one with a fancy degree slumming with a bunch of roughnecks. Hearing he had real issues was odd. He never thought he'd miss the long days on the rig when conversations were shallow and beer was forbidden.

"You don't have to get weird about it," Mud said, turning back to the corner. "Go if you want."

"No." Darius crouched beside him, tilting his head. "I'm . . . here for it."

Mud smiled down at him, then glanced back in time to see Rivera wave for his team to step out of the room, his rifle still slung across his back.

"Gentlemen," Cyril said, a calm, authoritative look on his face. "We don't bring guns to a peace talk."

Rivera groaned in obvious impatience, but still, he took his rifle off his back and placed it inside the room. Cyril led the way, taking Rivera and his airmen out of the bunk room, down the hall, and out of sight.

Mud spun the "lifter" and rounded the corner, moving quickly and quietly down the hall. Darius stayed close on his heel, nervous energy practically radiating from him. They reached the door and turned—only to find a soldier waiting for them.

Mud started, ready to run. Sergeant Booker, Monica, sat on one of the slats, her broken leg propped on a speaker taken from the stage. Her wide gaze moved from Mud to the lifter in his hand to Darius.

"If you're going to do something," she said, lifting her good leg onto the slat and lying down, "you should do it fast."

His muscles loosened. He activated the lifter, and they got to work, snatching the discarded rifles and tossing them into the invisible field. Ten in total, hovering haphazardly in the air. Mud saluted Monica, even though her eyes were now closed. He doubted she was actually asleep, though it would be a smart choice by her to claim she'd been out when Rivera discovered what had happened.

Mud's feet were as weightless as the lifter as he and Darius took the long way to the loading dock. He couldn't wait to tell Jonah what they'd done. They stowed the guns still floating in the lifter in a corner, and a few minutes later, Cyril returned and resumed his position on a nearby chair, watching the rain beat against the ramp. He gave them a polite nod.

"What do we do with them?" Darius asked.

"I don't know." Mud put his hands on his hips and walked off the energy still coursing through his veins. He hadn't got his heart pumping like that since the time his girlfriend Haley's husband came home early. He'd honestly thought he'd break a bone climbing out that second-story window. "Those jarheads don't know shit about this ship. We can put 'em anywhere, and they'd never find them."

"I guess." Darius mirrored his steps. He hadn't stopped panting yet. "By the way, jarhead actually refers to Marines, not Air Force."

And I was just starting to like you. Mud rounded on Darius—and saw Cyril pulling the lifter full of rifles toward the ramp.

"What're you doing?" Mud demanded.

Cyril gave the lifter the gentlest nudge, and it drifted out into the ocean. Mud rushed into the water, splashing in knee-deep, but the lifter was already out of reach. It rocked on the waves until it toppled over and sank. Mud dropped his head into his hands.

"It's always more dangerous when guns are involved." Cyril held his handkerchief to his mouth and coughed until he ran out of breath. Darius caught him by the arm and helped him back to his seat.

Mud tilted his head back, letting the rain splatter his face and drip down his neck. Okay, so he didn't get the guns. But the airmen didn't either. He'd call that a fair deal, except until Jonah and the rest of the crew got back, he and Darius were viciously outnumbered. He sloshed back into the ship. Looked like he'd be drying his shoes in hiding.

CHAPTER 14

Row sat on the diving pod's floor, his back against Kiki's wheelchair. At some point in the past fifteen minutes, she'd rested her hand on his head, fingers interlaced with his hair. He hadn't thought to pull away, as nervously excited as he was by her gentle touch.

How long are we going to be stuck here? he wondered. His dad paced in a tight circle while Cora leaned back in the captain's chair. Occasionally one of the serpents swam by, tearing chunks off the surrounding buildings with an absentminded sweep of its scaly body. Each time, Row's heart leaped into his throat, and he had to swallow to keep it down.

"How long until the ship leaves?" Cora asked. She kept running one hand up and down her armrest, and Row could see the long muscles of her forearms tensed to the point of straining.

"I don't know," Row said. "We can't understand all the displays yet, and . . . I'm sorry."

"There's no sense apologizing." Jonah tapped his fingers on his sleeve.

"Don't worry." Kiki smoothed Row's hair back. "They're animals. They'll move on, and we can head back to the surface."

"But they haven't moved on." Row stood and approached the front window, looking around like there was a chance he could see what else the monsters were chasing. "We can't be enticing enough prey for these things, right? Why are they hanging around?"

As if in reply, the plated serpent slammed into a building at the intersection ahead. Its carapace chittered as it melted the metal exterior and carved its way through the structure. A vibrant, holographic sign flickered out and broke from its supports on the wall, crashing into a cloud of dust and vegetation on the seafloor.

The serpent disappeared and the building crumpled in on itself. Row held his breath, and he felt Kiki's fingers still in his hair. The metal shell that once protected the building glowed red hot and bubbled the ocean around it. The support pillars exposed to the underwater city lights splintered and snapped, muddying the waters. If they fell toward them . . .

"We need to move." Cora settled herself and reached for the activation icon.

"Wait." Jonah put his hand on her arm. "Maybe we should wait until it's farther away."

The metal's glow faded, and the structure groaned, then settled. Everyone exhaled. Large metal containers slid out through the gap in the wall and thumped onto the ground. The containers collapsed and split under the intense pressure. Water rushed in and spilled out of the fist-sized cubes.

"Look at that." Row pressed a finger against the window, pointing to the cubes. "Didn't we see those in the mining operation? Only older."

"Much older." Jonah leaned over Cora's shoulder. "They looked like rocks. These are—"

The bone serpent tore across the dirt, knocking the broken containers aside and scooping the cubes into its mouth. The plated serpent dove in from above. It batted the other beast aside, snatching up one of the containers and dragging it into the dark ocean above. Cubes fell as it vanished, and the bone serpent snapped them up before taking chase.

Row's jaw hung open. *What just happened?*

"Oh! Oh! Oh!" Kiki slapped her armrests enthusiastically. "Fuel cells! Maybe they're not just attracted to movement, but the actual power sources. That's why they wouldn't leave at first."

"Because the city powered up when we arrived, drawing them in," Row finished. His face lit up, and he pointed at his dad. "You said this all looked like a refinery! That place we stopped at was supposed to dump fuel cells in the back, but it's broken. That's why the pod only filled with water. We have to go back!"

"Row." Cora gave him a look he'd seen a hundred times from some adult about to tell him "how the world works." "Our top priority right now is getting back to the ship safely before it jumps without us. Knowing what the fuel cells look like is nice, but it doesn't get them in the back of this pod and get us home."

"It could if we use it as bait," Jonah said. Row was a little surprised his dad was taking his side, and it felt . . . good. "They fought each other for those boxes, meaning they weren't trying to eat us. They wanted the fuel cells they assumed were inside. There might still be fuel back at that station." He turned to Cora. "Think you can get us there?"

"And what if there are no fuel cells?" Cora asked, adjusting her collar. "Or what if those boxes are just *things* they like?"

"Then we're in the same position we are now." He returned to his chair, expression still neutral and stoic, even as he alluded to a massive sea serpent cracking their ship open.

Row sighed and sat back in his own chair next to Kiki. He turned to her; she was nervously picking at her thumbnail, the other nails on her left hand already ragged. When Kiki saw him eyeing them, she squeezed her hands together and brought them to her chest, forcing her fingers to still.

"You're scared," Row whispered.

"Aren't you?" she asked.

"I . . . guess so." The way Kiki lit up with such excitement at figuring out the fuel cells, Row never thought just how afraid she might be. He was afraid, too, but he found his curiosity quickly outweighed his fear.

"Good. Great." Cora huffed and flicked some strands of hair out of her eyes. "Let's just drive really fast and hope we don't die." She

hovered her hand over the activation icon, fingers twitching in anticipation. "Hold on to whatever you can."

Kiki grabbed Row's hand and squeezed. His skin tingled at her touch.
Cora slapped the icon, and the interior lights flashed on. She gripped
the stick, slid her finger up the thrust panel, and the pod took off.

They kept low among the underwater city structures, skirting just
above the seaweed. Cora tore around corners like a street racer, scaring
off schools of luminescent fish. They were dipping under a walkway
when a rumble seemed to engulf them, and the bone serpent burst into
view. It clipped the corner of a building, smashing the stone like it was
Styrofoam, and charged at them.

"Shit!" Cora pushed the stick forward, and the pod ground into the
seafloor, slipping just beneath the serpent's unhinging jaw.

"Do you know where you're going?" Jonah shouted over the rumbling.

"Yes!"

"The tunnel's over there." He pointed to their right.

"The tunnel only slows us down!" She pulled back as they cleared
the serpent, lifting the pod off the seafloor. A second later, she veered
again as the plated serpent burst from the darkness.

A red icon flashed on the console near Row. No one else in the pod
noticed, focusing instead on the plated serpent tearing through the dirt
alongside them.

"Uh, hey," he said. "Something's blinking."

"Not the time, Row!" Cora banked hard left.

The bone serpent roared back, snapping at the plated serpent going
for its prey. Cora swerved side to side, trying to stay out of their way.
Still, they grew closer, their monumental teeth clashing at the windows.
The pod burst out from the city, leaving nothing but a straight and
open path to the cliff above the loading station.

Cora pushed the pod to its max, sweat dripping down her face.
Row tensed his jaw so hard he thought he might shatter his teeth, Kiki
still gripping his hand with all her might. Jonah grasped both chair
arms and stared dead ahead. The city lights dimmed as the dark ocean

crowded in, the ground disappearing beneath them, revealing the bright lighthouse of the refueling station. Cora dove hard. The serpents continued forward, flying behind them and crashing into each other as they attempted to reorient. Pulling up at the last moment, Cora skipped the pod off the ground and headed for the refueling station, driving the distance equivalent of a few city blocks.

"The tower!" Row pointed at the silo connected to the domed station. "That's gotta be where they store the fuel cells."

"Break it! Break the tower!" Kiki screamed.

The sea dragons streaked toward them, a double line of fanged death. Cora aimed for the silo and squeezed the stick until her knuckles cracked. The plated serpent's shell vibrated hungrily, but it was the bone serpent who gained on them. Cora's eyes were locked on the seaweed-covered metal. Anemone-like creatures retracted their tendrils as the pod approached.

She's going to hit it. Row's stomach turned to stone. He pressed his back into the chair. *She's going to run straight through it!*

Cora took in a sharp breath—and pulled the pod hard right. Their window kissed the edge of the silo, wiping off a layer of algae and leaving a streak of green down the metal. The serpents, meanwhile, struck the silo with full force, splitting it like a watermelon and sending a spray of fuel cells into the ocean.

The plated serpent scooped up a mouthful of cubes, taking a chunk of the bone serpent, too. Dark clouds of blood oozed from its tail, and the beast retaliated, wrapping its long body around its opponent, slamming the plated serpent into the seafloor and snapping up its own collection of fuel cells.

"Get us out of here, now!" Jonah shouted.

Cora had already turned the pod around and tilted it up, and they began speeding straight up. They cleared the cliff face and continued to the surface. The underwater city's light vanished behind them, and for a couple of minutes they sailed through the dark, lit only by the headlights and the pod's internal glow.

Finally, a dull blue light grew before them. The surface. They were close.

"Cora," Jonah said. "Are you going to slow down?"

She didn't. The blue turned to gray and with a thud that reverberated through Row's ribs, a cloudy sky greeted them as they shot like a breaching whale out of the ocean. Rain pounded against the pod's window, and a crooked lightning strike lit up the world as they flew. For a split second, everything froze, and they hung above the storm-swept sea like a fly suspended in amber. And then it ended. The pod's internal gravity kept them grounded, but Row's stomach still floated as they fell, slamming into the water's surface with a clap like the thunder that soon followed.

"Oh, my God." Cora shook her hands like they were covered in bugs, pacing around the pilot's chair in a tight circle. "Oh, my God, that was too fast. Why does my side hurt? Why do I carry stress in my side? Is this my appendix?"

"It's okay." Jonah ran his hands along his stubble. Sweat dripped down his temple, but he made no move to wipe it away. He gestured tiredly out the front window. "We're here. The ship's here. We're fine."

Row rushed to the window and was relieved to see the ship a few hundred yards away. He had no idea how they'd managed to launch out of the sea and land so close to their target. A gleeful cackle slipped out, and he pounded the glass victoriously. "Yes!"

"Holy hell!" Aleks's voice came through the pod's comms. "Was that you? We thought you were right behind us, dude. Where'd ya go?"

Jonah motioned for Row to open the line. "It's a long story, but we're—"

"You don't have time! The ship started humming a couple minutes ago! Hurry up!"

Cora lunged for the pilot's seat. Her bottom had barely touched down before she put the pod in high gear.

"Copy that!" Jonah left his seat and joined her at the front. "We're heading for the moon pool right now."

"No!" There was a thud on Aleks's end, and he cursed. "I'm there now. The doors we left through closed the second the ship started up, and I can't get them back open. Head for the main door. It's straight ahead of you."

"Got it." Dad leaned over the console as if by perching at the front he could somehow make the pod go faster.

Cora's hand rattled on the stick, fighting against the waves crashing into the pod's shell. Whatever gravitational manipulation propelled them forward when the pod was submerged seemed to struggle at the surface. The ship loomed before them, framed by dark storm clouds. It wouldn't be long before the large door started to close.

As they were getting closer, the pod slowed, even though they hadn't reached the door yet.

"Why are you stopping?" Dad asked.

"It's not me!" Cora ran her finger up and down the thrust pad. Though the visual level changed, the pod didn't react. It groaned against the water, then came to a complete halt, only the waves creating any motion.

Cora slammed her fist into the panel, then jerked on the stick, but nothing happened. Through the window, Aleks, Mud, and Frankie were visible on the ramp, shouting and waving their arms. Row's gaze drifted down to the panel where he'd seen the flickering red light earlier. It was now a steady glow.

"Uh, that blinking light is just on now," he said. "I think we broke something."

Dad stomped across the pod and kicked the wall where the door had once been.

"What're you doing?" Row asked.

"We have to swim for it." He ran his hands along the metal, searching for the door. "It's our only chance. Come on, open!"

He punched the wall, and it popped out, much to Row's surprise. The door hinged open into a small ramp, which splashed into the water. Waves sloshed into the pod, threatening to quickly fill the vehicle.

"Let's go!" Dad shouted, leaping clear over the ramp into the roiling ocean.

Cora muttered curses beneath her breath and followed. Row jumped to his feet and pulled on Kiki's arm.

"Wait," she said, her breaths quickening. "Look. I can't swim, Row! Even if I wanted to!" She tapped her chair's arm.

"I know." He slipped around her side and squatted. "I'm going to carry you."

Kiki's face reddened, but her expression stayed flat. A wave crashed against the pod. "Okay."

Row scooped one arm behind her back and the other beneath her knees. He took a couple of breaths, wishing he hadn't slacked off as much in gym class, then lifted her from the chair. Kiki threw her arms around his neck and pressed her head into his collar. Row tried not to get distracted by how close her face was to his. Slowly, he approached the open door.

The storm had only gotten worse. Saltwater sprayed his face, and lightning crashed every couple of seconds. The waves promised to drag them into the deep, back to the serpents and lost city.

"Do you know how to do this?" Kiki asked, muffled by his shirt.

"We had to take a lifeguard course at school," Row said. "It was that or bowling."

"Good choice."

Row chuckled. He stepped onto the small ramp, water filling his shoes, and crouched. "Take a deep breath," he said and stepped forward.

The cold hit him first, catching his breath in his chest. Next, the pressure threw him in a circle. Kiki tightened her grip around his neck. They broke the surface together, drawing in fresh air.

"I got you," Row assured her, holding her above the water as he kicked them toward the ship.

Each wave pulled them under for a moment, tossing them until they didn't know which way the ship was. All Row could do was reorient himself each time they resurfaced, grit his teeth, and keep

swimming. He heard Kiki still breathing, and that was all the motivation he needed.

His legs burned. His arms burned. His lungs burned. *I have to be
close.* Shouts came between the thunderclaps, backed by the ambient
hum of the ship's reawakening. Something touched his arm, and Row
seized up in fear. Then his dad, hair pasted to his brow and breathing
heavily, appeared from the waves.

"I got her," he said, taking Kiki from his arms. "Go! Get in the ship!"

Row opened his mouth to protest, but saltwater filled it. He
glanced at Kiki, and she met his gaze, her eyes now red and puffy. He
relinquished her to his father and swam for the door.

Water swelled as the ramp began to slowly lift. Voices shouted for
them to hurry. Cora had already crawled onto dry ground, heaving up
a mouthful of water. Saul helped her to her feet while Frankie rushed
out to assist Row. He got him by the arms and pulled him up.

"You okay?" Frankie asked, holding Row steady as the ramp
tilted upward.

"Where's Kiki?" Row spun around to face the angry ocean.
"Where's my dad?"

He saw his dad just a meter away, fighting against the swell, Kiki
braced on his side. Dad reached the ramp just as it broke the surface
and grabbed the edge. Row lurched toward them but stumbled as his
legs finally gave out. Frankie, Mud, and Darius rushed past and hoisted Kiki onto the ramp before pulling Dad up after her.

The ramp continued to rise, pouring water into the ship. Dad
scooped Kiki up, and everyone stumbled down the incline and
thumped against the floor. For a moment, no one moved or said a
word. The only sound was Kiki softly sobbing in Jonah's lap.

"I'm sorry," Dad whispered, getting his feet beneath him and standing, Kiki held in his arms. "I'm so sorry. I'll get you to your father."

The group parted, letting Dad pass. Row dropped his head and
rested his arms on his knees. Thunder crashed, and the door closed,
leaving at least one storm outside.

CHAPTER 15

Luckily, the caterers had provided plenty of towels for the swimmers to dry themselves off with, even if they were sized for hands. That was where the tablecloths came in. Jonah retreated to one of the living quarters around the scientists' lab, Row and Cora splitting off into two more. Kiki, despite insistence from her father and others, remained with Mbeki, sopping wet with towels clutched in her fist. Jonah barely got Row to leave her and go get dry.

Without anything to change into, Jonah's only option was to hang his shirt and pants off any edge he could find in the room. The space had a strange familiarity despite its alien design, a trend throughout the ship. With the living room in the center, a bedroom, and what he could only assume was a bath on the sides, it wasn't unlike the small apartment he'd lived in during his undergrad while getting his journalism degree.

Sitting naked in the corner of the living room, a hand towel draped over his head, Jonah felt a smooth breeze as a pleasant warmth wrapped around him. The ship's previous denizens, the human-ish people as the scientists explained, must've had similar tolerances. How alike could they have been? Jonah's head spun at the thought that long ago, a creature much like him might have sat in the same room, might have felt the same warmth.

A knock came at the quarter's main door. "Hey, Dad?"

"One second." Jonah grabbed the tablecloth he'd brought with him and wrapped it around himself, creating a toga-like covering. He unlocked the door using the panel Row had shown him, and it slid away, revealing his son, fully clothed, on the other side. Jonah frowned. "How'd your clothes dry so fast?"

"That's why I came over." He pulled at his collar. "They have a dryer."

"What?" Jonah glanced over his shoulder. Nothing looked like it could dry clothes.

"A dryer, it . . . Just grab your stuff. Come on."

Jonah snatched his clothes and followed Row into the quarter's bathroom. Row approached the far wall, and a series of icons appeared. He pressed one, and a two-foot-diameter circle popped out of the seamless metal wall, accompanied by a sharp click. He slid it out farther, revealing a hollow tube with an opening at the top.

"Drop your clothes in." Row stepped back.

Jonah placed his clothes inside the tube. Row slid the device away, and once again, it clicked into place, camouflaged in the wall. A smaller ring of light appeared in the center of where it vanished.

"It'll take about ten minutes." Row pointed to the circle, indicating where it had already lost a slice of its edge, ticking down like a clock. "It doesn't even seem to use heat or anything. Probably ultrasonic. I read an article about that, like, a year ago."

"How'd you figure this out?" Jonah inspected the remaining icons. They were all gibberish to him.

"I experimented. They're buttons in a bathroom. I couldn't imagine they'd do anything too dangerous. Look." He tapped another icon.

In a nook at the side of the bathroom, a few dozen tiny holes opened in the ceiling and unleashed a downpour of water. Jonah opened his mouth in a silent *ah*. He didn't need Row to tell him it was a shower.

"You're really getting good at figuring this stuff out." He remembered how easily Row had worked the coffee machine at his house back in Alaska, what already felt like a lifetime ago.

"I'm just pressing buttons." Row turned off the shower. "It didn't help us much down there."

"You mean in the sub, or pod, or whatever? You and Kiki figured out the fuel cells and how the refueling station worked. Hell, I only understand half of what went on down there because of you kids." Jonah massaged the knot at the back of his neck. "We only got outta there 'cause you figured out those creatures wanted to eat fuel cells."

Row scoffed, clearing his throat. "And Cora's driving."

"Yeah." Jonah had only just gotten his feet back under him after getting tossed around by that woman's piloting skills and the unexpected dip in the ocean. "That was unexpected. Look, we got through it. We're back on the ship. We're not locked outside. Couldn't have gone better."

"We could've gotten fuel."

"Right." Jonah wandered back into the main room. "One problem at a time."

"I can't think of one problem at a time. There's too much going on." Row followed, head down. "Besides, we didn't all make it back in one piece."

Jonah glanced back. He'd seen his son and Kiki holding hands in the pod, relying on each other for support in the direst of moments. He couldn't help but wish Lorri was here; she would have more to say, words of advice to offer. "Have you talked to her yet?"

"What?" Row's cheeks reddened.

"Have you talked to Kiki since getting back on the ship?"

Row hastily shook his head. "I wouldn't know what . . . I wouldn't know how to talk to her."

Jonah ruffled up his drying hair. "You'll figure it out."

"Yeah. Maybe." Row puffed out a mouthful of air and shuffled for the door. "The dryer will be a couple more minutes. It'll make a sound when it's done. We should probably tell Cora, too."

"I'll let her know."

"Cool." He kicked his shoe against the ground, the rubber sole squeaking from the water still inside. "I'll just, uh, I'll go see Kiki."

"Wait, Row." This was Jonah's chance. A chance to give his son some real fatherly advice. But as the words formed in his throat, they got stuck halfway. He couldn't possibly be the one to talk about love. Instead, he stepped back, his skin chilling as the distance between them widened. In the end, all he said was, "Good job."

Row nodded.

Had he seen the moment Jonah faltered? If he had, he said nothing and left the room. Jonah fell back against the wall.

Good try, he told himself. *You'll get it next time.*

Kiki watched the water pool around her feet. It had taken until Jonah had set her down next to her father to notice she'd lost her shoes somewhere in the ocean.

That's fine, she told herself. *I don't need shoes. I prefer to be barefoot.*

Her father sat next to her at the table they'd eaten lunch at hours earlier. How many hours, Kiki couldn't say. She had kept her phone in her wheelchair, and it had the only clock she owned.

That's fine. She gazed up at the steady white glow from the lights in the ceiling. *I'm on another planet. Time doesn't matter.*

"Perhaps we should go dry you off." Dad spoke softly as if his words could somehow break her. "You don't want to get sick."

"It's warm here," Kiki said. "I'll dry off soon. I don't want to go anywhere."

She also didn't want her father straining himself. With each jump of the ship, his gait slowed, and his hand shook more on his cane. She'd been able to ignore it for a time because deciphering the ins and outs of the alien ship with Row had kept her distracted. But sitting next to him, there was no denying how he trembled.

That's fine. She smiled at him. *He's strong. He always has been. He's just a little shaken from the experience.*

"Hey!" The oil guy with the friendly smile—Terrance, she thought, even though she'd only heard everyone's name once when they were introduced before the luncheon—shouted from across the room. He hopped onto the stage the dignitaries had once given their speeches from and waved at them. "We're rationing out some of the food from the luncheon. We got little sandwiches and little wraps. What do you want?"

"A sandwich!" Kiki exclaimed, then turned to her dad. "What do you want?"

"I'll go pick it up myself." He pressed his palm onto his cane's head and forced himself to stand.

"Dad. Please rest."

"I'm perfectly capable of walking. I've been doing it all day."

"You don't have to get up, sir," Terrence said. "We're still figuring out what we're sending over to the soldiers. We'll bring you your piece."

"See?" Kiki touched his arm. "Sit."

Dad huffed and planted himself again. "I'm not helpless, you know."

"I never said you were." Kiki was taken aback.

"I'm supposed to take care of you, Keneilwe. That's my duty as a father and I . . ." He clutched his cane with both hands and straightened his back. "I could do nothing for you. I should never have let you out of my sight."

"I'm not helpless either." She looked down at her thin arms and crooked legs; she'd never thought much—or any—of her possible limitations. "You've never coddled me before."

"We've never been in a situation like this before. You must know your limits."

"I am well aware of my limits!" She felt her face heat up in frustration. "More aware than you are."

"I am simply concerned for you." He kept his voice level but still powerful, like when he gave speeches. "You have no idea what it's like seeing someone you love confined to a wheel—"

"I am not *confined* to a wheelchair! That chair gives me the only freedom I've ever known! It's how I could be useful. Now, I'm . . ."

Her dad focused on something past her. When she looked, she saw Row paused in the middle of the room. Kiki couldn't help but grin; she liked seeing him, and the time in the pod, even with how it ended, had been so exciting.

"I . . ." Row's gaze flicked between the two of them. "I don't want to interrupt."

"You're not," Kiki said. "Honestly."

He nodded, but Kiki could tell he didn't quite believe her. "Are you doing okay?" he asked.

"Of course!" She pointed at her mouth. "See? I'm smiling. I must be okay if I'm smiling, right? You dried yourself off quick."

"Yeah. The rooms have these ultrasonic dryers. It's cool."

"Oh." Her stomach clenched for a moment. He'd figured something out without her. "That does sound cool."

"I was gonna head back up to the bridge. There's that entire wall we didn't even touch. Wanna come?"

Unconsciously, Kiki reached for her armrest, only to find nothing but the plastic of her cheap chair. She couldn't leave. "Thanks, but . . . I'm fine here. I'm tired, and I should stay with my dad."

"If you say so." Row frowned. "Maybe tomorrow, whatever that means. I'm getting tired, too, and we'll have jumped by then."

"Maybe." She pushed her smile out as far as it would go. "Maybe tomorrow."

Kiki forced herself to continue facing forward as Row left. Of course she wanted to go with him. She wanted to spend every hour with him because he made her pulse race. Because his enthusiasm for learning about the ship matched hers. Because he was nice to talk to, and he didn't treat her like something fragile, something to be protected.

But how can I help without my chair? she thought. *I would be in the way.*

She could see her father watching her out of the corner of her eye, but he didn't say a word. He didn't need to. She didn't need his vague platitudes.

I'm fine. She pressed her lips into a narrow line. *If I'm smiling, that means I'm fine. How could anything be wrong if I'm smiling?*

And so, she smiled.

The ship's hum grew steadily throughout the late dinner; it was a little after nine in Alaska, according to Row's phone, though that didn't matter much on another planet. The soldiers stayed in their makeshift home base, only one of them coming out to take their share of the rations earlier in the evening. Mud and Darius refused to get anywhere near them for reasons they wouldn't divulge.

With the meal done, everyone settled in for some well-deserved sleep, spreading out among the quarters, taking tablecloths with them for blankets or bundled up like pillows. For one calm moment, the ship didn't feel so alien.

Until the humming stopped, followed by a terrible thump. It wasn't the gentle pop they'd experienced on the previous two jumps. Row was the first to rush to the bridge, but he was quickly joined by Jonah, Cora, and the rest of the roughnecks.

The same torrential ocean spread before them. Row checked the displays, but it didn't take much to guess what had happened. Surrounded by an unending storm, the ship had just run out of fuel.

CHAPTER 16

Days droned by, or whatever could account for days on that water planet. The storm never ended, never revealing a sun through the cloud cover, and in all that time, the sky only darkened but never turned black. For a while, people kept their schedules by their watches and phones, but before long, the only meaning time gave them was when Terrence rationed out another meal of hors d'oeuvres. Row showed everyone how to get water out of the ship's taps. It tasted like warm metal, but Dr. Young assured them it was safe to drink. Still, they had plenty of water bottles to go through before having to turn to that option.

Running out of fuel turned the engine cold, but the ship didn't entirely shut down. The scientists surmised there was a separate energy source for general power—after protesting they weren't electrical engineers, of course. As more of the ship's layout became available to them, some of the travelers explored. They never spoke of why, though a silent hope among them was clear. They needed to find a way to power the engine.

The only ones who didn't tread the halls were the soldiers. They'd taken to shutting the door to their barracks, only opening it when food was brought. In there, Christopher held a mass of sorts. He'd stripped away his Air Force dress to his undershirt. No one dared to speak out of turn. They knew the natural order of things, something the people outside never could grasp.

The loss of their rifles was a setback, but the ship's engine stopping gave them new motivation, Christopher had realized once he had finished ranting about it, plotting out loud what he would do to those roughnecks who thought they had the run of the ship.

"What do we do now?" asked one of his subordinates, a short man with the last name Thomas.

"We adapt," Christopher said, sitting on a bunk with his back against the wall. "They're too cowardly and weak to use our guns, so our concern needs to be continued survival. They didn't mention what they found on their excursion, so it must be something good. In return, we get scraps."

He held up the last bite of his small sandwich. Ham, lettuce, mayonnaise. Barely more than a mouthful. The others wanted to starve Christopher and his team out. He was sure of it.

"They're pretending to play nice now," he said. "But it won't last. They'll get desperate. They'll crack. People always crack, then you really get to see what humanity is made of."

Christopher had seen the atrocities mankind could inflict when pushed, had witnessed it on too many battlefields. He needed to wrest control back before that happened. It wouldn't be pretty or nice, but it was what needed to be done. Not everyone survived hostile contact.

Booker sat across the room, her own sandwich untouched on her lap. She claimed to have been sleeping when the thieves came in and stole their guns. It sounded likely enough as she spent most of her time sleeping, her skin growing pale and green, but a voice in Christopher's head told him to doubt her. He didn't pay too much mind to it, though. For the time being, she was harmless.

"They'll be begging for my leadership once things start falling apart, but it may be too late by then," he continued, throwing his legs off the bunk and hopping to his feet. The soldiers similarly followed him to attention. He tapped the one who had asked the question earlier. "What do we do, you ask? We let them tire themselves out, then apply the pressure. Take control back before that driller makes a real mess of things."

He popped the last of the sandwich in his mouth and chewed.

The ship had no end, at least from Saul's point of view. Every wall looked the same, smooth and metallic, creating a mazelike quality he found more than a little unsettling. He and Frankie had been walking the newly opened areas for the last couple of hours, searching for anything that could help them. They'd come through a door into a long and narrow room, big enough for two more layers of catwalks but with massive amounts of empty space above metal slabs. Potentially for smaller ships, Saul reckoned.

Too bad there weren't any. Instead, he had to listen to the thumping of his and Frankie's boots echoing off bare walls. It put a tremor in his spine. Saul liked looking on the bright side but being locked in a spaceship on another planet tended to put a damper on things.

Frankie wasn't much company. More than the others, he seemed particularly quiet. Saul had gotten most of the crew's feelings on the situation pegged, but Frankie was so distant he was unreadable. He had every right to be distant, too. There wasn't an hour that went by where Saul didn't think of his wife and son Claire and Lon. Their faces drove him forward. To find a way to return home.

"This is dumb," Frankie said, the first words he'd spoken in half an hour. He kicked at the support struts for the catwalks. "We don't even know what we're looking for. Who knows what kind of weirdo food these aliens ate."

"You heard Jonah," Saul told him. "Humans built this ship. That means we can probably eat whatever they did. Though . . ." He cast him a look out of the corner of his eye. "You know we're not going to find food, right? This ship's, like, tens of thousands of years old."

Frankie shoved his hands into his pants pockets and trudged on. "Yeah, I . . . I know. I was just giving an example."

"Hey, kid, you okay?" Saul caught him by the arm. "I know that's a dumb question considering the circumstances, but we're all going through this together. Talk to us, man."

Frankie pulled away and took a few more steps before pausing. His breaths sounded like roars in the empty room. "Emily's pregnant."

"Your girlfriend?" Saul hurried to his side. "That's . . . good?"

"It is good, I mean, yeah. I don't know. We never wanted to get married, but having a kid? Yeah. We wanted kids. I thought it would take some time. She went off birth control last month, and now . . . she told me at the luncheon."

"Dang. How'd you react?"

"Not well." He forced a laugh, one that cut itself off, realizing it wasn't funny. "I think I said 'cool.' Then I rushed off to get a drink, and then we did a photo shoot, then all this. I panicked, Saul. It was all panic. Is that normal?"

"Maybe." Saul put a sympathetic hand on his shoulder. "I can only tell you how I felt when I found out I was going to be a dad. And, yeah, there was a moment of fear. Worry. Panic, even. Claire and I had been planning for a while, but even so, that moment hits you." He gave Frankie's shoulder a friendly pat. "How do you feel now?"

"I feel . . ." A slow smile spread across his face. "I'm going to have a kid. I'm going to be a dad!"

"Exactly." He tapped Frankie's chest. "That's the feeling that matters."

Frankie laughed, a genuine one this time. He stepped around Saul and whooped and hollered to the far reaches of the room. "I'm gonna be a dad!"

Saul watched him celebrate, but he couldn't join in. His family's faces had been his driving image to get home, but he wasn't the only one missing someone out there. The bright side he looked for grew dimmer. Everyone needed to get home, and they still didn't know how.

Row's heart pounded through his bones. With each step across the main hall, its beat grew stronger. He held a tablecloth tightly around the device he pushed in front of him. Its wheels squeaked every couple of seconds, and the structure rattled as metal hit metal, but he trusted it was secure.

Kiki sat in the same chair she'd been in for the past couple of days in the loading dock. She'd barely spoken to Row, claiming to be tired and staying with her father. President Mbeki had remained by her side and given Row a consoling look every time he passed.

As Row pushed, the device got caught on a chair, knocking it over and alerting Kiki to his approach. She frowned and cocked her head as he righted the chair and wheeled the device in front of her.

"What's that?" she asked.

"I made something for you. Let me just . . ." He pulled on the cloth, but it had gotten tangled around the back. "One second." He worked at the pinch point, trying to force the cloth free.

"Do you need a hand, my boy?" Mbeki asked.

"It's fine. Just a little stuck." With a jerk, the cloth finally tore free, and Row cast it aside, waving his arms over his big reveal like a magician. "Ta-da!"

Kiki and Mbeki barely reacted, aside from Kiki's awkward smile and her father's single raised eyebrow. The overly dramatic reveal had perhaps oversold the product, Row consoled himself. The device itself was admittedly rather simple, an upright dolly once used by the caterers with a chair tightly bound to the front. A wheelchair, though a crude one.

"Oh, it's . . ." Kiki squinted. "Nice."

"I don't wanna work without you." Row bundled the cloth up

against his stomach. "We only got this far together and . . . and it's not fair. I thought I'd make you something. I know it's not as good as yours."

Kiki just stared at him.

"Okay, okay." He grabbed the dolly, suddenly embarrassed. "It's stupid. Forget it."

"No." She reached out to stop him. "It's not stupid. It's just that I don't want to be a burden. I would slow you down."

"You won't!" He sighed. "Or you might, but why does that matter? Seriously? I may never truly understand what you're going through, but when I was ready to give up after . . ." He choked up for a moment and forced himself to swallow the lump in his throat. ". . . after Ethan, you convinced me to keep moving. Not *despite* what happened but *because* of what happened. I want you to move forward as well."

He offered his hand. Kiki's smile wavered, then dropped. Had he done something wrong? His stomach turned to stone until Kiki broke out into a quiet, sad laugh.

"This sucks," she said. "This all sucks. Okay, let's do it. You're the one who said these grown-ups are useless after all." She turned to her father. "Sorry."

He waved her off. "There is truth in those words."

Row slid his arms gently beneath Kiki's and helped her from her seat to the makeshift wheelchair. The straps groaned as her weight settled, and she held onto the arms with white-knuckled tension.

"I pushed Mud around for a bit," Row explained. "It held. But I could make a seat belt if you want."

"I'll get my sea legs." She laughed. "Thanks, Row."

"Row." Mbeki leaned forward. Each movement came like he was pushing through Jell-O. "Please take care of my daughter."

Kiki scoffed. "I'm right here, Father."

"Yes, of course . . ." He poised himself, sitting up a little straighter. "Kiki, you take care of him as well."

"Can do." She reached back and tapped Row on the arm. "Let's get some work done."

Row braced his foot on the rear of the dolly and tilted back. Kiki was much lighter than Mud, so he was careful not to move too fast. All he wanted to do was run, though. His legs shook with nervous energy.

He and Kiki. They could do anything.

CHAPTER 17

Time passed slowly on the ship, and Jonah found he'd lost all track of time. In fact, no one else seemed to keep a strict schedule anymore either, abandoning their phones, the clocks still set to Alaska time, and simply existing in the hours between waking and sleeping. That macabre peace soon shattered when Aleks cried out across the main room: "Those boot-stomping fascists!"

Jonah stepped through the door after checking the aft section with Terrence and jogged down the curving floor. "What the hell's going on?"

"They took the food!" Aleks kicked over a speaker from the stage.

"Who took the food?" Jonah glanced to the other roughnecks for help. Saul, Frankie, and Darius paused their card game while Mud propped himself up on an elbow and wiped the sleep from his eyes. Cora stood across the room, watching with confused interest, but none of them looked like they knew any more than he did.

"What do you mean 'Who took the food'?" Aleks jumped onto the stage and threw his arms wide. He'd changed out of his oversized suit into an oversized hoodie he kept in his backpack. "Count the people on the ship, Jonah! The goddamn military-industrial complex down the hall robbed us!"

"But we were all eating it," Darius said, stumbling to his feet. "Why would they steal something we were all sharing?"

"Maybe they found oil beneath the pastrami." He sneered at him.

Jonah circled the stage. The table they'd stored the food on for the past few days, all bundled up in plastic wrap, had been cleared. Only a single triangle sandwich remained on the ground in front of it. Jonah scooped it up and placed it back on the empty cloth. His blood turned hot. Christopher had gone too far. He shoved off the table and stomped across the back of the stage.

"Finally!" Aleks clapped and chased after him.

The rest of the roughnecks abandoned their game. Even Darius followed at their heels, albeit with a worried look. *At least Row and Kiki are in the bridge,* Jonah thought in a moment of clarity. *This isn't for them.*

"Mr. Wall!" Mbeki shouted. He braced himself against his cane and pushed to his feet.

Jonah kept his eyes and his thoughts pointed forward.

"Mr. Wall!" he shouted again. "Jonah!"

"I'll get him," Cora said, rushing after Mbeki.

Jonah and his men reached the hallways before Cora caught up, pushing through the group and matching Jonah's stride. He chewed on his cheek. He should've known she would get involved.

"Hey, buddy," she said with faux friendliness. "Have you considered what your approach is going to be for this?"

"I was thinking the direct one." He squeezed his fist until his knuckles cracked. "He's playing with everyone's lives."

"I understand." She stepped in front of him, forcing him to stop. "Do I need to remind you they have guns?"

"They don't have guns," Mud said from the rear.

Everyone turned to him. "What was that?" Jonah asked.

"Yeah. While you were all down in your submarines, me and Big D took their weapons."

The eyes shifted to Darius, who squeezed the bridge of his nose as if he had a headache suddenly coming on.

"Where . . ." Jonah took a second to gather his thoughts. Why hadn't they told him? "Where are they?"

"Cyril dumped them in the ocean." Mud scratched at his stubble. "It was unexpected."

"Well." Jonah turned to Cora and then stepped around her. "Direct approach it is."

"They're still trained soldiers," Cora said as the roughnecks pushed by. She sighed and followed the crew marching through the halls, eschewing subtlety in favor of thumping, angry boots. When they got to the barracks, Jonah strode into the soldiers' room. His foot came down on a bundle of plastic wrap with a sharp crackle. The garbage created a trail to the soldiers, where they'd set up a collection of boxes with a feast spread atop.

Rivera raised his head, sitting on one of the metal bunks. He grinned when he saw Jonah and popped a cheese cube into his mouth. The rest of his soldiers jumped to their feet, puffing out their chests to meet Jonah and his crew.

"What the hell are you doing?" Jonah asked, shouldering a soldier aside.

Resting forward on his knees, Rivera considered the remains of the meal. Over half of it had already been eaten. "Dinner."

"That's all the food we have!"

"I'm sure it is." He sneered, and the soldiers chuckled. Rivera slapped the bunk and jumped up. "It's not like you would ration out the scraps while keeping all the good stuff to yourself."

Jonah frowned. "What are you talking about?"

"All you people . . ." He swayed through his soldiers, pointing at the roughnecks without ever looking at them. "You're pretending you're some gentle society builders, but what do you do when you feel threatened? You take our weapons, and you starve us out. You want us weak, but you don't have the balls to shoot us. You'd rather see us crawl."

"We don't have the guns." Jonah stepped forward, only for two broad-shouldered men to cut him off. "They were dumped in the ocean. No one has them."

"What is the point in lying!?" Rivera slammed his fist against the wall, and blood spurted from his knuckles on impact.

"No one is lying!" Jonah huffed through his teeth. Saul laid his hand on his shoulder. *Calm down*, Jonah told himself. "We need to work together."

"You don't play *Kumbaya* in firefights." He inspected the wounds on his knuckles with disinterest. "I heard you've been to war. You've seen what people do in desperate situations, so you should understand that not everyone gets out of them."

"Oh, shut up!" Mud pushed his way to the front. "We're taking the food."

"Stay back!" One of the soldiers shoved him away.

Frankie caught him, and the roughnecks pushed forward. The soldiers met them in the middle, battering Jonah between the two groups. Someone swung an elbow, striking Aleks in the nose and sending blood pouring down his chest.

"Stand down!" Rivera ordered, his face turning red.

The soldiers obliged. Saul grabbed Aleks by the shoulders and forced him to tilt his head forward, letting his nose drain, before walking him to the back of the room. Jonah hoped he was all right, but the waves of anger coursing through his veins pushed him to focus on Rivera. He sounded like a madman.

"Who would you use the guns on?" Jonah growled.

He rubbed the blood between his index finger and thumb and paid no mind to Jonah's question.

"Goddamn it!" Jonah got up in his face, and to his surprise, none of the soldiers stopped him. Rivera truly had them on tight leashes. "It doesn't matter who you think is in charge."

"That's easy for the person wearing the boot to say."

"Jonah," Cora said. "Let's just get the food and go."

"Listen to the woman," Rivera said. "Keep playing the saint while we all stare at locked doors. Maybe you aren't hiding anything from us, but that means you don't have the control you need to get anyone through this. Things'll get worse, and you'll have to stop pretending your human nature is different from anyone else's."

Jonah's breath turned to iron in his throat. He'd never spoken to anyone who had so much in common with a brick wall. He glanced behind him at the soldiers and the roughnecks waiting. Aleks had his nose clutched in one bloody hand. Cora urged Jonah to leave with her eyes. Maybe she was right. He turned back to Rivera for one last snappy remark, and that was when he noticed movement in the far corner.

A coat had been placed over a shifting form. As the lapel fell away, he saw Booker, her skin pale—almost green. Her eyelids flickered, and her gaze slipped around the room. Never focusing.

"What is she—" Jonah's hand twitched. "You're supposed to be taking care of her. What happened?"

Rivera looked back and shrugged. "I told you, not everyone gets out of war."

Something snapped. In the next moment, Jonah had his hands around Rivera's head, and he slammed it against the edge of the bunk. Someone screamed.

Rivera tumbled back, his face a mask of blood. His left eyebrow had been split open, and he'd bitten through his lip. Still, he let out a laugh and pointed at Jonah.

"There it is!" he shouted. "That's what human nature looks like!"

"Shut your goddamn mouth!" Jonah tore himself out of the soldiers' grips. "You're not a soldier out here! Now, someone get that food and bring Monica to where somebody will actually look after her!"

No one moved. No one breathed.

"Jonah," Cora said, sliding a foot forward.

He looked down at his hands. Rivera's blood covered his palms. His vision blurred for a second. He'd had hands like that before. After a bomb had dropped on a school. He was just supposed to tell the stories; he wasn't supposed to help. But he tried. All he got was bloody hands.

"Is that a problem?" he asked, glaring at the soldiers. "He's not your commanding officer. Not anymore. Either you help all of us"—he looked at Booker—"or you just became another monster."

He tried wiping his hands clean on his shirt but only succeeded in spreading the blood around. His stomach twisted, trying to crawl up his throat and scatter onto the floor. Since when was the air so stale? He needed to breathe.

He turned on his heel and stomped out, head kept low, unable to look anyone in the eye. All the while, Rivera kept laughing.

Once Jonah was gone, Cora pressed her palms against her temples, trying to drive them through her skull. The soldiers just stood there— rigid, dumbstruck, and useless. The roughnecks weren't any more helpful. In fact, the only person not frozen in his spot was Christopher, cackling like a jack-in-the-box as blood poured from his face.

"What the hell are you all standing around for?" she demanded. "You heard Jonah. Get the food and Monica."

Mud and Frankie started gathering what remained of their food, finger sandwiches and room temperature cheese cubes, while Saul left Aleks with Terrence before sliding through the motionless soldiers and scooping Booker into his arms, one arm under her shoulder blades and the other under her knees. One of the soldiers, a young man with the starting of a beard on his chin, caught Cora's gaze. Like the others, he wore a stern mask, but something trembled behind his eyes. Something that grew as Cora stared him down.

"Is it true?" he asked, his voice much deeper than his youthful appearance indicated. "You don't have any other supplies?"

"Yes. This is it." Cora looked over the couple dozen mini sandwiches and few bowls of cheese and meat that remained. It could sustain them for a couple of days. A couple of hungry days. "We don't have any more food; we don't have any more guns. We aren't trying to hide anything from you. We're trying to keep us all alive."

Christopher chuckled, resting his body against the wall between two bunks. The soldier who spoke straightened his spine, then spun about to go help Saul with Monica. The others stuttered into movement, like old machines coming to life. They either assisted Monica or gathered up the tossed-about feast with Mud and Frankie. A few held positions, forming ranks around Christopher, but their bravado had faded.

"And somebody clean him up," Cora said, pointing a shaking finger at Christopher.

"We'll see how you feel once they start slamming *your* face into walls." Rivera spit out a mouthful of blood.

"For the last time." Cora turned for the door. "Shut up."

CHAPTER 18

Jonah lost himself in the ship's labyrinth. No matter how much time he and his crew spent looking, the twisting metal halls only grew larger around them. At moments he lost focus on what direction was up, simply following the ship's shifting gravity until he entered a room where the floor curved away.

Soon, he found himself in a massive spherical room, about the size of a basketball court, plus seating, with a series of concentric rings set into the ceiling. He'd passed by it before but could never figure out what it was for. This time, a catwalk had appeared over the concave depression that filled most of the center of the room, spanning the diameter with a ring section in the middle.

He stepped forward and grabbed the railing. Cold, like everything else on the ship. He pulled his hand away, leaving a red smear. Rivera's blood. He should've stopped to wash it off, but his mind spun at a million miles an hour. He wiped his hands on his shirt, again without thinking, and groaned.

He wandered to the middle of the walkway and leaned over the side, letting his mind drift. Something had struck the bottom of the dome far below, leaving a messy smudge and a collection of metallic shards. Some of those pieces had made it onto the walkway, even though it was fifty feet up.

Something had been blown apart. Pure, kinetic energy tearing through matter. He'd seen buildings the same way. He'd seen people the same way.

Damn. Why am I thinking this now?

It'd been years since he'd remembered his time as a war reporter. The journalist's life was far behind him. It needed to stay there. He took in deep, lung-filling-to-bursting breaths until his mind turned dark again, and time drifted away.

Soft thumps padded down the walkway, and he saw Cora approaching, her arms tucked behind her back like she was trying to act casual. All that wandering, and he still got found quickly.

"Is Rivera okay?" Jonah asked.

Cora stopped partially across the walkway. "He was laughing about it. Couldn't be that bad."

"I'd never done something like before. But that man, he's so . . ." He squeezed his fist until his fingers ached, the drying blood flaking off the skin. A towel landed on his head as Cora passed behind him.

"So that was something." She leaned her back on the railing.

"You should go." The towel scratched against Jonah's skin as he dabbed at the blood, leaving behind red stains in the creases of his palm and around his fingernails.

"You're not a bad person," Cora said.

"I just slammed a guy's head against a wall." Jonah looked around for a place to dispose of the towel. Finding nothing, he tossed it to the ground.

"At least you feel bad about it."

"Is that the bar we're setting now?"

"Come on. I saw you swim like Aquaman to help Kiki."

"She's a kid in a wheelchair. Anyone would do the same."

Cora curled her upper lip. "You'd be surprised."

Sounds like there are worse sharks in the boardroom. He squared up with her. "Why are you here? You're the one who said my problems aren't your problems."

"I also said people listen to you. Sure, they listen to President Mbeki, but even if he wanted to get involved, he's not looking well. I want to get back to Earth, and to do that, I need you to keep these people focused on something beyond their squabbles, so your goddamn man pain isn't helping."

Jonah took in a sharp breath. *I guess she has a point.* He pushed off the railing and headed back to the loading dock. "Fine, I'll get over it."

"Wait." She clasped her hands at her waist and regained her poise. "I didn't mean to come off as dismissive. He said you've been to war. Were you a soldier?"

"No." He gazed up at the rings set in the ceiling. "I was a reporter."

"How'd that come about?"

"How anything comes about. I went to school. Then I thought people needed to know what was going on over there. We had this vague concept of 'The Middle East,' but none of it seemed real, and I thought I could make it real." He winced. "It was very real."

"Did you ever get therapy?"

"I'm not suicidal." Something heavy clogged his throat, clawing to get out, bolstered by the thoughts driving through his head. "When my wife was pregnant with Row, she got in a car accident. I got the call while I was in Afghanistan, but she was fine. That's what they said. She was fine. And I thought 'good' and moved on with my work. It didn't even cross my mind that she was my wife and that was my kid until I got a second call from Lorri, rightfully pissed." He pressed his thumb against the spot where he once wore a wedding ring. When did he stop wearing it? He couldn't even remember. "How does a father do that? How does a person do that? At some point, I don't know when, I lost myself."

He looked at Cora, but she turned away. Not that there was much to say. He hadn't even talked about it with Lorri. Every time, they'd move on, and he'd vow to try harder in the future. Eventually, there was too much to talk about, and he couldn't try anymore. He still regretted so much.

Something whirred in the ceiling. An oculus opened high above them, and a series of nine cubes rained down. Jonah and Cora stumbled back, watching the objects pour from the ceiling, about to fall through the hole in the walkway, until they suddenly stopped, hanging like Christmas ornaments without a tree, suspended and spread out. An invisible force tugged against Jonah's chest from the inside.

"What's going on?" Cora's voice trembled, and she grabbed the railing behind her. She must've been feeling the same pull.

It could have been the groaning behind the walls, the fact Jonah recognized the falling objects as fuel cells, or even his years working around the metal grime of heavy machinery, but he knew exactly what was going on.

They were in the engine, and it had just turned on.

Row tore through the halls, Kiki directing him from her makeshift wheelchair like a charioteer. After an initial awkwardness, they got the hang of the more manual process of moving her around. She barely needed to ask for adjustments as they sped about the bridge, giving them plenty of time to talk about other things.

"I really like those story horror games," she said, holding on to the armrest as they took a right. "No combat. Just walking about. Getting spooked."

"I have a couple of those in my library. I don't think I ever finished any of them. I prefer multiplayer games."

"Other people?" She stuck out her tongue. "Gross."

"I have more friends online."

"Maybe we'll find something to play when we get back." She smiled up at him, and he couldn't help but smile back.

They blew past the lab. Row hopped to a stop, pulling back on the dolly's momentum. They weren't on a walk for a conversation. They'd found a potential lead in the bridge but also a wall. Time to call the professionals.

As they entered, Dr. Young looked up from his microscope while

Dr. Cooper rested on a large travel case, her knees held to her chest. She frowned as Row and Kiki thumped over the threshold.

"Hey!" Kiki leaned forward. "Which one of you is the space one again?"

Dr. Young cocked his eyebrow as Dr. Cooper raised her hand hesitantly.

"We have some questions. Could you come to the bridge?" Row wheeled Kiki around so they could head back out. "It's about space. Please?"

"Sure . . ." She eased herself off the case, stretching her arms with a groan. "I have some time between panic attacks."

"*I* have panic attacks." Dr. Young returned to his microscope. "She has depressive episodes."

"Rude."

"Could we go?" After losing track of how many days they'd been stuck on the water planet, Row ached to give the travelers some good news.

"Yeah, let's go." Dr. Cooper smoothed down her button-up and followed Row and Kiki, much slower than the near breakneck pace Row had taken to the lab. His feet wanted to fly, just so he could prove to everyone on the ship he wasn't a mess-up. That maybe he and Kiki had found a way out of there.

"So, what's all this about?" Dr. Cooper asked.

"We were going through the controls up at the front, but it's starting to get pretty technical," Row explained.

Dr. Cooper slowed further. "Are you able to read the language?"

"Kind of." Row's hands tensed around the dolly's grips. They were moving too slowly. "I have a cryptography app on my phone I used to figure out some of the sentence logic, but to do that, we had to have a sense of the language. You said humans were on this ship, so maybe we kept a piece of their language hidden in ours, and since Kiki speaks, like, six languages—"

"Five," Kiki said. "And a half. Can we go faster?"

"Sure." Dr. Cooper picked up her pace.

"So, we kept changing what language the app thought it was working with," Row continued, finally slowing down. They were almost back to the bridge. "That gave us some idea of what it could be saying, so we kept translating into different languages and treating some languages like other languages. I kind of jury-rigged the application. It's a pain without internet access, but we tested the process with some of the few words we already knew, and it worked well enough."

"Wow." She let out a low whistle. "You've been keeping busy. That's impressive. Please tell me you're planning on going to school for something in the sciences."

"Computer sciences."

She deflated. "That's disappointing."

They arrived at the bridge. Row and Kiki's experiments had left it in a mess of holograms and individual lights. They'd figured out the purpose of most of them, but nothing too exciting yet. Plenty of high-end specifications and readouts for a spaceship, so even if they knew the words, they couldn't do much with them.

"What did you need from me?" Dr. Cooper asked, approaching the front window and watching the infinite storm crash against the pane.

"I'm hoping it's not too complex." Row rolled Kiki to one of the side panels, and she deactivated the holograms one by one. They'd figured out the day before most controls could be moved freely between the consoles so that Kiki could puppeteer the entire bridge from one spot. "How does this ship . . . move?"

"That's not my area of expertise." Dr. Cooper leaned over the cloud-like hologram filled with tiny lights, revealed as Kiki removed the others. "These are stars and planets."

"It's just the engine—" Row started.

"You recognize it?" Kiki asked Dr. Cooper.

"Sort of. The orientation's off, but I think I see some familiar constellations here." She ran her fingers along a line of stars, jerking back when the map moved with her motion. "Oh. Oh! It's like a phone."

She pinched and slid her fingers across the air, moving the translucent map like an old pro. She found a thread-like light and followed. Row guessed it was the ship's jump path, connecting their current water planet to the mining operation from before.

"Whoa, we were on one of Saturn's moons before." Her eyes lit up. "Titan, perhaps? We're far out of our solar system now." Her brow furrowed. "That's odd."

"What?" Kiki leaned out of her chair.

"There's no Earth." She squinted into the projection. "There's no Mars, Venus, or Mercury either. That's weird."

"I'm really sorry, Dr. Cooper." Row needed to keep their minds on task, as interesting as he found the talk of planets. "But we need to talk about the engine. We're trying to figure out the controls for it, but without knowing how it works, we don't know what terms to look for."

"Right, of course." She shoved her hands in her pockets and paced the room, one eye still on the map. "As I said, it isn't my area of expertise. I was brought on for more theoretical reasons. Though, from what I've seen, whoever built this ship has a great understanding of harnessing gravitational forces; the structure utilizes curves in ways that to outside observers we would appear to be upside down."

"What about black holes?" Row leaned against a console. "Could that move a ship?"

Dr. Cooper paused and craned her neck at him. "Maybe. Or, theoretically, I should say, a very precise tear in space-time could appear as a jump."

"I knew it!" Row slapped the panel. "Dr. Cooper, I think this ship can create a black hole. I was thinking about how the ship pops around and how it pulls things around it with it when it does, and then Kiki translated something that could mean black hole—"

"Technically, I translated it as 'gravity pit,'" Kiki corrected.

"You also said it sounded like science fiction." He sent her a playful smile. "I told you I saw a TikTok about this."

"We're in a spaceship. Everything's gonna sound like science fiction."

She tossed her braids over her shoulder. "And I said it sounded like teleportation, and *that* sounded like science fiction."

Dr. Cooper chuckled. "You two are cute."

Row turned away, his face hot like a light bulb. Clearing his throat, he moved through the screens on his console. "So, what is a black hole but a 'gravity pit'? The translations aren't always one to one, but if you're saying it's possible—"

"Theoretically," Dr. Cooper said. "I have to stress, theoretically, yes, despite what some scientist on TikTok says."

"Okay, then *if* a gravity pit is how they refer to their engine, then I think we found the controls. And if this button between a full bar and an empty bar is what we think it is . . ."

"And I think it is!" Kiki exclaimed.

"Then . . . we have reserve fuel." His body tingled with excitement. "We're not stuck here!"

"Yes! Yes! Yes!" Kiki threw her arms in the air.

"Are you sure?" Dr. Cooper asked.

"Only one way to find out." Row hovered his hand over the icon he believed switched the engine to reserve fuel. "We take a leap."

Kiki nodded. Dr. Cooper tucked her arms behind her back and waited. It was up to Row. His fingers twitched with electricity. Days of work all for this moment. He steeled his stomach and pressed his palm against the icon.

The full bar drained while the empty bar gained a sliver. Not much at all, but the power consumption chart shot skyward, and the ship began to hum. Once a terrifying drone, now music to his ears. He laughed from the pit of his belly, a deep, unintended bout of joy.

They'd done it. The engine had just turned on.

CHAPTER 19

The engine room roared with mechanical fury. The fuel cells collapsed into a single cube that bowed and bent, space twisting around it. The towel Jonah had used to wipe the blood off his hands floated past his head until another pulse, and it slammed back into the walkway like a chunk of lead.

"We need to get out of here!" Jonah said. Every other step came with a shift in gravity, causing his feet to nearly float off the floor or feel like he was about to sink through the metal.

Cora clutched the railing as she pulled herself forward. Her hair floated above her head, then flattened to her skull in time with the cube. She was closer to the walkway back to the room's edge, but as she got within a few steps, it disconnected from the center ring, leaving the walkway floating on nothing.

"No, no, no!" She lunged forward, but a burst of high gravity caught her and slammed her to her knees. The walkway retracted beyond her reach.

Without the support of the two walkways, the center wavered under their weight, and Jonah worried it would send them crashing into the dome below. The three rings in the ceiling clicked and fell instead, slowing much like the cells had as they reached the middle of the room.

They thumped as if striking solid ground, and Jonah's feet flew out from beneath him.

Cora, the towel, the shards of junk, anything loose in the room shot up in line with the rings. As they floated, a couple of the fragments drifted by his face. They looked like pieces of computers, loose keyboard keys and bits of wiring. The innermost ring tilted into a spin, pulling the shards along with it.

"We need another way out!" Jonah pulled himself along the railing toward Cora. "Those pieces of junk are going to swing around like bullets."

"What?" She barely risked moving a hand to readjust her grip.

"We jump."

"What!?"

"It's low gravity!" He took Cora by the shoulders. "We push each other, and we both get back to the door."

"That's insane!"

The second ring tilted. "We don't have time! I'll count to three, then push!"

Cora paled but nodded and clutched his shoulders.

"One, two . . ." Jonah paused for the ring to pass behind Cora. "Three. Push!"

He shoved against her shoulders, and she did the same against his. They sailed back in opposite directions. Cora passed beyond the first ring with ease, thanks to Jonah's timing, but he flew slower than she did from the imbalance in their pushes. He crossed over the railing as the ring came around, striking him hard in the back.

He grasped at the metal of the ring, clutching for his life at large wires and knobs as pieces of metal clinked off the ring around him. He was pulled high into the air, floating nearly sideways in the low gravity. To his right, the second ring swept up along the exterior of the first. He ducked his head as it roared by, tearing at Jonah's grip with its own gravitational force. He needed to get out of there.

The central walkway shot past, each swing of the ring speeding up. Jonah aimed himself the best he could and let go. The world spun around him, turning into gray blurs until he landed chest-first on the railing. Air shot from his lungs, replaced by burning pain. At least he was on something, not spinning at what felt like a hundred miles per hour.

The fuel cube remained in its suspended state, spinning so fast he could barely tell its shape anymore.

Jonah hugged the railing, his legs dangling into space, and watched the cube spin. The three rings turned into blurs, and their terrible roar filled Jonah's ears. His thoughts faded. Blood rushed from his head. He didn't care that the junk shards still pounded off the railing around him. His fingers grew weak.

A heavy thump shook him awake. The rings slowed, and the pressure lifted off Jonah's skull.

Cora stood at the door, one hand keeping it from shutting while her other arm stretched out and held down a lever set in the wall.

"Emergency stop!" she cried out. "Come on!"

More like emergency slow, Jonah thought. He jumped his feet up to his hands with ease. Something between the low gravity and the adrenaline made him feel like Spider-Man. He timed the three rings and the cloud of junk as they passed.

The rings came together, and he saw his moment. They parted again. He pushed off the railing and let the void carry him on. There was no control once he let go. Only hope.

He covered his head as he flew past the junk, feeling the pieces of laptop and motherboards bounce off his forearms. He felt the wind ruffling his pants, and he didn't dare look at how closely the rings roared by.

The wall must be close. That one little wish rolled through his head. But he was taking too long. He couldn't even tell if he was moving anymore. *Maybe I'm already dead.*

He glanced up to see the wall closing in fast, only a couple of inches from his face. His forearms struck the metal, and he crumpled to the metal floor, the low gravity saving him from cracking his skull open.

Even there on the rim of the room, pressed against the pseudo-safety of the wall, he could hardly stop his heart from thundering. Each swing of the ring pulled on his bones, trying to yank them out of his skin.

"Jonah!" Cora braced her arm against the sliding door. Her feet slipped on the floor, the engine urging her back into the whirling rings even with the emergency lever flipped. "Hurry!"

Jonah half-crawled, half-ran for the door. He caught Cora around the waist, and she released the emergency lever, pulling them out of the engine room. The door slammed shut, and the roar vanished into absolute silence.

Cora and Jonah lay on the floor, their arms wrapped around each other, eyes locked and chests heaving. Her hand cradled his neck, her nails tickling his skin. His hand rested on her hip, feeling the heat from her body through her clothes.

"Are you all right?" Jonah asked.

Cora's pink lips parted as if she was about to say something. Her hands shifted behind his neck, and she pulled herself closer. Jonah pressed his palm against her waist. She smelled like sweat, but it was almost intoxicating.

He pulled her closer, but she pulled him harder. She kissed him hard and threw her leg over him, while he slid his hand up to her cheek to keep her in place. He forgot the fear from the engine room or how they were lying flat in the middle of the hallway. All he wanted was to feel her.

Cora's hands ran down Jonah's torso—then she jerked back, her eyes wide like headlights.

"Oh, shit!" She looked at her hand, which came away red. "You're bleeding!"

"No, it's Rivera's blood," Jonah said.

"It's not! You have a chunk of . . . I think a keyboard in you."

He propped himself up on his elbows. A black piece of plastic, about an inch long, stuck out the side of his stomach. A *J* key was visible just outside the tear in his shirt.

"Oh." He winced as he laid back. The adrenaline drained away, and the pain ramped up.

"We should look at that." But Cora didn't move, Jonah's shirt still clutched in her hands.

"Yeah. Maybe we should." He squeezed her thighs.

Cora's eyes stayed with his. *We can ignore it,* Jonah thought, even as the burning reached into his stomach. Every movement sent a spike across his skin, not helped by Cora straddling him.

"I mean . . ." Cora's gaze narrowed, and she shook her head. "No, no. It's blood. We gotta go."

She crawled off him and helped him to his feet. As much as Jonah wanted to stay there and see where their moment led, the pain was unavoidable now. Cora helped him walk, not that he needed it. But they could for a moment share each other's warmth.

Cora couldn't believe what had just happened. Nearly getting ground up in the ship's engine was one thing but mounting one of her employees in the middle of the hallway was almost worse. Almost. At least she didn't get squished.

She walked with Jonah to the scientists' lab, silently agreeing to pass around the loading dock rather than through. She didn't want anyone seeing her clearly flushed face.

Why should I be embarrassed? she thought. *He's an attractive man, and much less infuriating than he first appeared. He has a lot of depth and . . . demons I never expected.*

She had always had a soft spot for lost puppies.

Dr. Young greeted them as they entered the lab. "Good timing! I was gonna come get you in a little bit. Is that blood?"

"Yeah, it's blood," Jonah said. Cora cleared off a table with Dr. Young's help, and Jonah hopped up onto it. "Any chance you could stitch me up, doc?"

"Not that kind of doctor." He tossed his notes aside and dug around in the space beneath his workstation. "I do have a medical kit, though, if you wanna do it yourself, Rambo." He held out a red and white case.

"I'll do it." Cora took the kit.

"You know how to stitch a man up?" Jonah asked.

"Nope." She clicked the latches open and dug through the supplies. "But we can at least yank out the plastic and put a bandage on it."

"Ah, I thought I might be seeing another one of your secret skills."

"I think you've about seen all of those by now." She put aside a couple of large bandages and gauze. At least she was somewhat familiar with the supplies from all the times she'd needed to patch up one of her brothers after a scrap; as the oldest, she had always felt a familial obligation to take care of them, no matter how stupid they could be. "You'll need to take your shirt off."

Between Christopher's and Jonah's blood, the plaid button-up was a loss. Might be better to just burn it. He peeled it away, leaving behind a white long-sleeved undershirt, also stained with blood from Jonah's wound. Had it been cold back on Earth? She had barely noticed, too focused on ensuring the unveiling event went perfectly from PetroWave's end. *So much for that.*

Jonah pulled up the undershirt, too, revealing a decent-sized chunk of keyboard sticking out of his side. It bled slowly but constantly. Cora bit her tongue, hoping it didn't go too deep.

"What did you two get into?" Dr. Young asked, peering over her shoulder.

"An accident." Jonah adjusted himself on the table and groaned.

"Clearly." He tucked his shirt collar into his sweater. "Would you like to hear what I learned?"

"Is it good news?" Cora asked.

"Depends on your point of view."

Jonah and Cora shared a look as she pulled on a pair of latex gloves. "Let's hear it."

"I looked into that bone fragment you brought me." He pushed his glasses up his nose and snatched his notes. "As we suspected, this and the traces of DNA we found earlier are of the same flavor of human."

Cora mouthed the word *flavor* at Jonah, and he shrugged.

Not noticing, Dr. Young continued, "Notably, in none of the samples have I found evidence of any interaction with anything from Earth, no presence of the minerals commonly found in the minerals in Alaska's soil, for example. This ship was sealed up like a perfect time capsule until Jonah cracked its shell, so this means they've never touched down on our planet before."

That didn't surprise Cora. She would be more shocked if tens of thousands of years ago, humans built a spaceship. She placed a hand on Jonah's stomach, around the shard.

"Pulling now," she said.

Jonah bobbed his head and held his breath. Cora gripped the J and tugged. The shard came out easier than she expected, and Jonah gave little more than a soft grunt. Lucky him, most of the keyboard was outside the wound. She placed it aside and grabbed the bandages.

"The bone had some other strangeness about it," Dr. Young continued, unfazed by the medical show. "The marrow looks . . . eaten away. More so than just due to the passage of time. If I had to guess, it's some sort of unnatural biological decay."

"Like a sickness?" Cora glanced back at him over her shoulder. "Could we have caught it from being on that planet?"

"It was a mass grave," Jonah said. "And they didn't look like plague victims. Who would just put them there like that? It was on purpose. They were disposed of."

"It could be . . ." Dr. Young flipped through his notes. "You're saying a war? Maybe? If you're right about it being a mass grave—I wouldn't know, I was on the ship—this kind of decay could be due to a chemical weapon. A nasty one, if that's true, perhaps some heightened form of mustard gas or even nuclear. Did you see any other evidence of a battle?"

"No." Jonah clenched his jaw. "Don't forget to clean the wound."

"Yeah." Cora set the bandage aside and found the alcohol and wipes. Her hand knocked a bottle of liquid antibiotics out of the kit. Jonah snatched it up before it rolled off the counter and, after a quick glance at the label, took a swig and then handed the bottle off to Dr. Young.

"Can you take this to everyone else?" he asked. "A woman named Monica Booker is hurt. She might have an infection."

"I can do that." He tucked his notes under his arm and saluted with the bottle. He was nearly out the door when he paused. "Should I tell them about the chemical weapon?"

"No. In fact, if you find anything else out, you or the other doc, make sure you come to me first."

Dr. Young nodded and took his leave.

Good idea, Cora thought. *The less those idiots know, the less they can freak out about.*

"So, mass graves, huh?" She soaked a wipe with alcohol. Hardly casual conversation, but she knew so little about the man. "You've experienced that before?"

"Yeah." He winced as the alcohol touched his wound.

"Oh, come on, Mr. Quiet."

"I already talked enough. More than I usually do. And like you're an open book."

She scoffed. "I am very sociable. I talk a lot."

"It's easy to talk without saying anything."

She tossed the wipe, his words gnawing at the back of her mind. She stuck several gauze pads on his cut and got to taping the bandage.

"You called me a hypocrite, you know." She ran her finger along the tape. "Actually, you called me a dog in a crown."

"Sorry."

"No. You were right. I got this job because PetroWave wanted a new face for their big 'more responsible' rebrand after those spills in the twenty-tens. Someone who was not an old white guy."

"I'm sure that's not true." He watched closely as she finished with the bandage.

"It is. They told me. At the time, I thought I could use the position to make the company more responsible." She sat back on the opposite table and smiled. "I had big dreams."

"What happened?"

"I saw my compensation. I bought a house, way too big for me. My job was not to make PetroWave more ethical but to make the shareholders more money. In turn, I get more money. And if I don't, if I make a push for something that cuts into the profits and devalues the company, the shareholders will just sue me."

Jonah grunted and nodded, but his expression never changed.

"Something wrong?" she asked.

"Not sure how much sympathy you expect for the struggles of being rich."

"I know." There was a time a response like that would have driven her mad. A time before getting trapped on a spaceship with a bunch of people who were not afraid to speak their minds. "I just never thought I would become like this."

"What did you think you'd become like?" He risked the barest hint of a smile. "A submarine pilot?"

"Only in my wildest dreams." She leaned back on both hands. "It was a lot like the games I used to play at the arcade. We had an NES, but my brothers would never let me play, so the arcade was my space."

When she shut her eyes, she could smell the popcorn, cleaner, and something she learned later was cigarette smoke. It had been a decade since she last thought about Gold's Playland, yet the memories flooded in, fresh and vibrant in the turquoise, pinks, and yellows of the eighties bleeding into the nineties.

"It was supposed to be my space." The colors faded from her mind. "The boys there always made fun of me because I wore eyeshadow with glitter. So, I stopped. They made fun of my dress. So, I wore pants. But I kept saying it was where I belonged because I had fun. When I first started playing online games, I muted my mic for obvious reasons."

"I never really got into that stuff. My dad had a construction company, and I worked summers there."

"That makes sense." She leaned forward, letting her precise poise fall away. "You do not want to be a woman in online lobbies. Not in the two-thousands. When my brothers joined the military, I went to business school." She gave a mirthless laugh. "I was so scared someone there would learn how much I enjoyed smokey eye shadow and *Gran Turismo*. I would be too girly for the boys' club or too childish for serious business. So, I stopped. All of it."

The cleaning drone buzzed by the door.

Cora crossed her arms and chewed at the inside of her cheek. "I have never been able to be myself. I am wound up so tight in this shell, and if anyone ever sees beneath it, if I am too feminine or too nerdy or just not *exactly* what they want me to be, it will all unravel. My actual self has been stolen by some twisted idea of growth. And now I am this." She balled her hands into fists. "But no one would look at me in pity."

"Are you happy?" Jonah asked.

She scoffed. "In my business, happiness does not matter. We ask if you are successful."

"Are you successful?"

". . . Yes."

Something inside her broke at the word. Jonah placed his hand on her knee and squeezed.

She laid hers on top. His were rough but not hard. Her thoughts flashed back to when she'd straddled him, adrenaline punching through her veins, his taste on her lips.

"Dad!" Row came into the lab, pushing Kiki with Dr. Cooper at his back. His eyes fell on Cora's hand.

She yanked it away without even thinking. She had forgotten about Row. His eyes widened, but Jonah's hand moved more slowly. *Does he not notice how compromising this is?*

"We, uh . . ." Row shifted in his shoes. "We got the engine working."

"Your son is very impressive." Dr. Cooper stepped around Row, frozen in place, and sighed at the mess Cora left from cleaning out the medical kit.

"He knows his stuff." Jonah pulled his shirt down over his bandage and then hopped off the table.

"What happened?" Row asked.

"A railing broke. I'm fine."

He must not want his son to feel bad that he almost killed us. Cora fixed up her hair just to have something to do with her hands. Was Row still looking at her? She couldn't look at him.

"I'm glad you're okay. Uh." Row cleared his throat and grabbed the handles of the dolly. "We'll be jumping soon. Then we can . . . I mean, we'll be . . . I'll be in the bridge."

"What—" was all she got out before Kiki and Row tore away.

Cora's face felt on fire. Why had she said so much to Jonah while she was fixing him up? She had made herself look weak. Jonah, on the other hand, picked up his bloody plaid shirt with two fingers and looked it over with disgust. If only she could be that oblivious.

"Row!" Kiki shouted, clutching the armrests. "Row, stop! Where are we going?"

How could he answer that? He barely knew *why* he ran, much less where he was headed. His brain was doing backflips. He'd said he was going back to the bridge. That sounded as good a place as any. They thumped over the threshold. Row should've slowed.

"Come on, man!" Kiki reached back and shoved his arm. "What's going on with you?"

"I don't—I . . ." He released the dolly and circled her, nervous energy driving his feet forward. All he saw was his dad's hand on Cora's knee. "I thought there was a chance."

"For what?"

"For my mom. For my dad." He stopped, his arms limp at his side. *I'm acting like a little kid.* "I thought there was a chance for all of us."

"Come here." Kiki took his hand and pulled him down to her level. "Be realistic. No one knows how any of this is going to turn out. We may not even live through it. People will find ways to feel things, so just let them. Let yourself. Let it go."

He leaned forward and rested his head on her lap. "It's so much different in my head."

"What is?"

"Everything." He sat back on his heels again, Kiki still holding his hand. "Do you know what I like best about online games? I can mute people. I can block people. I could even pretend they're not real. They are exactly what my mind wants them to be. God, that makes me sound like a psychopath."

"No." She played her thumb along one of his knuckles. "I do that, too. Well, not *exactly* that, but . . . I thought if I just smiled, then everything would be all right. We all have our things."

"Well. . ." *When did it get so hot in here?* "When you smile, I think things *are* all right."

Kiki's mouth opened. Row sucked air into his lungs.

"That was lame." He started to stand. "I'm so sorry. We should go."

"No. I . . . I mean, it was, but . . ." She held on tight to his hand to keep him there. "Do you want to kiss me?"

Row's mind went blank. "Yeah."

She pulled him closer and pressed her lips to his. For a moment,

Row froze, confused. *What do I do? Do I lean in? Do I turn my head? Should I open my eyes? Are her eyes open?*

Then her hand brushed his cheek, and the thoughts faded away until it was only them and their kiss. His first kiss.

Row's ears popped, and he pulled away. Kiki stared at him with beautiful brown eyes, a smile dancing across her lips. They were both breathless. Row wanted to kiss her again. All he ever wanted to do from now on was kiss her. But that popping meant . . .

They'd reached the next planet.

CHAPTER 20

Jonah looked out over the new terrain. It was a stark change from the raging blue of the ocean world to a grim gray and white of concrete and ice—the cold, yet beautiful, stillness similar to the Alaskan shelf spreading miles into the distance, and still the mountains appeared massive even that far away. The ship had landed on a raised platform built into the side of one such mountain, displaying a distant white horizon.

Beneath them, about a half mile away at the base of the slope, were three gray-white boxes. The buildings, boring as they were, had been completely overtaken by snow, causing the larger one's roof to cave in while the smaller ones were barely more than tombstones. If there was any more to that old compound, it was long buried. They'd have to get closer to see any specifics.

"God," Terrence moaned. "Just looking at that makes my bones ache."

"At least it's not underwater," Frankie said, rolling a rubber ball between his hands.

"I prefer the water to the cold." Darius already had his shoulders hunched like he was blocking the wind. "Maybe not an ocean, but yeah. I miss my heater."

Aleks and Saul took in the view silently, Saul like a statue, and Aleks curled up on one of the bridge's chairs like a gargoyle. The scientists, too, had joined them. They claimed to be busy, though Jonah suspected, like the rest of them, they simply needed to keep their hands moving, so their minds didn't wander to darker thoughts.

"Something's moving out there." Cora pointed out the window toward a series of lights flashing down the mountainside and into the wilderness. A second later, the horizon rose. What had looked like shadowy sections of mountain split from the ground. Jonah's jaw dropped. Over the next minute, five fortresses shook off their snowy shells and took to the sky. The farthest were barely more than dots against the clouds, but the closest—which were still at least twenty miles away—were airborne, city-sized monstrosities.

"It's like the other planets," Kiki said, smiling. "It's waking up."

There came a thundering boom, like lightning snapping in the distance, and one of the closer fortresses tilted.

"Oh, shit!" Aleks jumped off his chair.

The fortress struggled to stay aloft, pieces the size of skyscrapers breaking off and crashing to the ground. When it couldn't take anymore, it crumbled. Quicker than it had risen, it plummeted, striking the snow and dirt with such fury the ship shook beneath their feet. Any closer, Jonah figured, and they would've been buried.

"Okay." Jonah rubbed his chin. "So, it doesn't all work."

"It is around fifty thousand years old," Dr. Young said.

Terrence grunted like a bulldog. "When're we gonna hop to the next place? When're we going to hop home?"

"That's the problem. We can't." Row pushed himself off the step he sat on and to his feet. "The reserve fuel was only enough for one jump. I guess it's supposed to be to get to a refueling station."

"And we used it to get here?"

"We didn't do anything. The ship's on a predetermined course, so whenever the engine hits max, it jumps again." He stuck his hands in his pockets and shrugged. "I don't know if we can stop it."

"Wait a sec." Mud cut in front of Terrence. "Does that mean we're still stuck in the ship?"

"No. We got stuck in the ship because the engine lost power late in the jump sequence after the door closed, and we didn't know how to open it. We know how to open it now."

Mud squinted. "How do we know that? How do you know any of this?"

"Because . . ." Kiki clapped her hands twice. "We made an alien translator."

Mud cocked his head and looked between her and Row. Jonah's boots squeaked as he turned around. He couldn't have heard that right. Mud let another second pass, then burst into a rib-rattling laugh.

"You translated the ship's nonsense?" He shoved his finger at the scientists. "Neither of you eggheads could figure that out. The kids had to?"

"For the last time." Dr. Cooper pointed at herself. "Astrophysicist." Then at Dr. Young. "Biologist. You're thinking of a linguist."

"If you can read the language, why can't you have the ship take us home?" Terrence asked Row, stepping closer with each question. "Or make us food like on *Star Trek*? Or just not let it almost kill us?"

The roughnecks crowded around Row, their voices becoming a wall of noise. Row shrank away, his eyes snapping between the men towering over him.

Jonah grabbed Terrence by the collar and yanked him away. "Hey! Step back!"

"It's not easy!" Row kept his dad between him and the crowd. "We have to put words through a code-cracker and then take those words to a translator, and sometimes we do it backwards. It's hours for each symbol, trying to figure out if it has any relation to English. I'm not a linguist, I'm sorry. It's a cobbled-together computer program on a phone."

Terrence stuck his jaw out then threw his hands up in surrender and peeled off. Jonah cast the rest of the roughnecks a hard glare and they similarly retreated to the other side of the bridge.

So much for keeping calm. Jonah took a breath. Row held his phone loosely between his fingers, all the energy he'd carried when they came in evaporating in an instant. Kiki took his hand, but he didn't react.

Jonah fumed. Row had been making great progress before the crew came in, pressuring him.

"What I'm gathering from all this is we still need fuel, and maybe supplies if we can find them." Jonah approached the window. "Maybe in those buildings? How cold do you think it is out there? Row?"

"There are external sensors." Row turned on the hologram readouts he'd shown Jonah earlier that week.

In addition to the fuel display, there were three with similar moving line charts and a separate window full of the alien language, some words were static while others changed every few seconds. Everyone in the bridge gathered around, staring up at the lights, confusion slapped across their faces.

"I . . . don't know what they mean." Row pointed at the changing words. "I think one of these is temperature, but we haven't been able to figure out which one. Turns out numbers are hard."

"We wouldn't even know the scale." Dr. Young approached the projection. "Celsius, Fahrenheit, Kelvin. Who knows?"

"Is that temperature?" Darius leaned over Row's shoulder and indicated one of the words. "I think I saw something like that in a small room Mud showed me, right off where the luncheon was held. It looked like it referred to some little disks, and the symbols look the same. Could be something for the weather."

"I don't know, man," Saul crossed his arms and considered the view. "Even if we get in there, those places are practically buried. How're you going to find anything?"

"We'll figure it out," Jonah said. "We have to."

"Row." Kiki touched him on the back. "What about the thing?"

"Oh . . . right." Row crept around Terrence, weaving through the roughnecks with his head down until he reached his father. "Remember how I took the sub off autopilot? I found a similar option here."

Jonah frowned. "I thought you said we couldn't get off autopilot?"

"From what we can tell, the system that makes us jump is different from the one that just moves us around. I can't get off auto-jump, but I could give us manual flight. It's been locked on automatic this entire time."

I can't believe all the things Row's been up to while we've been searching the ship. He'd figured Row staying in the bridge kept him safe, but he'd been making the best of it—with a few unintentional missteps. Jonah touched his stomach where the keyboard had pierced him. Still hurt.

"Good job," he said. If Row could figure all that out, Jonah could only imagine what his son could do with more time. And distance from any distractions. "If someone can fly us, we could look for signs of life. Maybe there are people out there." He looked at the floating fortresses. "Or supplies up in those things."

"You wanna go up after you saw one fall?" Saul asked.

"At least they aren't buried." He nodded at Row. "Give us control."

"You got it." He motioned for Kiki to use her console.

The holograms faded, and the ceiling opened. Mud danced back as a curved arm descended into the bridge, unfolding and extending until it formed a seat. One of the side panels opened, and a second arm swung out, creating an instrument panel with an array of holograms.

"All right, Cora." Jonah breathed through his teeth. "Wanna try flying this?"

Cora stepped toward the pilot's seat, only for the instrument panel to slide open and snap out a W-shaped yoke. Her eyes widened, and she retreated.

"That's a bit more than an arcade game," she said. "You probably want a real pilot."

"Fortunately, we have a ship full of the Air Force." Jonah leaned back on the front window.

A collective inhalation ran through the room. Jonah cocked an eyebrow. No one met his eye.

"We don't have to talk to Rivera. There's probably plenty of other pilots we can ask."

Those words lowered everyone's hackles. Jonah's crew and Cora took an extra moment of reflection. Their concern had a greater tinge of tension than disgust, at least in Jonah's eyes.

"Let's get to it." He clapped his hands. *Keep moving,* he told himself, and pointed at Darius. "Take some of the guys and go get those disks you mentioned. Saul, Cora, let's get us a pilot."

Overkill, but Jonah would rather everyone keep busy, even with little things. Frankie approached Row, where he was taking Kiki to see the new pilot's chair. Jonah instinctively moved to intercept.

"Hey," Frankie said to Row, "some laptops got left with the tech stuff. Do you want them?"

"Yeah!" Row's face lit up, and Jonah settled back. "That would be great! Thanks!"

"I'll grab 'em." Frankie bounced off, enthusiasm practically radiating from him.

Positive energy filled the room. Jonah moved, light on his feet for the first time since the ship had turned on, as though he had helium in his heels. They might have a chance at things going right.

The main door had indeed opened shortly after their arrival on the planet. The sun reflecting off the hills outside blazed like white fire, so much that Jonah had to squint as he walked into the loading dock. The same invisible wall that had kept the luncheon at a pleasant room temperature also kept the biting wind away. Snow occasionally blew in before melting away, leaving puddles along the edge of the ramp.

As cold as it might have been outside, the reception from the soldiers was colder.

"We can't," one said. She introduced herself as Farah Hardy, an Airman First Class, and insisted they call her Farah. She sat with two other airmen on the stage, watching over Booker as she rested on a pile of tablecloths and towels.

"We need to fly if we're going to find anything on this planet," Jonah said. Saul and Cora backed him up.

"I get that, I really do." She looked at her companions and shrugged. "But the only reason we came out here when you asked is that we're worried about Sergeant Booker and felt bad about the food. But it don't feel right doing stuff behind the lieutenant colonel's back."

"How is Monica?" Saul asked.

Farah glanced back. Booker barely moved. Her chest rose and fell in a painfully slow rhythm.

"I'd like to think she's doing better after taking those pills," Farah said, "but that may just be optimism. She's still got a fever, and her leg's not looking too good, neither."

Jonah placed his hands on his hips and stepped back. "Guess we're going to have to chat with Rivera."

"Sorry we can't be more help, sir." Farah nodded at him.

If you were sorry, you'd help. Jonah gave a polite wave and headed off.

Once they were a reasonable distance away, Saul took a big step and cut him off, whispering, "Are you sure about this?"

"Do you mean am I going to crack his skull open when I see him?" Jonah growled, insulted.

"Yes, I do."

Jonah squared up with him. He really wanted to push that button? Was that what Saul thought of him? That Jonah was a second away from lashing out?

"It's fine." Cora pushed herself between them. "I doubt Rivera wants to talk to him either. I'll take the lead. He doesn't scare me."

"Problem solved." Jonah kept his eyes locked on Saul.

"Cora, why don't you go on ahead?" Saul ran his fingers over his brow. "I need a moment with Jonah."

"Sure, whatever." Cora waved them off and walked away.

"What's going on?" Jonah asked, pushing through the frustration.

Saul considered him, from his messy hair to the blood on his undershirt and the stains on his old boots. "Are you okay?"

"Is anyone okay right now?" He wandered over to a table that, earlier in the week, had held a glorious food spread, and leaned on his knuckles. "I'm tense. Everyone's tense."

"Everyone's worried. The boys were talkin'. We've never seen you go off like that."

"Don't act like I haven't seen you all throwing hands at Anchorage barfights. What? Are you scared of me now?"

"We're not scared of you." Saul circled to the other side of the table. "I told you, we're just worried. You ain't playing cards with us. You're barely talking to us other than to give orders. That woman's got in your head, making you think only you can carry the burden or some nonsense."

"Now I'm confused. Do you want me caring more or less?"

Saul tapped his hands on the table, though the tension in his face said he'd rather punch through it instead. "I just don't want you driving yourself insane and forgetting about the people on the ship. We all want to get home, not just you. I'm happy you got those antibiotics for Monica, but have you even talked to her since she got hurt? Cyril's looking worse every day, Frankie's been a mess, Terrence hasn't stopped complaining, your kid lost his brother a week ago, *you* lost your son, and all I see you do is walk this ship like a ghost."

"Do you think I forgot about Ethan? Should I go back and cry in the bridge?" He prodded Saul in the chest. "You're the one who told me to get on my feet. You said I always know what to do, so here's what we do . . ." He checked over his shoulder to make sure no one listened in. "I can't get us home. Rivera absolutely cannot get us home. But Row and Kiki can, and I need to keep everything together until they do."

"That's a whole lotta pressure to put on some kids."

"I know. That's why I'm not going to tell them." He shook a finger at Saul. "And you're not going to tell anyone either. I need everyone focused. Those kids are smarter than all of us. They believe harder than we do despite everything. I wish it didn't fall to them, but sometimes you just need to get out of the way."

"So, your plan is to just not talk about it?"

"My plan is for everyone to stay in their damn lane." He ran his hand through his hair. "I saw how everyone jumped on Row back there when they learned he'd started translating stuff."

Saul pursed his lips. "I don't like it."

"You don't have to like it." Jonah brushed some dirt from the table off his palms. Saul had mentioned something about President Mbeki, and so had Cora back in the engine room. "What's wrong with Mbeki?"

"He's sick." Saul glanced over Jonah's shoulder, where Mbeki sat alone, playing solitaire. "Maybe not sick, but not well either. He refuses to talk to anyone about it because when he does, he ends up coughing."

Jonah hadn't noticed, but as he observed the old man pull a card off the top of the deck, he paused. The card shook between his fingers. Mbeki shut his eyes, took a deep breath, and built the walls of his indomitable façade up again. With great care, he set the card down and leaned back in his chair.

"What's wrong?" Jonah asked.

"What do you think? We're teleporting through space, and he's an old man."

"Terrence is old."

"Terrence acts old; Cyril is old. This can't be easy on his body." Saul leaned in and lowered his voice again. "Kiki should be with him, not mucking around up front."

Jonah glanced over at Mbeki again. "Maybe he doesn't want her to see him like this."

Saul backed off, a flat expression on his face. Jonah followed Cora. Saul could express his disappointment at the back of his head if he felt like it.

CHAPTER 21

Cora stared Christopher down, lips compressed. His three remaining airmen flanked him like sentinels while Christopher lounged in his chair, one foot propped on a black carrying case for audio equipment. He hadn't even attempted to clean up his face, letting his wounds breathe and the blood stain his face.

"Good to hear my people still have an ounce of loyalty," he said, cracking a red-tinged smile. "That's what real leadership gets you."

"Jesus Christ, Christopher." Cora pinched the bridge of her nose as though staving off a headache. "Do you even want to get back to Earth?"

"Not if it means submitting to your brand of tyranny."

Cora clenched her jaw until it hurt. *He's really calling this tyranny when he wanted martial law?* "Are you going to let one of your airmen fly or not?"

"Where is he?"

"Who?"

Christopher bared his teeth. "You know who."

"What is your deal with him?"

"He wants to be the big man in charge? He needs to act like it." He swung his leg off the case and leaned forward. "I want to talk to him. Not you."

Cora threw her head back. Of course, the men wanted to have their pissing contest. "Fine. I'll get him." She turned to find Jonah already standing at the door, his somber, intense gaze locked on Christopher.

"Thanks for trying," he said, stepping inside.

"There he is." Christopher scratched at some of the dried blood. "Do you like your handiwork?"

Jonah narrowed his eyes. "We need a pilot to fly the ship. See if there's anything else on the planet."

"Interesting idea." He nudged one of his airmen's legs. "We'd be like real explorers, huh? Traveling the stars. Meeting new people. Going where no man has gone before." He jumped to his feet and held a finger up to Jonah. "I think that's a great idea, and maybe I'll even fly for you myself. But first, I want an apology."

Cora rolled her eyes. *What an asshole.*

"And I want a *real* apology." He gave an exaggerated smile, his tone taunting and pouty. "I want to feel it deep from—"

"I'm sorry." Jonah stepped forward. "I'm sorry I lost my head, and you took the brunt of it. It shouldn't have happened, and I shouldn't have done it. So, I'm very sorry for that."

Cora hid her smile behind her hand.

"Well . . . good." Christopher huffed and smoothed back his hair. "Glad you're repenting. Suppose a deal's a deal. Show me to the stick."

Jonah motioned toward the door. With a flick of his wrist, Christopher's airmen stood down as he sauntered out. The soldiers looked grumpy, but none dared to speak up, instead fading back and sitting on their bunks. Cora shivered at how they wordlessly followed Christopher's orders, but at least for the moment, he was on their side.

They brought him up to the bridge, where Row and Kiki waited. For a moment, Cora caught them holding hands, with Row's in Kiki's lap. Christopher strode in, and Row jumped to his feet, starting to talk, only for his words to catch in his throat.

"Where'd the scientists go?" Jonah asked.

"Dr. Young said he had more work to do on a bone." Row focused on Christopher. "Dr. Cooper went with him."

"This is what everyone's been talking about? Looks cold." Christopher didn't give Row half a glance as he approached the window and faked a shiver. Then he chuckled and spun toward the pilot's seat. "That's awesome. I can see why you needed a real pilot."

"Think you can fly it?" Cora asked.

"I can fly just about anything." He slipped into the seat, one hand resting on the yoke while his other drifted over the holograms above the instrument panel. Cora figured they looked like clocks, but Christopher furrowed his brow. "Airspeed. Altitude. Turn coordinator. This might be vertical speed. This is very . . . familiar. Why is it familiar?"

"Because humans built it." Jonah peered over his shoulder.

"Weird." He took the yoke in both hands and rested his feet on two of the four pedals. "It's like a cross between a commercial plane and a chopper. Which I think means this is up."

He pressed the center-right pedal down. The ship groaned and vibrated in reply. Cora steadied herself on the nearby console to avoid being thrown to the floor. Christopher's foot flew off the pedal.

"Nope, that was down." He laughed, seemingly without a care that he had nearly put them through the landing platform.

"Hold on." Row tapped on the console nearest Kiki. "I'm closing the loading dock doors."

"Yeah, better the drawbridge is up before anyone falls out." Rivera squeezed the yoke and relaxed his shoulders. "Take two."

He eased his foot down on the center-left pedal. Soundlessly, the horizon fell before them as the ship took flight.

Kiki clapped her hands and shouted for joy before tugging on Row's jacket. Cora drifted forward in slack-jawed wonder. Even Jonah had a small smile on his face.

"This is insane." Christopher pulled back on the yoke, and the ship tilted its nose up.

He shifted his foot over to one of the outer petals and pushed down. The ship glided forward. Cora's breath left her chest. They were flying. They were actually flying the spaceship.

"All right, kids." Christopher grinned over his shoulder. "Where're we going?"

"Forward," Jonah said. "Until we find something."

Christopher opened his mouth, no doubt to reply with a snarky comment, but a strange voice filled the bridge, its speech garbled. At first, Cora thought it was English through a broken speaker, but it had too much form. Alien words from the ancient people who built the ship.

"Can we shut that off?" Christopher asked.

Jonah jogged to the door. "Sounds like it's going out through the entire ship."

"That's annoying."

"Welcome," a monotone voice said, "to the Unicanis System."

Everyone froze. Cora's heart slammed against her sternum. There were only five of them in that room, and none of them had spoken.

"You are late, but we have waited for you," the voice continued. "It's time to return home. To a place of peace, where you will find no pain, no hunger, no sickness. Beyond death. Your family waits for you in a place of peace."

Cora's eyes met with Jonah's. *What's going on? Why can we understand it?*

"You may find rest or experience anything you have missed in your life. You only need to come home."

The voice echoed down the empty halls. The ship glided on above mountain ranges, a silent, silvery cloud.

"It learned English from us," Row said. "It's been listening to us talk. While we've been translating it, it's been translating us."

"The ship's been listening to us?" Cora fell back against a console, her head swimming. "Everyone's going to freak out. They're probably on their way here already."

"What's home?" Jonah asked.

"Probably wherever the auto-jumping is taking us," Kiki said excitedly. "This ship is full of surprises!"

Christopher slapped the side of his chair. "Hey, there's something else in the sky."

"We know." Jonah kept his eye on the door. "There's a bunch of flying buildings out there."

"Yeah, I see those. This is smaller. And coming right at us!"

A silver blur shot past the window, and three hard thumps knocked the ship around. Christopher jerked the yoke to the right and tore off across the mountain range to avoid the sudden attacker.

"That thing just shot at us!" he shouted.

Two more impacts rattled the bridge, and the blur flew past on their left. It skirted the low-lying clouds, slowing enough so they could get a good look at it: long and slender like a dart, made of the same shiny material as the larger ship.

Unlike their ship, it had a clear source of propulsion. A set of five engines, a large one in the center surrounded by four smaller ones, roared pillars of blue flame as it turned back on them. Christopher banked left, but a series of crimson beams fired out of the dart's nose, scouring black marks across their hull as it took off at high speed again.

"Lose it!" Jonah shouted.

"This thing flies like a boat. What do you expect me to do?" Christopher punched the instrument panel. "Hey, kid, these lights came on when we got hit. What are they?"

Row moved to check, but Kiki held his hand tight. He gave her a reassuring nod. She smiled weakly and let go. Row rushed over to the pilot's chair. "I've seen this before."

The dart hit them with another flyby, at least one laser cutting across their window, cracking and burning the right side. Cora gasped, dropping to her knees in case it broke. The spiderwebbing crack repaired itself, and the large chunks of melting slag pulled back into their original shapes. Like what the investigators said happened to the roof after Jonah's team broke through the hull with their drill. Apparently, their opponent's lasers could break through the metal ship as well.

"What does it look like?" Kiki called to Row. "What word?"

"Not words, symbols." He snapped his fingers. "The snails! They were on the snails!"

"Did you say snails?" For a split second, Cora's half-panicked mind conjured a vision of alien snails roaming the ship's halls, and she had to fight a sudden inappropriate urge to laugh.

"If I had things activate in a combat situation—" Christopher grunted as another salvo struck. "I'd want them to be weapons!"

"Maybe they are!" Row sprinted back to one of the consoles along the edge of the room.

Cora craned her neck to see what he was working on, but he flipped through screens too fast for her to keep up. He slapped some symbols that looked like a Y inside a diamond and a chair, not unlike the pilot's chair, built itself out of the floor. The console screen changed to pure white, with an occasional flash of green and gray.

"It is the weapons! Kiki!" Row hopped back.

Kiki lifted her arms so he could pick her up and place her in the chair. A control stick flipped out of the console, and Kiki grabbed hold. As she moved it, the image moved too. A camera. Cora scrambled to her feet.

"Come on!" Row ran to each of the three remaining edge consoles, repeating the process he did with the first and creating another gunner's chair.

Jonah rushed for the one next to Kiki. Cora took the one across the door from him, and Row settled himself into the last. Cora's viewer showed blue sky and gray clouds, but as she moved the stick, she caught sight of the silver dart shooting across the horizon line. *It's so fast. How're we going to hit it?*

A red blast shot across the sky, but this one came from their ship. Kiki yelped in surprise. "The button on the stick fires it!"

"Looks like the arrows on the left move the gun forward and back." Row's foot nervously tapped on the floor. "It must be on a track on the outside of the ship."

Cora glanced over at Row's screen. He held down the top arrow and the sky became horizon, mountains, horizon, and sky again.

"I love that you're figuring out all this stuff," Christopher said. "But maybe do it while you're shooting that thing down!"

The four gunners pressed their buttons, and the sky lit up with crimson streaks. The dart danced between the laser show, deftly dodging their shots but unable to retaliate with its own. Cora stuck her tongue between her teeth, eyes locked on the crosshairs in the middle of her screen, the dart always just out of reach. For a moment, she was back in the arcade, pockets full of tokens for the first-person shooters. She was always better at racing games.

It took some time to get used to the strange moment of aiming the gun while moving it along the track. She turned the sights completely around and pressed forward, only for the gun to move back. She cursed under her breath. *Where'd it go?* The ship shook.

"Oh, no, no, no!" Kiki shrieked. "It got me!"

Cora risked a glance back. Kiki's screen had gone black.

"Damn it!" Christopher slammed his fist down. "I need one of you to give me an orientation on this thing. I'm gonna get us real close. Try not to miss it before it takes the rest of our guns."

Cora gripped her stick and took a breath, cutting out all other distractions. She circled the ship's hull until a silver blur shot past her screen. "Down!"

Christopher dove. Cora swung the gun at where she saw the dart fly until it filled her screen. She nearly jumped out of her chair but slammed her thumb down on the trigger. All three remaining guns tore into the lonely dart. Three of its engines popped like fiery grapes. Its shell melted under the intense heat, and with a gut-shaking thump, it bounced off the hull and went tumbling down. Black plumes marked its final descent. The bridge erupted into cheers.

"Yes! I got it!" Cora leapt from her seat, throwing her hands in the air. "I shot it first! That one counts for me!"

Row shot back to Kiki, sweeping her out of her gunner seat and spinning her about. Cora clasped her hands over her chest, trying to steady her heart, and looked over at Jonah. He watched his son dance through the bridge, then cocked his head in Cora's direction, a flash of a smile crossing his face before he slapped his knees and stood.

Christopher sighed, then pointed the ship's nose down.

"Where are you going?" Jonah asked.

"Following the wreck," he said. "You wanna find supplies? Fuel? Something was powering that ship. Hell, you could even find the pilot."

"That's a good idea."

"Better get your away team together, *cap'n*." Rivera cracked a smile, adding a bit of venom to the word. "Looks like you're going off the ship."

"Looks that way." Jonah turned and then stopped. "That was some real good flying, Lieutenant Colonel."

Christopher clicked his tongue. "You're damn right it was."

Jonah lingered for a moment, watching Row return Kiki to her wheelchair-dolly, then vanished out the door.

Cora flopped back into the gunner chair, catching her breath. One crisis averted, but she couldn't get the voice that had spoken to them out of her head. *Return home*, it had said. What was home? Did it still exist? Cora shut her eyes for a moment, taking in the squeaks as Row pushed Kiki around, the gliding of metal as Christopher piloted the ship.

When her heart rate returned to a comfortable level, she hopped out of the chair and chased after Jonah.

CHAPTER 22

Jonah returned to the loading dock to find the ramp discon- necting from the wall and lowering. The roughnecks near- ly knocked him down in their speed to meet him. Only Saul kept his distance, sitting with Cyril, though he did glance up as Jonah entered.

"What the hell was all that?" Frankie asked.

"We heard someone talking," Terrence added. "Was that some kind of joke one of y'all was playing?"

"What about the explosions?" Darius pushed his glasses up his nose, but they kept slipping down from sweat.

"We had a run-in with another ship," Jonah explained, pushing through the group. "It's fine now."

"Another ship like ours?" Mud asked, keeping pace.

"No, smaller. We shot it down."

Frankie stopped. "This ship has guns!?"

Jonah ducked his head and lifted his shoulders. Too many ques- tions. He'd only just gotten over getting shot at.

"What about that voice?" Terrence asked. "What about all that talk about home? What was that?"

Jonah drove his heel into the ground. "What makes you think I know any more than you?"

The roughnecks stopped and shared a look. Saul rose from his chair and crossed his arms but didn't move closer.

"Well, you're . . ." Mud pushed back his hair. "You're always up front."

"Here's the situation." Jonah pointed out the open ramp. "We shot down a small ship out there. It could have fuel, or it could have a person on it. We're going to go check it out and see what we can find."

The roughnecks grumbled in vague agreement. Aleks stuck his hands in his pockets and wandered toward the door. Jonah had hoped for a little more enthusiasm.

"Did you get those disks you mentioned?" he asked Darius.

"I did." He pulled out a hockey puck–sized black disk, only half an inch thick. He spun it between his fingers and then tossed it over. "We haven't figured out how to use it yet."

Jonah bounced it on his palm, surprised at how little it weighed. One side had a smooth glass center, while the other had a simple clip.

"How many did you find?" Jonah caught sight of Cora as she arrived from the bridge.

"A lot. More than enough for everyone here."

"Perfect. Then who's coming for a walk?" He headed for the ramp. No one followed.

Frankie dug the toe of his boot into the floor while Mud and Darius found something incredibly interesting on the back of their hands. Terrence waited with his lips pressed together and hands shoved into his back pockets.

"Come on," Jonah said. "You're gonna have me go out there alone?"

"It's dangerous, man." Mud rubbed the back of his neck. "It's the soldiers' job, not ours."

Farah and the other two still sat over Monica but made no move to come to Jonah's aid. A thought ran through his head to ask Christopher, but it left just as quickly. He didn't want to get laughed at again. Instead, he headed to the ramp alone. Saul remained standing, watching him as he made the long walk across the loading dock.

"I will come with you." Cora jogged to catch up.

"I need you to stay on the ship in case Christopher tries to fly off without me."

She took in a sharp breath to argue, then paused. "That is fair. I will get Row to take it off manual control. But you are really going to go out there alone?"

"Seems that way." He looked over the disk Darius gave him, turning it in his hands. There didn't appear to be any switch or button to activate it.

Aleks squatted next to the open door, his sweater's hood over his head and his backpack slung over one shoulder. He tapped a full cup of water against his knee. "Hey, Jonah. Check this out."

He wandered over to the door and splashed the water out. The second it crossed the threshold, it crystalized and shattered on the ramp. Jonah's stomach clenched.

"That's cold," Aleks said.

"Sure is." He squeezed the disk. "I really hope Mud and Darius are right about what these things do."

"Me, too." Aleks clipped his own disk onto his collar.

"Are you coming with me?"

"I figure why not? The ship's getting stuffy."

"I appreciate it." Jonah clipped his disk onto his belt. "I really do."

One of the airmen jumped off the stage. "Hey! Bet you wish you kept those guns now, huh?" He slapped his chest and laughed. Farah gave him a swift kick in the ass.

"Don't listen to them," Cora said. "We blew that ship out of the sky. Anything in it has got to be dead, right?"

Jonah gave her a flat stare.

"How do you figure this works?" Aleks tapped the glass center of his disk, which lit up bright green. A shock of shimmering light flowed out from the saucer and around his body, hovering just off his skin. Aleks recoiled and held his arms out, bracing for whatever was to come. A moment later, the aura faded.

"Are you okay?" Jonah reached out to touch him and met a strange pressure. Not enough to force his hand back, but enough to notice.

"I feel . . ." Aleks looked over his arms and legs, touched his face, and slapped at his stomach. ". . . the same."

Jonah tapped his own disk's center. The same flash covered his body. Electrical tension rolled through his muscles like the fastest-ever deep tissue massage. Just as quickly as it started, it faded.

"You wanna give it a go?" Aleks jerked his head toward the door.

The planet looked colder as Jonah approached the exit. They'd landed at the edge of a copse filled with strange trees, tall with thick branches like yucca, only covered from tip to root with pine needles. A plume of dark smoke rose from behind a nearby hill. Jonah reached out, stretching his hand past the threshold. Nothing changed.

He shuffled forward slowly. Still nothing. With a deep breath, he stepped full body out into the icy landscape, but no cold wind touched his skin.

"Awesome." Aleks hopped out next to him, craning his neck to see around both sides of the ship. "I was hoping for a cool spacesuit, but I guess a personal heater's fine, too."

"We won't be long," Jonah called back to Cora, walking down the ramp. Despite not feeling the cold, his breath still puffed out in large clouds of vapor. "If we don't come back . . . well, hopefully, someone comes after us."

"I'll make sure someone does." Cora stayed at the ramp, watching as Jonah and Aleks stomped across the tundra.

Each step pushed the snow down, but their feet never sank too far. Whether due to the temperature disks or the sheer compaction of the snow was up to Jonah's imagination, but at least he wasn't trudging through knee-deep drifts. Aleks took the phenomenon as less of a given, and shortly after they left the ramp, he started occasionally jumping, trying to force his sneakers deeper to no avail.

"Thanks for coming along." Jonah knocked a few needles off a tree as they passed. They splintered like dried wood. "Why are all the guys acting like children?"

"Saul thinks you're not telling us something," Aleks said, stomping one last time before giving up.

"Hell. You seem fine with me."

"Even when I'm talking with someone, I think they're not telling me something. That kind of paranoia is only tiring if you let it run your life." He climbed onto a fallen log, losing his balance for a moment before catching himself and walking it like a tightrope. "Out here, there's no corporate interests pulling the strings or government agencies looking through our computers. I thought this might be a plot or an experiment, some MKUltra shit, but this is just chaos. And that's beautiful."

"If you say so." Jonah skirted the log. Aleks seemed more cheerful than he did on the rig.

"Yeah, man." He jumped off and stumbled up to Jonah's side, adjusting his bag strap after it slipped. "Earth's a mess of conflicting and secret agendas from people with way more power than you and I will ever have. But on the ship, we're all playing with the same rules. And when you know the rules, the game can't hurt you."

"So, you're saying you don't necessarily trust me. You just don't care."

"I'm in a good mood because of, you know"—he snapped his fingers and pointed up—"alien planet. Alien spaceship. Aliens, in general. I always said we were visited by extraterrestrial life, and now we're visiting them back."

"You remember humans built the ship, right? And it was about fifty thousand years ago."

He rolled his eyes. "Fine. Maybe we didn't have extraterrestrials in Roswell."

"Coulda built the pyramids."

"Egyptians built the pyramids, Jonah." He clapped him on the back. "Don't be racist."

I'll never get a handle on this guy. They trudged up the hill and crested the top to a thin overlook above a narrow valley. The ship had impacted the far side, leaving behind a deep groove of ripped-up trees and stone before wedging itself at the bottom. In the sky, it was barely more than a pinpoint against the clouds, but in perspective, it was about the size of a private jet Jonah had once seen a PetroWave executive take into Anchorage. Black smoke curled skyward from its engines as the wind whistled over a hole broken through its hull, penetrating the mountain silence with an ominous cry.

"That guy was right," Aleks said. "I do kinda wish we kept those guns now."

Jonah spotted a branch on the lip of the overlook. He dislodged it from the snowpack and shook it clean. It was cold from the snow and had a thick, heavy knot at the end, not unlike a club. He showed it to Aleks and gave the makeshift cudgel a few hefty test swings.

"Yeah, that'll block a laser gun." Aleks flashed him a double thumbs-up and climbed down into the valley.

Jonah rested the club on his shoulder. Despite Aleks's sarcasm, he preferred a weapon. Even a wooden one.

They descended slowly toward the ship, scrambling to recover from the occasional slip as the snow gave way. Aleks held back once they reached the bottom, letting Jonah lead the way. Jonah braced one hand against the ship's shell, then immediately jerked it back. The metal was so cold it felt like fire.

"You okay?" Aleks asked.

"I'm fine." He shook the pain out of his hand. "I guess the temperature disk doesn't protect you from touching something."

"I'll keep that in mind." Aleks shrank away from the ship.

They continued to the hull. The far edge was burned black and partially melted, while the rest had been peeled away like a tin can lid. The floor sat at about Jonah's chest, so he poked his head in. Sunlight bounced off the surrounding valley walls to fill in the shadows, but it only reached a short distance down the central hall.

"Need a boost?" Aleks asked.

"I don't think so." Jonah backed up the slope a couple of steps, then jumped into the ship.

Aleks followed his maneuver but paled at the dark corridor leading from the aft to the bow and snapped out his phone, turning on the flashlight.

"Looks like this ship has the same temperature control as ours." Jonah exhaled audibly. "Can't see our breath anymore."

"For now. This thing took a beating on the way down." Aleks swung his light back and forth.

The smaller ship had the same smoothed-over-metal design as their larger vessel, with no exposed machinery aside from that revealed by the crash. Jonah straightened his spine. *Am I really calling it "our ship" now?*

"No one's popping out to kill us," Aleks said. "Wanna grab your own light and split up?"

"My phone doesn't have wireless charging. It's dead."

"Together it is." Aleks shined his light down a narrow corridor toward the bow. His head almost touched the roof as he crept forward. "What're we looking for anyway?"

"Anything." Jonah kept close to Aleks, his club ready to swing if anything jumped out. "Fuel is essential. Supplies like food would be nice since we're running low."

They passed benches with safety belts set into the wall, the kind Jonah had seen in troop transports. It certainly wasn't a luxury liner. At the end was a five-foot ladder up into a cockpit. Jonah grabbed Aleks by the hood, stopping him fast.

"The pilot could be alive," he whispered. "Just knocked out."

"Or waiting for us." Aleks nodded at the club. "You good to use that?"

"Yeah, stay here." Jonah crept past Aleks and grasped the top rung of the ladder.

He braced himself on the bottom rung, ready to leap up. Aleks gave him a nod, and Jonah threw himself upward, the club held over his head.

The cockpit was empty and dark. There was no window for a pilot to see and no chair for them to sit in. Remembering how their ship's hull could turn transparent, it seemed likely enough that the same could happen there, but that didn't explain why there was no space for a person to fly it.

"There's no pilot!" Jonah called down. He crept into the cockpit, ducking his head to keep from hitting the ceiling, and ran his fingers over the blank instrument console. "There are no controls either."

"It's gotta be a drone." Aleks rested his foot on the ladder and held his phone high, shining the light over his head for Jonah. "Maybe some automated defense system. Could be we're on a military base."

Jonah squinted into the shadows. Something had been scratched into the metal above the ladder. Some phrase in the alien language. If only Row and Kiki were there.

"Aleks," Jonah said. "I gotta borrow your camera."

Aleks handed his phone up, and Jonah snapped a picture of the message. He zoomed in while it was on the screen but still couldn't make heads or tails of it, only that it must've been done with a sharp piece of metal. He'd have to leave that up to Row. The only sign of life they'd found, an ancient bit of graffiti.

"Damn it." He kicked the wall.

"What's wrong?" Aleks asked.

"Nothing. I'm just . . ." He pressed the heel of his palm into his forehead.

"Frustrated? Hoped we'd find civilization?"

"Pretty much."

"Funny thing about life, you can always find something to be disappointed in." Aleks stepped back and mumbled under his breath, "I thought we'd find an alien."

Jonah climbed down the ladder and handed Aleks back his phone. "Let's check the rear. Maybe we can get something out of this."

Aleks led the way back down the corridor. Even having walked it once, the shadows remained oppressive, though in that direction, they at least had the daylight through the breach to give them a goal. The air already smelled of harsh smoke. The quicker they searched, the quicker they could get out in case the entire thing burned.

They passed by the hole into the aft. The corridor narrowed soon after as the walls became lined with vertical handles. Aleks was all business, walking as quickly as he could. Jonah took a moment to inspect the handles. Above each was a familiar symbol. An angry bee.

"Hold up," he said, leaning toward the wall. "When Row showed me the fuel gauge, this was on it. It must mean fuel."

He pulled the handle. While it shifted for a moment, something held it in place.

"It's got a latch on the top," Aleks said, flicking the symbol. As he shifted the light back and forth, it revealed a slight rectangular bulge.

Jonah placed one hand over the symbol, and it slid up easily. With another yank, the handle came free, bringing with it a section of the wall like a filing cabinet. It contained metal mesh and four fist-sized cubes.

"What're those?" Aleks asked. "Didn't we see those in the ocean?"

"They're fuel cells." Jonah glanced past him at the remaining cabinets. "Each of these contains fuel cells."

"Awesome!" Aleks shoved Jonah's shoulder. "Come on, act excited! We found fuel!"

"This *is* my excited face." Jonah pulled one of the cells free from the mesh. It was heavier than he expected. "Take as many as you can. We'll come back for the rest."

Aleks swung his bag off his shoulder and shoved in the three remaining cells. He unlatched the next drawer and piled them in, too. Jonah inspected the cell he held in his hand. The discovery tasted bittersweet. Finding fuel meant they could jump, but jump where?

Earth. They needed to jump to Earth. But to do that, they'd need control over the ship's navigation. That all came down to Row and Kiki. They needed time. They needed people out of their way.

Jonah squeezed the fuel cell. If his crew wanted to blame him for everything, he could take it. If he took on their ire as well as the airmen's, it wouldn't phase him. Row, Kiki, they would get the time they needed. Jonah would make sure of it.

CHAPTER 23

Three airmen. They were the last to remain by Rivera's side, right up to when he abandoned them, too. Klondike had joined Rivera's squad just after they got the orders sending them to the Alaska site, one of Klondike's first assignments after finishing Basic. He never told anyone how thrilled he was for the opportunity to see the spaceship the entire world had been fawning over or his excitement to work under Lieutenant Colonel Rivera. He'd heard he was a hardass but a man of honor.

That wasn't what he saw now.

He rubbed at a scuff on his boot with a towel, sitting on a crate while watching the two other airmen out of the corner of his eye. They all continued with similar menial tasks, all waiting for Rivera to return, none willing to wonder if he might not. None except Klondike.

"What are we doing?" he asked, tossing the towel aside.

"Waiting for the colonel," Airman Ruane said. She was a tall woman, currently partway through the unlacing and relacing of her boots.

"I mean, what are we doing about this ship?"

"The colonel wants us to wait." Airman Losey, a gruff-voiced bearded man, stood near the door, pretending he had guard duty.

"The colonel also said not to trust Jonah and his people." Klondike pushed off the crate. "He said they'd get us all killed, that we had to stay as a unit, but he's not here."

Airman Losey cast his eyes back over his shoulder. "What're you trying to say?"

"The colonel made it clear not everyone is surviving on this ship." Klondike shook his head. "I'm wondering if he left to save himself."

"You better watch your mouth!" Airman Ruane leapt from her bunk and shoved a finger against Klondike's chest. "I worked with that man for years. You ain't been here barely a month. You don't have the right to question his loyalty."

"We all have that right after what we've seen." He slapped her hand away. "If we need to take charge, why aren't we doing it? If those civilians out there are plotting something, why are we sitting around? All we have is what he tells us, and, man, he got his face cracked and he laughed like a madman. Did that look stable to you?"

"He laughed to show they didn't hurt him," Airman Losey said.

"You can't believe that." Klondike looked between Losey and Ruane. For a moment, he thought he was cracking their resolves. "We deserve answers without getting our asses beat. My neck still hurts from when he pinned me against that wall. I just wanna know that if I talk to him, you'll have my back."

Ruane checked with Losey, apparently coming to a silent agreement before they both stared back at him and nodded. It wasn't much, but it was better than nothing.

"Good." He sat back down on the crate and clasped his hands, one leg bouncing in anticipation. "We'll get him when he gets back."

Ruane returned to lacing her boot, while Losey turned his attention back to the door. Same places they were before. Same places they had been for a long time. As Klondike looked down at his boot, he spotted another scuff.

Nothing changed.

Jonah and Aleks returned with as many fuel cells as they could carry, which wasn't many due to their weight. Five in Aleks's bag and two for

Jonah, one in each hand; he couldn't help but envy Aleks's bag as his arms were sore before they got to the ship.

With the fuel cells as proof and the guarantee of no alien monsters, the rest of the roughnecks agreed to help retrieve more. Aleks emptied his bag onto the floor, and the guys emptied out several black plastic cases used to move audio equipment so they could carry as many cells as possible. Aleks ordered them to keep up as he led them back to the ship.

Saul never said a word to Jonah, barely casting him a glance as he unlatched an equipment case's handle and rolled it away. Saul had been on Jonah's crew since the beginning. While he hesitated to say he was close to any of them, Saul was about as close as he could be. Jonah went to Alaska for solitude, but Saul's bombastic spirit easily warmed up any rig. Losing his trust stung.

Whatever the look meant, Jonah stayed behind while the crew went to get the rest of the fuel cells. If he was such a sickness for them, better to stay away.

Remember, he told himself. *You just need to give Row time. Let them be angry at you if it keeps them unified and away from him.*

The thought of Row lingered for a moment. Was he still up in the bridge? Cora hadn't been there to greet them, presumably headed off to keep an eye on Rivera. Despite his impressive performance flying the ship, Jonah couldn't bring himself to trust the man entirely. Not yet. He chuckled and wondered if that was how Saul felt.

He'd turned to head back to the bridge when he saw President Mbeki sitting at what had become his standard table. Every day he held to the same routine. At nights he hobbled off to his quarters—the closest one to the loading dock and right next to Kiki's—and in the morning, he returned right to the same table to play solitaire, talk with people, or just take a quiet moment to collect his thoughts.

Jonah had kept his distance. Mbeki spoke quietly but powerfully, and Jonah liked him enough from a distance, but he had the air of someone who offered unsolicited advice, and Jonah had too many load-bearing problems.

Mbeki watched the roughnecks head off into the cold, each with their temperature disk clipped on their body, then turned his eyes on Jonah. He gave him a soft nod, then laid his cane on the table and shuffled his cards, the tremor in his hands looking worse. Jonah sighed and approached.

"Would you like to play?" Mbeki asked, cutting the deck. "I don't know too many two-player games, I must tell you."

"That's all right." Jonah leaned against the back of another chair. "I just wanted to see how you were."

"What an odd question at this time. How is anyone? There's hope, I think, but it's tempered."

Jonah knew an evasive answer when he heard one. He slid the chair back and sat down, facing the blazing white landscape outside. "I never got a chance to say, but I liked your speech. It was honest."

"Thank you." Mbeki set out his solitaire field. "It feels like a long time ago now. I must admit, when I tried to warn people about the dangers of uncontrolled progress, this isn't what I meant."

"I don't think any of us expected this, Mr. Mbe—I mean President, uh—"

"Cyril is just fine. No sense standing on ceremony this far out."

"I suppose." *What am I doing? If Cyril is sick, he can handle it himself. He's a grown man.* And yet, Jonah didn't move. "I'm glad to see Kiki's doing better."

"I believe your boy is partially to thank for tha—" He froze, one card in his hand. He stared off into space, acting like he was considering something, but the tightness in his neck told a different story. He was holding in a cough. A couple of seconds later, he placed the card down. "I apologize; something just crossed my mind. No matter."

"Right."

"He's a good kid, your Row is."

"They both are." Jonah leaned back, throwing his arm over the back of the chair. "They're really showing us old guys up, huh?"

"I always feared there'd be a day I couldn't keep up with Keneilwe." He riffled the edge of the deck of cards. "A child should remember their father as strong, so they can carry that example into the future."

"I don't know what Row thinks of me."

"Children have a fire in them. It gives them both their boundless energy and makes them hard to get hold of. Row has seen what I have seen. You're showing leadership, courage, and, yes, strength. He'll understand that in time, even if the fire inside blinds him to it now. You never showed weakness; he'll respect that."

"Yeah." He looked at Cyril. "Just like you."

Cyril met his gaze. Another cough tried to work its way up through his throat, but his chest and stomach clenched, holding it in. A minuscule flexing. It passed as he placed his next card. King of diamonds.

They sat, two strong men, alone at a table.

Cora stared Christopher down as he lounged in the pilot's chair. He'd grown too comfortable in his seat for her liking, with one leg swung over the instrument panel and through the hologram.

"Even if I did fly off, where would I go?" he asked.

"You misunderstand. I am not here to watch you." Cora dropped her stare and put on her most pleasant affectation. She had grown used to pulling it out whenever the board of directors waddled through her office. "I am simply enjoying the view from the bridge and keeping an eye on the kids."

"Please don't call us kids." Row didn't look up from the laptop Frankie had brought him. Kiki sent her a scolding glance.

Exactly what a kid would do, Cora thought.

"Any idea if this ship has more weaponry?" Christopher shouted over her head.

"That's not what we're looking for," Kiki said.

"We are trying to get back to Earth." Cora slid her body between Christopher and the kids. "I think we can all agree that is the best course of action."

"And how're we gonna do that? A 'can-do attitude'?" He slid his leg off the instrument panel and dropped out of the chair, his boots striking with a solid thump. "It's no coincidence that voice started talking to us after we got our first hands-on control of the ship. Then we were attacked. The further we push into the ship, the more trouble we call on ourselves." He leaned around her to talk to Row. "You said it yourself; the ship was listening to us. That's how it spoke English."

Row scratched his head. "I did say that."

A smug grin crossed Christopher's face, and he turned back to Cora. "We have an enemy out there, one we cannot comprehend. Weapons should be higher on the priority list."

"We can get back to Earth." Cora stood her ground, though for a moment, it sounded like she was trying to convince herself as much as him.

"You're deluding yourself. Survival is all that matters. We only use the ship as much as we need to. Jonah's idealist nonsense is not going to save anyone. Not Booker, not Kiki's sick father, no one."

"Shut up!" Cora said through her teeth, but it was too late.

"What did you say about Dad?" Kiki asked.

"Oh, come on." Christopher rolled his eyes. "Everyone knows President Mbeki has been looking worse. I've barely seen him, and it's still obvious."

"He's just . . ." Kiki sighed. "He's just a little shaken. He's getting stronger. I scared him when I got pulled out of the ocean."

Christopher sank back, a hint of softness coming through on his face. "Yeah. Sure." He shifted uncomfortably. "I gotta piss."

He left quickly, leaving Cora to gaze after him in shock. Even he had an ounce of humanity. The damage had been done, though. Kiki stared at the floor, hands clutched together at her chest.

"Hey, Row," she said softly. "I think I should go see my dad."

"Of course." Row tapped the top of the computer screen and forced a smile. "I'll keep working on this and when I need your language expertise, I'll . . . I'll see how you're doing." He shut his laptop and rose.

"I can take her." Cora stepped forward. "I should check to see if Jonah's back anyway. Not that I am interested in seeing your father, I just . . . it is the responsible thing to do."

Smooth, Cora.

"Okay." Row creaked the laptop back open. "You can go."

Kiki touched Row's hand. Cora noticed him return the squeeze, but Kiki was already zoned out. Cora grabbed the handles of the dolly and wheeled her from the bridge. The whole way to the loading dock, neither of them spoke a word.

The halls blurred together as Christopher walked in circles. He had said he needed to pee, but that was a lie. He needed to get out of that stuffy bridge with all the people in it before he lost his mind. Kiki's face when thinking about her father seared itself into his brain, and, if he wasn't careful, his thoughts would drift back to his own father. He could not let that happen. He needed to be strong. But for whom?

"Sir!" A voice cut the static in his brain.

He found himself outside his bunk room. His instincts must have taken him back there. The three airmen who had remained after Jonah's show of power stared at him, arms crossed and brows furrowed. "What is it?"

"What are you doing?" Airman Klondike asked.

"Going for a walk."

Klondike's expression turned angry. "I meant, what are you doing helping Wall and his people? You said they weren't to be trusted and now you're, what, being their chauffeur?"

"I am no one's chauffeur!" Rivera stormed into the room. Klondike had an inch of height on him, but Christopher held himself like he was nine feet tall. "I made a deal, that is all. Honor is what sets us apart from animals."

Klondike swallowed hard. "You turned your back on us."

"Since when?" He shoved a finger into Klondike's chest. "I got you food. I kept you safe. I took a beating for you. When did I ever turn my back?"

Klondike's jaw shook, but he took a breath and steadied himself. Christopher cast his gaze across the other airmen to gauge similar reactions. They were the ones he needed to be strong for, before they sensed weakness and gave in to fear.

"All he had to do was apologize to you." Klondike's voice trembled slightly, "and you completely flipped."

Christopher let out a pleased sigh. "Honestly, I thought he would put up more of a fight. But I gave my word, and I felt bad for him showing his belly so fast."

"Of course." Klondike bobbed his head.

When Jonah had said he was sorry, Christopher was stunned. He had been sure Jonah would come at him again and show his true colors. He had obviously antagonized him, and no one would apologize for something that was not their fault; few enough people apologized for the things that were. A man willing to sacrifice his pride was dangerous.

But the airmen did not need to know all that. They just needed to know that Jonah was a coward.

"Besides." Christopher spun to the door and shrugged. "Now we have a person in the inner circle. You heard that announcement, right?"

The airmen grumbled an affirmative.

"Home. A paradise. That is a trap if I ever heard one. Jonah, the idealist, is bound to get stuck in the honeypot, and we will be there to take hold of cold, hard reality." He glanced over his shoulder, eyes locked with Klondike. "Are there any other problems, soldier?"

"No, sir." Klondike spoke with a spike of poison Christopher couldn't ignore.

He rubbed the stubble on his chin and pulled back his fingers with flecks of dried blood. "Airman Klondike. Hand me one of those wet wipes."

Klondike tossed him a small package they had taken from the luncheon as Christopher walked out. He tore the sleeve open and worked at the blood stuck around his eye. His squad's loyalty was slipping through his fingers while he risked choking on the deadliest poison of them all: hope.

CHAPTER 24

The roughnecks carried the fuel cells toward the engine room. They had little idea of how to refuel the ship, but Jonah remembered seeing the cells drop from above, giving them a suggestion of where they could go.

They scoured the surrounding levels, but it wasn't until Terrence found one of the turning rooms that flipped them sideways that they caught a break. It let them into an industrial room of exposed piping, a stark change from the clean aesthetics of the rest of the ship. A massive machine of blinking lights and hologram readouts covered most of the wall facing the top of the engine room. Along its length were rows of removable shelves not unlike those on the smaller fighter, only with two handles and a box shape rather than a narrow drawer.

Jonah grabbed one with both hands and yanked it clear of the wall. It floated easily in his grasp, despite the nine cells inside. They lacked the signature green glow the other cells had. It was more like the gray ones he had seen under the ocean. The ones the serpents ignored.

"Guess they must be depleted." He placed the casing on the ground and took a cell out of the bunch. Once he touched it, the weight returned. "Seems likely enough this is how we fix the engine."

"And start jumping again, right?" Saul asked.

"The process is automated." He made eye contact with each member of his crew. "So, yeah. Is that a problem?"

"It is if we're gonna keep jumping farther from Earth." Saul motioned to the machine. "This thing's gonna burn all our fuel before we have a chance to get back."

"We were attacked on this planet by an automated drone. It's not safe here."

"Who says the next one will be any safer?"

"I do." Jonah thrust the dead fuel cell into Saul's chest. "We keep jumping. Let's fill it up."

He pushed through his crew, off to get the fuel cells they'd left a couple of levels below.

"We got it, Jonah," Saul said, rolling the cell over in his hand. "We don't need you looking over us like we're new hires."

Jonah stopped himself with one hand on the exit. He glanced back, and everyone but Saul turned their eyes away. "Good. Then do it." He left.

He didn't have the luxury of being offended by his crew's actions. A modicum of order had been established over the ship, and after running from the airmen to his crew to a trip out onto the alien planet, he finally had a moment to go check in on Row.

He took an elevator from the engine room to a couple of hallways from the bridge. Kiki kept mentioning there should be a command that took them directly outside it, but Jonah didn't have the same "press any button" courage she did. He was partway through the trip when the familiar hum of the engine spooling up greeted him.

At least they still listen to me, he thought as the doors opened and he headed for the bridge.

At first, he couldn't see anyone. It wasn't until he circled the entire room and came up on the left side that he noticed Row, alone, sitting cross-legged on the floor and typing slowly with one hand on a laptop. He didn't look up as Jonah approached.

"Where's Kiki?" Jonah asked.

"Hmm?" Row barely registered Jonah's presence before returning to his work. "She's seeing her dad. I guess he's not feeling well."

"I heard. Suppose it was only a matter of time before she did as well."
He leaned on the wall Row sat against. He'd meant to only go in and
check on him, but he couldn't rightfully leave him sitting in the bridge
alone. "We found some fuel in that ship we shot down."

Row paused as if he'd missed the engine's hum. His face lit up.
"That's awesome! We can jump to the next planet, then. Maybe we'll
get another message from the ship if we're getting closer to this 'home'
it was talking about."

"Unfortunately, it was just a drone." Jonah rubbed the tiredness
from his eyes. "There's still no sign of life."

Row had already returned to his computer. The laptop screen was
a mess of black windows with white text. It looked like the DOS system Jonah had to use to manage his crew hours before it was updated.
Row's phone sat at his side, plugged into the laptop's USB port. The
power cord ran for a few feet before the plug had been torn off and the
remaining wires taped to the wall.

"So, what is . . ."—Jonah waved his hands vaguely in the computer's
direction—"all this?"

"I'm trying to automate the process Kiki and I use to translate the
alien language into one program. I already have the built-in translation
software from my phone, but I need it to talk with the cryptography
app I downloaded back on Earth. The more we understand the alien
language, the more we can control the ship and maybe get it off whatever auto-jumping protocol it's currently on."

Jonah blinked. He'd understood most of that, surprisingly. "Why
did you download a cryptography app?"

Row gave him a deathly serious stare. "Because I'm a nerd, dad." A
smile broke through.

"Ah, of course." Jonah laughed and pushed off the wall, motioning
at the power cord. "And how's that working?"

"I don't actually know." Row considered the tape holding the wires
to the wall. "The power transfer in the ship seems to use the walls

themselves rather than any wires within them. I thought it might work, and it did. Everything always does. This ship is made to be used by us."

"Christopher did say the flight controls felt familiar."

"But it's not familiar." Row set the laptop aside and stood. "It's the future! Every piece of technology on this ship is so far ahead of anything we could imagine on Earth, but it's built for us! What if this is where humanity was always meant to go?"

"Space?" Jonah crossed his arms.

"Well, yes. And this technological progression." He approached the window, looking out upon the wild landscape, floating fortresses dotting above the horizon. "We can understand how to use this stuff because someday, we'll make it. We were always meant to be here."

Jonah stood at his son's side, at the threshold to another infinite landscape, but this one was broken. Pieces of it sailed into the sky and crashed down again if their systems failed.

Trees rustled at the base of the nearby mountain, and a flock of blue-gray birds took flight. Row smiled, but Jonah waited for something strange to happen. It never did. They were just birds like they'd find on Earth, flying in slow circles above a clearing half a mile away.

"Row, I . . ." Jonah started. Cyril's words drifted in his mind. Children need to see strength. Be strong. "I'm proud of you."

Row's head twitched slightly in his direction.

"I've always been proud of you. You're so . . . smart and clever." A smile drifted across his lips. "When you were young, we had these child-safe locks on the pantry. But without fail, you figured every single one out, and we'd constantly find you sitting on the kitchen floor eating graham crackers. To this day, I have no idea how you even reached some of them. Your mom always said, 'He can't be stopped. We can't stop him.' I ended up drilling into the jamb and installing a padlock. Still, I swore someday I'd find you sitting on the ground, eating crackers, the padlock mysteriously open."

Row looked at his dad, jaw offset and trembling, a hint of a grin hiding in his eyes.

"But all you've done here." Jonah scanned the bridge. "I shouldn't be surprised anymore."

"There's a part of me that likes it here," Row said. "Maybe that sucks to say, but for the first time, I know what I'm doing. And I'm doing it. And I'm good at it. On Earth . . ." His gaze fell to his feet. "Did Mom tell you I almost got held back?"

"What? How?" The last thing Jonah had heard about Row's schooling was he planned on applying to MIT.

"I wasn't doing my homework. I thought it was boring." He stuck his hands in his pockets. "No, it *was* boring. Why do I have to waste my time going over things I already know? I aced all the tests, and my teachers knew that, but this one class . . ." He stifled a growl. "Mom said she understood, but I had to do the homework as a show of responsibility. And she let me watch videos while I did because I could do it with an eye closed."

"Yeah." Jonah bobbed his head. "It's best to listen to your mom."

Through the window on the bridge, Jonah saw the birds break from their pattern and take off, disappearing against the overcast sky. Wind whipped through the trees below, thick limbs waving. Jonah took a deep breath as if he could smell the old pine forests and wet dirt. Instead, all he smelled was musty metal and human bodies.

"Hey, Dad," Row said. "Do you think you and Mom might get back together?"

"That's a complex situation, Row."

"We're on an alien planet, jumping through space using the power of black holes." He shrugged. "We may want to reconsider what a 'complex situation' is."

Jonah laughed. He hadn't thought much of his relationship with Lorri. Even if he could somehow convince himself to get back into society, would she want him back? And what about Cora? There were feelings there . . . at least, he thought there were. But he and Lorri had history and kids. They were only separated, and if it gave Row the hope he needed . . .

"Maybe," he said. "How about when we get back home, I promise to take you and your mom to dinner? Hell, we could even go on a trip. Somewhere Ethan would've liked. Does that work for you?"

"Yeah!" Row pumped his fist, his voice cracking a bit. "For Ethan."

They shared a smile, something they hadn't done in years. Row's optimism reminded Jonah of his own when his own demons weren't yet able to push themselves to the forefront of his mind. There were still moments like that for him, moments where he could let himself breathe, though they were few and far between these days. At least now he could spend some of them with Row.

As he stood beside his son at the bridge, watching the trees sway in the wind, Jonah thought he heard something move near the door, but when he glanced back, nothing was there.

Cora hurried away from the bridge, practically running before she realized how foolish that made her look. She did not have to sprint off into the night like some illicit lover. She slowed her pace but couldn't slow her swirling mind.

He could get back together with her, she thought. *Of course, he would. He has a kid.*

She stopped at an intersection and collected herself, visualizing her breathing as she had learned in meditation, in through the nose and out through the mouth. Sure, she made out with Jonah. Sure, she would have gone further, not in the hallway, of course, but she would have. But she would not be some trashy "other woman," like a stock character in a steamy soap opera.

Nothing has changed, she told herself. Clearly, there was no romance with Jonah. Physical attraction, yes, but not romance. She would need to find a moment to talk to him about how—or if—they should continue with . . . whatever they had.

She sighed, adjusted her skirt, and continued on her way. *Can't wait.*

***

Kiki scowled at her father while he played his fourth game of solitaire since she'd arrived. Her gaze flicked from his shaking hands to the sweat on his brow and the paleness around his lips. How could she have brushed these signs off so casually before? She waffled back and forth between being angry at him for acting so cool and furious at herself for not being there.

"I'm fine, my girl." Dad placed a seven and frowned. He huffed, scooped up his cards, and built the tableau again.

"No, you're not. You're more than just tired."

"I will not hear any more of this, Keneilwe." He held up his hand to stop her. "I apologize that my desire to be alone is being misconstrued as some mystery illness."

"Everyone!" Frankie shouted, cupping his mouth with his hands. "Dinner's up! It's a little . . . sparse today. Sorry!"

The travelers meandered into their positions for food, a haphazard line, one of the airmen running off to let their friends know. Colonel Rivera was already there, and Cora came in not long after the call went out. Last were Row and Jonah, wandering down from the bridge. Kiki felt like she should've been up there helping Row, but at the same time, she knew she needed to stay with her father. She had never wanted to split in half and live in two places more than at that moment.

"Will you be having dinner with Row again?" Dad asked, pushing away from the table. He held himself stiffly, throat clenched as he stifled another cough.

"Stop it!" Kiki screamed. Everyone in the room turned. "Stop acting like this!"

Dad gave a tight smile to the room, then turned back to Kiki. "Don't cause a scene. I'll get us some food." He started to move, putting nearly his full weight onto his cane.

"Don't walk away from me! It's not fair!" She struggled against the dolly, but of course, it wouldn't turn. "You're not fooling anyone. Everyone knows you're sick."

Dad froze. "I thought—"

"Stop it, please." Kiki clenched her fist until her fingers hurt. Tears flowed down her cheeks no matter how much she tried to keep them in. "Stop being a president for one second. You were the same after Mom died. Stop acting like nothing's wrong."

He bowed his head. The ship hummed on, and no one made a move. Finally, he braced his hand on his cane and settled back into his seat. His chest deflated, and his shoulders fell. He coughed into the back of his hand and let out a long sigh.

"Perhaps," he said, laying a palm against his chest, "I am feeling the effects of this trip. Perhaps I should lie down."

Kiki clutched her hands against her face. The tears wouldn't stop. She squeezed her eyes shut, and the drops flowed into her knuckles and down her arms. A hand fell gently onto her knee, and she looked to see her father smiling at her.

"I still miss your mother," he said, his voice raw. "In the quiet moments, I think of her."

"I know." She put her hand on top of his.

The ramp creaked to life, slowly cutting off the view of the frigid landscape surrounding the ship until it became a seamless wall once more. The travelers waited for the next jump, for the next planet. Kiki and Cyril were left together, neither sure of what would come next.

CHAPTER 25

Cora caught Jonah as they finished sorting their remaining rations of week-old luncheon scraps—pretty much anything that had not grown mold yet. Row and Kiki had taken her father to his room since he had finally admitted to being ill, and Jonah kept himself busy counting the meals they had left; she could tell he was simply using it as a distraction because he kept sorting the food into neat, numbered stacks before starting over, again and again.

"I thought Frankie already did that." Cora crept up behind him.

"He did." Jonah finished his count and groaned. "Three more days."

"Hopefully, the next planet will have some food." She sidled up next to him, looking past him as if she wasn't talking to him. "Can we have a chat?"

"About what?"

Her gaze flicked toward the roughnecks and airmen posted up on opposite sides of the loading dock. "Maybe in private."

Jonah cocked an eyebrow but didn't protest. They headed off to a far end of the living quarters, one of the many corridors of near-identical rooms they slept in, and settled on either side of a doorway.

"How are you?" Cora asked.

"Is that what you wanted to talk about in secret?" Jonah rolled his eyes.

"I was being polite." She picked at her nails. "I heard you with Row."

"What part of it?"

"The part about your wife."

A flash of realization entered his eyes. "Is this about us—"

"Taking a tumble on the engine room floor? Yup. I do not want this"—she swung a finger back and forth between herself and him—"to be a thing if it is not a *thing*. Does that make sense?"

"Kind of." Jonah tapped the back of his head against the door jamb. "Do you want it to be a thing?"

"Do you want to get back together with your wife?"

Jonah turned into the room. "I don't know how I would. We were different people when we got married. Or I was a different person. I left because I knew that was true. If I stayed, it wouldn't be fair to her or me. I . . ."

"What?" She took a final glance to make sure no one was coming, then joined him in the room. "Spit it out."

"I'm making excuses." He sat on the bed, elbows to his knees. "Or I was, earlier. I told Row we'd have dinner. I need him to have hope for Earth, but I don't have a lot of hope."

Cora sat next to him. "You lied to him?"

"I claimed something I wasn't sure about. How am I supposed to know the future?" He rubbed his forehead. "I guess that's a lie."

Cora leaned back on her hands. She had hoped for a straightforward answer, but with Jonah, nothing ever seemed to be straightforward. His mind was more labyrinthian than it initially appeared. He had doubts, but Cora knew she would get back to Earth. If everyone worked the way they should, it was inevitable. Or they would be dead, and then she would truly have no concerns.

Earth was the future. She always thought ten steps ahead, and it turned her brain into mush. She needed a moment of the present.

"Okay." She rose to her feet and sauntered toward the door. "Let us make this very simple. I like simple things."

She felt Jonah's eyes follow her steps and, as she reached the door and spun around, caught his gaze flicking up from her legs to her face.

He kept his eyes locked with hers, the former a strong, steely blue. She placed her hands behind her back and leaned against the door.

"We are here, a hundred million miles from Earth, and things might actually be working out for us." She tilted her head, letting her loose hair roll over one of her eyes and peering at him through the locks. "Would you like to find a quiet place and have sex?"

Jonah opened his mouth, shut it, then opened it again, only to shut it for the last time. Cora smiled. Men always acted so funny once the innuendos were left behind.

He took a moment to consider, then pressed his hands to his knees and stood. He closed in on her. Cora pressed out her chest, aware her shirt was unbuttoned lower than she normally kept it. Her skin turned hot. She had never known how much she needed him until he stood right in front of her. Her lips parted, anticipating the warmth of his mouth on hers.

But when he reached out, his arm did not draw her closer or even wrap around her waist. It went beyond her, just to her left, and her stomach filled with gravel. Had she misconstrued the situation?

"I know how to lock the doors," he said.

A smile filled her from head to toe. "You are a fun one."

She threw her arms around his neck, and the door slid shut.

Row stood in the corner of Cyril's room, stuck between a desire to give Kiki and her father some space and Kiki's insistence that he stay. Cyril had broken into another coughing fit, which rattled down the ship's corridors. Kiki sat at his side, taking his attention when she could with stories from home. They reminisced about trips they'd taken when Kiki was a child, or she regaled him with schoolyard gossip—who was dating who and what all her friends had hoped to do before summer ended. It was light enough conversation, and Row found he liked hearing what Kiki's life was like back home.

Cyril's next coughing fit nearly threw him off the bed. Kiki touched the back of her hand to his forehead.

"Oh, my God," she said. "How long have you been this hot?"

"Every planet brought with it a new pain and shake." He patted the saliva off his chin. "I didn't have long before you'd find out one way or another."

Row winced, watching Cyril try his best to keep Kiki's spirits up. If he was sick, he needed medicine. *Sergeant Booker had antibiotics.* He pushed off the wall. *Maybe the soldiers know where to find more medicine.*

"I'll be right back." Row headed out the door. "One minute."

"Where are you going?" Kiki shouted after him.

"One minute!" He took off down the hall at full speed. "I'm getting help!"

Cyril's room wasn't far from the loading dock, and Row tore through to find tables the airmen had posted. Booker had moved from lying flat on her back to sitting with the crew, though she still needed another airman to keep upright, the two sitting in chairs pressed together.

"What's wrong, kid?" The soldier—Hardy, by the name on the patch on her jacket—asked, folding up her hand of cards.

"President Mbeki isn't looking great." Row took a second to catch his breath. "You got those pills, right? For Sergeant Booker's leg? Do you have any more?"

"Those were antibiotics." Booker's voice sounded rough as sandpaper. "I don't think they're gonna help him. Your dad's the one who sent them along. He would know if there was any other medicine."

"Cool, thanks." He took off before any of the airmen could get another word out.

He sprinted up and down the halls where he thought his dad would be, only slowing when his lungs burned. He had to find help for Cyril. If he could do that, he could make Kiki happy. He couldn't stand uselessly in the corner anymore.

Dad wasn't in his room or any of the surrounding halls. The only place he could possibly be that didn't require Row running randomly through the ship was the bridge. Row jumped into the nearest elevator and rushed to the bridge. It was empty.

Row braced himself against the front console, drawing in dry breaths that hurt as they worked down his throat. *Maybe I should take up jogging,* he thought. *A quick break, then I'll find Dad.*

The planet was quiet, the tree branches swaying gently and a speckling of birds flitting among them, just like earlier when he and his dad had talked before dinner. A sense of calm overtook him, much as it had after he'd finally broken through Dad's shell.

It started as a slight ripple, as if someone had dropped a pebble into a lake, except in the air. Then, snapping out like a pop-up book, a massive ship filled the sky. Row stumbled back. It had the same silver metallic hull as their ship but was a darker tint made of hard angles and long like an insect's thorax. Several dozen tall, rectangular columns, each bigger than the entire ship Row stood on, stuck out from its bottom, shifting so slowly it looked at first like the ship was breathing. He couldn't even see the back; the ship's length faded into hazy clouds as it stretched into the horizon, casting a shadow across the land below, turning day to night and darkening the bridge to the point the lights came on.

Row's legs shook, threatening to drop him. His mind reeled at the size of the thing like some futuristic nightmare town had lifted from its roots and taken flight. Their ship might as well have been a ladybug. All the fear from its scale and cruel contours paled in comparison to a singular thought drilling through Row's head.

It exists. Another ship.

Row's ears popped, and the dreadnought was gone. So was the ice planet. Instead, the ship sat on an overgrown landing pad nestled between two massive trees, at the base of a huge city, with architecture similar to the outpost on the mining moon. The shells of collapsed skyscrapers littered a jungle floor, overwhelmed by the pure green fury of the land.

Row barreled out of the bridge, all his earlier exhaustion replaced by unfiltered adrenaline.

What the hell did I just see? He hammered on the icon in the lift taking him back to the loading dock. *I need to tell someone. Kiki.*

The elevator doors had barely opened before he squeezed through. Everyone in the loading dock was already on their feet and approaching the ramp door to see what the next planet held in store for them. No one noticed Row as he crossed through. Back in the halls, he caught the door jamb for Cyril's room and spun in, bouncing off the opposite jamb and hardly keeping his feet.

"Where did you go!?" Kiki shouted. "You said you were getting help. We jumped again, and he . . ."

Cyril clutched at his chest, his eyes nearly bulging out of his head, and while Kiki had her hand on his shoulder, he didn't seem to register her presence. Sweat poured down his face, soaking his shirt collar.

"Wet this." Kiki tossed Row a small towel.

"I was trying to find some medicine," he explained as he entered the bathroom and slapped the sink icon on the wall, missing the first time but catching it with his pinky on the second. A basin and tap folded out of the wall, and he ran cold water over the towel. "The soldiers said my dad had some, but I couldn't find him, so I ran all over the ship. I got to the bridge, and this—"

Cyril erupted in a wet coughing fit. Row rushed over with the towel for Kiki, and she laid it across her father's forehead. The cooling sensation took hold, and Cyril sighed in relief.

"And then what?" Kiki asked Row.

"I saw a ship." Row visualized the strange stutter and pop before the monstrosity appeared.

"Like, another one of those little drone-like ones?"

"No, this was huge. But it wasn't just big." He crouched next to her and lowered his voice. "It jumped in. It didn't fly. It jumped. Like we do."

Kiki's eyes widened. "Do you think it had people on it?"

"Maybe? I don't know. We haven't seen any people on any of these planets. They all look abandoned. But it's interesting how it appeared now." He waved a hand around vaguely, referring to the voice they'd heard. "After we got that message."

Kiki clutched her hands. Row nodded, understanding she knew the implication of why a ship of that scale would suddenly jump in right above them. It could be looking for them.

"We should tell your dad." Kiki turned to Cyril. "Will you be okay? I'll be gone just a moment."

"I'm not going anywhere," Cyril said, forcing a smile.

Kiki returned one of her own, weak as it was, and motioned for Row to push her. They left Cyril to rest and returned to the loading dock.

The roughnecks, a couple of airmen, and Row and Kiki waited at the ramp door, giving it a wide berth in case the planet ended up being even more dangerous than the last. Row pushed Kiki toward the front, but there was no sign of Jonah. Rivera came in from behind, cutting through the pack and approaching the door seemingly without a care. Row still froze up at the sight of him. He might know where Jonah was, but Row wasn't going to ask him.

The ramp popped out of its shut position, forming an arch of light. A burst of hot and humid air rushed in, smelling of moisture-filled growth and rotting vegetation. It only lasted a moment before the ship's systems adjusted and brought the temperature back to a familiar, healthy medium.

The open door revealed the lush jungle Row had seen from the bridge. A couple of people, including Kiki, gasped in amazement. Trees the size of buildings stretched into the sky. The canopy was thin enough where they'd landed to let in plenty of sunlight, though darker as the layers grew thick farther away. Some grew straight through stone and metal structures, binding them tightly in their roots, while others lifted all that stood in their path skyward.

In the center, where the trees split into a wide clearing, stood a thin, spire-like mountain. It looked like a termite mound, only hundreds, if not thousands, of stories tall. Metal structures jutted out of its sides like a giant had thrown skyscraper darts.

"Finally, a place with some life to it." Dr. Young appeared next to Row. "I was worried everything would be cold, dead, or wet."

Kiki reached back and clutched Row's hand. A flock of green birds burst from the undergrowth and vanished amid the trees. Row smiled, allowing a moment of peace to wash over him.

It quickly faded as Jonah rushed into the loading dock with Cora a short distance behind him. He slowed as he took in the new world, stopping at the edge of the ramp. Row tilted Kiki back and rushed them up to Jonah's side.

"Row, Kiki." Jonah greeted them with a small wave. "Why aren't you in the bridge?"

"Mr. Wall," Kiki said. "My dad's not doing too well. I heard you know where some medicine is."

"Medicine? There's a medical kit in the lab with the scientists. I don't know if it'll help, but it's there."

"There's also something else." Row glanced at the others crowded around the opening. Saul and Rivera looked their way, but they didn't look intent on eavesdropping. All the same, Row leaned in, and Jonah did the same. "I saw a ship before we jumped. A big one. It had just jumped in before we disappeared."

Jonah cocked his head, his expression like stone. His eyes flicked over to the group. "Okay. Keep that close to your vest for now. We don't need people worrying about something else."

"Sure, yeah." That made sense to Row, though he did wonder for a second if everyone didn't deserve to know. They were all in it together, after all.

Jonah patted Row on the shoulder and turned back to the jungle. He took in a deep breath, then faced the crew. "We're going to have to go out there. We'll run out of food sooner rather than later. The ship seems to have us covered on water, but if we run out of something to eat, it's going to get bad. It's not a choice anymore. We need all the hands we can get."

A grumble ran through the crowd.

"Come on!" Jonah threw his arms apart. "If anyone has a better idea, I'd love to hear it, but until then, stop acting like we're not in trouble. I don't care what you think about me but do it for each other."

Rivera let out an exaggerated scoff and wandered to Jonah's side. A couple of the airmen from the stage, including Farah, snapped to attention and joined him, leaving the last one back with Monica. The airmen who'd initially stayed with Rivera were a bit slower but eventually also joined. At the same time, Saul and the roughnecks shared a look of silent agreement before heading over. All in all, a dozen volunteers, nearly the entire group, prepared to head into the jungle.

"I'll stay with Kiki and Cyril." Row squeezed the handles of her dolly. "Be careful, Dad."

Jonah nodded sternly and turned to Cora. "Keep an eye on things."

"You got it," she said.

"Hold up." Christopher snapped a two-way radio off one of his airmen's belts and tossed it to Row, then held up his own. "If this thing starts to move, you let us know, got it?"

"Got it." Row handed the radio to Kiki.

"Everyone grab a couple bags, and let's get moving." Jonah clapped, and the group scattered, picking up every backpack, warming bag, and emptied-out equipment case they could find. Darius handed temperature disks to everyone making the expedition, figuring if the ship's system kept them cool as well as warm, surely the disks would as well.

A minute later, they marched down the ramp, Jonah at the head, eyes scanning the tree line. Row's heart pounded. Even though he wasn't going, he dreaded what could be out there. This planet already appeared much more alive than the others.

"Wait up!" Dr. Young shouted, pulling a little tote bag over his shoulder and chasing after the group.

They paused and looked back in unison. Christopher cocked an eyebrow. "*You're* coming?"

"Of course I am." Dr. Young practically skipped as he went down the ramp. "Have you seen the biodiversity of this place? I wouldn't miss it for anything." He scanned the airmen and frowned. "Don't you have guns?"

The group groaned.

"You really are in your own little world in that lab, huh?" Christopher shook his head.

Row, Kiki, and Cora waited at the ramp until the team disappeared into the brush, then waited a minute more. Another minute and Kiki squeezed the radio in her fist. Another minute and Cora patted Row on the shoulder before walking off.

"Row," Kiki said. "We have to get that medicine for my dad."

"Right." He shook the dark thoughts from his mind. They'd be fine. They'd survived everything every other planet had thrown at them.

Yet, as he and Kiki headed to the lab to check on the medicine supply, the image of the massive ship came into his mind. His father had shrugged it off, but he couldn't. All he could do was count the minutes and hope they got back soon.

CHAPTER 26

The temperature disks kept the heat off the team's skin but did little for the humidity. They'd hardly marched for half an hour before Jonah's shirt collar was soaked. The path he forged toward the massive tower never seemed to get any closer. All the while, he couldn't shake the feeling of a dozen eyes watching from a dozen directions.

"What's even the plan here?" Terrence asked. He hadn't stopped talking since they'd left the ship. "You said all this stuff is old? Are we looking for millennia-old Twinkies still on a shelf somewhere?"

"You wanna talk louder so everything knows where we are?" Mud said.

"Don't you read survival articles? You're supposed to be loud so you don't accidentally frighten a bear."

"Those are bears, not alien whatchamacallits."

"Maybe you can both shut up," Rivera said, ducking under a human-sized leaf. "Or at least carry on with your nonsense a hundred feet that way."

Despite Rivera's annoyance, Jonah knew there was safety in numbers. They weren't alone in the jungle, after all. Hoots and cries from animals they couldn't place surrounded them, and while leaves rustled in the trees, they saw no sign of what created that movement. Occasionally Jonah spotted a flash of fur, scales, or feathers, but as long as those creatures kept their distance, let them watch.

"He has a point." Saul took wide steps to reach Jonah. "What are we hoping to find?"

"Do you really want to get into this now?" Jonah asked. They passed by a vine-covered fallen building where the vegetation lay low enough that they could still see their feet.

"I don't want to get into anything." Saul gazed through the broken windows. The inside had nearly been rotted hollow, leaving behind only the metal bracing in the walls. "I just want to make sure you're thinking of everyone."

"Of course I'm thinking of everyone. The entire point of getting home is to get *everyone* home."

"I've seen too many people have tunnel vision and lose perspective." Saul glanced back at the group. "Do you know Emily's pregnant?"

Jonah ran through all the names he knew of the ship's passengers. Emily could be a soldier—he'd mostly caught last names rather than full ones. "Who's Emily?"

"Frankie's girl."

"Oh." *How am I supposed to know that?*

"He found out just before this whole thing happened. He's kind of freaking out about it."

"Is he freaking out, or are you freaking out?" Jonah skirted a thick root sticking out of the building.

"Why would *I* freak out?" Saul crunched the root with his boot and held it down, making it easier for the people behind them to pass.

Jonah stopped with Saul as the group caught up. "Because that's what you do."

"People have families they need to get back to. That's all I'm thinking about."

People stepped over the root one by one as Jonah wiped the sweat from his brow and waited for everyone to pass.

"What does this have to do with finding food?" Jonah asked.

"It doesn't have anything to do with that." Saul let the root snap back up into position. "You're the one who thought I was trying to start something."

"Right. I was thinking we might find, I don't know, bananas. The animals here have to eat something, right?"

"Check that out." Frankie pointed about fifty feet up a nearby tree.

A building's façade hung off the branches, complete with windows and a door dangling by one hinge with a limb sticking through. Farther up was another section, this one with exposed ventilation wrapped in moss. The tree's bark had grown around the metal supports.

"Guess there wasn't a jungle here when they built it." Frankie craned his neck to see higher. "We had a tree back where I grew up that had grown around an old bench. Not quite as impressive as this, though."

A couple of other trees had their own pieces of construction subsumed into their bark and pulled into the sky. Clearly, the wilds here had been free to overtake what must have once been a great city. Jonah couldn't imagine what could've caused people to suddenly abandon someplace so completely.

As the group gawked at the sight, a light came on above the hanging door. A second later, a flickering blue and green hologram faded in, unreadable due to the alien language, but unmistakably a marquee. All around them lights flashed on, and hologram advertisements appeared from the brush and canopy, turning the jungle into a neon-colored, haphazard main street.

With each step toward the great tower, the ground grew harder. Jonah pushed aside a patch of grass with his foot, revealing concrete, or something like it, below. Some buildings had remained flat on the ground, with greenery punching through their walls and roof, while others had been broken apart, pieces stretched out amid the limbs and stalks.

Aleks approached a vacant storefront, shards of ancient glass still hanging onto the edges. As he peered in, a screen projected in front of his face, and he stumbled back.

"Be careful," Saul said, mouth open in amazement.

The projection showed a humanoid figure, their features completely blacked out, wearing a gray jacket and pants with red accents along the sleeves. Aleks batted at the hologram, his hand passing through without disruption. The projection flashed and the outfit appeared on Aleks's body.

"Oh, that's cool!" He twisted around to see his back.

The group gathered around him, eyes wide and mouths agape. He swiped at the projection and the outfit's color on the screen changed to a red jacket with black accents and black pants. He poked at the new design and his outfit changed to match.

"No way this is real." Terrence approached, stretching out his finger to poke the projection, and the red and black outfit appeared on him, too. He leaped back in surprise, and the suit he wore to the luncheon reappeared.

"It's a hologram," Jonah said.

"A really good one." Aleks reached for his zipper, and it moved without him touching it, revealing a white shirt beneath. He zipped up, then down, up, and down. "I could do this all day."

"I'm sure you could." Rivera jerked his head to the side. "But it's not food. Let's keep moving."

He took two steps, then froze. A dark green blob about the size of a soccer ball rolled out from between a building and a tree. It bounced and squished across the road like a tumbleweed and stopped right where Rivera was about to step.

"What is tha—" he started.

The blob exploded in a deafening bang, covering Rivera and the two airmen closest to him in green goo. Jonah's ears rang, reminiscent of a couple of times he'd heard a flash-bang go off in an active warzone.

"That's a strange response." Dr. Young uncovered his ears and crept up to Rivera. "Are you all right?"

"I'm not dead." Rivera wiped the goo from his eyes and tossed it to the ground. "I guess."

"Why would it explode? What possible sort of biological advantage does that give it?"

One of the soldiers slapped his arms and face. "It's moving! It's still moving!"

The goo oozed down their bodies and pooled at their feet, leaving the airmen spotless. Jonah noticed a speck had landed on his shoulder and it similarly limped down his arm, hot and almost ticklish as it reached his fingertips and leaped to the ground. The various globs reformed into the large green blob before rolling off into the jungle.

Dr. Young snapped his fingers. "Ah, it's probably a collection of small organisms that acts as a larger group. Explodes to disorient its predators."

"Glad we got that figured out." Rivera covered his ear with his hand, wincing occasionally. "Someone else take point."

Jonah resumed his position at the front. If his head felt like it had taken a sledgehammer, he could only imagine what Rivera, who'd stood right over the blob, dealt with. Aleks took one last look at his outfit before stepping out of the hologram and jogging to catch up with the group. Jonah checked back to make sure they didn't miss anyone and nearly laughed as everyone's gaze went from staring up in amazement to watching their feet for any more exploding blobs.

They walked another ten minutes before Dr. Young caught Jonah by the shoulder. "Just a moment, please."

"What's up?" Jonah stopped.

"If we're trying to find the food the animals eat, we should go this way." He pointed to their right, indicating a long path of low-lying grass. "Some group has walked that trail long enough to make a groove. It could be a food source."

"Whatever made this looks kinda big," Saul said, inspecting the ground.

"So are we, relatively speaking." Young stepped forth and considered the way, brimming with a self-confidence he never showed on the ship. "We need to eat what the large herbivores and omnivores eat. Might as well go where they go."

"You're the expert." Jonah followed him in the direction he indicated.

"I was torn between being a wildlife biologist and an astrobiologist." Dr. Young explained. "I wanted to learn philosophy, but there's no money in that. I had a blog for a while, but it never really . . . never mind."

At least someone's enjoying the trip, Jonah thought.

They followed the trail through the broken husk of what might've once been a mall with clearly defined interior rooms. At the far end, they had to circle a field of narrow freestanding walls. These were set apart from the rest of the city and had a rougher design. They made Jonah think of barricades, but why would those have been needed?

He thought back to the mass grave he'd discovered on the mining planet. Something like that didn't happen accidentally.

The trail next led them to a wall of hanging vines. Dr. Young pushed a handful of them aside like a beaded curtain, revealing a tunnel at least four car lanes wide, descending gently. Lights snapped on, first at the mouth, then dipped into the ground below. When Jonah looked up, he found the canopy here was so thick he couldn't tell where they were in relation to the tower anymore.

"You've got to be kidding me." Darius spun on his heel and paced with his hands on his hips.

Dr. Young reached past the vine curtain and picked something up, bringing it out into the clear daylight. It was a rough semi-circle, about the size of a soccer ball, one side beige, the other with a bright-orange rim that faded into green near the back.

"These are teeth marks." Dr. Young ran his finger over the orange part. It squished slightly beneath the pressure and released a juice. "And this must be a rind. It's a fruit of some kind."

He looked at the juice on his finger. Jonah narrowed his eyes. He wasn't going to eat it, was he? The thought had barely crossed his mind before Dr. Young stuck out his tongue to taste it.

"How is it?" Darius asked.

"Sweet. More like an apple than a melon." He smacked his lips. "I don't feel like I'm having an immediate reaction, and I don't feel sick, but that remains to be seen. Well, if I don't start vomiting, I think we found ourselves a food source." He gazed down the tunnel. "It's down there somewhere."

Rivera grabbed the vines with both hands and tore down a sizeable chunk, giving everyone a clearer view of the path ahead. Vegetation covered the walls and ceiling, forming a great green throat curving out of sight. Another apple-melon rind sat rotting on the ground a dozen feet ahead.

"You know what I like about this?" Rivera wiped the sap from the vines off his hands. "Clearer sightlines."

Jonah never imagined Rivera would be the optimist, but he wasn't wrong. Jonah already felt safer knowing some otherworldly panther wasn't stalking them from the tree line. The group gripped their bags tighter and started the descent.

Row peered through the bridge's front window, over the lush foliage to the termite-mound tower beyond. The radio dangled between two fingers, swinging casually within his grip. *Should I check in on them? Just to make sure they're okay?*

He put the radio down on one of the consoles and pulled up his laptop. No. He needed to focus on his own work and let his dad and the others do theirs. Kiki had stayed with Cyril, watching over him as he struggled and sweated through his shirt. After half an hour, Row couldn't watch anymore. He'd gone back to the bridge. A place where he wasn't useless.

The translation program mostly worked. Between the cryptography app looking for sentence logic and the translator running through languages, he always eventually got something outputted. The problem was that most of it was nonsense. The phrase he knew turned on the lights gave him nearly a hundred variations, including activate, glow, float, and levitate. The program was only guessing, the same as Row.

He slammed the laptop shut and clutched his head. A sharp pain pounded into the center of his brain. Part of him wanted to go back to pressing buttons at random, but he had just as likely a chance to cause the ship to jump prematurely as he did to change its target.

If only I could connect to the ship's systems and talk to it. Row straightened and spun to face the front window. *That's it!*

"You've listened to us talk, haven't you?" he shouted. "You know English better than we know your language."

He waited. No response.

"Um." He wracked his brain. "Computer, I have a question."

Still nothing.

He looked like a fool, trying to talk to the ship. Then a flash of realization hit him.

"Ship," he said. "I have a question."

"What is your question?" The voice was different from the one from before, deeper and a bit rougher.

"Yes!" Row jumped and threw his arms in the air. Of course, since they had only ever referred to it as such, it's the only word it would know itself by in English. "Ship! Turn off the autopilot!"

"Autopilot is already disabled."

"No! Gah!" He slapped the side of his head. "Turn off the auto-jump."

"Auto-return control requires captain's authorization."

Row stared up at the ceiling, his arms limp. So close, and yet so far. He puffed out a lungful of air and recovered. "Okay. Ship, what were the captain's last orders?"

"After the auto-return function was activated remotely, the captain overrode the orders. During the ensuing battle, I was damaged and ordered to jump without a target. This would obliterate me and all crew on board."

"But you weren't obliterated."

"Affirmative."

Row circled the bridge. If the ship expected to be destroyed with the jump, why was it still around? *It could have something to do with how Earth isn't on the map. It thought it was jumping nowhere but landed on Earth.* "Were you deactivated?"

"Almost definitely." The voice decayed into only bass for a moment before recovering.

"I must've reactivated you when we took manual control."

"Likely. I am not required after auto-return functionality is active."

Row leaned on the back of a chair. "What other logs do you have?"

"Access to travel logs requires captain's authorization."

He tapped his finger against his forehead, trying to force out a better question. "Who turned on the auto-return function if not the captain?"

"Home."

There's that word again. "What's home?"

"I do not understand the question."

Row threw his head back. "Fine. Why did home want your captain to return?"

The bridge hung silent. Row gripped the arms of the chair.

"Heaven awaits."

A cold shiver ran down his spine. That had to be a mistranslation. Why would an alien ship mention heaven? Only if it *wasn't* an alien ship, was it? *Humans* crashed it into Earth, and they never left. *Until now.*

Row darted across the bridge and threw open the laptop. Back to brute-forcing it. He refused to believe he couldn't bring the ship home. Surely not only heaven awaited them, or why would their ancestors have tried so hard to run?

The empty halls of the ship had a bizarre tranquility to them, one Cora delighted in absorbing while everyone else was off on their adventures. She decided to return to the engine room. Once she got over the terror of nearly being crushed in it, it had a novel design she wanted to take a closer look at. It reminded her of something from a science fiction novel she read as a child.

As Cora approached, she discovered Dr. Cooper leaning against the door, watching the rings spin slowly through the glass. Cora considered turning back. The entire point of her walk was for some quiet, but Dr. Cooper had such a solemn look on her face, with one of the temples of her glasses held in her teeth, that Cora could not imagine she would be a disruption.

"Hello, Dr. Cooper." She peered through the window with her. "Fancy finding you outside your lab."

"Well, Samuel's off traipsing around in the jungle, and there's not much for me to do anymore." She plucked her glasses from her mouth and put them back on. "Can you imagine how fast that thing spins before we jump?"

Cora's eye twitched. "I can, actually."

"It creates a black hole, you know." She tapped her knuckle against the glass. "A mass so dense it warps space and time. And it's done with such precision that it casts us across the universe to land on a dime."

"Sounds like something from a book."

"It sounds like something from a theoretical textbook. But there it is." A sad smile crossed Dr. Cooper's face. "These people are ancient, and yet they harnessed such incredible power."

Cora put her back against the wall. She had heard scientists gush about the ship ever since they first pulled it out of the ground, but they did not know half of its capabilities like Dr. Cooper did. Everyone else in the meetings, the oil officials and financiers, had only talked about policies and business opportunities. That was before Cora got shut out, and the international governments stepped in.

"I always wanted to go to space," Dr. Cooper said. "I wanted humanity to go to space, even to be able to live among the stars one day. I thought once we did, we could solve all those problems we filled our lives with. We'd find perspective, and they'd seem so small and manageable, left behind on a fragile pale blue dot."

Cora squinted. "I have heard that before."

"Pale blue dot? It's a photograph of Earth taken by the *Voyager 1* before leaving our solar system. Carl Sagan pushed for a decade to have that photo taken and he wrote about it in his book." She put a hand against the engine room door. "'Our posturings, our imagined self-importance, the delusion that we have some privileged position in the universe are challenged by this point of pale light.'"

"That does not sound reassuring."

"It's not. It's a warning. It's a call to cherish the one planet we have."

"Not to speak ill of Mr. Sagan," Cora said, "but I do not think he expected us to find a spaceship. We are on another planet—our fourth—and, hey, you are now farther out than any astronaut has ever gone."

Dr. Cooper didn't laugh or smile. Her eyes followed the slow swinging of the engine rings. "They created such astounding advancement that their technologies still work even though the people who built them are gone. But look at what we've found: mines, refineries, and military bases. Strip away all the anti-gravity and jump drives and it looks the same as Earth. They reached the stars, and nothing changed. And now they're gone. Completely."

The rings whipped around, creating a slow whooshing sound with each pass. Cora bowed her head. Dr. Cooper was right; there were no more people. If the humans of Earth were these people's descendants, why were they the only ones who remained? Why was Earth the only planet still inhabited?

"What if we don't go back?" Dr. Cooper asked.

Cora's head snapped up. "We will figure out how to control this ship, do not worry."

"I mean . . ." Dr. Cooper's gaze grew distant. "What if we decide not to go back?"

"Why . . . why would we do that? Do you not have a life you want to return to?"

"I have a dog I left with my roommate when I went to Alaska. I have a sister and my parents. But maybe I don't care about going back."

"Do you want to start homesteading or something?" Cora pushed off the wall, heat flushing her face. "Post up on one of these planets and start a new civilization or something?"

Dr. Cooper laughed until she sighed. "No. I always think about the future of humanity and other nonsense like that. This is about me. Maybe there's no reason to go back if this is where we all end up. Vanished, with nothing but memoryless ships left behind."

Cora shook her head. She could not believe what she was hearing. "I am getting back to Earth. I am not giving up."

"If you think this is giving up, that's fine." Dr. Cooper rested her head against the glass. "I'll just watch the engine turn. I've never seen a black hole get made before."

Cora opened her mouth to chew her out again, but a single tear rolled down Dr. Cooper's cheek, stopping her. *Whatever.* Cora turned on her heel. The halls seemed less peaceful now, more constraining, like a noose tightening around her neck.

I am getting back to Earth. She slammed a fist against the fist in frustration. *I am getting home.*

CHAPTER 27

Jonah and the team descended into the tunnel, their footsteps crunching undergrowth and echoing down the passage. The farther along they went, the bigger the passage became, until they arrived at a massive solid metal gate. Vines grew up both sides, collecting in the center where the gate stood ajar wide enough for them to walk through. Jonah and Christopher took the lead, pushing through the vines. The doors were at least a foot thick, and as they stepped through, Jonah's mouth gaped.

In front of him lay a city unlike any he'd seen before. Buildings rimmed all sides of the tunnel, twirling in gravity-defying levels. A tower rose from one side, only to land at a second base on the other side. Smaller tunnels branched off from the central line where one could look up and see another street directly above. And all through-out, the same trees outside grew, twisting and shifting as they moved through gravity zones.

"Look!" One of the airmen pointed up at a hole in what could've been the ceiling. Instead, daylight streamed in, revealing the jungle trees.

"We're in the tower," Aleks said. "Holy crap, we're vertical right now."

Jonah looked at his feet as if expecting to suddenly lose grip and plummet. He'd experienced the twisting gravity in the ship, but never on such a grand scale and with this degree of perspective. His stomach churned at imagining walking straight up a wall.

A high-pitched roar split the silence, and the group ran for cover. Jonah and a few others dove behind the closest half wall into a small space, Dr. Young practically sitting on his lap as they dropped.

"So, what do you think?" Jonah poked his head over the wall, hoping to catch a glance at what made such a sound. "Was that an herbivore or a carnivore?"

"Bones." Dr. Young looked down, his eyes wide.

"What?" Jonah finally registered where they'd landed.

About five skeletons shared the little cubbyhole in which they found themselves, two lying in half-fetal positions, the other three leaning against the opposite wall. The two airmen who'd gone in their direction, along with Aleks, Darius, and Mud, stared in shock, no one daring to make a sound. The skeletons' clothes had degraded to practically nothing, but they still clutched rifle-like devices to their chests.

Jonah crept over and pulled one of the devices out of a skeleton's hands. Its wrists disintegrated at the first sign of resistance, readily giving up the tool. Jonah knocked some moss and vines off the rifle's receiver. Thicker than any gun he'd seen before and heavier to boot. Rather than a hole at the end of the barrel, it came to a pinpoint piece of glass.

All in all, it didn't look to be in bad shape, though Jonah had long ago stopped being surprised by how well these people's technology held up. He braced the stock against his shoulder and laid his finger over what he imagined had to be the trigger.

Aleks crept forward. "You don't think that's a—"

Jonah aimed at a building down the road, one with a glowing purple sign, and squeezed the trigger. There was no recoil, or at least not enough to matter. A flash of red light left the barrel along with a sharp *ping,* and, at the same time, a black score appeared on the distant building as a chunk of it shattered.

"Laser gun!" Aleks and Mud shouted in unison.

The rest shushed them. Aleks picked up a gun of his own and

aimed at the same building, pulling the trigger three times and putting two more marks against the far wall before the third punched clean through.

"Settle down," Jonah said. "These things are clearly dangerous."

Another laser shot went off, taking a strip out of the building they'd used for target practice. Jonah spun to find Rivera across the street, laser rifle resting in the crook of his arm and a grin on his face.

"Looks like we both found something useful." He stepped out into the street, as did the rest of the team who hid with him, each carrying their own rifle.

They regrouped at the metal doors of the city's entrance. Another roar echoed, and they snapped their rifles up. Nothing moved. Jonah had to admit he felt marginally safer searching with a weapon. Rivera gave him a nod and crept forth, rifle pressed against his shoulder. The airmen matched his movements. The roughnecks tried their best to do the same, but their lack of military training showed.

Dr. Young took up the rear. He didn't carry a rifle.

"There's probably an extra one back there," Jonah said.

"Hmm? Oh, no." His head practically vibrated he shook it so fast. "I'd just as likely shoot you as I would anything else."

"Good call, then. Stay close."

Jonah kept rear watch as they moved through the city. Rivera set their pace, stopping if he heard a strange noise or thought he saw something. Whatever had roared in the depths of the tower had been quiet ever since.

"Take a left," Dr. Young said. "The grazing path is to the left."

Rivera nodded and followed his directions into one of the smaller tunnels. Jonah looked up at the city hanging above them, and a rush of vertigo hit. He blinked away the disorientation, then nearly walked into Dr. Young's back. Rivera had stopped the group, his hand in the air. Jonah leaned to the side, trying to see what had caused Rivera to halt them dead in their tracks.

A familiar green blob rolled over the tree root ahead of them. Rivera waited until the thing was long gone before lowering his hand and pointing forward.

"I think that's what we're looking for." Rivera gestured at a clearing between the buildings above them.

A small pond glimmered beneath a hole in the tower's exterior, ringed by a collection of smaller trees. Each one had at least a dozen of the beige soccer ball–sized apple-melons hanging off their branches or sitting near their roots. Jonah's heart leaped into his throat. They'd found food. He could hardly believe it.

The roughnecks broke formation, scrambling over roots and ruins to circle the path.

"Hey! Keep in step," Rivera ordered.

None of them listened. Jonah decided not to either. He vaulted a low wall, barely touching it with his free hand, thanks to the adrenaline pumping through his veins. He ran up the wall, the world turning around him, dodging back and forth between buildings until he reached the pond. His crew had already arrived at the sparkling shores, laying down their rifles and shoving melons into their bags.

"We need as many as you can get." Jonah swung his backpack off his shoulder. "We may not get a chance to come back."

"There's gotta be more of these trees outside, right?" Frankie asked, holding an apple-melon above his head.

"If you wanna go searching around the jungle, that's your problem." Terrence maneuvered a third fruit into his bag, forcing the zipper shut best he could.

Jonah's pitiful bag, a backpack he'd found tucked under one of the stage chairs, could only hold two apple-melons. Saul had had the foresight to bring a large sack meant to lug around lighting equipment and got seven shoved inside.

"Is it necessary to do it that fast?" Rivera asked with a touch of sarcasm, jumping down from a chunk of foundation at the edge of the pond.

"The quicker we get the food, the quicker we get out of here." Jonah hefted his bag up and grabbed his rifle. At least the apple-melons weren't too heavy; they still had a sizeable trek back.

The airmen and Dr. Young filled up their own bags, but none could quite manage what Saul had. Still, between them, they averaged three melons each, enough to keep the ship fed for a while.

"We may get sick of 'em, but at least it's something," Farah, the airman, said.

"A varied diet would do us better." Dr. Young stroked his chin. "I wonder if we can eat those blobs Colonel Rivera found."

The group laughed. Even Rivera cracked a smile. The outdoor light faded from the cracks in the outside walls as the sun moved behind the clouds, leaving only the city's lamps.

"Shit." Mud suddenly scrambled away from the pond, looking straight up. The group followed his gaze.

Above, in the opposite gravity zone, sat a massive ape-like beast, its powerful, bulky frame covered in brown and white fur. Red eyes perched atop a shortened muzzle. As it took them all in, a vicious, thick tail ending in a scorpion's stinger curled out from beneath the lamppost it sat on.

The group backed up, holding onto their bags and rifles. Rivera hadn't finished packing his fruit away. He crouched near the root of a tree, his rifle sitting just out of his grasp. The creature turned its crimson gaze on him, its hunched-over form unfolding into something over nine feet tall. It grabbed the top of a tree on their side of the tunnel and pulled itself up, turning in the air before placing itself gently above Rivera, settling in the branches. Jonah could almost laugh at how gracefully the hulking beast moved. Almost.

Rivera's gaze darted to his rifle. He crept his hand closer, keeping one eye on the creature.

"Christopher," Dr. Young whispered. "Don't. It might just be curious."

The stinger curved over the beast's head, extending almost twice the length of its body. Rivera stopped with two fingers on his rifle's stock. The creature angled its neck down, sniffing at him. Jonah's fingers twitched at the edge of his trigger guard, praying the creature left Rivera and the rest of them alone.

The beast snorted, and Rivera lunged for his gun. It reared back and let out the high-pitched roar they'd heard earlier. Two pings sounded through the glade, and two blackened holes punctured the creature's chest. Its roar turned to a whine, and it tumbled out of the tree, landing in the pond and drenching Rivera.

A chorus of roars filled the city. Another ape creature pulled itself onto a building along the glade's edge. A second swung onto a pile of moss above. The city came to life with howls and shifting shadows, more colossal monsters moving.

"Run!" Jonah shouted.

They took off at a dead sprint. The tall, skinny airman with short blond hair moved too slowly, and a creature slammed him to the ground with a sickening crack. Rivera whipped around and shot rapidly, hitting the creature in the arm and neck, but foamy blood already bubbled out of the poor airman's mouth. A second creature grabbed the injured airman by the leg and dragged him away, swiping at Rivera at the same time. He dodged and ran to catch up with the group.

The city blurred around them, with Jonah at the head, focusing on the way out. They needed to get back to the gate; surely, the creatures couldn't squeeze past. He darted around and through buildings, barely slowing down to shoot at any creature that seemed like it was gaining on them. Afraid he might trip and it would all be over, Jonah only glanced back a couple of times to make sure he hadn't lost anyone. Every time, he only saw a light show of laser fire.

"Wrong side," Dr. Young said through heavy breaths. Without a gun and only a single melon in his tote, he only focused on running. "We're on . . . wrong side . . . of tower."

Jonah shot a creature off a nearby roof and checked the way ahead.

Dr. Young was right. They'd circled the tunnel when they'd gone for the fruit. But with creatures flashing by on their left and right, there wasn't much chance to turn.

Instead, Jonah looked up. A tree had grown through a building ahead of them, perching itself at the end of a natural ramp. A creature landed on its peak, sending a shower of leaves upward.

"Keep close!" Jonah shouted, firing a flurry of shots at the creature's head.

It covered its face to protect itself, but the laser blasts shot clean through its arm. It went limp and rose off its feet, crashing through the roof of a store above them. Jonah gritted his teeth and barreled forward, digging his toes against the collapsed wall and heading up. He pressed a boot against the tree branch and threw himself upward.

His head pulled down, chest lifted. Blood rushed to his head, and stars filled his vision. The world spun as his body turned, then fell. His feet landed on the edge of the building that had once been above him, and he tumbled off into a mass of moss atop a lower roof. A thankfully soft landing spot.

He let out a breath and looked up just as Dr. Young's scared face fell toward him. Jonah rolled away in time for the scientist to land next to him.

"That was exciting." Dr. Young spit out a piece of moss.

"Move!" Jonah pulled him out of the way as Aleks descended.

One by one, the group tumbled out of the city above. Terrence, face red as he huffed and puffed, took his turn at the jump. He'd gotten himself to the pivot point when, in a white flash, a creature shot by, and he was gone.

Jonah's heart fell to his feet, and only the threat of the creatures kept him from scrambling vainly after Terrance. *Oh, God.*

Rivera tumbled down after. The creatures encroached on the group's mossy perch, their steps eerily silent.

An exploding blob rolled through, sucking up flecks of greenery as it went. Rivera snatched it up and hurled it skyward. It crossed the gravity line and struck a creature across the snout. A pause, then a bang as it popped and covered the beast in goo and drove it away, at least enough for the rest of the jumpers to carry on.

"Keep running!" Rivera shouted, pulling Darius to his feet and shoving him onward.

Saul, who'd taken his jump before Terrence, locked eyes with Jonah. There was nothing for them to say, not at that moment. They ran on as the last of the airmen reached them.

They moved along the rooftops, jumping across the tight gaps between the buildings as they searched for a way down. At the end of the next block, they came to a stairwell exposed by a hole in the roof. Rivera hopped down first and waved for everyone to follow. Jonah glanced over his shoulder. The ape creatures poured out of cracks and crevices, swinging through the inverting gravity with natural grace. He jumped into the hole and landed on a staircase, the rest of the group already thundering down ahead of him.

Halfway down, the wall protecting them from the street stopped, leaving broken bracings where it once stood. Farah stepped too close to the edge, and the stairs crumbled. Saul reached out, but she slipped from his grasp, landing on the hard street two stories below, her rifle bouncing across the stone.

Jonah shoved his head out the window. She was still moving, though her apple-melons had broken, and juice and pulp seeped through the holes in her bag. A creature landed inches away with a resounding thump, snarling over her. Jonah fired, trying to give her cover while she scrambled for her rifle. He killed the first creature, only for a second to leap forward, and then a third, surrounding the airman.

Laser fire rained from the stairwell, driving the creatures back. Farah got her hands on her rifle and added her own lasers to the mix. One of the creatures broke from the pack, hurling itself across the street and slamming into their building. It grasped one of the airmen by the head and smashed him into the stairs, coating them in red. The lasers turned its chest into a smoking hole, and it toppled back, still clutching the now-headless airman with one hand.

Other creatures turned their attention to the stairwell. "We're being overrun!" Rivera shouted. "We need to get out of here!"

The group barreled down the stairs, finding a hole in the wall near the bottom that wasn't straight into the overrun street. Jonah kept one eye on Farah, firing shots when he could. He jumped over the section of the stairs slick with the dead airman's blood and brain matter.

Farah darted after the team, barely visible as Jonah jumped from the building and into an alley. The creatures circled her. Jonah rushed out, digging his heel into the street and firing in a desperate attempt to open a path for Farah. Aleks, Mud, and another airman joined him, focusing on taking down the closest creatures. The lasers tore chunks and filled the street with the smell of burning flesh, but the creatures had strong backs, even against directed energy.

Finally, one dropped, giving Farah a way forward. She made her move—and a stinger punched through her chest. She looked down, shocked. Her arm hung at her side, firing her rifling constantly into the ground, turning the street below her into slag. A creature leaped off the top of a nearby building.

An earth-shattering crack reverberated as the creature landed, and the ground under Farah gave way, dropping her and three of the creatures out of the tower before they took a hard right angle with natural gravity and vanished. The rest of the creatures recoiled at the sudden daylight, protecting their eyes.

"Goddamn it." Mud pulled at Jonah's arm. "We gotta go."

They raced to catch up with the rest, who'd already nearly made it to the door. Saul and Rivera had placed themselves in sentry positions, rifles up to keep the path clear. As Jonah, Mud, Aleks, and the airman showed up, they turned and fired. That gave Jonah an indication of what was behind them.

"Go! Go! Go!" Saul shouted.

Jonah pushed away the burning in his lungs and pulled out the last his legs would give him. He leaped through the door, Aleks barely behind him. Mud and the airman nearly took each other out trying to squeeze through. Jonah's legs gave up, and he collapsed.

Rivera spun through, setting off a series of parting shots. Then it was only Saul. He rushed through the door but stopped hard. He jerked at his shoulders, but the large bag across his back had gotten stuck. Jonah tried to stand, but his knees fought against him. Saul cursed and pulled at the strap. Jonah could hear the creatures closing in.

Frankie rushed forward, reaching through the gap between Saul and the door and twisting his bag free. He threw Saul aside just as the first creature crashed into the heavy metal. A stinger shot through the gap, striking Frankie in the back of the neck and retracting before anyone had a chance to react.

He grabbed at his wound, and his eyes rolled back. His knees wobbled. He took two steps, then collapsed. Green liquid seeped from the puncture.

"Frankie!" Saul shouted. He rolled him onto his back and shook him. "Frankie, talk to me!"

"I'm so . . . I'm . . ." His head lolled about. "I'm . . . I'm . . ."

He went quiet. Then still. Saul put his head against his chest.

"He's breathing," he said. "We have to get him back to the ship." He hefted Frankie onto his shoulders and trudged up the tunnel.

"One of us can carry him," Jonah said.

"I've got him." Between Frankie and the apple-melons, Saul walked with a couple of hundred pounds of weight.

"Saul . . ."

"I've got him!" Saul carried on, Frankie limp across his back. He didn't wait to see if anyone followed.

The radio on Rivera's hip crackled, and Row's voice came through. "Hey, uh, come in? The jump sequence is starting up. You should get back here. You got a couple of hours, probably, but it's quicker than last time."

Jonah forced himself to his feet. They left the creatures to slink back into their hovels, the team dishearteningly smaller than the one that had left the ship.

CHAPTER 28

Saul fell to his knees at the top of the ramp, setting Frankie down as gently as his sore body would allow. Jonah had made no more offers to carry him as they walked back, not sure what to say; nobody made a sound at all. They couldn't celebrate the discovery of food after losing so many lives in return.

Booker and the airman who'd stayed back with her perked up at the return.

Cora rose from her seat. "What happened?"

"Nothing good." Jonah handed her his bag and collapsed into a chair. His legs felt like jelly, and he could hardly draw in a breath without it stinging his throat. "We got food."

"That sounds good." She peeked in the bag, taking out one of the apple-melons and giving it a once-over before turning her gaze to the team.

Jonah could see her counting in her head and noted the exact moment she realized there were fewer of them. He let his head drop back and ran his hand over the sweat on his neck. Row entered the loading dock, taking in the entire scene before his eyes landed on Jonah. Jonah leaned forward.

I have to keep this together. He slammed his palms into his knees. *Just keep the threads together.*

"Let's put the food into the coolers." He rose and took the apple-melon from Cora. "Might make them last longer."

"Give people a second, Jonah!" Saul slammed his fists into the floor.

"We have to get prepared for the next jump." Jonah collected more fruit to take to the stage.

"Prepare what?" Saul stumbled to his feet, grabbing Jonah by his collar. "We have nothing to prepare for! Our only hope is your kid stumbling on the right button to push while the rest of us stand around with our dicks in our hands!"

"Saul. Calm down."

"Why? It doesn't matter what we do. We're useless out here. We're a bunch of idiots stuck in a tin can flying through nothing, and we can't *do* anything."

Everyone watched, their expressions falling at the truth they all knew but were afraid to admit. Row shook, holding his hands to his mouth. Jonah needed him to keep hopeful. He had to say something, but his throat turned to stone.

"Now Terrence and Frankie and . . . and . . ." Saul squeezed his eyes shut, tears running down his cheeks. "Frankie was gonna be a dad. He was supposed to be a dad. This wasn't supposed to happen."

He let go of Jonah's collar and fell to his knees again, his weeping filling the loading dock and bleeding out into the uncaring jungle. Jonah continued on his original path, placing the apple-melons on the stage. He needed to keep it together. For everyone. Frankie, Terrence, the airmen. All could be mourned when they were safe.

Saul picked himself up off the floor, face wet and eyes red. He cradled Frankie in his arms and trudged through the loading dock, everyone giving him plenty of room.

"I'll find him a soft place to sleep," Saul muttered. "He never liked camping on the ground."

His footfalls thumped down the hall, and still, no one made a move.

"Look," Jonah said. "Let's get these—"

"Someone stop him!" Kiki shrieked from down the hall.

Cyril stumbled into the loading dock, barely keeping himself upright with his cane. He coughed, drips of blood running down his chin. Row looked between the old man and the hall he came from and sprinted for Kiki.

"Where are you going?" Cora placed herself in front of Cyril, but not enough to stop him.

"I'm leaving," he said, sliding around her.

Row shot back in with Kiki on her wheelchair. "Dad! Stop!"

"Sir, there's nothing out there." Rivera held Cyril back with a hand.

"There is more out there than there is in here." He slapped the other man's hand away and continued unabated, eyes locked on the ramp. "I will not die on the floor of this spaceship."

"Please stop," Kiki begged. Row kept her moving at the same pace as her father. "You're not going to die."

"Keneilwe." He brushed a braid from her face. "I cannot survive another jump. I know each time it takes my life from me, and as this infernal engine hums, I know it comes for the last time. Just let me know the feeling of soil beneath my feet at the end."

Kiki pleaded with the rest of the group. "Why don't any of you do anything? Stop him!"

"He can make his own decisions." Jonah kicked off the stage and stomped out before he lost it altogether.

Kiki sat across from her father as he pulled off his shoes and pressed his bare feet into the dirt. He'd found a fallen tree not too far from the ramp, and Row kept watch from the ship. At least he'd given them space and wouldn't see her in such a state. She couldn't stop the tears rolling down her face. How could her father make this choice? Even though touching the dirt did seem to slightly invigorate him.

"See? Now you're feeling better." She touched his hand. "Let's go back on the ship."

He gave her a soft smile, the same one he'd given her when she'd told him she'd broken the banister in their front hall after taking too hard a turn in her chair. And when she'd gotten in trouble for sticking her tongue out at her teacher. Now he gave it to her when he was about to tell her he was going to die. More tears welled in the corners of her eyes.

"It's not fair." She swiped the back of her hand across her damp cheek.

"I know." He placed his hand over hers, letting warmth flow from his skin. "It should never be this way. But think of this adventure we just had!"

"You never left the ship, Daddy."

"But I heard about it!" He stroked her cheekbone with his thumb. "When you and Row told your stories, I felt like I was there."

"I'm not a very good storyteller. I keep getting distracted and losing the point."

"That just makes your stories that much more interesting to hear." He settled back and took in a deep breath of clear air. "I will always be there in the stories you tell. I tried to be strong for you, but you are stronger than I could have ever believed. My only regret is that I did not see it until now."

Kiki hung her head, tears dropping free and wetting her pants. Her father shifted off the log and took her in his arms. She held him as tight as she could, afraid that if she let go, he'd immediately drift away.

"I'm not worried about me. I'm worried about you," she said. "You're going to be alone."

"No, he won't." Sergeant Booker limped down the ramp, another airman—a tall woman with a stern face—helping her. "I'm gonna stay, too."

"I do not need company," Dad said, shifting back to his spot on the log.

"It's not about you, sir." The airman placed Booker next to him. In the daylight, Kiki could clearly see how pale and yellow she'd become. "You're right. It is a lot better out here than it is in there."

"Look, Daddy." Kiki smiled, tears running along her lips. "You have a friend now. I bet she has some fun stories, too."

"Do you?" Dad asked.

"I promise you won't get bored."

Dad motioned for Row to come down and leaned toward Kiki. "Now, I want you to go up into that ship. I want to see you right there." He pointed at the part of the bridge visible from his position. "And I am going to imagine you flying off to your next adventure, okay?"

"Okay." The tears threatened to reappear, but she bit her tongue and held them back. She would be strong for her next adventure. For him.

"Good." He kissed her on the forehead as Row arrived. "Take care of the boy."

"I will." She grabbed Row's hand as he turned her back toward the ramp.

The door began to shut just as they and the airman reached the top. Kiki looked back in time to see Dad and Booker waving as the ramp hid them from view.

"It's okay." Row wrapped his arms around her from the back.

"It's not," Kiki whispered. "But it will be."

The door clicked shut.

Christopher found solace in the empty halls. Every jump opened more doors, and he could push deeper and deeper into the ship's twisting innards. For too long, he had sat in that bunk room, surrounded by vacant-brained soldiers who could never grasp their situation. That was why they died—and he lived. That was why he would survive the new world.

The world of the ship.

A door slid open for him, letting him onto a balcony overlooking a large piece of machinery made of pipes and containers. It hummed and grumbled like nothing he had heard on the ship before. Most of the technology had been quiet and sterile, peaceful machines designed for aesthetics. This was raw, built for purpose, and choked with the smell of dusty hardware.

That was not all that was there. Christopher was not alone. Jonah stood on the balcony, leaning against the railing with a distant look on his face. He had taken a verbal beating from the commoners in the loading dock, one he did not deserve.

"What do you think it is?" Christopher asked, sliding up next to him and looking down into a spinning generator.

"I don't know," Jonah mumbled.

"I think it is life support. I think this is what has been keeping us alive." He clicked his tongue. "Well, not the only thing."

Jonah pushed off the railing as if he meant to leave, only to turn back and square up on Christopher. "Why'd you change your mind about helping us?"

"I am a man of my word." He raised his hands in mock surrender. "You apologized, and I said I would."

"No." Jonah chewed on the inside of his cheek. "No, I don't believe you. You've been up my ass from the moment we met. How'd that change?"

Christopher tapped his fingers along the railing. The spinning generator below slowed until he heard each swing of the turbine. Jonah would not leave until he got an answer. One that Christopher had never put into words.

"Because I figured you out," he said. "I thought you were this bleeding heart who was going to get everybody killed, who could not do the hard things. But you are clever. When you bashed my head against that bunk, I could only laugh because you finally let the real you show. But that was not what changed my mind. Anyone can be cruel."

He leaned toward Jonah as if to share a secret. Jonah had not reacted to a single word.

"What these civilians who have never seen war cannot understand is just how vile humanity can be." The twitch in Jonah's eye told him everything he needed to know. "You understand. I have seen mothers pitch their own babies into fires to save themselves. That is selfishness, pure and simple. But, if doing that saves a hundred lives, the morality starts to waver. That is what most people cannot see."

Jonah curled his lip in disgust and turned away.

"But as I said, cruelty did not change my mind," Christopher continued, following at Jonah's heel as he walked down the balcony. "It was when you apologized. I did not expect it! Truly! Took me off guard. What kind of man would drive someone's face into a piece of metal to the point of blood, then turn around and say he was sorry? No man. That was when I figured it out. It was a ploy. You were not sorry. You did not have to be. I should have been mad that you tricked me, but I was not. I was impressed."

Jonah stopped. The turbine wound up again into a hum, and a pipe rattled in its fastening. Jonah scowled, meeting Christopher's gaze. "Do you honestly believe the things you say?"

Christopher recoiled. "I do not follow."

"Are you that scared of losing control? You twist yourself into knots?"

What is he talking about? Christopher thought. Jonah still played his game. Christopher had not gotten his trust yet. It made sense. He had missed the signs for so long, Jonah could not know if he belonged in his inner circle.

"You have a strength in you," Christopher said. "It scares most people, but it is what keeps you alive. I can see it."

Jonah never gave him an answer, he just walked out. Christopher lingered, listening to the workings of the ship. An answer was not what he needed from Jonah because he had all the answers he needed. Of course he believed everything he said. It was the truth.

Row wheeled Kiki to the bridge, placing her at the window where they could see Cyril and Monica waiting below. She'd stopped crying once they'd left the loading dock but hadn't said much.

I wish I could say something to make her feel better. Row placed a hand on Kiki's shoulder.

They weren't in the bridge alone for long. First, Mud and Darius arrived, their conversation stopping once they saw the kids there. The last trio of airmen was next, followed by Rivera, and finally the scientists, all taking up Row's air.

His hands shook, so he stuck them in his pockets. His neck grew hot. Everyone stared at him. He didn't need to look back to know. Why wouldn't they be? Jonah had been telling everyone Row was their only hope.

That's not fair. He squeezed his eyes shut, trying to force the sound of whispered conversation away. *I'm just a kid. I'm trying my best, but it can't be all on me. But . . . who else could it be on? I wanted this.*

Row's father was one of the few people who hadn't joined them in the bridge. They needed to talk. Truly talk.

"I need to find my dad," Row whispered to Kiki.

"Okay." She pressed her forehead against his cheek and held it there for a moment. "I'll be right here."

Row turned, and it felt like everyone else looked away. He clenched his fists and hurried out the door, gaze lowered. He'd spent so long avoiding everyone he could, only for them to choke up his space.

Jonah sat on his bed, fingers tented and pressed against his lips. Deep in thought, he considered their next move, but nothing came to him. The cleaning robot puttered around his room, and he tracked it absent-mindedly, letting time drift away into the hum of the engines.

"You have a bad habit of running away." Cora leaned against the doorframe.

He couldn't remember her arriving. "Find someone else to keep everyone in line. Maybe Rivera. At the very least, he'll believe he deserves it."

"That is not why I am here." She stepped into the room. "Are you okay?"

"I'm not doing great." He rested his chin on his knuckles, watching as the cleaner reached the corner and started moving up the wall. "I didn't want Row to know he was our only chance at getting home. I wanted to keep everybody separated and distracted, but now they all know. It's all they're going to think about."

"Come on. Row knew." She rested her hands on his shoulders. "He is a smart kid. Do you really think he did not realize the rest of us are not at his level? If he did not know, then I am sure Kiki told him."

"I was afraid he'd crack under the pressure. I wanted to protect him."

"You did protect him."

"I didn't protect Frankie." He turned his head against her stomach. "Or Terrence. Or Farah, or all the airmen whose names I don't even know."

"Those were not your fault! Oh, my God, for someone who is worried he is heartless, you take so much of the world on your shoulders." She tilted his chin up, her luminous brown eyes nearly black in the dim light. "You need to stop trying to control everything."

Jonah cast her a flat stare. "Are you really the person who should be telling me this?"

She rolled her eyes. "Fine. Have you considered that you do not care too little, and instead, you care way, *way* too much? You need to stop taking it personally when things do not go the way you think they should." She played her fingers along the nape of his neck. "You asked me if I was happy. Ask me again."

Where is this going? Jonah wondered. "Are you happy?"

"I am not." She shook her head. "I am absolutely not. I should be. I have everything that says I should be, but I am not. But I will be. I am going to tear this shell off myself and be that little girl who liked sparkly makeup and comic books and believed she could make the world a better place. And I am going to do that on Earth. Because now I have seen out here, and that pale blue hellhole is all we have, so I am gonna damn well be happy on it."

Jonah couldn't help but believe her. Her energy infected him, pouring through his skin from her smile, a smile she'd long hidden.

"We are going to get back. Do you know how I know?" She leaned in, her lips hovering just out of reach of his. "Because we are going to work together. And I am going to stop trying to be anything and just *be*. So we can both take a step back. Find perspective."

"I like the sound of that." He ran his fingers up her legs to her waist and pulled her against him.

She kissed him then, her hair falling from the messy bun at the nape of her neck and draping across the sides of his face. The world faded. The hum of the ship, the thoughts of Earth, the people they'd lost. Everything except Jonah and Cora, alone.

"Dad!" Row's voice drove like a spike through the silence.

Jonah pulled away from Cora, but not soon enough. Row stood at the door, eyes wide with shock, then anger. Cora stumbled back, smoothing her rumpled clothes back into place. Jonah leaped to his feet as Row darted off.

"Row, wait!" he shouted, chasing after him.

Row reversed direction halfway down the hall, stopping Jonah in place with a point of his finger. "You told me you were getting back together with Mom!"

"I just said we'd have dinner." Jonah shrugged. "I didn't mean to imply anything more."

"Stop lying!" Row sprinted away again.

"Row!"

He hurried to keep up, but Row ducked into the elevator. Jonah got there in time to see his son's furious face before the doors shut. He grunted in frustration and kicked the wall.

"Jonah." Cora crept out of his room. "Is he—"

"Stay there!" He threw his hands up. "Or go anywhere. It doesn't matter!"

Cora frowned, but Jonah didn't wait for her response. He took off down the hall, figuring Row would go to the bridge. That was where he always went. Jonah had to catch him. Talk to him. He knew he hadn't done anything wrong, but why did it feel like he had?

He barreled around a corner, bouncing off the wall, and spotted Row about to enter the bridge. "Hey!"

"Leave me alone!"

He jogged toward his son. "I need you to understand—"

"Understand what? That you're a liar? That all you do is lie?"

"I'm trying to protect you."

"How is lying protecting me!?" Row pounded his hand against his chest and walked onto the bridge. "You have *never* been honest with me. Or Mom!"

Jonah ran his fingers through his hair. How could he make Row understand?

"Your mom and me are complicated." He followed his son into the bridge, immediately struck by how many people were already there watching in shock at their emotional explosion.

"Stop saying that!" Row slammed his fist on a console and spun on Jonah. His eyes were misty, but red rage filled his face. "You left us, remember? You said you still loved Mom! You said we'd see you more than once a year!"

"Everything I did was to make a better life for you!"

"By not being in it?" He stumbled back, his arms falling limp at his sides. "What did we do to make you hate us so much?"

Ice sliced through Jonah's veins. "I don't . . ."

"What the hell!?" Mud shouted.

A shadow fell across the bridge, and everyone's eyes shot to the window. A massive ship of sharp angles hovered over them.

CHAPTER 29

The foreign ship descended closer to the ground, its shadow growing darker over the jungle. Birds and climbing creatures fled as it threatened to crush them. When it was almost directly overhead, it stopped. Nobody dared move lest the dreadnought somehow see them.

"It can't land, right?" Darius whispered. "It's too big. Surely it can't land."

"Anybody wanna shoot them a text?" Mud asked with a shrug.

Jonah had no doubts it was the same ship Row had seen at the military base, following them in their jump. That couldn't be good. They'd yet to find anything friendly in their whole journey. Cora caught up to them, her gaze drifting over Row and Jonah before finally spotting the ship, too. Her jaw dropped open.

A green cloud formed beneath the dreadnought, spreading across the sky as it drifted down. Little droplets of vibrant water struck the bridge's window like rain. Terror gripped Jonah's chest, and he rushed forward, the rest of the group trailing after him.

Outside the ship, Cyril and Booker looked up in awe from their positions on the fallen tree. Jonah slammed his fist against the window to warn them, but it was already too late. The first droplet struck Booker's face, and she seized, clutching at her mouth and then tumbling off the log. Cyril was next, grabbing his neck, digging as if he could pull the spray from his throat.

The bridge erupted into shouts, all paling in comparison to Kiki screaming, "Open the door! Open the door!"

Booker pulled herself across the grass, leaving chunks of melting flesh in her wake. Cyril held still, hands clutched in prayer, as his skin pulled away from his bones. Row threw himself over Kiki and covered her eyes so she couldn't see. She could still scream.

"Open the door!" Her voice cracked.

"If we do, we'll all die!" Rivera said.

If the door stayed closed, they'd be protected from the mysterious aerosol spray. The fact did little to calm Jonah's heartbeat after seeing what happened outside. The neon cloud swallowed up the jungle, yet the frightened animals didn't exhibit the same effects. Jonah swallowed over the lump in his throat. A poison made to kill only humans.

"How long until we jump?" he asked.

"A couple minutes, I think." Row held a weeping Kiki in his arms.

A series of panels opened at the ends of the dreadnought's rectangular protrusions, unleashing a swarm of silver dart ships. It seemed a couple of minutes was too long. Jonah grabbed Rivera's collar.

"Get us out of here!" He shoved the other man toward the pilot's chair.

Rivera caught himself on the instrument panel and, after a quick scowl in Jonah's direction, settled himself to fly. The darts swept past, rocking their ship with laser fire. At least two dozen flew in tight clouds, with more pouring out of the dreadnought every second.

"Row! We need those guns!" Jonah ordered.

Row stayed wrapped around Kiki. Rivera slammed his foot on the pedals and sent them skyward, knocking a dart off its axis before orienting on the horizon and giving it full gas.

"Row, now!" Jonah glared at him.

Row glared at him for a moment then let go of Kiki and went to work. He set three outer consoles to weapon mode. The fourth gun had been destroyed. Cora, Jonah, and Row took their positions on the guns and let loose a storm of hot plasma.

"What do we do?" Mud seemed barely able to pull his attention away from the window.

"Hold on to something." Rivera put the ship into a nosedive. "We're gonna see how well these drones fly."

Mud clutched onto Darius, and they both dropped to the ground. Dr. Young and Dr. Cooper joined them a second later, along with the airmen. Only Aleks stayed standing, holding on to the front console with both hands and watching in amazement as Rivera dodged among the trees.

The ship curled around trunks and through branches. Jonah took a moment to appreciate how quickly Rivera had grown accustomed to flying the ship in this new environment. His eyes danced between the window and a holographic sphere on his instrument panel, indicating where the darts were incoming. He'd said before that the ship flew like a boat, but now he moved it like a dragonfly, using gravity manipulation to drift in all directions, playing with shifts in momentum like physics was a suggestion.

Rivera took a hard left but drifted the ship right, spinning the ship through a narrow gap in the canopy. Thinner branches snapped off as he cut through, flying into the jungle. Three darts attempted the same turn, only to go wide and strike the tree, exploding into brilliant blue flames.

Jonah turned his focus back on his guns. He aimed for the center of the drone fleet and opened fire, tearing through a pair of darts and sending one crashing into a third. A stark difference from chasing down a single ship, they had a target-rich environment and let fly. But for every dart they popped, two more swooped in.

Their ship rattled with blasts from the dart's guns. An alert blared through the bridge. Jonah may not have known the language, but he knew an emergency alarm when he heard it. The ship wouldn't hold up forever.

"Why aren't we jumping?" Rivera yelled. "Shouldn't we be jumping?"

Row checked the power chart. "We should be. But we're not."

"We can't jump while we're moving!" Dr. Cooper used Dr. Young as a brace as she poked her head up. "Using a black hole requires extremely precise—"

"I got the technobabble!" Rivera cursed as another laser volley seared the front window. "I don't think they're going to let us stop!"

"I have an idea!" Row leaped out of his seat and started tapping on one of the center consoles. One of the airmen took his place, awkwardly trying to figure out the controls.

"What are you doing?" Rivera leaned out of his chair to see. The ship clipped a tree, tearing out half its width, and he scrambled to keep control.

"I took your suggestion and looked for some weapons."

Jonah glanced back when he could, but all he could make out was an indecipherable menu of selections and Row shooting through them at light speed. Row snapped his fingers when he found what he was looking for and a large targeting reticle appeared on the front window. Row's smile turned to confusion.

"Oh." He scratched his head. "I guess it only fires from the front. We'll have to turn around."

"What only fires from the front?" Rivera asked. The ship shook and dropped a dozen feet. He pulled back, keeping them from grinding against the jungle floor.

"The gun!" Row clutched onto the console. "The gun I found!"

"What does it fire? How long do we need to face them for? What's the load?"

"I don't know!" He gestured wildly at the reticle. "Big!"

"Then let's stack 'em up." Rivera pressed a pedal, and they shot above the tree line.

More and more dots appeared on his readout until the space behind them was one solid blue light. The ship rattled and whined, its

alarm bells screaming for someone to listen. Jonah and Cora shot down
as many darts as they could until in a flash of red, Jonah's view shut off.

"They got my gun!" he said.

Rivera puffed out a breath of air and slammed the yoke to the side.
They pivoted and resumed backward. Silver darts filled their view, un-
loading sprays of red straight at them.

Row slammed his hand on his screen. A thin laser, barely more
than a string, shot out from just below the bridge, cutting through the
middle of the formation.

Nothing happened. The darts kept firing. Jonah's stomach
turned to stone.

A dull thump sounded outside, not unlike a sledgehammer striking
a metal barrel. The air around the string of light rippled. The darts
slammed together. Their shells crumpled under the immense gravity
pulling them into the light. Those at the edge of the pack were sheared
in half before being pulled in. Where the laser got close to the jungle,
its gravitational pull ripped up trees by their roots, turning them into
pulverized dust.

In less than a second, it was all over. The thin light faded, and pieces of metal and wood fell to the ground below.

"Whoa," Row said. An understatement.

Rivera took his hands off the yoke. "Now we jump, right?"

"Yeah. Give it a second."

The dreadnought remained on the horizon, another wave of darts
pouring from its underbelly. Jonah rose from his chair, wiping sweat
from his forehead. The alert faded into the hum of the engine. The
darts grew closer. Rivera's fingers twitched, ready to grab the stick if
they needed to run.

The darts were almost within firing range. Jonah took a deep breath,
and his ears popped.

The darts disappeared. The planet disappeared. Everything disappeared. All they saw out the bridge window was a smoky, roiling storm
of iridescent colors and pinpoint lights. No planet.

Nothing.

Mud heaved a sigh of relief, audible from across the bridge, but no one celebrated. They'd survived, but all Jonah heard was the sound of Kiki softly crying into her hands. Row crept across the bridge to console her. Jonah approached the window, watching a strand of blue light change to green, then yellow, and drift out of view.

He looked over the group. Everyone gazed back at him, a dozen accusing eyes.

Saul wandered in, gazing at the spectacle outside before joining the crew in staring Jonah down. "What's going on?"

Jonah leaned against the front console. His body felt like it was a million years old, ready to crumble into dust. Tension had kept him together for as long as he could remember. Since the atrocities he'd witnessed in the Middle East, on live battlefields choked with dust and gas and death. He had to let it go. Let the pieces fall where they may.

"This is everything I know," he said. "I already told you we found human DNA in the ship. We also looked at a bone I found in a mass grave back at the mine. It has signs of unnatural decay, possibly from a chemical weapon." He gazed out the window, images of Cyril and Sergeant Booker melting in his brain. "Possibly what we saw that big ship spewing back there."

"Did you know about the ship?" Darius asked.

"Yes. But only recently."

He scowled. "How'd you know?"

"I saw it." *No need for them to turn on Row.*

"*I* saw it." Row stepped forward. "It appeared as we left the ice planet."

Jonah chewed on his tongue. His kid was as stubborn as he was. But he was right; they couldn't keep lying. "Also, the ship's been listening to us. That's why that message came in English."

"That's not all." Row lifted his chin. "Ship, can I ask you a question?"

"What is your question?" The voice came from all parts of the bridge.

Jonah spun around. *That must be recent.*

"It's not perfect," Row said with a shrug. "It can't turn off the auto-jump."

Darius practically fell over a chair as he stepped forward. "Can it tell us where we are?"

"Ship, where are we?"

"Home."

Everyone groaned. Row gave a sheepish smile. "I told you it's not a perfect translation. It learns from us talking. But I did find out the ship was in a battle and jumped to Earth. That's all it knows because it thought it was destroyed. Earth isn't even on their star maps."

"Why didn't you tell us?" Saul asked.

"You needed to stay focused." Jonah ran a hand through his hair. "Focused away from Row. To give him time. I saw how you all swarmed him once you learned about the possibility of a translator, and he . . . and *I* thought you couldn't handle it. So, I kept the little things secret."

"Little things?" Mud let out a single barking laugh. "Like how everyone on these planets we've been visiting was wiped out by a big ol' ship spewing poison? Sounds like the people on this ship were running home because they were getting slaughtered by the same thing trying to melt us! Aliens versus aliens, and here we are in the middle!"

"I didn't realize the scale." Jonah winced. He needed to stop making excuses. "Fine, I didn't want you focused. I wanted you distracted. I thought all you needed was hope, even if it was blind."

"That's not your decision to make," Saul said.

"I'm sorry." It was the best he could give them. "You didn't need blind hope. You needed trust. We all needed to trust each other."

"We weren't hopeful, Jonah," Darius said. "We were scared."

Saul shook his head and tramped out. The roughnecks turned from Jonah, shuffling across the floor toward the door.

"Does anyone else think that big ship was compensating for something?" Mud asked on the way out.

"Goddamn it, Mud," Darius said, clearly exasperated.

"What? Who needs a ship that big? And who's piloting it? It's ridiculous."

Darius urged Mud to keep walking. One by one, the bridge emptied of roughnecks and soldiers until only Rivera and Cora remained with Jonah, Row, and Kiki.

Row headed over to Kiki. "Let's go."

"Don't touch me!" She slapped at his arms, and he jumped back in surprise. "I should've spent more time with him! You ate up all my time! We were never going to fix this. You wasted it all. Someone else, take me to my room."

Row's mouth hung open, speechless, as Cora approached the dolly.

"I've got you," she said, giving Row a pitying look as she rolled Kiki away.

Rivera tapped his hand against the stick and then stood. "Well, let me know if we are gonna be flying anymore."

Then it was just Jonah and Row. They met eyes and then turned away. Jonah had done everything he could and still failed. Row hated him. Maybe he should.

Jonah drifted up the stairs, more ghost than man, hoping to lose himself in the ship.

CHAPTER 30

Soft sobs echoed from Kiki's room. She sat in the chair Row had made for her, arms wrapped around herself. She'd thought she was ready to say goodbye to her dad, but he wasn't supposed to die like that. They were supposed to jump away, and she could dream of him finding peace in nature or dare to imagine they'd come back after figuring out how to move the ship.

But he died choking on his blood, and figuring out the jump-engine was a fool's dream all along. So, she sat alone, crying until her eyes turned red and itchy, wondering when it was her turn to die.

She heard a sound at the door and thought Cora had returned, only to find Rivera standing there, hands in his pockets and eyes downturned.

"I wanna be alone," she said. Rivera had always bugged her.

"I know. I just . . ." There was something different about him, about how he held himself. He didn't have the same bravado he usually wore like a blanket. "I wanted to say something to you."

Kiki waited.

"My, um, my dad . . ." He sighed. "Can I sit down?"

She motioned to the bed.

"My dad died when I was a kid." He sat gently on her covers. "I was thirteen. He stepped on a nail at his construction site. Now, we did not have insurance or money for a doctor, so he just wrapped it up and kept moving on with his life. A couple of weeks later, his muscles started hurting, and he got these painful spasms in his neck. Turns out he had tetanus. At the end, he could not even breathe."

He crumpled forward, his elbows resting on his knees. His back rose and fell with each inhalation and exhalation.

"He died because of a nail. The strongest man I knew. Could lift me over his head like I was made of straw, and a little nail got him."

"I'm sorry," Kiki said.

"No, I am sorry." He sat up straight. "I am not asking for pity, never had it, never wanted it. All I am saying is you had a lot of good years with your pops. Just like I had a lot of good years with mine. Those are the years that matter, not however they ended."

Kiki did have fantastic memories of her father. Though she wished she could make more, she would never lose those. *It's like he said, he'll live on through me.*

"You take all the time you need." Rivera clapped and jumped to his feet. "And if you wanna go anywhere, give me a shout."

"Thank you."

"Oh." He spun around and tossed her his radio. "And don't blame the kid."

Kiki laughed. She'd never thought she'd do that again. "I don't."

Rivera nodded and went on his way. Kiki held the radio to her chest. She had to make the best of what she had. Her entire life was a fluke, no sense in wasting it. She held down the "speak" button and brought the radio to her lips.

But nothing came out. She couldn't find the words. She let her hands fall to her lap and released the button. She would take all the time she needed. She only needed a little more.

Christopher found himself walking in circles. He hadn't talked or even thought about his dad in years. He was supposed to be over it. He was supposed to be stronger than that. But seeing Kiki in that way, he couldn't help himself.

He was so wrapped up in his head, he nearly crashed headfirst into Klondike and the two other airmen going the other way. The last three of his team to be alive, the rest lost to mines and jungle creatures. They had the laser rifles they'd found in the tower hanging off their shoulders. It looked like they had repurposed straps from equipment cases and attached them to their guns.

"Sir, we've been looking for you," Klondike said.

"What is this about?" Christopher stood tall, hiding the weakness that crawled through his mind.

"We're just wondering when we're going to make our move."

Christopher cocked his head and slid closer to him. "What move?"

"You were right, sir. There's no way back to Earth." He didn't flinch as Christopher got right up in his face. "It's time to take control. We have guns. We have food."

"They have guns, too." He turned to the other airmen. "And they outnumber us."

"They don't carry their guns. They left them in the loading dock. We can grab them before they even know we're there. Besides, they're not soldiers, sir."

Christopher nodded. The two airmen behind Klondike had wide eyes like stunned deer. They were the same ones who had left with Airman Booker, cowards following the orders of whoever gave them. Klondike had gotten himself a fair group of cronies.

"Sounds like a plan." Christopher nodded at Klondike. "Give me your rifle."

Klondike blinked. "Uh, yes, sir." He slipped the strap off his shoulder and passed it over.

The rifles were in good shape, despite the uncountable years they had spent in the dirt. Christopher ran his finger over some rusting around the trigger guard and up to a thin indicator on the side. When the gun was fired, it went down, and afterward, it recharged. A gun that never ran out of ammo. Ingenious.

Christopher smiled at Klondike, then cracked him with the rifle's butt. Blood exploded from his nose, and he fell back, screaming in pain. Christopher stepped on his chest. Klondike struggled, and he pressed down until the man went quiet.

"You think that is who we are?" Christopher said, resting the rifle on his shoulder. "We are going to sneak around and ambush these people when they least expect it? You wanna be the man in charge so much you will give up your honor?"

"You goddamn hypocrite!" Klondike spat out the blood running from his nose into his mouth. "You're the one who told us to steal their food!"

"You have no idea what I am because you cannot comprehend people like me and Jonah. Strong people."

"You're insane." Klondike's arms flopped to the side, his nose split at the bridge.

"Yeah, maybe." He rubbed some blood off the end of the rifle's stock and handed it to one of the airmen. "But I am surviving. That is all that matters. And it is Jonah who keeps me surviving." He patted Klondike on the cheek, spreading the crimson around his face. "You do not make the plans, got it?"

"Got it, sir." He pulled away.

Christopher wiped the blood on Klondike's shirt and walked away. *Vultures always circle when they sense death.* He whistled an old lullaby. They were not dead yet. He did not care that Jonah had kept things from them, though a couple of days ago, he might have. It took him too long, but he had finally figured out what Jonah was. The real truth. Not a naïve idealist and not a slave to human cruelty. He was strong, just like Christopher's father.

He just had to watch out for nails.

***

The bridge sat quiet once again, the only sound the occasional click as Row's fingers struck the laptop's keyboard. He studied the coding in his translator system, using one of the consoles as a desk. There was little left to do, and that would require a sudden, huge leap in understanding the alien language. Even if he did get to that point, he knew turning off the auto-jump required the captain's permission. They had no chance. They never had.

And yet he worked. It was the only thing that kept Kiki's voice out of his head. He wanted to see her, but he knew she'd just yell at him again. Everyone would yell at him. It wasn't his fault his dad had promised them a miracle. Row never would have. *Yet, that's the exact reason he isolated us on the bridge. To keep Kiki and me working without the others distracting us.*

He glanced away from his screen as Aleks entered. He waved at Row and pulled down his hood.

"Hey, you got a minute?" Aleks asked.

"I guess." Row rubbed his tired eyes. "I haven't figured anything out."

"It's not about that." He hopped down the steps and held out his phone. "Your dad took a picture of some scratching in that drone you shot down. I think he was gonna have you translate it, but I guess it slipped his mind. My curiosity is just running wild, so at the very least, I'd like to know what it says."

"Sure." He took Aleks's phone. It had a photo of a metal wall with letters scratched into it. "It probably won't work, you know. It's a pretty rough system."

"Whatever." Aleks kicked back in the chair across the center aisle from Row's. "No harm in trying."

Row had always thought Aleks was high-strung. Now he acted like a slacker with nothing better to do. Row watched him out of the corner of his eye and scanned the photo with his phone. The system ran the words through its database.

"Is it working?" Aleks asked.

"It always gives something." Row tapped his foot against the underside of the console. "It just gives a lot of translations, and I never know which is the right one."

"So, you guess?"

"Pretty much." He turned his phone over in his hand. The process always took forever, but it felt even longer with Aleks waiting. He must've expected Row to figure out the ship, just like the others did. "I'm sorry my dad told you I could bring us home."

"Hmm?" He cleared his throat. "Naw, your dad never told us anything. I think that's what pissed the others off so much."

"I thought you all were waiting for me to pull off a miracle."

Aleks shook his head. "We were all surviving the best we could. The guys trusted Jonah. Even when they thought they didn't, they really did. So, we followed his lead. Turns out you're the real brains behind the operation, huh?"

"Yeah . . ." Row fingered the edge of his phone.

Maybe his dad *had* been protecting him. It didn't change the fact that he'd caught his dad making out with Cora, though. It wasn't that Row didn't like her. If anything, she was one of the coolest people he'd met on the ship. But she wasn't his mom. She wasn't a part of his family.

A beep from his phone brought Row's attention back to the present. A list of translations appeared on the screen.

"See?" He showed Aleks. "I got, like, twenty or more, and that's after it parsed out anything that didn't make sense grammatically. I don't know which one—" A familiar phrase appeared five translations down the list. His throat dried. "Though, there is . . . Heaven Awaits."

Aleks seemed to take that in for a moment, then cleared his throat and spun out of his chair. "I know we're doing this whole 'trust' thing"— Aleks clapped his hands—"but maybe we keep this one between us."

"I'm fine with that." Row handed Aleks his phone back, thinking that finding those words carved into an empty ship had all the markings of a horror story.

Aleks headed for the door but stopped at the threshold. "Heaven awaits . . . us?"

"I can't imagine who else."

Aleks shivered. "Better not to think about." He flipped his hood up and headed out.

Row chewed on his thumbnail, staring at the two words on his translator app as they burned into his mind. The same two words the ship had said the former captain had run away from. Heaven awaits. What could possibly translate into that?

A chime rang through the bridge. "Scan of contaminants complete," the cheerful electronic voice said. "Connecting to master system."

Row's ears popped. The smoky exterior vanished, and bright white light streamed through the window. Row held up a hand and blinked through the sudden brilliance. As his eyes adjusted, towers came into focus, then smaller buildings at their bases. A city stretched before him.

"Welcome home," the voice said.

Row's breath caught, and he sprinted out of the room shouting, "Dad!"

CHAPTER 31

The ramp tilted down, opening the ship to its new destination, somewhere bright and white, as light spilled into the ship. The travelers, battered as they were, stepped out and breathed still air. Most of them had laser rifles at the ready, surer than ever nothing could be trusted. Row looked over at Kiki, with Cora managing her wheelchair. Rivera and his airmen took up the rear. One of them had a bandage over his nose. Row briefly wondered what had happened before moving on.

Mud, Darius, and Aleks thumped down the ramp, first to touch ground on the landing pad. This one was whole, made of a shiny white material Row thought could be metal. A train of cleaner drones, larger than the one from the ship, puttered by on a pristine, paved walkway.

"They're really rolling out the red carpet," Mud said, stepping out of the way. He slapped Row on the back as he passed by. "You're sure this is the end of the line?"

"The jump engine's shut down. There's no sign it's powering up for another planet," Row said.

He caught sight of his dad standing alone, hands in his pockets as he took in the gleaming city before them. He had told him the same thing when the ship first touched down. Dad had said nothing in return. All Row had caught was a single moment where the severity of it all came crashing down. The ship was done moving. Then Dad had simply clapped his hands and gone to inform the people in the loading dock, Row following behind.

"This is it," Dad had said flatly, his eyes on the floor. "This is where the ship was heading all along."

"Then there has to be something here, right?" Cora asked. "Why else would it stop here?"

"We should all go. Someone get Rivera. The doctors. Kiki." He swept his hand across the controls for the ramp. It hummed and shifted forward, letting the gray daylight in. "Ship's dead. Food's gone. No sense staying here."

"*And* there might be something out there that can help us get home." Cora glanced across the roughnecks' dejected faces. "Right, Jonah?"

"Yeah!" Darius leapt to his feet. "There's gotta be something!"

Dad didn't reply. At the time, Row had wondered if he had still decided on no more lying, but he had come to accept his dad had given up. They were passing by each other on autopilot, just as they always had.

"And if this city does not work . . ." Cora forced a smile. "We will fly to the next one. The planet is big; plenty of places to search."

Row blinked out of his memories as Dr. Cooper and Dr. Young rushed past, smiles stretching across their faces like they were kids at an amusement park. Dr. Cooper bounced to the end of the landing pad and craned her neck back to take in the towers.

"Finally!" she said. "Now *this* looks like an advanced civilization!"

"Try not to have too much enjoyment at our grave," Mud muttered as he walked by.

Row shook his head in disbelief. *At least someone is keeping their spirits up.*

A flock of drones flew over their heads toward the skyscrapers. Monorail lines and skywalks braided between the structures as high as they could see. The landing pad itself was filled with ships just like theirs, their doors closed and exteriors still shining silver from the cleaner drones spinning over and over across their hulls.

There was a grunt of exertion, and Saul arrived at the door, Frankie's body over his back.

"Saul. He's—" Dad began to say.

"Still breathing." Saul shifted Frankie's weight. "He's still alive. I'm not leaving him behind."

Instead of arguing, Dad just nodded at him and headed into the city. The rest of the team followed, though no one made a sound. Row had never seen everyone so quiet. It made his skin itch.

Large vehicles without wheels rested on the sides of the street. Row figured they were cars; they had the right shape and contained varying numbers of seats. He ran his hand over the chassis of a dark brown one, catching his fingers on the occasional dots of rust. The city had no trees or grass, only a fleet of drones in an endless dance of maintenance.

"Where are we going?" Darius asked, using his rifle to knock the glass out of a broken window as he passed by.

No one answered. No one knew. They walked without purpose through a ghost town. For a while, Row could manage a spark of hope every time they passed a new block of buildings, but it faded in time as each building proved empty and eerily similar to the one before it, blocky and plain. Only the doctors kept up any semblance of excitement.

Row stopped at a building with a large window and peered in. Ceiling lights glowed as he approached, revealing a long counter with stools built into the floor in front. Along the left wall was a line of booths and tables leading back to doors at the far side. A cleaning drone drifted across the tiled floor.

A small restaurant. Quaint even. Row imagined people seated at the counter, swapping stories of their days and drinking whatever they had for coffee on this planet. In his mind, they looked like the people he saw through the window of the family diner he passed on the way to school.

"Row." Kiki's voice crackled through the radio on his hip, the loudest thing in existence in the silent city.

He jumped in surprise and unsnapped it from his belt. He'd almost forgotten he still had it. "Kiki?"

"Turn around."

He spun to see Kiki and Cora waiting a short way down the road, near one of the abandoned vehicles. Kiki waved.

"I wanted to tell you I'm sorry," Row said through the radio. "I'm sorry I kept you from your dad. I should've told you earlier, but I'm not good at this."

"Just come over here," she said, then laughed.

Row clipped the radio back on his belt and jogged down the road. He couldn't help but smile at Kiki, but still cast a wary eye at Cora.

"Hi, Row," Cora said.

"Hi." He pulled at his sleeve.

Cora pursed her lips and nodded, double-tapping the handles of Kiki's wheelchair before practically sprinting away. "I'll leave you to it then."

That's never not going to be awkward, Row thought. But he let it go when Kiki took his hand. "I'm—"

"Don't say you're sorry again." She squeezed his fingers to her chest. "I don't . . . I don't blame you. I don't know what happens now, if it's the end or if we have another jump ahead of us. I just know there's no one I want to be with other than you. Even at the end of the world."

Row brushed a braid behind her ear and kissed her. The world lit up around him. There was nothing to fear when they were together.

Jonah walked alone. *This can't be the last stop,* he thought. *What's the point of it?* They'd been to a mine, a refinery, a military post, and a city, but this planet, lying on the other side of the smoky space sea, just felt wrong. Both alive and dead.

Drones flitted between buildings, some cleaning while others moved pieces of material from place to place. Jonah climbed to the top of a vehicle to get a better view and saw two drones carrying a thin, black panel into the sky, the whining of their rotors fading as they disappeared behind a tower. From his vantage point, he could see in a few windows on the buildings that sat back from the walkway; the rooms within were just as plain and clean as the rest of the city so far, but with their identical countertops, chairs, and low tables, they could have easily been kitchens and living rooms in any Earth city.

From his perch, he saw the distant buildings shift, but not from haze or wind. Rather, sections of the city moved from their places, sliding aside and connecting with other fluctuating architecture. A piece of wall three stories up lifted out of its setting, allowing a flood of spider-like robot crawlers to swarm into the mechanics below. Welding sparks poured out, and a trio removed a piece of machinery in time for another trio to bring a similar one in.

They weren't just cleaning the city; they were maintaining a machine. But for whom? Who was still around to need such a massive engine built into the very walls and streets? Indeed, the more Jonah watched, the more drones he saw replacing damaged parts. Ahead, where the city converged at the base of a singular shining monolith, the drones were practically a locust swarm.

"You see anybody?" Mud asked.

The crew had caught up, wandering past with stunned looks on their faces. Saul still carried Frankie on his back while Row had taken up position as Kiki's driver. Rivera and his airmen took circuitous paths through the alleyways and buildings.

"Not yet." Jonah hopped down from his perch. "Maybe not at all."

"Who was calling us here, then?" Mud rubbed at his forearms. "They coulda at least set out a beer or something."

"Everything we've seen has been automated." Jonah gestured at a group of drones flying by, carrying wire in their pincers. "Maybe no one called us here."

Mud's gaze fell. He cursed under his breath and kicked a cleaner drone as it rolled by, sending it crashing into a wall and shattering. It had barely struck the ground before a flying drone swooped down, snatching it up, and a second cleaner came out to tidy up the pieces.

"Feel better?" Jonah asked.

"Kind of." Mud spat on the ground, then hurried to catch up with the rest of the group.

The cleaner rolled in, wiping away Mud's spit and carrying on unabated. As they grew closer to the central tower, the variation in the surrounding buildings disappeared. White cubes with plastic sliding doors lined both sides of the street, stacked a hundred high with no way to reach the upper ones.

A door Jonah pushed on glided aside without resistance. Pleasant warmth met him, joined by a sweet scent both pleasing and unplaceable. The single-room cube he stepped into had simple furnishings: a chair, a bed, and a desk with a computer screen smaller than the ones on the ship's consoles. A collection of four metal squares hung over the head of the bed, attached to the headboard by a central wire.

He backed out and checked the next box. Same thing. All down the line, each box contained a carbon copy of the same chair, bed, and desk.

"Maybe we should go back to the landing pad," Cora said, approaching from behind. "See if we can open one of those other ships and have better luck with its computer."

"Unless you have a tri-head drilling bit laying around somewhere, I think we're out of luck," Jonah said.

"That was almost a joke. Maybe you're not out of the fight yet. You still want to return to Earth, right?"

"Of course I do." He checked another cube and added silently, *I'm just not sure that's possible anymore.*

"Good. I think some people are . . ." She glanced over her shoulder at the doctors chattering excitedly about a drone repairing the road. "Some people are losing focus." She slid open a cube door and grimaced. "And I thought my first apartment was dour."

"I don't think these are apartments." Jonah stepped inside another cube. They even all smelled the same. "It's a different design than all the rooms back near the landing pad. Why change it here?"

"They look like hospital rooms. My grandma spent years in a room just like these," Darius said, carrying on as if he didn't realize he'd said anything at all, eyes up to the sky.

These little boxes would be terrible to die in, Jonah thought, pressing his hand against a firm bed. *Watching the world as it watched you.*

"How're you doing?" Cora slid in next to Jonah.

"Managing." He looked over her shoulder as Aleks wandered past. "Everyone's on their own now, huh?"

"We don't have to be." She started to put her arm around him.

Jonah shifted away just enough to get his point across. "I think we should take a step back."

"We barely took a step forward."

"Just for the moment." He squeezed her forearm, running his thumb over her warm skin. "I'd like to know you more when we aren't about to die."

"Is that the dream?" She looked around the room. "If all this is for medical reasons, why would they need so many? Do you think that poison-spewing monstrosity attacked them, too?"

"I don't know. But I think we can find out." The screen on each cube's desk had lit up when they passed, bearing the same unknown phrase. He leaned out of the cube. "Row! Come over here!"

Row froze mid-step. Kiki glanced over while he dropped his head and shuffled to his father, pushing her in front of him.

Jonah had barely spoken with his son since the blow-up in the bridge, only a couple of words when Row told him they'd arrived on the planet. Judging by the slow trudging and severe expression, Row hadn't forgiven him in the interlude.

"What, Dad?" he asked, stopping with Kiki at the door.

"All these computers say the same thing." He swept his hand over the desk. "Do you know what it says?"

"I can try to find out." Row pulled out his phone and scanned the screen.

The translator ran. Jonah looked at Kiki, who smiled. Kiki looked at Cora, and she smiled, too. Cora looked at Row, and he looked at his phone. Time ticked by like a broken clock. Rivera slowed as he passed, taking in the awkward show with fleeting amusement.

Finally, the phone dinged. Row hummed as he scrolled through the results.

"I guess . . ." He tilted his head from side to side. "Virtualization complete."

"What does that mean?" Kiki scrunched her nose.

"No idea." Row backed out of the cube, frowning, and checked all directions. "Every room says this?"

"Yeah." Jonah looped his thumbs into the belt loops of his jeans. "Weird, right?"

"It's all weird." Row shoved his phone back into his pocket and grabbed Kiki's wheelchair's handles before moving along.

Cora patted Jonah on the back. "He is a teenager. They are like this."

"Do you have any kids?" Jonah asked, brow raised.

"Well, no." She looked away and fiddled with her shirt. "But I watch a lot of teen dramas."

"Hmm." Jonah scoffed. "Maybe I should do some research."

At the end of the cube stacks, they found a grand plaza ringed with stone totems of strange design. Dr. Young bounded up to the closest, hovering his hands over carvings of unearthly creatures and primitive depictions of humanoids. Dr. Cooper peered over his shoulder.

In the center of the plaza sat a great metal dais polished to a mirror-like gleam. Jonah peered into his reflection. The distortions in its surface gave him wide cheeks and a flattened chin. He frowned, and the distortions changed, squishing his face together. Soon the entire surface rippled like water.

Mud caught onto the display next, watching in awe as the dais undulated. He reached out to touch the metal waves, only for Rivera to grab his wrist and pull him back.

"How about we don't touch the strange device?" he said.

A spiderweb crack started near Jonah's feet and spread across the dais. A million metal shards bulged out of the center, forming into a pillar before whittling down into a figure. The group raised their rifles. Jonah ensured Row was safely behind him.

The figure stretched back, the broken pieces of metal folding over each other into a scale-like shell. A light began at its feet and drifted up its body, scanning in a human façade like a printer until a dark-skinned woman with delicate features wearing a pure white suit stood before them.

"We've been waiting for you." Her voice came from everywhere at once, echoing through the empty city streets. As she walked toward them, the dais hardened beneath her feet before splintering apart again, joining the roiling mass behind her. "You are late."

"She looks like us." Darius turned to Mud. "She can talk like us."

"I can see that."

"Around you is the culmination of centuries of work." She lifted a hand to the drones buzzing above. "Your brave ancestors spread out from this planet to the stars, planting roots in every inhabitable land, forming a network that stretched throughout thousands of solar systems."

The dais followed her words, creating two moving sculptures of ships that launched between planets. They split into two more ships, then four, then eight. A thousand little lines weaving a tapestry behind the speaker. Goosebumps prickled the back of Jonah's neck. All of them came from that central point. The planet they stood on. The cradle of humanity.

"You flourished, unbound." The dais created tableaus of villages becoming towns becoming cities. "You conquered space. You conquered gravity. You conquered until there was no need to conquer anything else. And so our technology turned inward, for death had remained unconquerable."

She held her hands to her stomach, fingers together, and waited, letting the moment hang as she looked out over their heads, speaking to an imaginary crowd.

"Which is why you answered our summons," she continued. "All colonies to return home, to flee a galaxy no longer ours. We are leaving this physical world behind. Your minds will be transferred into this computer, powered by the sun that gave us life all those eons ago, and the core beneath our feet. Inside, you will create your own world. Beyond strife or struggle or disease. Beyond conquest and war, famine and pestilence. Beyond death!"

The shards of metal leaped from the dais like a cheering crowd.

"Inside, you can have whatever you want. Live however you want. Be another person. Be a beast. Journey on clouds and beautiful rivers. Create everlasting art. Talk with our greatest scholars. And, of course, you never have to age and watch your loved ones die. You will find peace, there, in the arms of"—the speaker paused, her head twitching—"God."

Jonah and Cora shared a look somewhere between horror and confusion. The rest of the group looked similarly flummoxed.

The speaker recovered from her momentary glitch and stood straight. The dais grew a spike from each side, stretching high above her head into a triumphant arch.

"Welcome." She spread her arms wide, glittering shards dripping from her fingertips. "To an infinite world."

Jonah stepped forward. It was just a machine, a recording to bring in ancient humans, but he was so tired. His head, so heavy. The reason every planet lay empty, the reason lives and foundations had been abandoned, right there in front of them. They'd left it all behind to upload their minds to a computer. A paradise, so it claimed, to escape those who were trying to poison them all.

"We just want to go home," Jonah said.

The arch retreated, and the speaker looked down at him, meeting his eyes for the first time. She blinked twice and bowed. "Of course. This decision must be made of your own free will. If you wish to go home, march on." She extended her right arm to the side. "Enter the Citadel, and we'll take you home."

A series of lights flashed in the ground, creating a looping path around the dais and up the steps into the tower's base. The Citadel, as the speaker had called it, seemed apropos. A grand enough name for a grand structure. It stretched forever into the cloud cover and rotated almost imperceptibly, like the ticking of a clock. It had taken Jonah the entire walk down from the landing pad to realize it followed the sun's movement.

Darius bounced on his toes. "We're going home! We're actually going home!"

"Wait," Jonah started. "Maybe we—"

No one listened. The group chattered excitedly as the speaker disintegrated, returning the dais to a smooth plane. Mud raced along the lit path, kicking off a chase to the Citadel's entrance. Kiki clutched her chair's arms, cackling with glee as Row tried to keep up with the group, finally falling behind with a surprisingly excited Rivera.

Aleks took a single step toward the Citadel before looking back.

"You have to know this is a trap or something, right?" Jonah said.

"Honestly." Aleks rubbed the back of his neck and sauntered on. "I'm just exhausted."

Only Jonah and Saul, Frankie held tightly to his back, remained at the dais. Saul stared at the tower, his jaw tight as a spring.

"You know what I'm thinking, right?" Jonah asked.

"Most likely." Saul huffed and lumbered after the group. "That everyone's just blinded by hope, and we're walking into a meat grinder. Even if they can help, we already have their enemies trying to kill us. And they won last time."

Jonah gazed up at the Citadel's height, squinting against the sun bouncing off its exterior. The speaker had said it was a way home. Finally. But a voice in the back of Jonah's mind told him to be cautious. To watch where he stepped. They'd been let down before.

CHAPTER 32

Within the Citadel, shifting statues of the same metal shards greeted them. They flowed from esoteric depictions of winged beasts to raging waves and unknown symbology. The high ceilings boasted opulent chandeliers that rotated freely with no chains holding them aloft. How far had they come that Jonah considered anti-gravity decorations unimpressive?

The floor lights flashed, leading the group between rows of the chaotic living metal and deeper into the Citadel. With the quiet atmosphere and cavernous size, it reminded Jonah of when Lorri had dragged him to a modern art museum in Boston. He'd spent the entire night squinting at nameplates that seemed unrelated to the paintings in front of him.

They came to a smaller door leading into a dark room, and Rivera peeled off in a different direction from the group.

"Where are you going?" Jonah asked.

"Gotta piss," he said, skipping around a podium.

"Do not pee in the building!" Cora shouted.

He flipped her the bird and disappeared around the corner.

"Could he not have held it?" she asked Jonah.

"Whatever. Let him mark his territory."

The dark room lay before them. Mud approached, peering into the blackness to no avail. If the speaker were to be believed, there'd be a way home inside. Jonah's muscles tightened. He held his chin high and pushed past Mud, taking the first step inside, his eyes straining against the shadows. Faint shapes lingered in the light trickling in behind him. Too small to be a ship.

Once the last straggler, the airman with the broken nose, stepped in behind Jonah and the overhead lights flashed on.

Fourteen beds were laid out before them. The same ones they'd seen in the cubes, with the four dangling metal pieces at the headboards. On a raised platform behind them, eight human figures crafted of liquid metal materialized, dressed in identical white coats; they were as detailed as the holographic galaxies on the bridge of the ship, but they looked more solid, as if Jonah touched them, his hand wouldn't pass through. A man with a tightly trimmed gray beard and sloping posture stood apart from the rest.

With both hands, he motioned to the beds. "This is your home."

Jonah grimaced. The group looked at each other, panic filling their eyes. He'd known it was too good to be true.

Christopher did not need to pee. He had spotted something around the corner, and, before they wandered off into God knew where he needed to confirm his suspicions.

Past the moving sculptures was a display of model ships. At the front, hovering just above its podium, sat the one they had been flying in, egg-shaped and silver. Its ramp descended as Christopher passed by, revealing a tiny version of the loading dock.

Next were the thin dart drones and a series of sleeker designs, more akin to a jet than their bulbous behemoth. They had truly found themselves the clunker of the bunch, probably designed to haul cargo. He swung his rifle's strap over his shoulder. He was not there to learn about their ship. He was there for the dreadnought.

In the center of the display, in a place of pride on its own pedestal, the dreadnought loomed over him, three times the size of any

competing ship, even in model form. His breath grew loud, domi-
nating all other sounds. That ship had dropped a chemical weapon
on Cyril and Monica. It had tried to shoot them out of the sky with
unending drones. And it belonged to the same people who preached
about paradise and promised them a way home.

"What a crock of shit," he muttered.

A stream of metal shards rolled across the floor and formed into a
humanoid form at Christopher's side. He swung the rifle off his shoulder and snapped his gunsights on the figure. It clutched its hands at its
chest, cocking its head like it should have been smiling.

"You are viewing a model of the Intimidator Class grav-ship." Its
voice came from the podium rather than its blank face. "The king of
our fleet."

Christopher tapped his rifle's barrel against the figure's head. It
didn't react. It was simply puppets for the computer to use.

"That thing tried to kill us." He lowered the gun but kept his finger
near the trigger. "Why?"

With a great flourish, the figure put a finger to its chin. "Interesting.
Most likely, it assumed you were a rogue element."

Christopher narrowed his eyes and leaned in, his reflection breaking
apart in the many shards of the figure's face. "What 'rogue element'?"

"Hold on," Mud said, "this thing wants us to put our brains in a computer? That's how they got away from the big bad ship? That's crazy, right?"

Jonah wasn't so sure, and judging by the silence, some of the others
were considering it, too. What the speaker had described had sounded
pretty good at first blush.

"Yes!" Cora exclaimed. "Of course that's crazy! We are supposed
to be getting back to Earth! That is the goal. That has always been
the goal."

"I'll do it," Kiki said, so quietly it almost slipped by without notice.

Everyone's attention slowly turned to her as she sat smiling in her chair. Row squeezed her shoulder, but she didn't need his support for this. She made her choice without flinching.

"Kiki," Cora said, "you understand what this means, right?"

"Of course I do. It sounds like a pretty good deal, doesn't it? For me, it's a no-brainer. My muscular dystrophy will kill me. That much is assured. A world without disease? Why would I say no?"

"But you could live a full life," Cora continued.

"I use a wheelchair because it gives me freedom from my condition. This . . ." She sat back and looked over the beds. "This is a way better wheelchair."

"I'm going to do it, too." Row took Kiki's hand in his.

"What are you talking about?" Cora swung her head around, searching for some sign that anyone agreed with her that this was madness.

Mud draped his arms over his head, a vacant look on his face while Aleks and Darius paced frantically. The airmen whispered to each other, occasionally glancing at the beds and the figures above. Dr. Cooper and Dr. Young were suspiciously quiet as they stared into the middle distance. That left Saul, who laid Frankie on the floor, and Jonah.

Jonah's mind spun in circles, asking questions with no chance for answers. Was it a trick? Could it truly be anything he wanted? Was it their only option? If they got uploaded, there'd be no coming back. What if he hated paradise like he hated everything else?

"Look at all we've seen. All we've experienced." Row swung his hand up at the figures. "This is where humanity was always going to end up. We're walking the same path as them, but we might not reach the end. Why would I go back to Earth? It's burning up. It's self-destructing. We may never reach this part of our destiny. Let's take it while we have it."

"Row, I . . ." Cora growled in frustration and spun to Jonah. "Talk to your son! He is making a mistake."

Jonah looked at his feet. *What's the right choice?*

"Jonah!"

A bolt of electricity shot through his heart, shocking him to attention. "Everyone should make their own decision. No judgments, just a choice."

Cora shut her eyes and sighed. That was not what she wanted to hear. A heavy tension lingered above their heads, apparent in every furrowed brow and darting look. The elder waited, his arms still extended to display the beds. Saul laid his hand on Frankie's chest and then scooped him into his arms. He sniffed against some oncoming tears as he carried his motionless body to one of the beds and laid him down.

"His mind is alive in there somewhere," he said, straightening Frankie's arm. "If this gives him a chance at something better, I want him to take it."

One of the airmen darted in, taking position next to another bed. "What they said sounds amazing." She ran her hands over the hard surface. "I could be whoever I want to be."

Dr. Cooper put her hand on Cora's shoulder as she passed by. "I did say I might not want to go home."

"And immortality is an incredibly attractive proposition." Dr. Young followed behind, picking the bed next to hers. "I would love to talk to our ancestors about life before us."

"There's no biology in a virtual world." Dr. Cooper gently flicked his chin.

"There's no space either, but I think we both know how much fun simulations can be." He planted a quick kiss on her nose.

"Ugh. Nerds in love." Aleks stuck out his tongue. He took a bed farther away from the group, flicking at the metal pieces hanging above.

"*You* want to live in a simulation?" Saul asked incredulously.

"Have you seen *The Matrix*?" Aleks unzipped his hoodie and tossed it aside. "Flying through the air, awesome kung-fu fights, stopping bullets with your mind. Knowing it's a simulation is the important part." He pointed at Jonah and winked. "If you know the rules, the game can't hurt you."

Jonah nodded, but slowly. Aleks continued to be a master of chaos and confusion—the one person he never would have thought would want to be virtualized. And that was it. No one else chose a bed. On one side: Dr. Cooper, Dr. Young, Aleks, Frankie—though with some extenuating circumstances—an airman, Kiki, and Row. On the other: Cora, Saul, Mud, Darius, two airmen, and Jonah. Rivera had yet to turn up after taking a leak, but that still left the numbers fairly even between those who wanted to be uploaded and those who wanted to stay.

Cora looked around in disbelief, but the fire to fight faded. "I cannot do it. I am not done out here. Not yet."

Jonah and Row met eyes. They were the same young eyes Jonah had seen the morning he'd left for Alaska, when he'd lied and said he'd see him again soon. Alaska. Far from humanity, where eyes like that couldn't hurt him. Standing there, dirty and exhausted, Row had become a man without Jonah noticing, too focused on the sad boy he couldn't care for.

"Dad! Please!" Row rushed to his father, his face wracked with pain. "There're no more jumps. What are you going to do?"

"Struggle through it, like humans always do." He bit his tongue to keep from crying. "I gave up once. I gave up when I left you, Ethan, and your mom. I thought I wanted to be alone, but all I cared about this entire terrifying trip was keeping you safe. And you will be." He nodded at the beds. "In there. This is right for you, but it's not right for me."

Tears welled in Row's eyes. "It can be."

"I don't want to go to a place my mind creates. It will be cold. And alone. The real world is messy, but it's not done with me just yet." He tried to continue, but the words caught in his throat. He stammered on syllables, his vision turning blurry as the tears won the battle. "I l-love y-you, Row."

"I love you too, Dad." Row threw himself forward, taking his father in a final embrace.

Jonah squeezed back. He held his son close and cried. He'd never see him again, and he knew it was too late to change the past, but in that one pure moment, nothing else mattered.

"You inspire me," he said. "I'm not ready to be where you are, but I hope someday I will be. I'm sorry I'm not brave enough to follow you."

Row clutched the back of Jonah's shirt. "I'm sorry I'm not strong enough to stay."

They broke the embrace. There were no more words to say. The ones who chose to virtualize took their positions on their beds. Row eased Kiki from her chair. She nuzzled into his chest as he lay her down, ensuring her head rested comfortably on the slightly upturned "pillow" at the top. He glanced back at Jonah, and a flash of realization crossed his face.

"You need this," he said, tossing his phone to him. "The app's just called Translator. It's on the home screen. You'll need to put in my passcode. It's zero-one-nine-zero, and then hold the camera up to what you want to translate. Make sure it's in focus, press the middle button—"

Jonah held his hand up. "Row. I got it."

Row smiled and lay down on his bed. He took Kiki's hand and looked deep into her eyes. Saul patted Frankie's chest and retreated next to Mud and Darius. The metal pieces hanging above the beds drifted down and enclosed the volunteers' heads.

"Let the pain of this world drift away," the elder said. The machine he stood on began to hum. "You are entering paradise."

Red lights appeared on their helmets, and the humming grew louder. The lights turned yellow, then green. Jonah stepped forward, wanting to be close before they left. Row squeezed Kiki's hand. The hum reached its peak, becoming a single ringing note.

Silence. The green lights vanished. The volunteers went limp, Row and Kiki's fingers still intertwined loosely.

"Virtualization complete," the elder said.

Jonah covered his face. It was best for Row, he'd found a place he belonged, but it still hurt. An icy dagger to his gut that would only melt with time. Cora wrapped her arms around his neck and pulled his head to her shoulder, stroking his hair.

Heavy footsteps pounded down the outside hall. Jonah pulled

away from Cora as Rivera charged in, rifle already at his shoulder. His eyes spat fire and his mouth twisted into a wrathful scowl as he waved Jonah over.

Jonah met him halfway.

"These things are trying to kill us!" Rivera said. "They are trying to put our brains in computers!"

"We know!" He stepped back, keeping his eyes on the rifle.

Rivera's gaze fell on the vacant bodies in the beds, helmets set around their heads. The past couple of minutes dawned on him. He blinked, processing the information, then grimaced. "We have to destroy it!"

"They're all in there!" Jonah shouted. "Row is in there! Stop!"

"Get out of my way!" Rivera shifted to the left, Jonah matching his movements. The rest of the group stood, shocked, unsure of what to do.

"I'm not going to let you hurt them."

"Do you know what they do to the people who don't do what they say?" Rivera thrust a finger at the elders. "Why don't you tell them?"

"In paradise, there is no pain or death. We want for nothing," the elder said. "The only danger is from outside. Intelligent life is messy. A threat. After many were brought into the computer, we learned of the rogue element, those who refused to enter paradise. So, we manufactured drones to protect ourselves. To protect our people, all intelligent life must be digitized . . . or exterminated."

Jonah's throat went dry. The mass graves, the signs of battle, the chemical weapon. The elders didn't only call their colonies back. They fought with those who refused. The final piece of the puzzle. He looked around, seeing the same reaction cross everyone else's face.

"That's why we have to kill them first." Rivera aimed at the computer.

"Stop!" Jonah raised his rifle in turn. "We still have friends in there. There's an entire civilization of innocent people in there!"

"They'll kill all of us, Jonah!" His eyes flicked to the rifle barrel stuck in his face. "All intelligent life, what do you think that means? They'll come to Earth and wipe us all out. I'm saving Earth!"

"Stand down!" He turned to the elders. "We don't want to hurt you! We aren't a threat!"

The elder shook his head. "All intelligent material life is a threat."

"Shut up!" Rivera aimed at the council and pulled the trigger.

"No!" Jonah slapped the gun aside.

The shot missed the head elder and struck one in the back row, shattering him into a spray of metal shards. The rest of the holograms dropped. They froze, some with their heads held in their hands, others with their arms lifted to the sky. Curled and wretched, they let out a symphonic whine, locked in a tableau of despair.

"Don't hurt us!" they cried, their voices echoing over each other. "We don't want to die! We're scared!"

Something was wrong. They didn't sound human anymore. The lights in the room dimmed and flickered.

"Enough." Rivera readied for another shot. "I'm breaking this—"

A flash of light and a black dot appeared on his neck. He choked out a breath, and blood spurted from the hole. A spider-drone crept down from the ceiling, a miniature version of their rifles attached to its back. Rivera dropped his weapon and fell to his knees, clutching his throat, desperately trying to hold the blood in before collapsing, dead.

Jonah stared in horror, registering the moment. Three more spider-drones click-clacked in through vents in the ceiling. The time for talking was over.

CHAPTER 33

"**R**un!" Jonah shouted.

They took off like gazelles in the grassland, spider-drones firing red lasers at their heels. Cora took a moment to grab Rivera's fallen rifle, letting off a few shots before catching up. The sculptures in the main hall twisted into spiky serpents, looming over them as they fled into the street.

The city rose to meet them, the twisting and shifting structures and walkways intensifying into a churning ocean of metal. The group had a straight shot back to the ship, down the long promenade to the landing pad. Flying drones joined in the chase, raining hell upon them. There was no cover and no way to lose them, not when the living city wanted them dead. All they could do was run.

Cora grabbed the side of her skirt, where it already showed wear and tear, and ripped a long strip up her leg to run more easily. The airman with the nose bandage broke ahead, planting himself at the edge of the plaza and firing at the oncoming drones, one of which took a shot to one of its four rotors, toppling over and nearly taking Jonah's head off before smashing into the ground.

Jonah fired his own rifle when he could, blasting a spider-drone off a car as they ran past, but there was no end to them. They'd reached the last of the cube stacks when the second airman took a laser through his back, dead before he hit the ground.

"Come on!" the first airman shouted, waving them into a nearby building. "There's a path here."

Jonah remembered seeing Rivera and his team weaving through the buildings earlier and broke a hard right to join him. They must've found something, and it had better cover than the open street. He paused at the door, waiting for Cora, Mud, Darius, and Saul to get inside. He glanced back at the Citadel and instantly regretted it. Drones flooded down the street and through the sky, their shadows creating a wave of darkness rushing toward him.

"Jonah, come on!" Cora shouted, rushing into the next room.

The airman led them through restaurants and houses, a couple of shops, and a library with empty shelves. A window shattered behind Jonah, and spider-drones bounded into the stores, lighting off a flurry of laser fire.

"What the hell?" Mud exclaimed.

Jonah peered ahead, catching a door vanish as a wall shifted in the way. The airman veered left and jumped through an open window instead. More and more, the buildings shifted around them, cutting off paths and trying to trap them with the drones.

They fled through an elegant kitchen, the airman reaching the far door just as the floor in the next room began to rise, starting to close off the passage. Saul and Darius got through, though Mud had to slide between the floor and the top of the door jamb. Cora reached the wall just as the crack of light at the bottom vanished. She swore and kicked at the blocked-off way forward.

The wall within the door frame kept descending. The floor wasn't rising; the whole building was lifting out of its foundations.

Jonah turned and raised his rifle, blasting a drone off the counter. A flying drone came rushing in, its rotors sparking against the pots and pans dangling from hooks. It whipped around, trapped like a cat in a box. Jonah grabbed Cora and pulled her down just as a rotor tore above their heads.

"Look." Cora pointed at the door.

They'd cleared the next building and could see its roof. The landing pad wasn't far, only a couple of buildings away. The flying drone continued to roar, letting off sporadic shots, taking out a spider-drone in its panicked flailing.

Cora rushed out the door, falling a couple of feet to the roof below and landing on her feet. Sending a few parting shots at the flying drone, Jonah followed. As soon as he struck the roof, it tilted. He and Cora toppled sideways off the front, landing hard onto a vehicle below. The air shot from Jonah's lungs, and his rifle rattled away.

The building turned over the street, acting like a pitcher pouring water. Saul tumbled out of the front window first, followed by the airman with the bandage, then Mud and Darius practically knotted together.

"Keep moving!" The airman grumbled and got to his feet, limping toward the landing pad.

Jonah caught his breath and checked on Cora. She groaned in pain but had no visible injuries. A laser scored the car hood next to them, a reminder that they weren't clear yet.

They leaped from the pavement to the landing pad. A flock of cleaner and unarmed spider-drones fled as they approached. Thankfully, the ramp was still down and waiting. The airman's feet pounded up it. He turned back at the top to cover the others' approach.

Saul cleared the ramp like a track star, Cora a short distance behind him. Jonah reached the bottom as Darius took a glancing laser to the leg. He dropped and fell across the pad. Jonah moved to help, only for a flurry of laser fire to drive him back.

Mud took Darius by the collar and belt, dragging him to his feet and practically throwing him onto the ramp.

"Get up!" Mud cried out, right before a laser pierced his shoulder. He gasped in pain. A second caught him in the stomach. A third through the chest. The drones rattled him down. Darius tried to help, but Jonah caught him by the midsection and pulled him into the ship.

"We have to go back for him!" Darius screamed.

"He's already dead." Jonah choked at the words. "It's done."

Mud's smoking corpse lay at the bottom of the ramp. The drones continued to fire into the loading dock, splintering tables and tearing away the stage. Jonah pressed his hand against a panel next to the ramp, and it began to lift into the air. The drones didn't stop. Jonah planted his feet and fired, Darius, Saul, Cora, and the airman joining him at his side. Their laser fire burned the air, knocking away any drone that got too close to the ramp and searing the edge pitch black. Even as the ramp continued to tilt up, spider-drones tried to crawl in.

"Shit! Shit!" Saul slammed his hand against the side of his rifle. The indicator on the side had turned bright red.

The ramp reached its peak, spider-drones sticking their vicious spike-legs through the gap. Their bodies rattled against the hull.

Come on. Jonah sniped a drone out of the corner gap. *Close. Just close.*

The ship groaned like a grizzly bear, and then, with a snap like bubble wrap, the ramp slammed shut. A hundred spider legs rained down from its edges, clattering to the floor like a hi-hat solo.

Cora put her hand to her chest to catch her breath and cast Jonah a confused look. "So, we can just shut the door now?"

"Row showed me how to close it." Jonah leaned on his knees and puffed.

Laser fire thumped against the door. Saul approached it carefully. "What do we do now?"

"We fly away." Jonah let out a final huff. "Let's get to the bridge."

Battered and exhausted, they made their way there, the ship rattling under the never-ending barrage. A maddening display of laser fire and drones could be seen through the window as they arrived.

"Do you think you can fly this?" Jonah asked the airman.

"I kinda have to." He laid his rifle against a console and hopped into the pilot's seat. His hands shook as he took the yoke, but they had little choice.

"The rest of us shoot." Jonah passed between the outer consoles. He may not have understood the language, but he remembered the movements Row had made. He set up the gunner seats, surprised to find the drones had repaired the two broken guns while they were gone. *I guess they didn't expect us to turn on them.* "Get in there, and don't stop firing."

Cora hopped into her usual position. Saul and Darius took the sticks, a little more cautious as they hadn't used them before.

"What's your name?" Jonah asked the airmen as he took control of his gun.

"Klondike," he said. "Airman Nathan Klondike, sir."

"All right, Klondike. Don't stop moving."

Klondike took a sharp breath and slammed his foot down on the forward pedal, sending them rocketing off the landing pad. Spider-drones rained down as they took to the sky. The gunners unleashed everything they had.

The particle accelerators spun along their tracks around the ship. Jonah barely had to aim, each sweep of his gun tearing through a line of drones, turning the air around them into a fireworks display of destruction.

Klondike cleared them of the Citadel only to find the city stretched out far beyond the horizon. They passed smaller versions of the tower they'd visited, all surrounded by cube stacks. The entire planet had been turned into one large city machine, and it was trying to kill them.

The ground opened, releasing a swarm of silver darts to take the place of the flying drones. Klondike did his best to dodge their fire while the gunners lit them up. Despite all efforts, there were too many to stop them all. Their ship rocked, whining and screaming as the danger alert sounded.

Klondike took them close to a tower, only for it to change shape, twisting to allow an anti-air emplacement to form out the side. A massive cannon turned its sights on them. Jonah's eyes widened. A red light glowed from within the barrel, then streaked across the sky. Klondike took a hard right, but the laser sheared their tail.

"Stay away from the towers!" Jonah shouted.

"No shit!" Klondike punched it out to the shorter buildings.

Without the protection of the towers, though, the drones swarmed. They danced around, firing with complete disregard for whether they got destroyed.

"What about that big cannon?" Cora asked.

"Hold on." Jonah abandoned his gun and hurried over to the console Row had used.

His fingers hovered over the screen, a mess of icons and options, none of which he could read. He planted his feet and calmed himself. He'd watched Row go through the options; he could do it, too. The smell of smoke drifted into the bridge. He had to do it now.

He tapped through the choices, trusting his memory and what he had learned from Row to guide him. Just as Row had said, sometimes you just need to push buttons. He touched the center icon on a screen that looked familiar, and a reticle appeared on the front window.

"Yes!" he exclaimed. "Line 'em up, Klondike."

Klondike pulled a hard turn and Jonah fired. The thin string swept across the sky, pulling an entire unit with it as it went. Many drones sheared apart at the gravitational pressure. Others got cast away, smoking and tumbling to the ground.

Still more came. A ring appeared around the reticle, ticks slowly rounding it as the cannon recharged. Jonah's heart fell into his stomach. They couldn't win this. They could only fight.

Cora blasted a drone away, knocking it into the others. Saul and Darius whooped in excitement as they tore chunks from the attackers. Klondike swept the ship low, driving a couple of reckless ships into the city. There was no end, but at least they could go down swinging. Jonah hovered his hand over the cannon's activator, waiting for the recharge to end.

Klondike yanked the yoke to the right, and nothing happened. He slammed his fist against the instrument panel.

"My gun's not firing!" Saul shouted.

"Mine neither!" Darius spun around in his chair.

Cora looked at Jonah fearfully. She had no weapons, either. The ship kept moving forward, but they had no control.

"What do we do?" Klondike asked.

Jonah had no answer. The drones continued to bombard them. The smell of smoke grew stronger. Their view was nothing more than flashing red lights. There had to be a way to fix this, Jonah told himself. Row would find a way.

"I'm not afraid." Darius stumbled out of his chair, shouting at the fiery display. "You're afraid! You said you were scared! You lit up the whole damn planet! You're the scared one, not us!"

A laser struck the window head-on, sending a spidering crack across the surface. Still, Darius stomped forward, sweat and tears streaming down his face. Jonah shook his head. Darius had lost his mind.

"Mud was right! You're just ghosts!" With each step, Darius grew emboldened. "He would say this is ridiculous, and it is! A dead civilization so frightened even your ghosts are scared!"

"Hell, yeah!" Saul clapped his chest. "I ain't scared either! Machines running around with nothing to do, it's ridiculous!"

"They are scared!" Cora hopped to her feet. "They are so lame!"

The bridge filled with shouts rivaling the pounding of laser fire. Klondike practically threw himself out of the pilot's chair when he joined in. A claxon sounded. Jonah looked at the four—Saul, Darius, Klondike, and Cora—in slack-jawed amazement.

At the end, when hell fell upon them, they would meet it with the purest distillation of humanity. They were brash, loud, and taking the wins where they got them.

"I'm not scared!" Jonah approached the window with his arms wide. The cracking spread from one side to the other. At his voice, the crew went quiet, though they held pained smiles on their faces.

Cora went to his side and rested her head on his shoulder. The claxon warbled and then went silent. With a thump, the lights shut off. Jonah wrapped an arm around Cora.

"Are you happy?" he whispered.

Cora nodded. Jonah shut his eyes.

Silence.

Death was quieter than Jonah expected. He still felt Cora's warm hand in his. He opened his eyes. The clouds of drones swarmed, but none fired. The ship glided along in peace. They flew past a tower, and its anti-air cannon retracted, returning the building to its natural form.

"What's happening?" Saul ran his fingers over his scalp.

"It was fighting back." Cora released Jonah and stumbled forward. "Like an immune system. The more we hit it, the harder it hit back."

"Maybe." Something about that didn't sit right with Jonah. The drone swarm split and took wild circles across the sky. "They can't see us. Something's hiding us. Something stopped us from shooting them so we *could* hide."

"Who?" Cora asked. "Who . . . what could do that?"

The question ate into Jonah's mind. Had they gotten lucky? The ship glided left, circling a tower and landing in a crooked alley in its shadow. Jonah tapped at the screen with no response. He tried another console. Same thing. They were locked out. They'd survived the planet's defenses, but he wasn't sure that was any better. They were stuck in the ship. Again.

A hum grew in the bridge. Familiar; they'd heard it many times before. The floor shook under their feet.

"Are we jumping?" Klondike asked, clutching the yoke.

As if in reply, the graph projection of power use, the first one Row had ever shown Jonah, appeared between them. The line rocketed to the top of the graph, the fastest it had ever climbed.

"Where are we going?" Cora looked around the room for an answer.

The front window cleared. A sentence, the words projected on the glass, typed out one letter at a time.

YOU OWE MOM THAT DINNER

"Row," Jonah breathed.
The ship vanished.

CHAPTER 34

Jonah Wall stood at the precipice of two worlds. In front of him, the Alaskan wilds he never thought he'd see again, spread out from the front window of the ship to the hole it had been dug from and beyond to unbroken wilderness. Behind him, the bridge of an alien vessel that had become his life and the people he'd lived it with.

Row had brought them home. Jonah's breaths came so hard he thought he'd vomit. Row had saved them.

"We're home." Darius fell to his knees, clutching his hands over his head. "We're actually home!"

Saul cheered and grabbed Cora around the waist, lifting her into the air as she shrieked and laughed. Klondike jumped out of the pilot's chair, sprinting up to the window to make sure he wasn't imagining it.

"People!" he shouted. "Actual, real, people!"

Down at the dig site came a flurry of movement. Distant dots rushed out of trailers and into trucks, tearing up dirt and snow as they kicked into gear toward the ship. Klondike pushed off the console and charged for the bridge door. Saul let Cora down and followed.

"Hold on," Jonah said. "What are we going to tell them?"

"What d'you mean?" Klondike caught himself on the pilot's chair as he passed. "We tell them what happened."

"We tell them there's an alien computer that wants to kill all intelligent life in the universe?" He rolled his shoulder, a week of pain catching up to him. "It doesn't know Earth exists, but it found us because of this ship."

"Jonah," Saul said, "we have to trust people, remember?"

He opened his mouth to respond but caught himself. Cora, Darius, Klondike, and Saul, the ones who'd returned to Earth, beaten as they were, looked back at him. Jonah had trusted them at the end, just as he'd trusted Row.

"Okay." He stretched his neck. "Let's get off this ship."

Darius hopped around the edge of the bridge, overtaking Klondike and Saul as they all rushed out. Cora lingered for a moment at the door, looking back at Jonah before joining them. Jonah took one step and turned to the window.

Row's final message had disappeared once they jumped, but at least he'd settled into the virtual world quickly. Jonah shook his head and smiled. *Row living in a computer? He's gonna be a real hellion.*

He waved at the window, a final goodbye to his son, to both of them, and walked out into the world again.

Dinner ended up being a burger and fries at an Anchorage bar. Lorri cried the whole time. Jonah told the story over and over, hoping he'd hit the iteration that would help her. But he never got it right.

"The instant he learned about Ethan, Row went tearing off to find him," Jonah said. "You couldn't stop that boy. And I told you about that translator he made. We wouldn't have survived at all if not for that."

The servers took a wide path around their table, eyeing Lorri as she cried into her hands. One of them pointed at Jonah. The bar TVs showed the news, still in their near-twenty-four-hour report on the ship's disappearance and return. Footage of the five survivors being picked up cut to newscasters interviewing whoever could be considered an expert on the situation. At least it was muted so Jonah didn't have to hear it all again.

"Row was incredible." He poked a finger at his cold, untouched burger. "He was a hero."

"I don't want a hero," Lorri said. "I want my sons. You were supposed to take care of them."

Jonah's heart shattered. He sank into his chair. "Row found the place he'd be the happiest. He'd want you to know that."

"Just go." Lorri shook her head, tears falling into her drink.

Jonah pushed his chair back with a sharp squeak. He left enough money to cover the bill and a nearly fifty percent tip before walking out, leaving the intensifying whispers of the other patrons behind. The streetlights turned on as he stepped outside. He picked through his keys, and a cold breeze cut through his coat. Glancing up, he caught his reflection in a hardware store's darkened windows.

Dry-eyed and alone. Lorri would come to understand. Row was happy where he was.

He turned to walk toward the parking lot, and Row was happy where he was.

He stepped into the shadows left between the streetlights, and Row was happy where he was.

His knees gave out. He fell against the brick wall, his hand scraping down the rough exterior. He clutched his hands around his head, but he couldn't keep their faces out of his mind. Ethan, Mud, Terrence, Booker, Cyril, and all the others whose bodies lay on distant stars. Some were alive—Row, Kiki, Aleks, Frankie, Dr. Young and Cooper— but in a way he couldn't comprehend. If they were alive, how could they be so far gone?

He squeezed his eyes shut, willing his brain to understand. Row had saved their lives from inside the computer, but Jonah wanted him beside him. He wanted everything. He was supposed to be the strong one, the rock, but he cracked. He failed Ethan. He failed Row. He failed Lorri. He would walk on while their shadows lingered behind him.

In the darkness where no one could see, he wept, soundless and alone.

***

Jonah leaned over the coffeemaker, smartphone in hand, as he scrolled through its app. He'd found out he could set up different alarm times for each day, perfect for when he wanted to sleep in on the weekends. He also read an online article that said if he had a virtual assistant, he could tell it to make the coffee for him, but he figured he'd take things one step at a time.

He popped the pod out of the top of the machine and tossed it into the garbage, only for it to bounce off the top and skitter across the floor. The bag had been sitting there for days, stinking up the place with food thrown out before the press event. He put his phone down and spotted Row's old one sitting next to it.

His skin grew cold. His fingers twitched. The boys' luggage still sat in his guest room. He hadn't opened the door; he might never open the door. He'd burn down the house first with himself inside so he could feel his skin bubble, his bones turn to ash, and feel a moment of the pain he knew still lingered in the dead shadows on his back.

The doorbell chimed, bringing him back to reality. He caught his breath, unaware he had lost it, and went to see who it was. He threw the door open with a bit more force than he intended.

Cora stood on the other side. She recoiled. So did Jonah. They stared at each other like two stunned cats until Cora forced a smile.

"Hi," she said.

"Hi." For a moment, Jonah wanted to slam the door shut. He didn't need anyone coming around acting like they knew what he was going through. "This is a surprise."

"I thought I would call first, then I . . . I do not know." She laughed awkwardly. "I was driving past. Can I come in?"

"Yeah." Jonah stepped aside and then shut the door.

Cora unbuttoned her coat as she took in the room. "So, this is where *the* Jonah Wall lives. It is . . . empty."

"I'm trying to fill it more." He adjusted a crooked landscape painting he'd put up earlier that day. The emptier it was, the bigger it felt. The bigger it was, the easier for it to swallow him whole.

"Did you have that talk with your wife yet?" She wandered through the kitchen, inspecting the faucets and backsplash.

"Tonight, actually."

Cora stopped with one finger on the counter. "Ah. I'm sorry. How did she take it?"

"Lorri's a tough woman, but this would be hard for anyone."

"Like you?"

"Row's all right. He's where he wants to be, and we wouldn't be here if he wasn't, so he, um, and Ethan . . ." He leaned against the couch arm and gazed past Cora at the window that looked out into the backyard, where he had once watched his sons playing. He didn't understand why no matter how much he cleaned it, the blood wouldn't come off the glass. "Lorri will get through it. Lorri will . . . we all will."

The silence hung heavy, and the blood oozed.

"Jonah," Cora said. "I—"

The coffeemaker chimed, and Jonah practically leapt off the couch to grab his mug. "Perfect timing. We should have a drink, right?"

"Isn't it a bit late for coffee?"

"I'm not planning on sleeping." He poured half the coffee into a second mug and offered it to her. "How about you?"

She took it apprehensively, and they sat at the kitchen table. Jonah ran his hand over the hot ceramic, waiting for the steam to fade. A car engine rumbled by outside before fading into quiet night. If one of them didn't say something soon, surely Jonah would follow it.

"How about you?" he asked, tapping his fingers along the handle. "Are you doing okay with all this press and pressure?"

"Didn't you hear?" A hint of a smile appeared at the corner of her lips. "There was an accident at the ship. No one was hurt, but the engine room was practically destroyed. No one knows how long it will take or if they will ever get it put back together. They blamed some anti-space extremists."

Jonah cocked an eyebrow. "I didn't realize there were anti-space extremists."

"There are anti-everything these days."

"I thought we were going to trust people." He crossed his arms.

"I do trust people. To an extent." She slouched back in the chair, her expression solemn. "That thing knew we were out there because of the ship. As long as it exists, it could find us."

Jonah didn't need to ask what "thing" she was talking about. The dreadnought. "Well, what's done is done. I'm sure you'll keep moving on."

"No." She clasped her hands in her lap. "There were rumors and accusations, nothing substantial, but I *did* take personal responsibility for the ship, and while the government cannot do anything, the board—yadda yadda yadda—I was asked to resign from my position as CEO of PetroWave."

"Oh. I'm sorry."

She shrugged and tucked a stray hair behind her ear. "I don't know how much of a future I see for myself in oil and gas, anyway."

"And what future do you see?" Jonah asked, staring down into his coffee mug.

"I know what future I see. I have already seen it." She took a deep breath and met his gaze. "Not every piece of technology from that ship was lost."

"Then what's the plan?"

"Something that does not make me hate myself. Or maybe just see what it's like to relax for a bit." She eyed Jonah. "You were right. I think we both need to take a step back and process."

Jonah nodded. A tightness grew in his chest, and he fought it as it crawled into his throat.

"I've been wondering if I'm going to suddenly wake up still on that ship," she said, gazing into the blackness outside the windows. "It seems impossible sometimes to remember I'm here. We're here. The five of us."

The walls shattered, and Jonah fell forward on his elbows. Tears flowed freely from his eyes. Cora looked at him in surprise.

"It's not stopping," Jonah said through gritted teeth. "It doesn't get better. It just hurts more. I don't know what I'm supposed to do. Row should've come back. Ethan should've never been there. Frankie . . . Terrance . . . Their families are here, and everything is so heavy now. How do I do any of this?"

"I don't know. I . . ." She scrunched up her face, her own eyes filling with wetness. "I guess we hurt for a while."

Jonah pressed his chin to his chest, taking deep breaths to stem the flow of tears. The air in the house had become stifling. The walls reached out to crush him. And yet, it felt good to feel it all. Cora sat beside him, not judging, not talking, just letting their emotions wash over them. The way he wished he had with Lorri. He caught another whiff of the overflowing garbage and, in a sudden burst of energy, pushed to his feet.

"I, uh . . ." He left his mug on the table, and while Cora watched, she didn't try to stop him. "The trash is . . . I need to take it out. Be right back."

A brisk wind whistled through the trees like a low symphony. Jonah tossed the bag into the bin under a bright streetlamp. He let the clean air flow into his lungs and wiped away his tears. An owl hooted in the distance, followed by a rustle as it took flight. Jonah stopped at the edge of the orange pool of light, in a spot of darkness between his front porch and the street, and gazed into the sky.

Somewhere out there, Row lived his best life. Everyone who'd decided to move on to paradise did. But Earth, messy as it was, was Jonah's home for now. He'd have to make the best of it and let the hurt run its course.

A meteor crossed the horizon. The stars stretched out as far as he could see, pinpoints between the dark fingers of space. He'd looked up at them many times, staring into the Arctic tundra and thinking of the void and the emptiness.

It didn't look empty anymore.

EPILOGUE

A shadow moved through the dark halls of space, barely more than a shifting reflection. The dreadnought loomed, lumbering far above a quiet planet.

Its halls were empty. Nothing living had ever touched it. Drones rattled about in empty rooms, maintaining the ship to fulfill its one cold, robotic purpose: to protect the people in paradise. And so, the destroyer of intelligent life, a ghost of death, shambled on.

A single light glowed in its bridge, expanding out into a field of stars. The stars faded away until only the inhabitable planets remained. Next, the hologram flew through the map, stopping on its home world for a second before flying on.

It stopped at a green world, overrun with biomes full of life, too simple to pose a threat. Though it had once been one of the great colonies, the dreadnought had already fulfilled its purpose there. The rogue element wasn't present anymore.

Next was an icy planet. A military base, some colonies rebelled against unification used in the early wars. Most people left when the recall message was sent. The rest were exterminated. It moved on.

A planet of nearly one hundred percent water. Refineries for the creation of fuel cells were built under the endless ocean. The colonists fought amongst themselves over the recall message, resulting in many of their deaths when the walls broke. It moved on.

A moon around a gas giant. Mining operation on the edge of known space. Many did not want to return. Some violently stopped the willing colonists from leaving, believing they would turn on them once they arrived on the home planet. Reinforcements were sent to assist. Both the violent and the peaceful rebels needed to be treated the same. One ship had been listed MIA, with its wreckage never found. It moved on.

The map scrolled into the empty parts of space, past a belt of asteroids, and past a red planet, to where no habitable world had yet been found.

Here, in the dark void where once there was nothing, a pale blue dot appeared.

Stay up to date with Alex Schuler:

Follow Alex on Amazon & Goodreads

https://www.amazon.com/author/alexschuler

Other books by
ALEX SCHULER

Code Word Access

In a near-future world dominated by artificial intelligence, the country's leading scientist has programmed "ethics" into the decision-making of all machines, but when his algorithm suddenly finds that he is a threat to mankind, he must go on the run (and off the grid) to escape execution.

Faster

The birth of self-driving cars through the eyes of a brilliant but self-destructive machine-builder and the computer programmer who helped revolutionize the technology . . . while breaking his heart.